"I don't like the way we left things between us," Nate declared, taking a step in her direction.

Mia took a matching step backward. "You asked for something I couldn't give you."

"I asked for you to come back to Las Vegas with me."

"We'd barely known each other two months." It was the same excuse she'd given him three weeks ago and it rang as hollow now as it had then. "And I couldn't leave Ivy."

"She could've found another assistant." He'd said the same thing the morning after the tour ended. The night after she'd stayed with him until the sun crested the horizon.

Their last stop had been Sydney. Following his final encore, Nate had made sure Ivy was busy and then stolen Mia away to a romantic hotel suite overlooking the harbor. They'd sipped champagne, toasted each other, laughed and made love for the first time. But as sunlight filled the room, Mia was on the phone with Ivy making excuses for where she'd been.

"I'm not just her assistant. I'm her sister," Mia said, now as then. "She needs me."

I need you.

He wouldn't repeat the words. It wouldn't do any good. She'd still choose obligation to her sister over being happy with him.

And he couldn't figure out why.

An exce.

LITTLE SECRET,
RED HOT SCANDAL

BY
CAT SCHIELD

MILLS & BOON

First Published in Great Britain 2017
By Mills & Boon, an imprint of HarperCollins*Publishers*
1 London Bridge Street, London, SE1 9GF

© 2017 Catherine Schield

ISBN: 978-0-263-92820-4

51-0517

Our policy is to use papers that are natural, renewable and recyclable products and made from wood grown in sustainable forests. The logging and manufacturing processes conform to the legal environmental regulations of the country of origin.

Printed and bound in Spain
by CPI, Barcelona

Cat Schield has been reading and writing romance since high school. Although she graduated from college with a BA in business, her idea of a perfect career was writing books for Mills & Boon. And now, after winning the Romance Writers of America 2010 Golden Heart® Award for Best Contemporary Series Romance, that dream has come true. Cat lives in Minnesota with her daughter, Emily, and their Burmese cat. When she's not writing sexy, romantic stories for Mills & Boon Desire, she can be found sailing with friends on the St. Croix River, or in more exotic locales, like the Caribbean and Europe. She loves to hear from readers. Find her at www.catschield.com and follow her on Twitter, @catschield.

For my daughter,
who keeps me current on
all things pop culture.

One

After telling the sound engineer to take a break, Nate Tucker lay down on the couch in the control room of West Coast Records' LA headquarters. Closing his eyes, he listened to the playback of the song he'd just recorded. Over the years he'd trained his ears to pick up every nuance of a performance. His mind then went to work adjusting the frequencies, boosting or cutting EQ, feathering in a touch of reverb to improve the natural sound.

Nothing, however, could fix what Nate was hearing in his own voice. Proof that he'd pushed too hard on the final leg of his twelve-month tour.

He'd hoped that three weeks of rest might have allowed his vocal cords to fix themselves, but his reduced range and the hoarseness that plagued him weren't going away. The vocal cord surgery he'd scheduled for tomorrow was unavoidable. Nate's curses echoed through the room. One more damned thing he didn't have time for.

Since returning to his home in Las Vegas after touring all over the world with his band, Free Fall, he'd been inundated with work. Thank goodness he'd been able to do some songwriting while on the road, because he was all out of space and energy to compose for Free Fall's next album. Maybe that wasn't such a bad thing. With his voice out of commission he wasn't going to be singing anytime soon.

His phone began to ring. Nate checked the screen before levering himself off the couch. In the last three days he'd made a half dozen calls to Trent Caldwell, his business partner and friend. In addition to being partners in Club T's, the premier Las Vegas nightclub that Nate, Trent and Kyle Tailor owned, Nate and Trent were partners in Nate's label, Ugly Trout Records in Las Vegas, as well as West Coast Records, the company Trent had recently bought from his family.

Dropping into the control booth's comfortable leather chair, Nate silenced the music pouring from the speakers and answered the call.

"It's about time you checked in." Nate wasted no time with pleasantries. "Where have you been?"

"Savannah starts shooting next week, so I took her and Dylan to a spa hotel up in Washington." Trent sounded more relaxed and happy than ever. Being engaged to the love of his life obviously agreed with him. "We both turned off our phones for a few days."

Ever since Trent had rekindled his romance with his former lover and found out he was a father, he'd become a whole new person. Nate understood the transformation, after what had happened between him and Mia. It was easy to be cynical and even suspicious about stuff like that until it happened to you.

"Sounds nice." Really nice.

Envy shot through Nate. It wasn't like him to want something another man had. He already had fame and wealth. They didn't drive him. Nate loved what he did and didn't really care if he made tons of money. The music mattered.

And then he'd watched his friend and business partner fall hard for Savannah, and suddenly making music wasn't enough anymore.

"I got your messages about the meeting with Ivy Bliss," Trent said. "Have you lost your mind?"

"What do you mean?" Nate knew perfectly well what Trent was referring to, but decided to pretend he'd been motivated purely by business.

Ivy Bliss was a former child actress turned pop princess with an impressive four-octave range. Five years ago she'd signed with West Coast Records and released two albums. They'd done okay. Thanks to the label's poor management, the production work on the albums hadn't been stellar and the release dates had been pushed back so many times that fans had lost interest.

That was before Trent and Nate had taken control of his family's label the previous month. They intended to turn the record company around and make it a huge success. Ivy Bliss's new album was a great place to start.

But that wasn't the reason Nate had reached out to Ivy's manager-father about producing her new album.

"You did nothing but complain about her the entire eight weeks she was on tour with you."

"Oh, that."

"Oh, that?" Trent mimicked. Nate could hear a baby babbling in the background. "Just a second." There was a pause. "Dylan, Daddy's on the phone with Uncle Nate. Do you want to sing him your new song?"

Nate couldn't ignore the growing ache in his chest

as he listened to Dylan jabber along with his father's soft singing. Ever since Nate had decided on a career in music, every bit of his energy had been focused on writing, performing and producing. Now, he enjoyed all the money and success he'd dreamed about and yet something gnawed at him.

"That was terrific," Nate said when the song was done.

"He's barely a year and already starting to say a few words."

"Have you been teaching him the signs I showed you?" Nate had learned American Sign Language as a kid so he could communicate with his hearing impaired mother, and had taught Trent a few signs Dylan could use to communicate, for words such as *more, done, eat, play, finish* and *tired*.

"Yes, he's really taking to it. Now, back to Ivy. Why would you want to produce her new album?"

Nate sighed. "I don't need to remind you that she's a huge talent and poised to break out. She just needs one great album."

"She's a twenty-five-year-old nightmare."

"Yes, well…she's not that bad." Nate winced at the bald lie.

Seven years earlier, when she was seventeen and starring in a Broadway musical after her show on KidZ Channel was canceled, she'd gotten Nate's phone number and for four months she'd sent him impassioned texts and sexy pictures of herself. At first he'd responded with polite rebuffs and then silence. At last he'd contacted her father and warned him that this wasn't going to play well if it got out. All contact stopped.

"She's a little silly and spoiled," Nate continued, "but superstars can get that way sometimes."

Trent ignored his friend's self-deprecating jab. "Why don't you point her toward Savan or Blanco?" Both had worked with her on collaborations with other artists and produced hits.

Nate didn't need to remind Trent that Ivy Bliss had a reputation for being "challenging" in the studio. She didn't take suggestions, and criticism sent her into hysterics. Neither of the producers Trent mentioned would want to work with her again.

"I'm doing this for West Coast Records." Another lie. There were a couple dozen guys who could produce the heck out of Ivy Bliss and make an album that would rocket to the top of the charts.

"I'm not buying it." Trent hadn't made a major success of every one of his business ventures by being dense. "Wait a second, are you into her? Damn. That's crazy, but my sister said you fell for someone on the tour. I never in a million years thought it was Ivy Bliss."

"It wasn't." With a shudder, Nate changed topics before Trent could press further. "The other reason I called is that I'm going in for surgery tomorrow."

"Surgery." Trent's tone sharpened. "What's wrong?"

"I've got these polyps on my vocal cords." He tried to keep the tension out of his voice. The situation was serious, but he didn't want to make a big deal out of it. "I need to get them removed."

"That sounds bad."

"It's outpatient surgery. A couple hours max. I just wanted to let you know that I'm going to be out of commission for a few days."

"Do you want me to take you?"

"And do what?" Nate injected as much sarcasm as he could into the words to hide how embarrassed he was at his mounting anxiety. "Hold my hand? Please."

"Fine." Trent sounded doubtful. "But if you need anything, just let me know."

"Sure."

An hour after hanging up, Nate strode into the conference room for his two o'clock meeting with Ivy Bliss. Only it wasn't Ivy and her manager-father who awaited him, but Mia Navarro, her twin sister and personal assistant. His heart raced across the room toward her. Nate plunged after it for two strides before coming to a stop. What did he think he was going to do? Wrap her in his arms and crush her against his chest? Whisper that the last three weeks had been a living hell without her? That he ached to hear her voice and sulked without her smile to brighten his day?

She'd made her choice and it hadn't been him.

"How have you been?" He searched her face for some sign she'd suffered as he had, lingering over the circles under her eyes and the downward turn of her mouth. To his relief she didn't look happy, but that didn't stop her from putting on a show.

"Things have been great. Ivy's been busy with appearances on *The Tonight Show* and *Ellen*. She's stoked about being asked to perform at the AMAs on the twentieth. And of course she's really excited about working with you."

Nate reined in his impatience, unable to believe that he was nearly back to square one with Mia. He'd spent weeks chatting her up on the tour, afraid if he pushed too fast that she'd retreat into the persona of personal assistant to Ivy Bliss. Many times he'd asked himself why he was working so hard to draw out someone who didn't want to be noticed. Then she'd smile at him and make his entire day.

If only he could convince her to leave Ivy… Mia had

more to offer the world than just being her famous sister's flunky. For one thing, she was a ridiculously talented songwriter. When he'd discovered that she had written all the songs her sister had recorded and that she'd been denied credit on the albums, he'd been seconds away from storming into Ivy's hotel room and demanding she go public with the truth.

Mia had been mortified. She'd claimed to be okay with the lies and Nate could understand letting the error stand for the first album, but not the subsequent one. As someone who nurtured artists, he'd been appalled by what had been done to Mia by her own family, and saddened by how she'd been bullied.

"I didn't ask how your sister is doing. I asked about you."

"I'm fine. Never better." Mia could go on for hours talking about Ivy, but when it came to talking about herself, she was fond of two-word sentences.

"Tell me the truth." He was asking after her welfare, but what he really wanted to know was if she'd missed him at all. It seemed crazy that he'd known her for less than three months and in that time she'd become like breathing to him.

"I'm great. Really."

"What have you been doing since the tour ended?"

Mia shrugged. "The usual."

Meaning whatever occupied Ivy was what Mia had been doing. As her sister's personal assistant, she lived and breathed Ivy Bliss, pop princess.

"I hope she gave you a little time off."

"Ivy was invited to a charity event in South Beach and we extended our stay a couple days to kick back and soak up some sun."

Ivy demanded all Mia's time and energy. That Nate

had been able to spend any time at all alone with Mia during Ivy's eight-week stint on his tour was nothing short of amazing. They'd sneaked around like teenage kids. The danger of getting caught had promoted intimacy. And at first, Nate had found the subterfuge amusing. It got old fast.

For a while Nate wondered if he'd initially been drawn to Mia because he felt compelled to rescue her from her sister's clutches. When Mia was around Ivy, she was a quiet mouse in the corner, fetching herbal tea, being ready with Ivy's favorite snack, loosening her tension with a quick shoulder massage. And it had bothered Nate that Ivy treated Mia like an employee instead of a sister. She never seemed to appreciate how Mia's kind and thoughtful behavior went above and beyond the role of personal assistant.

"I don't like the way we left things between us," Nate declared, taking a step in her direction.

Mia took a matching step backward. "You asked for something I couldn't give you."

"I asked you to come with me to Las Vegas. I wanted to spend more time getting to know you."

"It was all happening was too fast. We'd barely known each other two months." She'd delivered the same excuse three weeks ago and it rang as hollow now as it had then. "And I couldn't leave Ivy."

"She could've found another assistant." He'd said the same thing the morning after the tour ended. The night after she'd stayed with him until the sun crested the horizon.

Their last stop had been Sydney. Following his final encore, Nate had made sure Ivy was busy and then stolen Mia away to a romantic hotel suite overlooking the harbor. They'd sipped champagne, toasted each other, laughed and made love for the first time. But as sunlight filled the room Mia was on the phone with Ivy, making excuses for where she'd been.

"I'm not just her assistant, I'm her sister," Mia said, now as then. "She needs me."

I need you.

He wouldn't repeat the words. It wouldn't do any good. She'd still choose obligation to her sister over being happy with him. And he couldn't figure out why.

"Your sister is a spoiled brat." Frustration and impatience got the better of him. "The only reason I agreed to work on her album is because of you."

Mia's beautiful brown eyes went round with shock, and although her mouth dropped open, no words emerged.

Her phone rang, interrupting the heavy silence between them. "It's Ivy." She looked almost relieved by the interruption. "I should get this."

Nate had grown weary of her sister coming between them. He crossed his arms over his chest and let sarcasm slide into his tone. "By all means, take it."

To his surprise, she put the phone on speaker. "Hey Ivy, I'm with Nate right now and you're on speaker."

After a short pause, Ivy's soprano voice came over the line. "Hi, Nate. Has Mia apologized for me missing the meeting and asked if you could meet for a drink later to chat about my album?"

Mia winced and wouldn't meet his gaze.

"Not yet," he answered.

"Then I'll ask." He could hear the seductive pout in Ivy's tone. "Please come by my house at eight."

He understood the invitation for what it was and barely restrained a growl. "If you wanted to talk about your album, you should've come by today."

Mia's large dark eyes went round with concern. *"Don't upset her,"* she told him in sign language.

Nate pretended that he hadn't seen the plea. While on tour they'd discovered they both knew how to sign. Something he'd used to overcome her reluctance to talk to him. That they'd shared a secret language had drawn them together.

"Didn't Mia explain that I had a conflict? I'm meeting with a representative for Mayfair Cosmetics. It's all hush-hush, but they're looking for the new face to represent their beauty line."

"Can you meet for dinner?" Mia signed, her eyes worried.

Nate reined in his temper, reminding himself the reason he'd offered to work with Ivy was so he could spend time with Mia and hopefully convince her to pick him over her sister this time.

"How about I make a reservation for dinner at eight," Nate said.

"Sure. Dinner would be wonderful."

"I'll text Mia with the details and this time you'd better show up." While Mia stared at him in horror, Nate reached out and disconnected the call. "Studio time costs money. I have a dozen artists I'm currently working with. If Ivy's not going to show up ready to work, then she needs to find a different producer for her album."

"Oh, no, please. She's counting on working with you." Mia was breathless and anxious. "I'll make sure she's where she needs to be exactly when you say."

"Promise?"

He held out his hand, impatient to revisit the feel of her. From the first Mia had appealed to him. She was as natural and competent as Ivy was artificial and flighty.

But it was that electric charge that sizzled through him when they touched that he craved.

Her eyes were solemn and earnest as she placed her palm against his. "Promise."

Mia hoped Nate wouldn't notice the way her fingers trembled as they shook hands. In those delightful seconds, Ivy Bliss faded from Mia's mind. There was only this tall, charismatic man with eyes the color of storm clouds.

For as far back as she could remember, Mia had been invisible. Why would anyone pay attention to the ordinary-looking child standing beside and a little behind the beautiful, charismatic, talented Ivy? And the difference between the twins had only intensified when Ivy had gotten a role in a television series and gone on to Broadway and a pop music career. Mia had become the quiet shadow at her elbow.

And then she'd met Nate. Never in a million years could Mia have believed that someone as talented and charismatic as the lead singer of Free Fall would notice she existed, much less be attracted to her. He'd seen her as a distinct individual with interests and goals. That was pretty heady stuff. No wonder she'd tumbled head over heels for him. What woman with a pulse wouldn't have?

Then the tour ended and the real world overcame the fantasy one she'd dwelled in for two months. She'd had no choice but to turn down his offer to go with him to Las Vegas. Nate had been so angry with her that last morning in Sydney. He'd accused her of leading him on. It struck her as impossible that a nobody like her could be anything more than a momentary distraction to someone as incredible as Nate Tucker.

Given all that he'd accomplished in the music industry, it amazed Mia that he was only thirty-one. An accomplished singer/songwriter and producer, he'd had six Grammy nominations for producing and won two. His band had been nominated for twenty-nine assorted awards and won eight, including several Grammys and an AMA award for favorite pop/rock band/duo/group.

"Are you okay?" he asked, peering at her.

They were still holding hands. Mia's cheeks heated as she released her grip. "Sorry." She took an awkward step back and bumped into one of the chairs surrounding the large oval conference table. "I was just thinking how lucky Ivy was for getting to work with you."

The dimple flashing in Nate's scruffy cheek vanished. "Mia, about what happened in Sydney—"

"You don't need to go there," Mia said, forcing lightness into her voice. "It was a crazy tour. So much fun. I won't ever forget it."

"That's not what I meant and you know it."

"Please, Nate." She longed to surrender to the intense glow in his eyes and fall into his arms. "You need to focus on Ivy. And so do I. She's really freaked out about this new direction in her career. I told her you were the best producer in the business and that together you would make platinum."

"I couldn't care less about her or her album. I'm only doing this so I can spend more time with you."

His words sent a spear of yearning through her, but Mia shook her head. "Don't say that. Ivy needs this album to be great." Maybe if she had a hit Ivy's insecurity would stop consuming her, and Mia could begin to live her life far from her demanding twin.

"How long are you planning to keep on being her lackey? Don't you want to be free to explore what makes you happy?"

"Of course." And she would have that life if Ivy's new project catapulted her into the big time. "And someday I'll have that chance."

"For your sake I hope someday is soon." The intensity in Nate's gaze made her shiver.

"I have to get going," Mia said, although now that she'd seen Nate again, the last thing she wanted to do was leave. "You'll text me the details about dinner tonight?"

"Yes."

As Nate escorted Mia to the lobby, she noticed he didn't touch her again.

"It was good seeing you," she murmured awkwardly. She wanted to throw herself into his arms and declare how much she'd missed him. But that would only make the problems between them worse.

Mia maintained a firm grip on her impulses. The connection they'd share on tour had been packed up and put away with the instruments, lights and sound equipment. Sneaking around behind Ivy's back had been necessary and exciting, but it wasn't something Mia intended to do any longer.

While on tour Ivy had been distracted by the traveling, flirting with Free Fall's single band members and blowing up social media for her fans. In Las Vegas, she would be completely focused on her music and on Nate. Mia wouldn't have any opportunities for time alone with him.

Ever since Ivy learned that she was going to work with Nate, she'd been more agitated and demanding than Mia ever remembered her being. Mia wasn't a fool. She understood why Ivy was so reluctant to give her space. Heaven forbid Mia would get a life and walk away.

After leaving Nate, Mia was halfway through the errands she was running for Ivy when her phone began to play Ivy's latest hit, her special ring tone. Mia held off answering for several seconds. But she'd already ignored a bunch of Ivy's texts, and her sister would have a fit if she didn't pick up now.

"OMG. Where have you been? I've texted you, like, a dozen times." Ivy's voice poured from Mia's smartphone, scattering her thoughts to the wind. Behind closed doors the sweetheart pop star became a demanding diva. "I've been dying to hear all about how excited Nate is that we're working together."

"Sorry I didn't respond." In fact, she'd been lost in thought and hadn't heard the alerts. "Traffic was crazy and there was an accident…"

"If you were sitting in traffic you should have called." Ivy barely gave that a second to sink in before continuing, "Whatever. Tell me. Tell me."

"Of course he's excited to be working with you."

"What did he say exactly?"

"That you're going to make the best album ever." It was lame, but her sister would freak if Mia shared what Nate had actually said. "But listen, Ivy—"

Her sister's squeal interrupted her. "I knew it. He is into me."

"I'm sorry. What?" Mia almost rear-ended the car in front of her when the driver stopped abruptly to avoid hitting an SUV that cut him off.

"Nate. He's into me." Ivy sounded quite pleased with herself. "I told you how he was hitting on me on tour."

"Nate hit on you?" Mia's stomach clenched in dismay at Ivy's words. "When was that?"

When it came to her sister, Mia was like one of Pavlov's dogs. She panicked at the first sign that her sister was scheming. Ivy made an art form out of keeping the focus on her. Even before Ivy became famous she knew how to manipulate a situation to suit her and often Mia received the full brunt of the backlash. Since then Ivy had pulled several stunts to stay in the spotlight. Mia had learned to keep her head down.

"All the time. How did you not notice?"

"Sure. Of course." Mia was glad her sister couldn't see her expression.

"And I never told you, but that last night in Sydney…" She let the confession hang in the air to build suspense.

"What about it?"

"We were together."

A curse shot from Mia before she could stop herself. "Sorry, I almost hit the car in front of me. This traffic is—"

"Whatever. Did you hear what I said?"

"About you being with Nate that last night in Sydney?" Mia was torn between a laugh and a groan. Good thing she'd already put her romance with Nate behind her. Now that Ivy had decided she wanted him, any hint that Mia had feelings for him would be disastrous.

"I should've told you."

Mia's voice was uncharacteristically sharp as she asked, "Why didn't you?"

"You don't need to be such a bitch. I'm sorry I didn't say something sooner, but I wasn't sure if what we had was going anywhere."

"And now?" Mia turned into the parking structure closest to the stores she needed to hit.

"Ever since I found out he asked to work with me on my new album, I've been convinced what we have is the real deal." Ivy sounded at the same time dreamy and triumphant. "When will you be getting back to the house?"

"I'm heading to Rodeo Drive to take care of the stuff you wanted me to return." Ivy loved to shop, but she could be fickle when it came to liking things once she got them home. "It shouldn't take me more than half an hour."

As self-absorbed as Ivy could be, when it came to her twin, she liked knowing everything Mia was up to. It had gotten to the point where Mia gave up on having secrets of her own. Or that's the way it had been until Nate came along. That they shared the ability to sign had enabled Mia to have something all to herself that Ivy couldn't barge in on and take over.

Mia realized she'd been counting on this album to launch her sister, hoping that it would be enough of a distraction to allow Mia to escape.

Was that how she viewed Ivy? As someone Mia needed to run away from? The relationship between Mia and her sister hadn't always been so strained. Until the last three or four years, when Ivy's career really took off, Mia and Ivy had been as close as two people who shared the same womb for nine months could be.

If anything demonstrated how much Mia craved a chance to get out of Ivy's shadow, it was her clandestine flirtation with a man her sister had shown an interest in. And now Mia realized that despite the way she'd left things that last morning in Sydney, a part of her hadn't given up on pursing a relationship with Nate.

In the beginning she'd simply enjoyed Nate's charismatic presence. Not only was the lead singer of Free Fall a musical genius, he had killer dimples that rendered her speechless, and the sort of lean muscles that made her all too aware of her vulnerable heart, unsteady knees and tendency to blush.

At first she hadn't taken his attention seriously. Fate had seen to it that Ivy was granted all the beauty and most of the talent. Most people outside their family didn't even know Mia and Ivy were sisters, much less twins. Ivy had taken their mother's maiden name because she liked the way it sounded, and Bliss worked great for marketing.

And then one day Nate had been backstage while Ivy rehearsed. She'd stopped the sound check and was shrieking at the drummer for messing with the tempo. Across the ten feet separating them, Mia saw the gesture Nate made, and amusement must have shown on her face because he snagged her gaze and winked.

Mia had signed, asking him if he knew what that particular gesture meant, and he signed back that he absolutely did. For the duration of Ivy's sound check, they'd discovered through sign language that each had a hearing-impaired family member. That day something unexpected had happened to Mia. She'd made an unlikely friend. And in the weeks that followed, it became more.

Ivy broke into her thoughts. "Can you stop and get me a coffee on your way back? You know how I like it."

Keeping up with Ivy's demands required Mia's full attention. For most of her life that hadn't bothered her. But ever since Nate had come along and actually noticed her, not as Ivy's twin or her assistant, but as a desirable woman, Mia spent more and more time thinking about a life away from Ivy.

"Sure." Now all she needed to do was find a way to explain to her family that she wanted to strike out on her own. And that was not going to be easy. "I know exactly how it needs to be."

Two

As soon as Mia left the studio, Nate got on the phone with Trent's sister. Melody had been on the tour with him as the opening act for Free Fall the entire twelve months.

Because he knew her as not only a fantastic songwriter and singer, but also as the little sister of his best friend and business partner, when she'd asked what was going on between him and Mia, he'd told her. Melody didn't like the way Mia was treated by her sister any more than he did. She'd grown up with a father who liked to bully people and had a particular sensitivity to such treatment.

Once she'd been clued in to what was going on, Melody had helped keep Ivy distracted so Nate and Mia could have as much uninterrupted time together as possible. At first Nate wasn't sure if Mia had any idea how Melody was helping them, but she'd caught on quickly. Mia and Melody shared a talent for songwriting and during the hours they spent collaborating became good friends.

The difference in Mia when Ivy wasn't around showed Nate how unhappy Mia was being her sister's personal assistant. Yet whenever he broached the subject of leaving her sister's employment to do something for herself, he hit a brick wall.

"You told your brother I met someone while on tour?"

"I might have mentioned that you were a bit distracted." Melody responded carefully, but there was laughter in her tone.

Nate closed his eyes and rubbed his temple. Melody had a romantic nature and succumbed easily to simple gestures of affection, like the dozen handwritten notes her boyfriend, Kyle Tailor, had tucked amongst the clothes in her suitcase. She'd discovered them halfway across the country and been over the moon that Kyle had done something so romantic.

Unfortunately, the strain of separation for so many months had led to trouble in their relationship. Nate blamed himself. If it weren't for him, Melody never would've gone on tour. He'd been the one who persuaded her to leave behind the anonymity of songwriting and to join him onstage. She had a fantastic voice and deserved to shine.

Fortunately, Kyle didn't blame him. If he had, it might have put a strain on their business partnership in Club T's.

"He thinks it's Ivy." Nate spent the next minute listening to Melody's laughter. "It's not funny."

"Oh, it is. Why does he think that?"

"Because I suggested I produce her next album. It's the only way I could think of to spend more time with Mia. She's determined we're over."

"I think that's fantastic. The girl has a killer voice and needs a producer who can showcase it. Besides, no one but you can stand up to that father of hers and make sure her next album kills it."

"I'm flattered that you think so." Nate's tone was as dry as the Mohave Desert.

"So how did the meeting go?"

"It didn't. Mia showed up without her sister and father. Apparently they were taking a meeting with someone from Mayfair Cosmetics. They're considering Ivy as their next spokesmodel."

"Are you kidding? They stood you up? Don't they realize who you are?"

"Obviously someone they can skip a meeting with." Nate thought about his stern words to Mia about her sister and regretted taking his frustration out on her. It wasn't her fault how her sister and father behaved. "I'm taking them to dinner tonight. Hopefully, they'll show up this time. I'm going to be out of commission for a few weeks starting tomorrow."

"Out of commission? What's going on?"

"I'm going in for surgery on my vocal cords."

"What? When did this come up?"

"I started noticing a problem on the tour, but we were so close to the end, and I didn't want to cancel any shows." In part because to do so meant shortening his time with Mia. Their relationship heated up a lot in the last two weeks and he wouldn't have missed that for anything.

"This is serious. Why didn't you say anything to me? Does Trent know?"

"I told him earlier today."

"Is he taking you to the surgery appointment?"

"He's out of town. I have a car scheduled. It'll be fine."

"No it won't. I'll get on a plane and be there to take you back to the hotel."

"That's not necessary. You need to stay in Vegas and work on your album. I've given you a deadline, remember?"

"A couple days isn't going to matter one way or another."

"Humor me." Letting anyone baby him was not in his nature. "It's outpatient surgery. I'll be in and out in a few hours."

"Why do you have to be so strong all the time? It wouldn't kill you to accept help once in a while." Melody let loose an exasperated sigh. "You are so stubborn."

After a childhood spent bouncing from one backwater town to another, Nate had learned to take care of himself. Sometimes his dad would be gone for months, sent all over the country to whatever oil fields needed his expertise the most. If the job required an extended stay, he might bring Nate and his mom along. Nate's dad never cared if this meant his son had to fit in at a new school or that his wife would have to take whatever job she could to make ends meet.

"I could say the same of you." Nate knew of only one way to get Melody off this particular subject. "How are things between you and Kyle? Have you talked yet?"

"Did you know that Trent hired Hunter to DJ twice a month at Club T's?"

"He mentioned something about it. I told him it was a bad idea."

Hunter Graves was Melody's ex-boyfriend. Several months ago he and Melody had run into each other in a New York City club. As they were leaving, to keep from getting separated while passing through the raucous crowd outside, Hunter had taken Melody's hand as they headed to a waiting car. The paparazzi had snapped several pictures of the couple and the media had ruthlessly promoted its theory that the former lovers had reunited.

Back home, while Kyle hadn't really believed Melody was cheating on him, he hadn't appreciated seeing the woman he loved hand in hand with her ex. And the months of separation had created tension for the couple, making Kyle even more reactive.

Melody sighed in Nate's ear. "And to answer your earlier question, Kyle and I have exchanged several texts, but we haven't sat down to talk."

"Don't you think that should happen soon?"

"I'm afraid if we have the talk we'll just end up fighting and the subject of us being over will come up."

"Kyle hasn't come to Las Vegas and taken over temporary management of Club T's because he's ready to give up on you two."

"He's here because Trent's in LA with Savannah and the club needs a manager." Melody's voice had a ragged quality that tore at Nate's heart. "Sorry," she muttered. "I really hope you're right about him, but I can't stop feeling like he's going to use what's happened between us since that photo came out to rationalize that we're not really meant to be together."

"He's not going to do that," Nate said. "Especially after he finds out what's really going on."

"What do you mean by that?" Melody sounded more wary than confused.

"You forget how hard it is to keep secrets on tours."

"You and Mia managed."

"That's because the only one we had to keep in the dark was Ivy, and in general she's so preoccupied with herself that she isn't sensitive to what's going on around her." Nate circled back to Melody's problem. "When are you going to tell Kyle he's going to be a father?"

"Damn. Who else knows?"

"Both Dan and Mike commented that you were looking a bit off and mentioned that their wives had both been sick like that when they were pregnant."

"Why did they tell you?"

"Because you're like my little sister and I've made it pretty clear all along that anyone who messed with you would get their ass kicked by me."

Melody huffed out of a breath. "I can take care of myself."

"Aww, that's cute," he mocked. "But you really can't. You are too sweet for your own good and people take advantage of that."

The same could be said of Mia. And his mother. Nate recognized he had a pattern when it came to women. He didn't actively seek out those most in need of protecting, but he did tend to gravitate to the ones who had a hard time sticking up for themselves.

"And you don't let anyone take care of you," Melody countered. "Case in point, tomorrow's surgery."

"Okay, we've both poked at each other's shortcomings long enough," Nate said with a laugh. "I'll shoot you a text tomorrow after it's done and let you know how it went."

"I'm not kidding about coming to LA to sit at your bedside."

"And I appreciate the offer, but I'd rather you take care of things there." He paused before delivering his final bit of advice. "Talk to Kyle. He's going to be thrilled."

"I will. Good luck tomorrow."

"Thanks."

After talking with Melody, Nate made a reservation for four at WP24, Wolfgang Puck's contemporary Asian restaurant on the twenty-fourth floor of the Ritz-Carlton. He selected this particular restaurant knowing Mia would love the downtown LA views and the blackberry soufflé with key lime ice cream for dessert. Once that was done, he texted her the details and then headed to grab a late lunch with his former buddy whose music career had nosedived six years ago, thanks to a drug problem, but who was making a small comeback.

Nate didn't return to his hotel until nearly six. He spent the time before dinner Skyping with his mother and letting her know in rapid ASL about the surgery the following day. At least he wouldn't have to worry about being able to communicate with her over the next two to three weeks while he was on total voice rest. If only the rest of his clients understood sign language, he might be able to maintain his work schedule with barely a hitch.

At a little before eight, Nate stepped off the elevator on the twenty-fourth floor of the Ritz-Carlton and approached the hostess. His pulse kicked up as he looked around for Mia, but he didn't see her or her family. The hostess confirmed they'd not yet arrived, and escorted him to a table by the windows. When the waiter arrived, Nate ordered a vodka on the rocks with a twist of lime. Normally he'd wait until his party showed up, but he expected Mia and her family to be late and they didn't disappoint them. What he hadn't expected, however, was Mia's absence.

Nate stood as Ivy approached. She wore a strapless emerald dress that clung to her slim body and brought out the gold flecks in her brown eyes. Her five-inch heels put a sexy sway in her stride.

"Nate," she cried in delight as if they were the best of friends. "It's so wonderful to see you."

They hadn't gotten along particularly well on the tour. She'd made demands on everyone from the roadies to the tour manager, and some of her requests had been ridiculous. The amount of time Nate had spent running interference hadn't sat well with him. And he had a particular distaste for how she treated Mia.

"Hello, Ivy," he said, pushing down his annoyance at how he'd been stood up earlier. "Good evening, Javier." He reached out his hand to Ivy's father, a handsome dark-haired man trailing in the pop star's wake. One member of the party was missing. "I made the reservation for four. Will Mia be joining us?"

Ivy settled into the chair beside his. "She wanted to come, but what's the point?"

The annoyance that flared in his gut was familiar. Everything about this spoiled narcissistic brat made him long to hand off her album project to another producer, but his whole purpose in working with Ivy was to have time with Mia.

"The point is I invited her."

"I thought the point of this meeting tonight was to discuss Ivy's album," Javier said, coming down on his daughter's side. "Mia's presence is unnecessary."

"Of course." Giving in was exceedingly painful. Nate could only imagine the conversation that had kept Mia away, and his heart ached that she'd received yet another slight from the people who should have had her best interests in mind.

The waiter approached before Nate could say anything more. Ivy ordered champagne and Javier ordered a gin and tonic.

"I've heard the food here is quite good," Javier said.

Ivy rolled her eyes. "If you like Asian."

Nate was pretty certain no matter which restaurant he'd chosen Ivy would've found something wrong with it.

Without Mia's presence, Nate had no desire to linger over the meal. As soon as they'd ordered he cut straight to business. "I have some ideas for how to proceed with your new album."

"I want to go in a completely different direction," Ivy said, cutting him off before she even heard what he had to say. "I'm not going to write my own music this time. I'd like to record some of Melody Caldwell's music. I heard what she was working on during the tour and I think it suits me."

While Nate agreed, he was dismayed that Ivy had no plans to record her sister's songs. Few people knew Ivy didn't write any of her own music but claimed credit for what Mia composed. Nate had discovered this during the tour and couldn't believe Mia let her sister get away with it. He suspected that part of the reason Mia stayed with Ivy and acted as her assistant was to have her music heard by millions. Did Mia know that Ivy was cutting her out? Would this at last be the catalyst that encouraged Mia to sever the bonds with her sister and strike out on her own?

"I can see if Melody would be open to working with you."

"Why wouldn't she?" Javier demanded. "Having Ivy Bliss record her songs would be a good career move for her."

"Currently Melody is working on an album of her own. A song list hasn't been finalized and I can't promise what will be available for you until that happens."

"I have several songs I'm interested in. I'll have Mia

send her a list in the morning. I'm sure Melody will understand that I can do them justice."

"Perhaps you and Melody could collaborate on some new stuff," Nate suggested, hoping the offer made Ivy squirm. "I've worked with her on several songs she's recorded. I think you two would enjoy collaborating."

He smiled through the patent lie. If Melody caught wind of what he'd just offered, she'd probably kill him. Nate doubted anyone on the planet enjoyed working with Ivy Bliss.

"I'm afraid my daughter will be too busy to write any music this year. This afternoon she signed a deal to become the new face of Mayfair Cosmetics. This will entail many media appearances beginning a month from now. We'd like to get in and get her album recorded as soon as possible."

So they expected him to clear his schedule? Nate wasn't surprised. And he would not be bullied. "I'm afraid the next month will not be good for me. Let's look at something after the first of the year?"

"Ivy is doing a movie in January."

Once again Nate reminded himself that the reason he'd agreed to produce the album was to have time with Mia. And then something occurred to him. It was brilliant, and he kicked himself for not coming up with it sooner.

His lips slid into a genuine smile. "Perhaps we could work something out. I'll need to rearrange my schedule and would appreciate having Mia's help to pull it off."

"Mia's help?" Ivy frowned. "What could she possibly do for you?"

"She understands sign language, doesn't she? I could use her as a translator."

Javier frowned. "A translator?"

"I'm going in for vocal cord surgery tomorrow and won't be able to speak for at least three weeks. I can sign and Mia can relay my instructions."

"Couldn't you find someone else to help with that?" Ivy demanded. "An actual interpreter?"

No one else but Mia would do. "Mia knows the music industry and will understand what I'm saying."

"Daddy?" Ivy's dismay was palpable.

Nate fixed Javier with a flat stare. "Surely you can spare her for a month if it means getting Ivy's album done."

Javier glanced at his daughter. "W-well," he stammered. "Of course. If that's what we need to do."

Nate gave a satisfied nod. "It absolutely is."

Mia sat in a chair beside the window of her bedroom in Ivy's house and stared at the front lawn. An hour earlier she'd watched her father's Mercedes retreat down the driveway, and still couldn't believe that she'd been forced to stay behind. More than ever her role as Ivy's personal assistant grated on her.

Though Mia felt trapped by her responsibility to Ivy, she knew that her sister carried an even heavier burden: the weight of their parents' expectations. Mia barely remembered a time when her sister didn't sing. She recalled their modest house in San Diego, where the twins had shared a bedroom with their older sister, Eva. Their mother had homeschooled all three girls, which offered the flexibility for Ivy to audition anytime an opportunity presented itself. And their parents were able to buy a bigger house when Ivy signed a contract for a new TV show on the KidZ Channel. While she wasn't the star, in the show's four-year run Ivy had demonstrated star potential, which had led to her landing a role in a

Broadway musical and eventually a record deal with West Coast Records.

With each rise in her career, the family home got bigger and better. Their father had quit his job with the post office to manage Ivy when she signed with KidZ Channel. Ivy became his whole focus.

Which brought Mia to tonight, and the business meeting her father and sister were attending with Nate. And just as her presence hadn't been needed at the Mayfair Cosmetics meeting earlier that day, Mia wasn't included now.

She wondered if Nate's choice of WP24 had been for her benefit. She'd mentioned how she'd always wanted to try the restaurant, but that had been a couple months ago. Had Nate remembered?

Mia's stomach grumbled, reminding her she hadn't eaten anything since noon. Even though her appetite was nonexistent, her body still needed fuel. Time to stop brooding and scrounge up something for dinner. Ivy's housekeeper usually cooked some chicken in case Ivy felt like supplementing her junk food diet with something healthy.

After pulling out the fixings for a salad and chopping up a chicken breast, Mia splurged with an extra tablespoon of ranch dressing. Too bad she gained weight simply by looking at French fries. As she headed into the den to watch some TV and hopefully take her mind off what was going on at WP24, she reminded herself that Nate had appreciated her full breasts, small waist and round hips.

Both Mia and Eva took after their mother with their dark brown hair and eyes, pale skin and curvy bodies. Ivy was built like their dad, lean and sinewy, but she had their mother's hazel eyes, smoldering charm and singing ability. Sharon Bliss had been an opera singer in her youth, but happily traded a career on the stage for being a wife and mother when she got pregnant with Eva.

Mia had barely sat down when her cell phone rang. She smiled when she saw that the caller was Melody. "I feel as if I haven't talked to you in ages. How are you doing?" she said by way of greeting.

"I'm doing great. Working on my album."

"How many songs are you up to now?"

Melody was a prolific songwriter with a powerful voice and distaste for the spotlight. The two women had become close while on tour. Mia didn't realize how much she missed having a friend until she and Melody had clicked.

"I don't know," Melody said. "Maybe around fifty. They're not all good, but many of my favorites are the ones with the biggest flaws. How am I supposed to choose between them?"

"I know the feeling. Some of my best stuff will never be heard." Until she'd gone on tour, only her family knew that she—and not Ivy—was the author of Ivy's hit tunes. Then she'd met Nate and Melody, and both of them had figured out her secret. Or maybe she hadn't tried very hard to conceal it. Both were such talented songwriters that Mia couldn't resist the urge to talk to them about their process.

To preserve the illusion that Ivy was writing her own songs, Mia was always careful to work when no one was around. But sometimes a tune got into her head and she caught herself humming it. The same thing happened with lyrics. It was why she always carried around her journal.

The notebook contained bits and pieces of songs and

snippets of lyrics. It also included doodles and miscellaneous thoughts. She filled one every six months or so.

"Nate could help you with that. I'm sure he'd be happy to work up some demos with you that you could shop around the industry. You never know what might get picked up."

"Actually, he's already offered."

"And what are you waiting for?"

Mia hadn't explained to anyone the real reason she stayed at her sister's side despite the way she was treated like hired help instead of family. It wasn't Mia's story to tell and she knew neither Ivy nor her parents would appreciate the information getting out. Not that Melody or Nate couldn't be trusted with yet another of her secrets.

"I'm not waiting for anything. It's just that I barely have enough time to write, much less create demos." But with Ivy scheduled to record her album at Nate's Ugly Trout studios in Las Vegas, perhaps she would have time to do something for herself for a change.

"Speaking of Nate, did you know he was going in for throat surgery tomorrow?"

"No." Mia's heart gave a worried thump. "I knew he was struggling while we were on tour, and that he pushed through because he didn't want to cancel any shows, but we haven't spoken much since the tour ended."

Nate had made it perfectly clear that he wanted to continue the relationship. As intoxicating as their affair had been, Mia knew it was only a matter of time until their paths diverged. He wanted her to choose him over Ivy, but she just couldn't leave her sister. Would the time ever be right? It was the question Nate had posed that last morning in Sydney. Mia had no clear answer.

"I'm worried about him. He's using a car service to get to and from the doctor's office tomorrow, and he doesn't have anyone staying with him at the hotel to help him after the procedure. I was wondering, since you are in LA, if you could check on him."

"Of course." It was something a friend would do and they'd parted on reasonably good terms. Why hadn't he said anything to her when they'd met earlier?

Mia ran through what she would say to her sister tomorrow about taking care of Nate, and decided she would simply tell her that she needed some time off. It wasn't as if Mia got to take vacations like a regular person. All the time she spent around Ivy was work, even when she was technically off. They might head to the Caribbean or the beaches of Europe together for a little R & R, but it wasn't as though Mia got to party all night, drink too much and sleep in.

"Do you know what clinic he's going to?" Mia asked. "And what time the surgery is?"

"No. I'm assuming that he's using Dr. Hanson. He's the best vocal cord surgeon in LA. Nate mentioned the appointment is first thing in the morning."

"How about where he's staying?"

"He usually gets a suite at the Four Seasons Beverly Hills when he's in LA. It's close to West Coast Records' offices."

"I know it well. Ivy stayed there while renovations were being done on her house."

"One more thing. Don't tell Nate you're coming. You know how he hates accepting help."

"I've got it covered. He'll never know what hit him."

"You're a doll," Melody said. "I've been sick, thinking about him all alone after the surgery."

"Don't worry," Mia said. "I'll take excellent care of him."

"I know you will. And he might never admit it, but I think he'll be really glad to have you there."

Three

The morning of his surgery Nate's thoughts were running on a hamster wheel, getting him nowhere. Not being able to talk for several weeks was going to make communicating with his clients a challenge. Although he'd asked for Mia's help from her father and sister, he hadn't approached her about acting as his voice for the next three to four weeks.

It wasn't that he couldn't hire an assistant with ASL experience, although it might be tricky finding one on such short notice. He also wasn't worried that the studio was booked solid and people were counting on him. He dreaded getting turned down by Mia again.

Pushing all that to the side, Nate left his suite and headed to the elevator. When the car arrived at his floor, a young couple with a baby stroller were already inside. Nate stepped to the side of the elevator and gazed from the infant to the happy parents. Almost against his will, his thoughts turned to Mia.

During those days with her on tour, for the first time ever, he'd contemplated what it would take to balance life on the road with a family. With the amount of touring Free Fall had done for the first few years when they were making a name for themselves, Nate hadn't even considered settling down.

Promoting an album meant grueling months on the road. It wasn't the sort of thing where you dragged a wife and kids along. Well, some people did. But unless it was the right sort of relationship, traveling from one end of the country to another put a lot of strain on a couple.

And then he'd met Mia. She was used to long months of touring and being away from home. As Ivy's personal assistant, she was on the go constantly. In fact, he wasn't entirely sure if she had a home of her own. He'd easily pictured them working together in the studio and then going out on tour. If they had a baby, the whole family would travel. It had been an appealing fantasy.

The elevator opened on the lobby and the couple with the stroller exited. Nate's mood, already battered by his anxiety about the surgery, took another hit. Damn, he was tired of being alone.

Suddenly every muscle in his body ached. He hadn't felt a sweeping depression like this in ten years. Back then he'd fought off the darkness with pills, booze and sex. None of it had helped, but for a while he'd been able to forget.

Nate stepped into the lobby, calling himself all kinds of coward and idiot for trying to handle things on his own. He was always the first one to lend a hand if someone needed it. Why did he have such an awful time accepting help?

Shame. Admitting that he wasn't strong enough to protect his mother when he was a kid or conquer an addiction to drugs when he was in his early twenties had led to both situations becoming worse. If he'd reached out for help, maybe his mom wouldn't have been nearly beaten to death by his father and he wouldn't have ended up burning bridges in the music business.

Nate headed across the hotel lobby and outside to where a car should be waiting to take him to the doctor's office. He'd turned down Trent's and Melody's offers to help, and he wasn't feeling great about his decision. But he hated being a bother. Trent was out of town with Savannah and Dylan. Melody was in Las Vegas. And while his mother would have happily flown in from Dallas to baby him for a few days, Nate didn't want to put her out. The surgery was delicate, but not overly invasive, and he was perfectly capable of taking care of himself.

And then the most amazing thing happened. A familiar brunette got up from a chair near the front door and started walking in his direction. Her appearance was so unexpected that he rubbed his eyes to determine if he was hallucinating. If so, she was the most beautiful, wonderful, perfect figment of his imagination he'd ever experienced.

"Mia?"

"At last," she said, gliding into step beside him. "I was worried that I'd missed you. How are you doing?" She peered up at him as the lobby doors opened with a whoosh and fresh air poured over them. "Are you nervous?"

"What are you doing here?"

"I'm here to take care of you." She gave him a stern look. "Why didn't you tell me you were having surgery?"

His first impulse was to tell her he didn't think it would matter to her. But that was a crappy response. He also hadn't thought she'd be available since her sister kept her so busy.

Instead he asked, "How did you know?"

"Melody told me. She said you didn't have anyone to help you after the surgery and she was worried." The look Mia shot him was pure accusation. "And so was I."

"I'll be perfectly fine."

"Ridiculous. A doctor won't release anyone going under anesthesia unless they're being picked up and watched over by a responsible adult. So, I'm going to sit in the waiting room while you have your surgery. And then I'm going to bring you back here. Tuck you in. And keep watch over you."

All that sounded like pure heaven. Having her fuss over him for the next few hours would speed his recovery along.

"You don't need to wait," he told her as they settled into the back of the town car. "The procedure could take up to six hours."

"I'm staying." Her tone was firm. "I brought stuff to read."

"Thank you." Such simple words didn't convey his full emotions. He was so damned glad to have her with him. But she smiled as if she understood.

Nate didn't feel much like talking on the way to the clinic, so they sat in companionable silence. The surgery was the most terrifying thing he'd ever faced and that included the night his sixteen-year-old self had gone up against his drunk, knife-wielding father.

Singing was more than just Nate's livelihood. It was how he'd comforted himself as a kid in an abusive home and the way he communicated who he was to the world.

No matter how successful he became as a producer and songwriter, he'd give up every penny he had to be able to perform on stage. This was something he hadn't realized until he was faced with the grim prospect of throat surgery.

When the nurse came to take him into the back, Mia gave him a reassuring smile. It was her face that filled his thoughts as he was wheeled to the operating room and injected with something to put him to sleep.

And when he woke what seemed like seconds later—in post-op, he guessed, based on the dim lighting and hushed silence—her name was the first thought that popped into his head. He floated in post-surgery haze, happy that she was waiting to take him back to his hotel As the residual anesthesia wore off, Nate lifted fingers to his throat, but the discomfort was all on the inside. Had the surgery been successful? He wouldn't know for several weeks, maybe months.

A nurse came to check on him and asked yes-or-no questions he could answer by nodding or shaking his head. She reiterated what the doctor and all the nurses before her had drilled into him: no talking of any kind for two to three weeks and minimal use of his voice after that. He'd start working with a vocal coach in a month, which would be a new experience. In all the years he'd performed, Nate had never had any formal training. He just got up on stage and let 'er rip.

They wanted him back in three days for a checkup, after which he could return to Las Vegas to continue healing. The nurse recommended Throat Coat tea with honey and gave him a prescription for pain meds.

"Your throat will probably grow more uncomfortable as the day goes on. Drink lots of fluids and remember, no talking."

Nate nodded. He might suck at taking advice on most things, but this he intended to follow to the letter. He couldn't imagine losing the ability to sing and perform.

While he had songwriting and producing to fall back on, the energy that came at him from a packed stadium was a high he craved.

From post-op they sent him back into the waiting room, where Mia was still waiting, and gave him a glass of water. It slid down his throat without too much irritation and he grew hopeful.

"Are you okay?" Mia asked, giving his hand a gentle squeeze. "Let me know when you're ready to head to the car."

He nodded.

The trip back to the hotel was a blur. When they arrived at his suite, Nate fumbled out his key card and tried to focus on getting it into the slot. He wanted to curse, but knew better than to speak. And then, Mia plucked the key from him and within seconds the door swung open. He took a step forward and his head picked that second to swim. With his reflexes not quite back to normal, he swayed and made a grab for the doorframe just in time to prevent himself from pitching forward.

Her arm went around his waist to steady him. "I've got you," she said, but she wasn't as calm and collected as she sounded. Her brown eyes looked huge in her pale face.

"I'm okay, really."

She looked so appalled that he almost laughed, but he knew better than to make a sound.

"You okay?"

She gave a husky laugh. "I'll be better once you're in bed and resting."

"I knew you'd been dying to get me back into bed." His dry smile didn't help ease the tense line between her brows. And then, becoming more serious, he signed, *"It means a lot that you're here."*

He wanted to follow it up by asking how long she could stay, but again sensed the answer wouldn't make him happy. For now, he'd enjoy her company and take what time with her he could get.

"I'm sorry things between us didn't work out…" She was prevented from saying more by his fingertips against her lips.

He didn't want to talk about the failure of their relationship or argue about Mia's inability to escape her sister's demands. His arms ached to hold her. At the moment he didn't have energy to do more than sit on the couch with her snuggled against him, though.

"Come." He patted the cushion beside him.

"You should go to bed."

"I'm not tired."

For an instant he worried she might call him on that, but then she joined him on the couch.

"At least lie down."

He obliged by shifting until he lay on his back, his head in her lap. She ran her fingers through his hair. The soothing caress made his whole body ache. Damn, but he'd missed her. How many times in the last month had he relived those precious few hours they'd spent together that last night in Sydney? Over and over the memories tumbled through his mind as he recalled every touch and kiss. The ravenous hunger with which they'd come together that first time. The ache in his chest as the sun lifted above the horizon. The glorious, joyful goddess he'd held in his arms, who faded before his eyes as the morning grew brighter.

He'd sworn then that he would have her. All of her. He intended to do whatever it took to make her happy. Only she would have none of it. None of him. She didn't understand what it meant to be selfish. To demand happiness. Her family had molded her into someone who put her needs after everyone else's.

He closed his eyes and enjoyed the silence. With Mia he'd learned to appreciate being quiet, for it allowed him to be fully in the moment. Almost immediately, however, Nate found himself drifting off, and fought to stay awake. He'd learned during those long weeks on tour to savor every minute with Mia, because all too often their secret rendezvous were interrupted. But with what he'd gone through earlier today, his body craved sleep.

The next time he woke the suite was dim. His head remained cushioned on Mia's lap. He rubbed his face and sat up.

"What time is it?" he signed.

"Six. How are you feeling?"

"Sore."

"I'll get you some water." She got to her feet and headed for the wet bar consisting of a mini-fridge behind a white panel door. When she returned and handed him a chilled bottle, she asked, "Do you want to take something?"

He shook his head. Although the pain in his throat required medication to take the edge off, he didn't like the way the drugs made him feel. Early in his career he'd gotten caught up in the highs and lows of the music scene and had partied too hard. He'd relied on booze and pills to jack him up and mellow him out. And then there had always been girls. They were relentless. He'd signed boobs and butts. He'd taken two to bed and woken up with a third. And all this had happened before Free Fall had their first hit.

Then one morning, Nate had woken up with a thick head and a sick feeling in his gut that had nothing to do with how much he'd consumed the night before. There was a fist-size dent in his hotel room wall and a descriptive expletive written in lipstick on his bathroom mirror. He remembered being angry, but not why. It had been perfectly clear, however, that he'd struck out in anger. Just like his old man used to do.

Nate didn't have any luck tracking down the girl he'd brought back to his room. She'd just been one of the faceless hangers-on who liked to party after the concerts. He'd been twenty-three and the wake-up call had changed his life. He took a break from the band and returned home to Las Vegas, where he'd spent the next twelve months writing music.

It hadn't been an easy time. For the first two months neither the words nor the music would flow. The urge to lose himself in alcohol or drugs had been a constant nagging presence. Much of the songwriting he'd done to that point had been while he was under the influence. He was afraid he didn't know how to write any other way. At that time his mom had still been living in Las Vegas. Being around her kept him from backsliding. He had only to look at her to remember how his father had gone after her with fists and eventually a knife.

At long last the music came more easily. The words took a lot longer. What he wanted to say came from his pain and his isolation and his sense of failure. These were not easy places to visit. He'd never really come to terms with the young boy who'd been too afraid to defend his mother. While a rational part of him knew it was ridiculous to expect a kid to take on a drunk, belligerent adult with a murderous temper, Nate knew there were things he should have done.

Like tell someone. His teacher. A cop. Anyone who could help. His mom had never learned to read lips and had had a hard time communicating. Nate became her voice from the time he could speak. But when it counted, he hadn't spoken for her.

"Are you hungry?" Mia asked. "I can heat up some soup. I brought you some of my famous chicken broth. And I have Throat Coat tea with honey."

Nate gazed up at her in bemusement. If this was what it felt like to be the beneficiary of Mia's nurturing, no wonder Ivy kept her sister on such a tight leash. How wonderful to have someone so focused on your every need.

I could get used to having you around all the time, he thought, but instead signed. *"I'm hungry."*

He hadn't noticed his empty stomach until Mia mentioned the soup. The thought of eating something she'd prepared with her lovely hands made him smile.

"What?" she asked, taking in his expression.

"I can't believe you're here."

"Well, don't get used to it," she teased, heading to the fridge once more. "You only get me for three days."

She busied herself pulling out a plastic container and ladling soup into a bowl. The suite had only the bare minimum of supplies—a coffeemaker, cups and a microwave, in addition to the small refrigerator—but somehow Mia presented a lovely tray with silverware, a linen napkin and even a tiny vase with a daisy in it.

"All this for me?" he signed as she placed the tray on his lap.

"Eat what you can. And there's vanilla and caramel gelato for dessert if you think you can manage it."

Instead of joining him on the couch, she sat in a chair nearby and watched him like a hawk as he tasted the soup. "Is it okay? Not too bland?"

"It's delicious."

"You should be able to switch to thicker liquids and

soft foods tomorrow. Maybe some creamy cauliflower or broccoli soup?" He'd once told her he hated any sort of pureed vegetable, and wondered if she was taking perverse pleasure in his situation. When he scowled at her, she laughed. "Macaroni and cheese?"

"Better." And then, since he had her full attention, he added, *"It means a lot to me that you're here."*

Mia drew her knees to her chest, making herself as small as possible. He would have no idea how much his heartfelt words meant to her. Actually, it wasn't his words as much as the look in his eyes that warmed her from the tips of her fingers down to her toes. In the weeks they'd spent apart, she didn't remember ever feeling so alone and empty.

"We promised to be there for each other always," she reminded him, proud that she sounded so steady. He couldn't know what a struggle it was for her to keep from throwing herself into his arms and confessing how miserable she'd been without him. "What sort of friend would I be if I let you go through this alone?"

She knew Nate had trained himself to catch all sorts of subtle nuances in a singer's voice: pitch, strain, emotion. And he could do the same with her. While on tour, it had been pretty obvious that she'd been an open book to him. And he'd capitalized. If it had been another man, Mia might have worried that she was being manipulated into falling into bed. But Nate was a straight arrow. Not one person in the industry had anything but glowing comments about him, personally or professionally.

"We did promise." He gave her a lopsided smile. *"Which brings me to something I spoke to your father about last night. How would you feel about acting as my translator for the next month until I get my voice back?"*

How would she feel? Thrilled. Honored. Slightly terrified. Spending an extended amount of time with him, she was bound to let slip that she was massively crazy about him. Would she have the strength to stick by her original decision if once again he demanded she choose between him and her sister?

The way things were with Ivy at the moment, Mia couldn't leave her. But the opportunity to sit beside Nate while he worked his magic on Ivy's album was worth the risk.

"You talked to my father about this?"

"I wanted to make sure you couldn't use your sister as an excuse to turn me down."

Mia made a face at him. "And both Ivy and my dad were on board?"

"Your sister wasn't thrilled, but she understands in order to have me work on her album in a time frame that fits with her schedule, I'm going to need your special skills."

This arrangement seemed perfect. Ivy would get her album recorded. Mia could keep an eye on her and at the same time spend hours and hours with Nate. A month. It wasn't a lot of time, but it was more than she'd ever expected to have with him after they'd parted in Sydney.

"When do we start?"

"I'm heading back to Vegas on Tuesday after I check in with Dr. Hanson."

"I haven't had a chance to ask. How did your dinner with Ivy and my dad go last night?"

"Did you know your sister wants to record some of Melody's songs?"

"No." Ivy had been acting weird since the tour ended. She'd become more demanding than ever, driving Mia half mad with her quicksilver moods and indecision. And now this. "I guess I shouldn't be surprised. Melody is a talented songwriter and Ivy wants to work with the best."

"I tried to talk her out of it. What you composed during the tour was fantastic."

"She thinks my songs are what are preventing her from moving to the next level." Mia picked at a button on her blouse. "What if she's right? Maybe trying something new will get her that superstardom she craves."

"And what about you?"

"What about me?"

"Are you ready to take your career to the next level?"

"I don't think there's a level above personal assistant." Mia shot Nate a wry grin. But his question had merit.

What did she want to be doing ten years from now? The thought of continuing to cater to her sister's every whim made her stomach churn. Mia supposed their father wouldn't want to manage Ivy forever. Mia could step into that role. Did she want to? If she was honest with herself, she'd admit that more than anything else she wanted to write music.

"I was thinking more in terms of songwriting."

"It's not the easiest way to make a living."

"You might need to combine it with something else to support yourself. Like producing."

"Do you know how many female producers there are in the industry?"

Nate shook his head.

"Neither does anyone else," Mia said with a touch of reproach. "Because the number is so small no one bothers to keep track. But it's around 5 percent."

"How do you know that?"

"When *1989* won the Grammy for album of the year, Taylor Swift talked in her acceptance speech about empowering women and how we should take credit for our own success."

Mia had been sitting alone in Ivy's house, watching the show and feeling a little sick to her stomach at how she hadn't fought for songwriting credit on either of her twin's albums.

"Afterward," Mia continued, "she was criticized for how few women she'd had working on her album. Nineteen people, excluding Taylor, worked on *1989*. Of those, only two were women. That means 11 percent of the production team were female. That's double the percentage of women in the industry."

"Women are underrepresented. How do you feel about changing that? Do you want to?"

"I won't lie and say I've never thought about it. I've been creating beats since Ivy recorded her first single. I know what I would have done to make the song better. Although I've sat in on every one of Ivy's studio sessions, most of what I know about the technical side is from watching other people."

"Is that a yes or no?"

"That's a hell yes, for spending several weeks sitting beside you and learning the ins and outs of what makes you such a fantastic producer. Beyond that I can't say what will happen."

Nate gave a satisfied nod and didn't try to push for anything more. Mia was glad for both their sakes. He'd been so frustrated with her that last morning in Sydney when she dug in her heels and refused to even consider taking time off from her sister and spending it with him. She hadn't seen the point in furthering their relationship when it was all bound to come to an end.

She might have given him a different answer if Nate had been the sort of guy who wanted something casual and would be happy to walk away at any point. If she could've sneaked away here and there for a long weekend with him they might still be involved.

But that wasn't the sort of guy he was. At least not with her. He'd been pretty clear from the start that she was special to him. While he hadn't minded keeping their blossoming romance a secret during the tour, everything had changed after they'd made love. He'd wanted to see her openly and as often as possible.

Ivy would freak if she ever found out Mia and Nate were involved. Especially now that she had some crazy idea that she and Nate were destined for each other. Mia wasn't ready for the upheaval it would cause for her family.

"How's your throat?" She cleared away his tray and brought him some gelato.

"It's great."

But she could tell from the tension in his facial muscles that wasn't true. "Where are your pain meds?"

"I don't want to take them."

Mia was torn. As much as she hated seeing him endure the pain, she had selfish reasons for being glad he'd refused to take the drugs. "Let me get you some water. Everything I've read advises staying hydrated."

She handed him a full water bottle and he signed his thanks. For no good reason, Mia's eyes prickled with sudden tears. Damn this man for turning her into a sappy mess with a simple thank-you. Not trusting her voice, and since saying "you're welcome" wasn't done in American Sign Language, she responded by signing *"no problem"* before turning away.

Despite his short nap earlier, Nate seemed tired, so after watching television together for an hour, she shooed him toward the bedroom. He caught her hand and, before she knew what he intended, dropped a kiss in her palm.

"Are you going to stay?" he signed, his lips curved into a hopeful smile.

The entreaty in his gray eyes messed with her pulse. She'd come prepared to spend the night, but hadn't intended on forcing her presence on him.

"I can."

He wrapped his arm around her waist and drew her against his solid body. Lean muscle shifted beneath her fingertips as she put her hand on his upper abdomen to keep a little space between them.

"On the couch," she added with a shaky laugh.

He shook his head and then tipped it to the side and put his free hand against his cheek to sign *"bed."* Her toes curled at the thought of lying beside him while he slept, listening to his even breathing, tormented by his powerful frame mere inches away. If they shared a bed there was no way she was going to get any sleep tonight.

Every time she shut her eyes she relived that night in Sydney. Sneaking kisses in out-of-the-way places during the early stages of their secret tour romance had been wildly exciting, but nothing had prepared her for the intensity of his mouth on her breasts or the surprising way his muscles shivered beneath her questing fingers.

The memory of making love with him hadn't grown the least bit fuzzy with each week that passed. Nor had her feelings for him dulled. For the last month and a half she'd thrown herself into everything that could take her mind off Nate for even a fraction of a second. Sticking close to Ivy made this pretty easy. And late at night Mia wrote music. Heartbreaking songs of love and loss that belonged on a country music album. They weren't the pop styling of Ivy Bliss.

"Go to bed. I'll be in after I call Melody and let her

know you're okay. I sent her a text while you napped earlier, but she'll want some details."

He kissed the top of her head and stepped back. *"Don't be long."*

"Tyrant."

"This is nothing. Wait until you see me in the control booth."

Mia called Melody and gave her an update on how Nate was doing, and shared that she'd be translating for him for the next month so he could keep his production schedule.

"What a great idea. I know Nate signs because his mother is deaf. How did you learn?"

"My older sister, Eva, lost her hearing when she was two." While Mia and her mother were fluent, Ivy and their father never learned to sign beyond some basic words.

"You haven't talked about her much. Does she live in California?"

"Chicago. She's a psychiatrist and a lot of her patients are hearing impaired." Talking about Eva made sadness swell inside Mia. With her sister so far away and both of them so busy, she didn't get a chance to see her as often as she'd like.

"How did Nate know you could sign?" Melody jumped in and answered her own question before Mia could say a word. "That's how you two communicated when Ivy was around."

Heat crept into Mia's cheeks. "Sometimes."

"I never did understand why you and Nate were so determined to keep your relationship a secret."

"Things like that get complicated around my sister."

"I mean that crush she had on him was, like, seven years ago. And it's not as if he encouraged her. Nate said he deleted every one of her texts."

"Wait…" Mia shook her head and tried to assimilate what Melody was saying. "Ivy had a crush on Nate?" Why hadn't he ever mentioned this to her?

"I thought you were glued to her every second of every day."

Mia rolled her eyes. "Now I am. Seven years ago I was finishing high school, like every other normal eighteen-year-old, while my twin sister was singing and acting on Broadway." That had been around the time when Mia's life stopped being normal. "Tell me what happened?"

"Apparently she got ahold of his phone number and sent him a bunch of texts, telling him how much she loved his music and begging him to come visit her in New York. Didn't Nate tell you?"

"No." Why not? Was that why Ivy had gotten so excited about the prospect of working with Nate? Because she'd had a crush on him a long time ago? "Did he go to New York?"

"Ohmygod, no. He wasn't interested. She isn't his type. He said he had to talk to your dad before it stopped."

Was this a contributing factor to why Mia had had to rush to New York and take a GED exam instead of graduating with her class?

"You should ask Nate about it," Melody continued.

"I will. And speaking of Ivy, Nate said she wants to record some of your songs." Mia was relieved no grief sounded in her tone. Although she was sad and disappointed that Ivy no longer wanted to record her songs, the fact that Ivy and their father had made the decision and not bothered to tell her was what really hurt.

"Which ones?"

"I have no idea."

"I guess I'd better decide which songs I want for my

album or Ivy will snap up all my best stuff." Melody laughed, but there wasn't much humor in it. "Tell Nate I'm thinking about him."

"Will do."

After Mia hung up, she picked up her overnight bag and headed into the bedroom. Nate was propped up on the pillows, his eyes alert and intense. Mia tried to keep her gaze from lingering on his bare torso, but his broad shoulders and muscular arms awakened her hormones and stirred up her desires. His lower half was hidden by the sheet and she prayed that he was wearing pajama bottoms.

"I'm going to change," she murmured awkwardly, heading into the bathroom.

"I've seen—" he began signing, but she was through the door before he could finish. One nice thing about his inability to speak was that all she had to do to get in the last word was not look at him.

She took her time changing into pajamas. She wasn't primping, but hoping that he might fall asleep while waiting for her.

He hadn't. And as she stepped into the bedroom and saw the glint in his eye, she wondered if either of them would feel rested come morning.

Four

"*Sexy,*" Nate signed, grinning as Mia's expression contorted into chagrin.

She dodged his mocking smile and glanced down at her bright blue sleepwear. "What did you expect?"

If she thought covering herself from chin to ankle was going to distract him from her luscious body, she'd underestimated her appeal. Then he sighed. Isn't that what she always did? Undervalued her worth.

"Something see-through and short."

"Ha. I didn't ask what you wanted." She set her bag on the chair next to the window and circled the bed like a wary alley cat confronted by a rival tom. "You're here to recover and I'm here to make sure you get lots of rest."

"Boring."

"I suggest you appreciate the peace and quiet. You're going to have my sister in your recording studio for the next month."

"Come here." He motioned her closer. *"I don't want to talk about your sister."*

Mia crossed her arms over her chest and shook her head. "Why didn't you tell me Ivy had a thing for you seven years ago?"

If Nate could've made a noise, what would've come out of him was a groan. *"Because it was seven years ago. And no big deal."*

"You rejected my sister. Do you seriously think she lets things like that go? She's still mad because Jimmy Reynolds picked me to be his buddy the day we went to the zoo in second grade."

Nate had little trouble believing Ivy couldn't let things go, but surely Mia was exaggerating about her sister holding a grudge because of a second-grade field trip.

Mia threw up her hands. "No wonder she was so cool to you on tour."

Had Ivy been cool? He must've looked puzzled because Mia asked, "You didn't notice the way she flirted with everyone except you?"

He shook his head. In fact he hadn't noticed much about Ivy at all. His attention had all been focused on Mia.

"It explains a lot," she said. "And now she thinks because you want to work with her that you're interested."

Nate wasn't particularly worried. He was a professional and would treat her as such. *"I'm only interested in you."*

Mia's color was high as she approached the bed. "You can't be interested in me. We've been through this already."

"And it didn't end the way I wanted to." He paused to read her expression. *"I don't think it ended the way you wanted, either."*

"What I want hasn't mattered since I was seventeen years old."

"Why?"

She waved her hand, batting his question away. "It's a complicated family thing. Ivy isn't as strong as she appears. She needs me to be there for her."

For how long? The rest of her life? Mia had so much to offer. If only she'd stop hiding behind her sister.

"When you say she needs you to be there for her," Nate began, bringing up something he should've probably saved for another time. *"Does that include making excuses for her when she doesn't feel like doing something?"*

To his mind, Ivy could stand to concern herself with something more than her immediate needs and desires. Maybe she'd grow up a little if she took some responsibility. He wasn't sure that Mia was doing her sister any favors by shielding her.

Mia pressed her lips together and held still for a long moment before offering up a long sigh. "Yes."

He made a rude gesture.

As always Mia was quick to make excuses for her sister. "She's an artist and artists are sensitive."

Nate wanted to point out that he was an artist, as well, and that didn't stop him from dragging his ass out of bed when he was exhausted or showing up on time and ready to work even when he didn't feel like writing or singing or being interviewed.

"That's not going to cut it in my studio. My time is money."

Mia's resistance crumbled. "I know. I'll warn her about that."

"Come here."

This time she didn't resist. Once he had her beneath

the covers, he slid down until he lay flat on his back. The urge to reach across the foot of space separating them on the mattress and touch her overpowered him, but she shook her head, as if she could read his intentions.

"We can't."

"You want to."

"Yes," she whispered, even as she shook her head. "But I can't." And then she turned onto her side and put her back to him with a mumbled good-night.

He signed his response, knowing she couldn't see it, and rolled onto his side away from her before temptation had him rolling her onto her back and covering her mouth with his. Not that he had the energy to make love to her. Damn it all. It figured that he'd get her back into bed when he couldn't capitalize on it. On the other hand, she wouldn't be here at all if not for his surgery.

Nate drifted off to sleep, keenly aware that bare inches separated his back from Mia's. However, at some point during the night, they both shifted, and when he woke up she was nestled beside him, her softness warming his left side, her cheek pillowed on his chest. His arm was around her. He'd buried his nose in her sweetly fragrant hair.

From her deep, even breathing he decided she was still asleep, so he kept perfectly still and savored the moment. Outside, the sun was kissing the balcony railing. Nate closed his eyes and pretended that he still had hours and hours to enjoy having his arms around Mia.

He guessed it was no more than twenty minutes later when she woke. Her body tensed as she became aware of their position, and almost immediately she began to disentangle herself. He tightened his fingers.

"How long have you been awake?" she asked, resisting his hold for several seconds before her muscles went limp once more.

He signed *"twenty minutes"* with his right hand and then placed his fingers beneath her chin to shift her head back. Their eyes met as he lowered his lips to hers.

She sighed into his mouth and he deepened the kiss, tracing her lips and teeth with his tongue until she let him in. His heart ached as her fingers stroked his cheek before latching on to his hair to pull him closer. She groaned against his mouth. Her morning kisses were sweet, with just a hint of sexy. Since he couldn't tell her how amazing she tasted or how soft her lips were, he did his best to let her know with his fingers against her cheek and neck.

"I don't think this is what the doctor ordered," she half moaned as he worked his lips down her throat. With a breathless laugh, she ducked away from the hand he'd slipped beneath the hem of her pajama top and half rolled, half shimmied off the bed.

"I was told not to speak. He said nothing about sex."

"I'm sure you were told not to exert yourself."

Her color was already high and his wicked grin drove the brightness in her cheeks even higher. She caught her lip between her teeth and stared at his bare chest for a long moment before shaking her head.

"I'm going to make you some Throat Coat tea and order you a smoothie for breakfast."

Nate watched her go before rolling out of bed and heading into the bathroom for a shower. When he came out, a bottle of water awaited him on the countertop by the sink. Mia was serious about keeping him hydrated. He dressed and headed into the living room, wondering how he was going to keep himself occupied and his hands off Mia for the next couple days. Idleness wasn't something he did well. If he wasn't working in the studio, he was writing music or promoting the band.

"I don't suppose you want to share what you've been working on lately with me?" he signed after breakfast.

"I have a couple beats I recorded the other day. When Ivy decided she wanted to change things up a bit, I started playing with some synthpop sounds." Mia frowned slightly. "Of course, that was before I learned she wants to record Melody's music."

"Let me hear."

She pulled out her phone and scanned through until she found the track she was looking for. When she played it for him, his eyes widened. It was very different from anything Ivy had done. Perhaps a little too different for the pop princess?

"Has Ivy heard this?"

"I can read your mind," Mia said with a self-conscious sigh. "I know it's different from her usual stuff. And no, I haven't played any of this for her."

"I know a couple singers who might be interested in what you have there." Nate paused and gave her a second to digest that. *"I can give them a call. Or send them a text,"* he amended.

"I'll think about it. It's all pretty rough at the moment."

"Maybe when we get into the studio you can play around with it some more."

"Maybe." She gave a noncommittal shrug. "By the way, I mentioned to Melody that Ivy is interested in recording some of her music, so she can prepare."

"I'm sure she appreciated the heads-up."

Mia's phone buzzed and she glanced at the screen. From her grimace, Nate assumed it was her sister calling. She got up and took the phone out to the small terrace.

"Hi, Ivy, what's up?" Mia stood with her back to him, but it didn't prevent her voice from carrying back into the suite. There was a pause, during which she paced from one end of the terrace to the other. "I can't, because I'm out of town. I drove up the coast for a couple days."

She turned in Nate's direction so he signed at her.

"Liar."

"Shut up." And then she sat on one of the chairs and leaned her forehead on her hand. "Dad hasn't talked to me about the direction for your new album."

Nate wondered what it would take for Mia to come clean about their relationship. What was the harm in explaining that she'd spent last night helping him out after his surgery? The dynamic between the sisters continued to baffle him.

"Of course I understand that you want to work with Melody Caldwell. She's incredibly talented." A long pause, then, "No, I'm not upset. I just needed a break... from LA. Can we talk about this later?"

When Mia hung up with her sister, she blew out a big breath.

"What did she want?"

"For me to run some errands."

"Your talents are wasted on your sister."

"It's more complicated than that." But she didn't defend her situation as adamantly as she'd done in the past. "She really does need me."

Not wishing to spoil their limited time together with an argument, Nate held out his hand and gestured Mia toward him. There would be plenty of time in the next month for them to discuss her future and for him to convince her to leave her sister and stay with him.

"Come play more of what you've been working on."

* * *

A week after Nate's surgery, Mia found herself in the lobby of Ugly Trout Records with her sister and father. The spare, utilitarian space was like Nate. Unpretentious and purposeful. There was a beige leather sectional beneath the company logo rendered in copper on the wall. On the opposite wall six guitars hung in a neat line. It wasn't designed to impress executives or big name stars. Musicians came to Las Vegas to record and work with Nate. His stellar reputation was all the promotion the label required.

Mia followed Ivy and their father through the glass door that led from the lobby into the empty conference room. They were late and Mia grimaced, wondering how upset Nate was at the moment.

"I'm surprised he isn't here to greet us," Ivy said, pulling a small mirror out of her purse to check her appearance yet again.

"Me, too, especially since we're fifteen minutes late."

Ivy shot her a dirty look. "What's gotten into you all of a sudden?"

Mia bit the inside of her cheek and reminded herself that this session would not go well if Ivy was upset. "It's just that I promised Nate we would be here right at ten." The second she used "we" Mia knew she'd screwed up.

"He's expecting *me*."

"Of course." Mia used her most soothing tone. "But you need me to translate what he's saying."

Ivy went back to checking her appearance. "If you think this makes you special, it doesn't. Remember that it's me he asked to work with."

Because he wants to spend time with me. But Mia didn't dare speak the truth out loud. Ivy wouldn't believe her. She barely believed it herself. Why was someone as talented and successful as Nate Tucker interested in a nobody like her?

A couple minutes later Nate, Melody and two men entered the room. The very air seemed to change with Nate's presence and Mia's eyes were glued to him as he came around the conference table to shake hands with Ivy. The rest of his team followed suit. When all the introductions had been made, Nate's gaze sought Mia.

He raised an eyebrow before signing. *"Let's get started, shall we?"*

Mia translated, and for a while the only sound in the room was her voice as she followed Nate's hands. He spoke about Ivy's previous two albums with West Coast Records and how the songs had been great, but the production had been rushed on both.

When Ivy had originally been signed by the label, the company had been run by Siggy Caldwell, Trent and Melody's father. In the past month, Nate and Trent had purchased the failing record company and planned to restore it to its former glory.

"We're going to develop a better marketing strategy for releasing her music this time," Nate signed.

"I'm glad to hear that," Javier Navarro said. "The delays in releasing her last album really hurt the sales."

"Trent and I agree."

"I've been dying to work with you and Melody," Ivy said. "When can I get into the studio?"

Nate glanced toward Melody. *"Studio C is open right now. Why don't you two run through a few songs. I want to give Mia a tour and introduce her to some people she'll be working with this next month."*

Ivy's eyes narrowed. "I thought she was going to translate for you."

"She is."

"Then why does she need a tour?"

"Your sister showed an interest in sound production and she's going to need to learn what I'm talking about in order to make people understand what I'm asking for."

"Whatever."

When Melody led Ivy and Javier out of the conference room, Mia turned to Nate. A blend of resignation and anxiety caused her chest to tighten. Conscious of the production assistants that remained in the room, Mia signed, *"You and I working together is going to make her crazy."*

"I don't care."

"I do. And you're not the one who has to live with her."

"You don't have to, either."

"Please tell me we're not going to have this discussion every day for the next month."

"It's not my fault that your sister misunderstands our relationship."

"By 'our relationship' do you mean yours and mine or yours and hers?"

"Both." Nate's eyes were liquid silver as his gaze settled on her lips. *"Now let's go find an empty studio so I can kiss you."*

"You are nothing but trouble," she declared.

The next four weeks were going to be heaven and hell. As much as it delighted her to be working so closely with Nate, keeping him at arm's length was going to be a nearly impossible task.

"When it comes to you I am very determined." He put his palm on her back and nudged her toward the door.

Just that fleeting touch sent her pulse skyrocketing. A nagging twinge in her chest bloomed into a sharp dig, but she smiled through it. Three days ago she'd woken in his arms and for a few minutes her world had been perfect. But the reality was that they couldn't be together. He wanted something that was impossible for her to give right at this moment. And she couldn't bring herself to hope that he'd wait around long enough for Mia to be reassured that her sister was strong enough to go it alone.

Mia's hands shook as Nate escorted her into a control room. She was relieved to find it occupied. On the other side of the glass, a group of studio musicians were jamming. The intensity of their concentration broke as the song came to an end. Smiles and high fives were shared all around.

Nate signed and then pushed a button. Mia stared at him until he made a gesture and she realized he wanted her to speak.

"Sounds good. This is Mia," she translated, then waved. "She's going to be my voice for the next month."

"You should keep her on permanently," a bald, barrel-chested guy with a goatee called out. "She sounds way better than you ever did."

"Looks a lot better, too."

Once the sound engineers introduced themselves, Nate indicated the door across the hall, which led to another control booth. In the studio a young man rapped to an intricate beat that Mia recognized as something Nate had been fooling around with during the tour.

"You wrote that."

He nodded before introducing her to the guy manning the booth. His name was Craig.

"*Moving on.*"

Nate opened the door to another studio and gestured her inside. The control booth on the other side of the glass was empty. The studio held a set of drums, a couple keyboards and several guitars.

As expected, he spun her around and pinned her against the door. He'd promised to find them an empty studio where he could kiss her, and he'd delivered. She didn't resist as his lips found hers and he stole her breath away. Damn. The man knew how to kiss. His tongue traced her lips until she parted for him. She expected him to deepen the kiss, and when he continued nipping and nibbling her lips, she was the one who pushed up onto her toes and took the kiss to the next level.

Both of them were breathing hard and flushed when he stepped back and signed.

"Feel like fooling around?"

"Depends…" She tucked the hem of her shirt back into her pants and drew the word out, wondering what Nate had in mind.

"Give me a taste of what you've been working on. Just play around a bit with some of it and see what happens."

"I can play some of the melodies." Mia glanced at the instruments.

"And the lyrics."

This wasn't what she was accustomed to. Usually she recorded all her demos using her laptop, alone in her room with a keyboard, synthesizer and a guitar. She was free to make mistakes, and stop and start if things didn't work. She often danced around, as if that somehow could make the creative juices flow.

Nate was watching her closely. *"Okay?"*

She gave a reluctant nod. While on tour, Mia had written several songs inspired by her growing feelings for Nate.

She sat down at the keyboard, but with Nate watching, her mind was blank.

"Can you maybe go sit over there?" She indicated a stool behind her. "You're making me nervous."

"Why? You've played your songs for me before."

"That was messing around. This is your studio and you've kinda put me on the spot."

"Fine."

With him out of her line of sight, the music came rushing back. Mia set her fingers on the keys and played a chord. The notes filled the space, a comfortable cushion for her emotions. She stopped worrying what Nate might think and just set her songs free.

They were two ballads. Some of her best work. Not only had her romance with Nate infused her lyrics with deeper emotion, his musical genius had encouraged her to innovate. To say she was proud of them was an understatement.

But the songs were too personal. Mia had been speaking the truth of her heart. And as she finished playing, she realized she'd written them for Nate. Suddenly, she was very glad Ivy wouldn't record them. To hear her sister sing those lyrics before Mia had even come to terms with what they meant to her would have been awful.

As she turned to face Nate, she found herself holding her breath. His thoughtful expression gave her no clue to his opinion. At last she couldn't take it anymore. "Well?"

"I'd like to run both of those past the guys. Free Fall might be interested in recording one or both."

Mia couldn't stop the tears that flooded her eyes. It was the nicest thing he could've said to her. Nate got to his feet and took several steps in her direction, but she waved him off.

"I'm fine."

"I can't guarantee anything."

"I know." She gave a shaky laugh and wiped moisture away from the corners of her eyes. "It's just such a thrill that you'd even consider..." She trailed off and regarded him suspiciously. "This isn't a bribe to get me to sleep with you, is it?"

His mouth popped open, but he caught himself just in time and signed instead. *"If only I was that devious."* He headed for the door and motioned her out.

The last studio they entered was occupied by Melody and Ivy.

"How's it going?" Mia translated for Nate.

"She likes this one." Melody cued a demo. As her voice poured from the speakers, Melody caught Mia's gaze and gave her head the smallest of shakes.

"I thought you were looking to take your next album in a new direction," Nate signed. *"That's similar to what you did on your last two albums."*

"I don't want to be too different. The fans have certain expectations."

"What about 'Love Me More'?"

Melody cued another song and Mia immediately saw where Nate was going with his suggestion.

An unhappy line formed between Ivy's brows as the chorus started. Mia recognized the warning signs and glanced toward their father, but his expression was thoughtful.

"You'd kill this," Melody agreed.

The song would take Ivy in a whole new direction. It was less sexually charged, more empowered and upbeat. Her sister had mad dance skills and enjoyed moving around the stage. Recording music like this would demonstrate that Ivy could do more than just pout and smolder as she sang.

Unfortunately, Ivy was comfortable pouting and smoldering, and as much as she claimed she wanted to grow as an artist, she retreated back into the same old tricks, where she felt safe.

"Let's give it a try," Mia translated for Nate.

"Now?" Ivy's eyes widened. She hadn't come prepared to record anything. Usually she took weeks and weeks to rehearse a song before she entered the studio. Not only was she a perfectionist, she hated looking foolish.

"Let's see what we can do."

"I don't know the song."

"We'll take it slow."

When Mia repeated what Nate had signed, Ivy shot daggers at her. Mia recognized that Ivy wanted her to speak up on her behalf, but a thousand trifling slights and mistreatments held Mia's tongue. Ivy had claimed Mia's songs as her own on the last two albums and now she wanted a new sound. This was it. Mia glanced between her father and Nate while the tension built in the room.

Finally, after seeing that everyone expected her to agree, Ivy nodded reluctantly. "I'll give it a try."

"Wonderful."

Melody handed her the sheet music and Ivy shot Mia one last scowl before leaving the control booth for the recording studio. When Ivy stood in front of the mike, Nate cued a track and let the music play. Ivy listened for a while and then began to sing. Her vocals were soft and sexy like what she was used to performing and not at all what Nate was looking for.

He signed and cued the mike.

With a silent groan, Mia translated. "Don't be afraid to let go. This is a girl telling a boy to really love her. Get in his face about it."

Nate's eyes were on her as she finished speaking. One corner of his mouth twitched as their eyes met.

Ivy started again. Mia could tell her sister was tense

and uncomfortable. At the halfway point of the song she quit. "This isn't working."

"I'm the producer. Why don't you let me judge what is and isn't going to work. Just sing," Nate signed. Mia translated, painful reluctance in her voice.

She was going to pay for this later.

Five

Nate almost felt sorry for Mia as she told her sister what he wanted. He understood the dynamic between them well enough to know that Mia was miserable relaying his suggestions for Ivy's performance. And Ivy was equally unhappy to receive them. But it had to be good for Mia to be the one in command for a change, even if only by proxy.

And in truth, as the hour went on, Mia's manner grew more confident and Ivy's interpretation of Melody's song evolved into what the songwriter had intended. It wasn't perfect, but it was a start.

"That's much better," Mia translated. "Why don't you come in here and listen to the playback."

"How did it feel to boss your sister around?"

"I wasn't. All I did was tell her what you said."

"Not word for word."

Mia rolled her eyes. *"Did you want her to storm out or keep singing?"*

"What are you two talking about?" Javier asked, breaking into their silent conversation.

"Sorry." Mia shot her father a rueful look. "I'm use to signing with Eva and I forgot that Nate can hear."

"Nice save."

"Nate was just saying how happy he is to be working with such a talented singer." Mia smiled in a way that dared Nate to argue.

As if he could. For all she caved to her sister's domineering ways, Mia had spunk and backbone. During the next four weeks, Nate intended to figure out why she let Ivy push her around, and to do whatever it took to steal her away.

"I enjoyed kissing you earlier."

Ivy entered the booth and sat beside her father on the couch.

"I enjoyed your singing." Obviously rattled, Mia blurted out the awkward translation. She pointed at Nate. "That's what he said."

"That's not what I said. By the way, you're blushing. How long do you think you can keep our relationship a secret?"

"Stop it," she signed back. *"And what relationship?"*

"The one where I tear your clothes off every chance I get."

Although he wanted to stare at Mia and see how his declaration affected her, Nate nodded to the sound engineer, who queued the playback. Beside him, Mia radiated heat, but without glancing at her expression, he didn't know if she was struggling with annoyance or lust.

Ivy's voice filled the space. She'd sung along with a simple piano track that Melody had recorded for the demo. Nate heard the potential in what Ivy could do with the song and the hairs on the back of his neck rose in reaction. It was a good sign. Whether she believed it or not, the music suited her voice. The question remained whether she could get behind the words and sell it.

A collective sigh filled the control booth when the last notes tapered off. Nate nodded in satisfaction and pinned Ivy with his gaze. The woman was ridiculously talented. Pity she was such a diva.

Javier looked pleased with what he'd heard. "I think that's a keeper."

"I'd like to record the other song we discussed earlier, as well," Ivy said, obviously not willing to concede quite yet.

Nate wasn't about to negotiate with the pop princess. He looked at Melody. *"Give her the music for those five songs we talked about."* When Mia translated what he'd said, he turned to Ivy.

"Take the rest of the week and get a feel for the songs. I want you back in the studio on Friday. We'll work on all of them."

"You're only giving me three days. That's not enough time," the pop princess squeaked, shooting a panicked look toward her father.

Javier shrugged. "If we want to get the album done in a short amount of time, you're going to have to commit to working hard."

Nate could almost hear Ivy's thoughts. She didn't want to work hard. She wanted to shop and party and boss her sister around.

Nate began signing again. "You have three days to learn five songs. They don't have to be perfect," Mia translated. "But you do need to have a feel for them."

"Fine." Ivy tossed her head and made her way to the door.

Before Mia could follow on her sister's heels, Nate

caught her by the arm, stopping her. *"Want to be my date to the AMAs?"*

Free Fall had once again been nominated for favorite pop/rock duo or group, an award they'd won two years earlier, and favorite pop/rock album. The competition was especially stiff this year and he didn't expect they'd win. Having Mia sitting beside him would take the sting out of the loss.

"The AMAs?" Mia breathed, beaming at his invitation.

Ivy had reached the hall, but when she heard her sister speak, she whirled around. "What about the AMAs?"

Mia's delight dimmed. "Nate asked me to go with him."

"Why? To translate?"

Nate could tell she was about to lie to her sister once again. He caught her hand to get her attention and shook his head in warning. *"Tell her the truth."*

"As his date."

"Your date?" Ivy looked scandalized as she fixed Nate with her stare. "That's not possible."

"Why not?" Mia translated for him.

The pop star set her hand on her hip and thrust out her lower lip like a toddler. "Because she's my assistant."

And he was sick of the way Ivy treated Mia. *"She's also your sister,"* he signed, but Mia didn't immediately translate.

Both Nate and Ivy glared at her as she stood frozen in mute silence, gazing from one to the other. She deserved so much better than to be at Ivy's beck and call. What was wrong with the entire family that everything revolved around Ivy and her damned career?

"That means she'll already be there," Mia said at last, playing diplomat and not translating his exact words.

The last bit of Nate's patience was draining away. *"Don't let her bully you."*

"But it's Mia," Ivy stated, as if that would convince Nate to change his mind.

He nodded.

Mia finally found her own voice. "I'd love to go."

She spoke softly, but her eyes glowed. In moments like these she was more beautiful than her twin.

"But I need her backstage. I'm performing and presenting."

"You'll have Yvonne to help with your changes and makeup," Mia said. Now that she'd accepted his invitation, she appeared unwilling to back down. It was a nice change from the way she normally catered to her sister's every whim.

"She doesn't own anything that she can wear to an award show," Ivy said to Nate. Clearly, she wasn't giving up.

As a featured artist, Ivy would have her choice of gowns sent over by designers eager for the publicity. Mia didn't have that sort of celebrity and Nate doubted she had the pull to arrange her own red carpet gown.

"I have a stylist in LA who can hook you up," Nate signed. *"I'll give her a call."* He sighed. *"Send her a email."*

"That would be great," Mia breathed, without bothering to translate.

Her reverent expression left Nate wondering how often anything good came her way. It spurred him to work even harder to make the entire event something Mia would want more of. She'd spent far too much time being invisible, not thinking she deserved her moment in the sun. Getting her used to being treated like a celebrity was a step forward in his plan to wrestle her away from her sister.

"I'll make the arrangements. Don't let her talk you out of going with me."

"I won't." And then to Ivy she said, "We'd better head out if you want to make your massage appointment." And as her sister stormed away down the hall, Mia gave Nate one last glance and signed, *"Thank you."*

Mia carried the cup of Throat Coat tea into Ivy's bedroom. Their father had rented a five-bedroom house with a pool in a gated community for the month Ivy would be recording at Ugly Trout. It had been a week since meeting with Nate at the studio and whatever progress her sister was making with Melody's songs was negated by the fact that when Ivy wasn't at the studio, she was either out shopping or partying with her friends Skylar and Riley, who'd shown up from LA.

The appearance of those two raised Mia's concern. The party girls, whose only source of income was their sketchy modeling careers and fashion blog, weren't good for Ivy, who was far too prone to be distracted from what she'd come to Las Vegas to do. Mia had convinced their father to chase them out of the house early that morning so Ivy could work on the songs Nate wanted her to record, but from the pile of high-end shopping bags on the floor at the foot of Ivy's bed, he hadn't persuaded them to leave town.

The fact that her sister wasn't trying on her latest purchases or even admiring what she'd bought told Mia something was wrong. The curtains were drawn over the sliding glass door that led out to the pool. It took a second for Mia to spot her twin. Ivy had pressed herself into a corner of the room, her knees tucked against her chest like a small child trying to make herself invisible. Tears streamed down her face and Mia's heart crashed to her toes.

"What's the matter?" She set the teacup on the bureau and went to sit before her sister. "I brought you some tea. Why don't you try to drink some."

Ivy stared right through her. "I can't do it. Nothing feels right. They're all expecting me to do something amazing and none of it is me." Ivy blinked and her eyes gained focus. She met Mia's gaze. "When we were on tour, I heard the songs Melody was working on and they sounded so wonderful. I want wonderful, but it's not happening."

"That's not true. I've been there, listening to you record. Everything you do is wonderful," Mia assured her sister, speaking from the heart. So often lately when she complimented Ivy it was because her sister expected the praise. But when Ivy was like this, when her demons crowded in, it was easy for Mia to give her twin every bit of support she had in her.

"Dad's expecting me to go platinum with this album, so it has to be perfect."

Mia had always thought having their father manage Ivy's career added extra pressure for her to succeed. In the same vein, if it hadn't been Daddy calling the shots, Ivy's image might be different. Mia was pretty sure her twin never would've had plastic surgery at seventeen and probably wouldn't have become addicted to the painkillers that almost killed her.

"Don't worry about Dad or Mom or what anyone else thinks."

No matter how well Ivy did, she always wanted to do better. And when she wasn't recognized, which was what had happened with this year's American Music Award nominations, things went downhill fast.

Since mid-October, when the nominations were announced and Ivy's name hadn't appeared anywhere, Mia had been scrambling harder than ever to keep her sister happy. As ambitious as she was beautiful and talented, Ivy had grown positively obsessed with making her next album grittier, sexier, more over-the-top than anything she'd done so far.

Mia thought her sister was on the wrong track. It was why Ivy and Nate were butting heads. If Ivy wanted to be taken seriously as an artist, she needed to become more authentic rather than a caricature of the personality she'd become.

"Make music that's in your heart," Mia continued. "Let it speak to who you are."

Ivy's lips curved into a sad smile. "What if I don't know who that is?"

"You'll figure it out. Just believe in yourself."

"Is that what Nate is telling you to do?"

Mia hesitated before answering. Nate was a treacherous topic for her to discuss with Ivy. "It's the message of every positive affirmation ever written. Believe in yourself. Do what you love."

"Are you doing what you love?"

"Sure."

"I mean with me."

"You're my sister. I love being with you."

"I bet you'd love it more if you were with Nate."

Mia sensed the mines beneath her feet, and stepped carefully. "I've enjoyed working with him at the studio. I'm learning a lot. It's something I could see myself doing in the future."

It was the closest Mia had come to sharing her aspirations with Ivy. That she'd dared to confess something so personal terrified her. Ivy didn't like change and might view her twin's dream of having her own career as a threat.

"I wasn't talking about working at the studio. I was talking about Nate himself. You like him." Ivy's voice had taken on a coolness that made Mia shiver. "You like him a lot."

With a shaky laugh that wouldn't fool anyone, Mia said, "Everybody likes Nate."

"But everybody's not sleeping with him." Ivy's eyes glittered in the dim light. "You know he's using you, right?"

"I'm not sleeping with him." How many times had she lied to Ivy to keep her sister in the dark about Nate? A hundred? More? When was she planning to stop? Mia's chest tightened. She was barely able to draw breath enough to defend Nate. "And he's not like that."

"Did you do it because you knew I liked him? Have you been saying bad things to him about me? Is that why he criticized everything I did in the studio? I'm trying really hard to make him happy, but nothing makes him look at me the way he looks at you."

How did Nate look at her? "We're colleagues," Mia said. "That makes things easy between us. With you he's pushing so he can get the best possible song. It might seem like he's not happy, but he thinks this will be some of the best work you've done."

But Ivy wasn't listening to her. Mia had seen that look before. She got up and went to Ivy's purse. Her sister noticed what she was doing and protested. Mia ignored her and started digging through the bag, unsurprised when she came up with a small bag of pills.

"Who gave you these? Skylar or Riley?"

Ivy stuck her lower lip out and stared mutinously at Mia. "Give me those. It's none of your business."

"What's the matter with you?" Sorrow and rage collided inside Mia's chest. "I thought you were done taking prescription meds. Damn it, Ivy."

"I just need something to take the edge off after being in the studio all day. It's exhausting and the pressure… You just don't understand."

"I understand that you almost died because you were taking this stuff."

Mia took the bag into the bathroom and dumped the contents into the toilet. When she turned, her sister was glaring at her from the doorway.

"You had no right." Ivy's voice slashed at her.

Discovering a bag of pills in her sister's possession both angered and frightened Mia. "I'm your sister and I love you. I'm always going to do what's best for you. Even if you hate me for it."

"It's your fault, you know. The reason I have the pills. You haven't been around for me lately."

"I'm with you all day at the studio and when you're working with Melody on the songs you're planning to record." Mia was having trouble catching her breath. She hated conflict and usually gave in to whatever Ivy wanted, but not when it came to her addiction. "The only time I'm not around is when you go out with Skylar and Riley. They're bad news, Ivy."

"They're fun." Ivy scrubbed the tears from her cheeks and shook her head. "I can't have any fun without you being all over me. You used to be fun. We used to hang out."

"That's not my fault." Mia's temper flared at the unfair accusation. It hurt that the two of them had stopped spending time together as sisters and friends. "You're the one who treats me more like an employee than your sister."

"You left me to go to high school."

Mia regarded Ivy in dumb silence. "You were in a show on Broadway. I wanted to be normal." Because she'd been just an average kid with no particular talent or ambition.

If Ivy had never become a pop star, Mia might have ended up like Eva, in a job she loved far from the music industry with its bright lights and soul-crushing pressure to make it big.

"You don't think that's what I wanted?" Ivy's pupils were like pinpoints, something Mia had learned to watch for. "To go to school with my friends and just worry about passing a chemistry test or what boy might think I'm cute?"

"So why didn't you say no?" Though Mia asked the question, she already knew the answer.

"You think it's because I love all the money and fame."

"I do. Ever since we were kids you always needed to be the center of attention."

"It gets old. Sometimes all I want is to be invisible."

"So quit."

"And do what?" Ivy glared at her. "I don't write music like you do. All I have is my voice and this body."

Mia wished her sister could look beyond show business. "What about going to college. You could get a degree. Or you're passionate about fashion. Start a clothing line."

"Sure." Ivy gave a bitter laugh. "Like Dad would let me quit singing and acting to become a fashion designer."

"You don't have to quit. Do both. See how it goes."

For the first time in what felt like forever Mia saw the old Ivy peering out at her. She impulsively took her sister's hands. "Why don't we take Saturday and go do something fun? Just you and me. Like when we were kids and we used to sneak off to the park."

"I'm flying to LA with Skylar and Riley tomorrow to meet with the guy who is going to manufacture their line of purses."

"Tomorrow?" Why hadn't she been told any of this? "But you're scheduled in the studio tomorrow. When are you coming back?"

"I don't know. Skylar and Riley really need my help."

"And by help you mean they want you to invest money." If Mia had disliked Skylar and Riley before, the discovery of the pills made things so much worse.

"I don't care what you think." Ivy glared at her. "I'm going."

"Then I'll go with you." If Ivy was taking painkillers again, Mia really couldn't afford to let her sister go back to LA without her. "I'll message Nate and explain everything."

Well, not everything. She'd shared a lot of her secrets with him, but couldn't tell him her fears about Ivy without explaining about Ivy's near death overdose.

"Sure, whatever. But do it somewhere else. I'm tired and I just want to sleep."

"Then you're not going out tonight?"

"Geez, Mia. It's only seven. Nothing gets going around here until at least midnight." And then Ivy lay on her bed and buried her face in a pillow.

After covering her with a throw, Mia took the now cool cup of tea and went to her bedroom to Skype with Nate. To her surprise, he was fine with the change of plans. He told her he'd head up to LA as well to meet

with Trent, and would arrange for Ivy to do a bit of recording at West Coast Records with a producer friend
of his so they could keep the schedule moving forward.

By the time Mia signed off an hour later, she was feeling a whole lot better. Nate had that effect on her. But
her equanimity lasted only until she went to check on
Ivy and found her sister's room in an uproar of rejected
outfits, but otherwise empty.

Mia hesitated just a minute before starting a system-
atic search through Ivy's room. The last time her sister
had given into her addiction, she'd squirrel away pills in
all sorts of places. Mentally crossing her fingers that she
wouldn't find anything, Mia began going through Ivy's
drawers and closet. After forty-five minutes of searching, she'd unearthed no contraband, but that didn't mean
Ivy couldn't hit up Skylar or Riley tonight.

Mia would have to keep a close eye on her sister to
avoid a repeat of the relapse that had happened three
years ago, while Ivy was on her first concert tour. Mia
had been in LA working on a demo for one of the songs
Ivy hadn't wanted to record. Preoccupied by the opportunity to have a career as a songwriter, Mia hadn't been
paying attention to her sister and Ivy had started taking pills again.

Sometimes it seemed that every time Mia tried to
grab something for herself, Ivy found a way to spoil it.
Which explained why keeping quiet about her relationship with Nate was so important. But at what cost? The
question roused a host of emotions ranging from frustration to guilt. She'd already lost Nate to her sister's
demanding personality.

Was she planning on sacrificing her entire future to
it, as well? How long could she live in Ivy's shadow before dissatisfaction with her situation turned love into

animosity? Choosing her sister over Nate had been hard the first time, even though she'd known him only a short while and could dismiss their fling as a tour romance. But now that she was working with him every day and accepting his help to develop her music, she was discovering richer layers to her feelings for him. Not sexual or even professional, but a complicated stew of romance, friendship and respect.

He was a brilliant musician and a wonderful man. When the time came to choose, how was she going to give him up again?

Six

Nate glanced Mia's way a hundred times during their drive to Santa Monica, where they were having dinner with Trent and Savannah. She looked beautiful in a navy-and-white abstract print sundress, paired with sandals and wavy beach hair. For a dramatic evening look, she'd applied eye shadow and red lipstick. He couldn't keep his eyes off her.

As he pulled into the parking lot, Mia gave the restaurant a doubtful look. "Are you sure this is a business meeting?"

He nodded, playing innocent when she frowned. He knew what she was thinking, but it wasn't really a double date. Just a quiet dinner with two couples, at a seaside restaurant with lots of good food and wine. Nope. Not a double date at all.

"It seems a little…"

He fitted the car into a parking spot and cut the engine. *"Out-of-the-way?"*

"I was thinking more in terms of romantic."

"Now that you mention it, I see what you mean. But I didn't pick it. Trent did. I think it might be date night for him and Savannah. That's not a problem, is it?"

"Sitting across the table from a newly engaged couple won't bother me a bit."

"Good. I wouldn't want you to get any ideas."

Mia shook her head. "I wouldn't dream of it."

They were fifteen minutes early for the reservation, but the hostess seated them at a wonderful table overlooking the Santa Monica pier and the ocean. The sun had already dipped below the horizon and the sky was saturated with rich gold, red and deep blue.

"Tell me more about Trent and Savannah." Mia's eyes held a wistful glow as she turned from the view. "Start with why they both have the same last name if they're only engaged."

"Savannah is Trent's former sister-in-law."

Mia's eyes widened adorably. "That has to be a tricky situation."

"It's quite complicated. They've known each other since Savannah was a kid. She came to live with her aunt, who happened to be the Caldwells' housekeeper, after her mom died and her father couldn't take care of her. From what Melody tells me, Savannah had a thing for Trent for a long time. When she went off to model in New York City he went out to visit her and they began to..." Nate paused and thought for a moment. *"Date."*

"Why the pause?"

"I don't think Trent realized how he felt about her until after they broke up and she married his brother."

"So why did she marry him? To get back at Trent?"

"That's not her style. She was pregnant and Rafe

wanted a legitimate heir to carry on the Caldwell name. He was dying when he married her, but no one knew."

"How old is her son?"

"Just turned a year. And the boy is Trent's. How that happened is also complicated, but let's just say Trent was a huge idiot for ever letting her go."

"Did Trent know about the baby before she married his brother?"

Nate shook his head. *"I think if they'd been able to talk to each other when she found out she was pregnant they might have saved themselves a lot of heartache."*

"Why didn't she tell him?"

"That would be a good question to ask her. I don't honestly know."

\"I'm glad Trent and Savannah found each other again." Mia paused while Nate ordered a bottle of pinot grigio from the waiter. "I don't remember Trent being a part of West Coast Records when Ivy signed with them. How long has he been involved? It's his family business, isn't it?"

"That's another complicated thing. Trent and his father never got along, so he wasn't involved in the record label. His brother, Rafe took over when their father retired, and mismanaged an already floundering company."

"My dad told me there were rumors that artists weren't being paid. That never happened with Ivy, but she was one of their bestselling artists."

"Trent brought in auditors to look over the books. There was some embezzling on top of everything else. Hopefully, within the next six months everything will get straightened out and people will be paid what they're owed."

The waiter brought the wine, and as it was being

poured, Trent and Savannah arrived at the table. Quick introductions were made and the newly engaged couple sat down.

"You two are early," Trent said, his gaze sliding between Nate and Mia.

"They didn't have a baby to get ready for bed," Savannah said.

"How is your throat?" Trent asked. "Are you speaking yet?"

Nate shook his head and glanced at Mia.

"I'm his voice."

Savannah's eyes widened. "How does that work?"

Nate demonstrated. *"I want to lick every inch of your body."*

"He just said you look lovely and asked how your son is."

"I don't think that's what he said." Savannah laughed. "You just turned bright red. Did he say something naughty?"

Trent cocked his head and regarded his smirking business partner. "So are you two…?"

"Lovers?" He nodded.

"No."

Nate had little trouble conveying his feelings on that situation. *"Not at the moment."*

Savannah grinned. "This feels a little bit like watching a silent movie without subtitles."

"We're being rude," Mia said, shooting Nate a severe look.

"Tell them the truth. It won't go anywhere."

She gave a big sigh. "Nate and I became romantically involved while on tour, but nobody knows that."

"Because?" Savannah prompted.

Nate began to sign, but Mia ignored him. "I work

for my sister and she wouldn't be happy if I was dating Nate."

"Because?" It was Trent who prompted this time.

Mia looked as if she wished the floor would open up and swallow her. "My sister can be a bit needy."

The sign Nate made needed no translation.

"So you're not allowed to date?" Savannah asked. "That seems a bit much."

"It's not that I can't date." Although from what she'd told Nate, her sister had a knack for ruining every chance at romance that came Mia's way. "It's more that I don't have much time for a life outside my work."

"Mia is a fantastic songwriter. I found out on tour that she wrote all the songs Ivy claimed to have written from her first two albums." Nate finished signing and gave her a hard look until she translated his words.

Trent gave her an equally hard look as he listened, but there was regret in there, as well. "You weren't given credit? How did that happen?"

"I don't know," Mia said. "When the first albums came out I wasn't mentioned at all. When I asked my dad about it, he said it was a group decision. They thought it looked better if Ivy was writing her own music instead of some nobody."

From the throb in Mia's voice, the slight continued to pain her.

"If it was something that happened because of my family's mismanagement of the West Coast label, I would be happy to set the record straight."

"No." Mia added a head shake for emphasis. "It would cause too much upheaval. My family would never forgive me if word got out."

Trent nodded. "If anyone understands how complicated family and business can be it's me. You have my word that this stays here."

"Thank you."

Mia gave Trent a wobbly smile and it hit Nate hard. He wanted badly to be able to make everything right for her, but she'd never let him. The best he could hope would be to get her away from Ivy so that her future looked brighter.

They dined on the fresh catch of the day and went through several bottles of wine. Trent, Savannah and Mia carried the conversation. Nate enjoyed his forced muteness and spent most of the dinner watching Mia's confidence bloom beneath his friends' attention.

"Dessert?" Nate asked as the waiter cleared the plates. He wanted to prolong the night as long as possible.

Savannah looked regretful. "I wish we could, but we promised the sitter we'd get home by ten."

Nate turned to Mia, but she was shaking her head. *"How about a walk on the beach?"*

She glanced out the window at the dark water. He knew she loved the ocean. They'd sneaked off to the beach a couple times while touring Australia. He would've liked to steal her away for some snorkeling along the Great Barrier Reef, but the schedule had been too tight for that sort of excursion.

"A short one. If I'm too late Ivy will wonder why."

After settling the bill the two couples separated in the parking lot. Mia maintained her smile as she stripped off her sandals and put them in the car. The temperature had dipped into the upper fifties, but the breeze blowing off the Pacific was light.

Nate took her hand and they made their way toward the sand. As they crossed the broad expanse, he revisited how easy it was to be with Mia. She had an ability to stay tranquil no matter how crazy the people around her became. No doubt it was a trait she'd cultivated in dealing with her sister's demanding ways.

Mia didn't expect conversation or feel compelled to fill silences with chatter. Even before his surgery, they'd spent long silent hours enjoying each other's company, physically connected by the touch of her foot on his thigh or his shoulder against hers, or at opposite ends of a room, content to occupy the same space.

If it weren't for Mia's peculiar attachment to being her sister's assistant, he could've delighted in having found the perfect woman. Instead his patience was worn to the thinness of onion skin by his constant need to resist the craving to pull Mia into his arms and kiss her. He was tired of pretending his interest in her was professional.

Fingers knitted together, they walked at the water's edge, heading away from the bright lights of the Santa Monica pier. The quarter moon gave them enough light to see by. Nate stopped and used Mia's momentum to turn her into his arms. Sliding his hand into her hair, he cupped her cheek and brought his lips to hers.

She tasted of the peppermint candy she'd snagged on the way out of the restaurant. When he licked at her lips, they parted for him, and he swept his tongue against hers, stealing her breath and the last bit of the candy disk. He'd always been good with words when it came to writing music, but this rush of emotion that hit him whenever he put his arms around her smothered his ability to form cohesive thought.

"I have a few more hours before Ivy will be home," she murmured against his cheek as he grazed his lips down her neck. She trembled as he nipped her skin. "Feel like going back to your hotel? I'm dying to be alone with you."

* * *

Nate didn't bother signing his answer. He grabbed her by the hand and pulled her toward the car. Mia laughed at his eagerness. It matched the impatience burning in her chest. Why hadn't she said something sooner? They'd wasted fifteen minutes on this walk.

Nate had one hand on the steering wheel and caressed her shoulder with the other while he drove. There was little conversation on the trip back into the city. It gave Mia time to think about what was to come and to work herself into a fine state of frenzied anticipation.

At the hotel, Nate turned his car over to the valet. When he would've put his arm around Mia for the walk through the hotel lobby, she shook her head.

"We can't be seen together like that," she cautioned, thinking what would happen if a picture got out of the two of them linked romantically. "I don't want to show up on social media and invite speculation."

"I think you overestimate my star power."

Mia rolled her eyes. The man had no idea how incredible he was. "I think you underestimate it."

"I'm pretty low-key off tour. And I don't really have one of those faces that everybody knows."

"Are you kidding? You're gorgeous." She covered her mouth with her hand and laughed self-consciously. "I don't know why I'm embarrassed admitting that to you. You already know how I feel."

"I'm not really sure I do." Nate frowned down at her for a long moment.

They joined several other hotel guests in the elevator and got out on the twelfth floor. He took her hand and brought it to his lips. The way he watched her turned her bones to mush. She spent so much time hiding how he made her feel. It was a relief to let her emotions shine.

His eyes widened. *"I never thought I'd see you look at me like that again."*

"I've been fighting this for two months," she murmured as they walked toward his suite. "It's been hell wanting you and knowing—" Her voice broke. The last thing he deserved was to hear her say again that she'd chosen being there for her sister over him.

His fingers tightened against hers as he slid the key card into the electronic lock. As soon as they crossed the threshold he kicked the door closed, gathered her into his arms and kissed her. Mia sighed against his mouth, her lips parting to welcome the plunge of his tongue. She filled her fingers with his soft wavy hair and held him close.

I love you. The words reverberated in her mind, but she didn't dare say them out loud. As much as she wanted him, wanted this, she couldn't commit to anything beyond this night. Soon she would have to consider Nate's place in her life. This connection between them had grown so fast and Mia wasn't accustomed to recklessly throwing herself into any situation. And then there were the doubts that rose after Ivy voiced her opinion about Mia not belonging in the limelight by his side.

Mia took Nate's hand and drew him toward the suite's bedroom. He deserved someone beautiful and confident to walk the red carpet and make other public appearances with him. Mia was too used to hiding in the background, and she knew he wanted to partner in everything private and public. But with his hands sweeping down her spine, his palms sliding over her butt cheeks to lift her against his hard body, it was hard to think about all the reasons she wasn't right for him.

"I'm going to do all the talking for you tonight," she told him, panting as his lips found the sensitive skin on the side of her neck. "You just tell me what to say and I'll say it."

There was a mischievous glint in the depths of Nate's gray eyes as he made an okay sign. He snagged the hem of her dress and skimmed it up her body. The cool air struck her overheated skin and Mia shivered. For a couple seconds the cotton material tangled in her hair as it went over her head and she was blinded. The loss of her sight awakened her sense of smell and she breathed in Nate's familiar scent of soap and aftershave.

Immediately she was transported back to that night in Sydney. She'd been a little intimidated by the discrepancy between their levels of sexual experience and what he might expect of her. And then she'd forgotten to be nervous as his mouth traveled over her body and he introduced her to pleasure she'd never known. After having nearly two months to relive that night over and over, Mia was more than ready to do to him all the things she'd been dreaming about.

His shirt followed her dress to the floor. Once his gorgeous chest was bared to her eyes, she went after his pants with a vengeance. Teeth gritted in concentration, she worked his belt free and had her hands on his zipper when he stopped her.

"What are you doing?" She tugged, trying to free herself from his grip. "I need you naked."

Nate set his forehead against hers and brought her hands to his lips. His breath puffed against her skin as he feathered kisses across her knuckles. Then he turned her in his arms and shifted so they were facing the mirror.

"Before we do this, I want you to know it's never been just about sex for me."

"I know." She relaxed against Nate's strong torso. The hard ridge of his erection nudged against her backside and she resisted the urge to rub against him. "But can't we talk about this later?"

"Now. It's important you understand how much I need you in my life. This isn't something I'm doing lightly. Can you say the same?"

"If you're going to ask me to choose you right now, I can't. Is it possible for you to accept that I care about you and want this to work between us? I'm not leading you on, but I need time to sort everything out."

"You're asking me to be patient."

"And I know it's a lot. You're so wonderful and I don't want to hurt you."

"I wish I could tell you I will make it easy on you, but I'm a selfish jerk who wants you all to himself." He met her eyes in the mirror and gave her wolfish grin. *"Now repeat after me…"* He began simultaneously signing and caressing her body to act out his words.

"I love your breasts and the way your nipples go hard when I touch them," she translated, quaking in reaction to his touch. "Nate, you're killing me with this."

He stopped signing long enough to pop the clasp of her strapless bra. Mia watched it slide off her breasts and hit the floor. Next he skimmed his fingers beneath the elastic of her panties and sent those plunging to the floor, too. Mia stepped out of them. Although she was no stranger to her naked body reflected in the mirror, seeing Nate's large hand fanned over her stomach was an erotic image she'd never forget.

"Keep going."

"I can't wait to taste you." A vivid blush dotted her cheeks as she repeated what Nate had signed. "I love how sensitive you are. It makes me crazy to hear you moan."

He trailed the tips of his fingers along her neck and into the hollow of her throat, all the while watching her in the mirror. She half closed her eyes as each of her senses demanded her attention. The silky drag of his lips across her shoulder competed with the tantalizing view of his fingers circling her belly button before skimming downward.

"Nate." His name was a plea as she shifted her hips, seeking the promise of greater pleasure beneath his hands. "Yes."

"Yes, what?"

"Am I ready for you?" she repeated, her voice a husky moan. "The answer is yes."

He laughed, a brief huff of air against her neck. *"I'm ready for you, too. Can't you feel it?"* He rocked his hips forward and drove his erection against her.

"Then what are you waiting for?"

She dropped her hand to his thigh and slid her palm along the sinewy length. His muscles bunched and jumped beneath her touch.

"I like taking my time with you," Mia repeated, watching as he lifted his fingers to her breasts and brushed the aching tips. She arched her back. "Later you can take your time. Now I want you to make me come."

"My pleasure."

While one hand cupped her breast, the other slid between her legs and dipped into the heat generated by his tantalizing caresses and sexy words. He touched her with tender confidence, sliding his finger around the sensitive nub until she quaked and groaned.

"Oh, yes. There."

He knew exactly what turned her on.

With his hands otherwise occupied and his voice out of commission he had no way to convey how he was feeling, but Mia could guess from the wonder that bloomed across his features and the ragged nature of his breathing.

"Kiss me," she pleaded. Although it pained her to pull his hands from between her legs, she needed his mouth on hers.

She turned to face him and his hands slid into her hair, fingers pressing into her scalp as he tilted her head and brought his mouth to hers. She gasped at the joy and welcomed the plunge of his tongue, meeting it with her own. Her toes curled at the shudder that ran through him when her hands smoothed over his back and down his spine.

During their night together on tour, Nate had proved to be very vocal in bed, crooning encouragement and telling her how she tasted and felt. She could tell his need to remain silent was very frustrating, because his hands tracked over her bare skin with feverish longing.

Mia broke off the kiss and pushed him to arm's length. "Pants off. Now."

With a snappy salute, Nate made short work of his zipper and sent his trousers sliding down his legs. Mia didn't wait for him to take care of his boxer briefs. Her fingers were already on the waistband, yanking them down to free him. His breath was ragged as his fingers formed the sign for a curse word, making Mia smile.

"Get ready," she said. "You haven't yet begun to swear."

She dropped to her knees before him and took him into her mouth before he had a chance to realize what she intended. She closed her eyes to savor the warm, smooth skin stretched over his rigid erection. His hips jerked as she rolled her tongue around him and smiled as his fingers bit down on her shoulder. It must be killing him to remain silent. As much as she didn't want to cause damage to his voice, she knew the fight to stay quiet would only enhance the tension building in him.

He double tapped her shoulder, indicating he wanted

her attention. She lifted her gaze and met his eyes, letting him see how much she enjoyed what she was doing to him.

"You're killing me."

In answer, she took him deeper, using her hand at the base of his erection to provide sensation along the full length of his shaft. She thought about all the things they hadn't done that first night, and not getting to do this for him had been her biggest regret.

The tension in his body built as she worked her mouth on him, but even as his pleasure soared, he broke free and pulled her to her feet. For a long moment he held her cradled against his chest, her ear atop his pounding heart. When he seemed to get himself back under control, he pushed her to arm's length and signed, *"When I come it will be inside you."*

She shivered and took his hand, walking backward toward the bed. Nate reached into the nightstand and pulled out a condom. He brushed her hands aside when she tried to help him. With him otherwise occupied, she let her fingers drift over the taut muscles of his shoulder and biceps.

Once he finished putting on the protection, he turned to her and pointed to the bed. *"Up you go. I'm going to make love to you now."*

"That sounds about perfect."

She shifted onto the middle of the mattress and he stalked right after her, his hot gaze raking over her.

"You are so beautiful." His fingertips grazed her breast, circling the puckered tip.

"So are you." The words were barely a whisper as he closed his mouth over her nipple and sucked hard.

She gasped, the sound escaping her like a half cry as his tongue flicked the sensitive bud. She skidded her fingers along his cheeks and down his shoulders to his back. Muscles bunched and loosened beneath her touch as she investigated each rib and bump in his spine. How often had she watched him move around the stage, his long lithe body filled with such energy and emotion, and wondered what it would be like to be up against his rock-hard abs, a heartbeat away from those mobile, smiling lips?

And then she had been. After one of the shows, Nate had drawn her into a dressing room and kissed her. It was like being embraced by a power line. All the hyped up energy he'd received from performing had translated into a passionate kiss. It had been crazy magic.

He grabbed her hand and now pulled it to his mouth. His eyes captured hers as if asking for permission. Her voice was gone so she nodded.

"I want all of you. Right now. As deep and hard as you want it. Fast or slow," she finally said.

Nate closed his eyes and set his forehead against hers. He gave her the sweetest kiss on the corner of her mouth. *"I don't deserve you."*

You deserve so much better than me. She didn't dare speak the words for fear it would ruin the moment. Instead, she framed his face with her hands and brought his lips to hers. They kissed and passion overwhelmed them once more. He shifted to lie between her spread legs. Once again his fingers drifted between her folds and found her wet and aching. A shudder raged through him as he slid a finger inside her, making her moan. Mia's hips lifted off the bed.

She grabbed his wrist, intent on doing…something to satisfy the tension building inside her. Her gaze flicked to his face and she found him watching what he was doing to her. Her heart tripped and stopped at the level of joy mingling with lust in his expression. And then she was over the edge, her hips bucking as she rode the release Nate had brought to her body.

She barely noticed when he guided himself into position, but as she experienced the last spasms of her orgasm, Nate drove his hips against hers, filling her.

Seven

Air hissed between his teeth as he stopped moving. He was now fully seated inside her and he took a second to appreciate the moment with this spectacular woman. Mia's internal muscles clenched around him as aftershocks reverberated through her. He stroked strands of hair off her cheek and peered at her flushed face and passion-dazed eyes. She was beautiful and sweet. And all his.

She blew out a breath and lifted her gaze to his. He saw a hint of the shyness that always intrigued him. As if she couldn't quite believe he'd noticed her.

As if that was possible.

He raised his eyebrows in a silent question.

"I'm perfect. You're perfect. This—" Mia purred as she ran the soles of her feet along Nate's thighs "—is perfect."

It was all he needed to hear. He began to move, pulling out slowly, before driving back in, loving the way her breath caught and her lashes fluttered. Two months without her was two months too long. Already he could feel pleasure tighten in a frantic ache that pulled him toward completion.

"Harder," she begged. Her nails dug into his back. The tiny pain shot straight to his groin. "Yes," she moaned as he picked up speed. "Like that."

Staying silent during sex was way more frustrating than anything he'd experienced in the last two weeks since his surgery. Curses flooded his mind as he sank into Mia's tight, hot body over and over. He wanted to tell her how good she felt. How she was unlike any woman he'd ever known. Instead, he kissed her, letting his mouth speak in other ways.

His orgasm was close, but he needed her to go first. As their breath rushed together in frantic pants, he slipped his hand between them and cupped her. She uttered a soft cry that sounded like a garbled version of his name and then threw her head back. Her muscles clamped down on him hard and she was going over the edge.

Nate kept himself from climaxing long enough to watch her, and then he couldn't hold it back any longer. He buried his face in her shoulder as his body exploded in pleasure. His lips moved, forming her name against her skin as he gave one final thrust and spilled himself inside her for what felt like endless seconds.

As he became aware of the room again, Nate rolled onto his side, taking her with him.

"Incredible," he signed.

"You can say that again."

He made the sign a second time and she laughed. Brushing aside a damp strand of hair, he made another sign. *"Stay."*

She shook her head. Already he could feel her starting to disengage.

"I can't."

He fought down his disappointment. *"An hour more?"*

When she gave a reluctant nod, he brought his lips to hers. It wasn't much time, but enough to make certain that the next time he asked her to stay, she'd have a much harder time refusing.

Club T's was in full swing when Ivy and three of her besties were escorted past the line of attractive twenty-somethings waiting by the velvet ropes for their chance to get in. Mia trailed behind the group, anonymous and forgettable in a sleeveless black dress that skimmed her curves but left everything else to the imagination. In contrast, Ivy wore a red sequin romper with a plunging neckline that showed off her long legs, toned by hours of dance rehearsals and yoga.

The group bypassed the dance floor and headed straight for the VIP area. The DJ was cranking great tunes and with Ivy preoccupied for the moment, Mia let herself fall a little behind.

Their private table was set up with bottles of vodka, champagne and assorted mixes. Flanked by her entourage, Ivy slipped into the booth. There was enough space between the couches and the table for the women to rock their hips to the music and fling their hair extensions around. Ivy was in high spirits, yelling that she loved every song that played.

Mia perched on the far end of the couch, suddenly overwhelmed. By the concussive beat. The dazzling light show. The hyped-up customers all around them, whooping, dancing and sucking up all the oxygen. Dizziness consumed her. Mia closed her eyes, wishing she were somewhere tranquil and quiet.

Someone shook her shoulder. Mia's eyes opened and she spied Ivy bent over the table and frowning at her.

"Did you order this?" Ivy demanded, pointing to the bottles. "It's Grey Goose. I wanted Belvedere."

"You always drink Grey Goose," Mia said, feeling very much like screaming.

"Not lately." Ivy rolled her eyes. "You never pay attention."

"I'll go find someone and get it fixed." Mia was glad for the chance to escape. "Be right back."

With the mixes disguising the taste of the liquor, Mia doubted whether Ivy could distinguish one type of vodka from another. Most often she made demands to remind everyone that she was the celebrity. Mia was probably one of the few people who recognized she did it out of insecurity.

And Ivy was feeling all too anxious at the moment. She was fighting the direction Nate wanted for her album and the stress had sent her running for the comfortable fog of prescription meds. This meant Mia needed to be more vigilant than ever. She just needed to get Ivy through the album and then her sister would calm down.

Mia headed to the first floor in search of a waitress and cleared up the vodka situation. She was standing on the edge of the dance floor, wondering if it would be possible to locate Nate in the crowd, when an arm came around her waist, startling her. Mia tensed, intending on twisting away, when a familiar cologne danced past her nostrils. She glanced down as Nate's hands moved.

"Relax. I've got you."

A thousand butterflies took flight in her stomach as he drew her into the crowd on the dance floor. Twisting, grinding bodies surrounded them, driving Mia against Nate so they had no choice but to touch. He turned her so her back rested against his chest and his hands could roam over her.

"I can't." But her words were lost to a groan as his lips trailed along her neck and his hot breath spilled across her skin. "Ivy and her friends are just…over…" She sucked in a jagged breath as his thumb grazed her nipple.

"Damn, I've missed you."

Me, too. She didn't bother with the words. Her muscles trembled as he grazed his hands up her sides and over her ribs, telling him everything he needed to know.

Earlier the music and crowd had bothered her. But away from Ivy and her friends, Mia wanted to get lost on the dance floor for an hour or two, gyrating with the rest of the crowd to the bass-heavy music until her feet had blisters on top of blisters and she was drenched with sweat. How long had it been since she'd done something fun or crazy just for herself?

Two days.

She shut her eyes, blocking out the million-dollar light show, and whisked back in time to the hotel suite and Nate's naked body sliding against her skin as they made love. Placing her hands over his, heat blazing in her cheeks, she pressed him closer.

His familiar scent wrapped around her and she filled her lungs until her chest ached. Nate's body aligned with hers was perfection. It banished her loneliness, stripped away her inhibitions and demolished her dependability until she became someone else. Someone who excited her. Someone filled with poignant emotions of such perfect joy that they terrified her.

That was why she'd broken off with Nate when the

tour ended. She couldn't be two people. She had to choose. In the end, she'd shied away from embracing the daring, impulsive woman she became around Nate and retreated back into the familiar territory of being Ivy's highly efficient, but mostly ignored PA.

Hips swaying in sync, Mia and Nate rocked to the music pouring over them, but all she could hear was the sound of her heart crying in joy. Nothing made her happier than being with Nate. But her life had never been about being happy. It had been about obligation, selflessness and patience.

Sleeping with Nate while in LA had been foolish and reckless, but she wouldn't trade it for anything.

Against her side, her purse buzzed, jolting Mia back to responsibility. She offered up a huge sigh and tugged Nate's hands away from her body. Turning, she signed.

"I have to go."

She made a fist with her right hand to form the letter *A* and then circled it clockwise against her chest twice. Her apology did little to ease the irritation that tightened his lips into a relentless line. Green and amber lights played over his face, highlighting his unhappy expression as he signed a rude response.

"Ivy will wonder where I am."

"I don't care."

"I know."

She grabbed his wrist and dragged him off the dance floor. She thought to leave him near the bar and return to Ivy, but he was on her heels as she ascended the stairs to the VIP section. At the top, Nate was hailed by a pair of tall men, Kyle Tailor, the third partner in Club T's, and Hunter Graves. In the last five years Hunter had become increasingly in demand as a DJ and a producer.

"You have company." Mia indicated the two tall men heading their way. "I should get back to Ivy."

"In a second. Come translate for me."

Before she could refuse, Nate caught her hand and towed her to meet the two men. Mia had never been formally introduced to either of them, but thanks to Melody she knew the story behind Kyle's annoyed frown.

Kyle was the first to speak. "Hey, Nate."

Hunter Graves stuck out his hand with a broad grin. "Good to see you. Kyle was just showing me around. This place is great."

Kyle checked his phone. "I have to take care of something," he said, sending a meaningful glance Nate's way, obviously eager to get away from the DJ. "You don't mind taking over for me, do you?"

As Kyle retreated down the stairs, Nate shook Hunter's hand and glanced at Mia as he indicated his throat.

"He had throat surgery," Mia said. She put out her hand. "I'm Mia Navarro, his translator."

"You're more than that," Nate signed, while she and Hunter shook hands.

"Nice to meet you," Hunter said. "I can't wait to get up there and spin for this crowd." He indicated the DJ booth that overlooked the dance floor. "They're on fire."

"We're glad to have you here," Mia repeated.

Hunter's eyes widened as he gazed from her to Nate and back again. "You weren't kidding about the translating. That's cool. Your own secret language."

"It's been handy having her around the studio these last few weeks."

Mia translated what Nate signed, and then added her own two cents. "His handwriting is terrible. I don't know what would've happened if he'd been forced to write down everything he wanted to say."

Hunter laughed and Mia could see why Melody had been hung up on him for so long. His engaging grin made it easy to smile back. Nate nudged her with his elbow and she shot him a questioning glance.

"Stop flirting with him."

"Did Trent mention to you that I'm interested in booking some time in at Ugly Trout?" Hunter asked, his keen gaze missing little of their exchange.

Nate nodded.

"I've got a couple artists I've started working with and thought it might be good to have them come to Vegas while I'm here."

"Speaking of artists," Mia said, "Ivy's here tonight. Why don't we head over there and you can say hi." Mia glanced at Nate as she finished speaking and sent a mischievous grin his way.

There'd been a very brief flirtation between Hunter and Ivy a year earlier. Hunter might be the perfect anecdote for Ivy's stress. If nothing else, he'd be a good distraction. Although Hunter liked to play as hard as he worked, he was an advocate for clean living. Maybe reconnecting with him would convince Ivy to send Skylar and Riley packing.

"It would be great to see her," Hunter said. "Lead the way."

As he gestured for Hunter to follow Mia, Nate could tell she had something up her sleeve. By the time he reached the table, introductions were being made and Ivy's girlfriends fell over themselves swarming the DJ. Not only was Hunter charismatic and good-looking, but his net worth was in the high seven figures, making him a player worth pursuing.

Ivy didn't seem to be as impressed, but she was the

star and, as always, wanted everyone to know it. But when Hunter gave her his best wicked grin, she thawed and patted the cushion beside her.

Mia signed an explanation. *"They had a brief thing and I think she still likes him."*

Now Nate understood. *"So he's a distraction?"*

Her smile was all the answer he needed and it gave him an idea. Maybe having Hunter in Las Vegas was going to be a good thing, after all. Having him spend time with Ivy might kill two birds with one stone.

The friction between Nate and Ivy in the studio meant that recording the album wasn't going smoothly. He could put it down to artistic differences, but more likely she'd picked up on his disgust for the way she treated Mia, or any number of the other things that irritated him about her. Whatever the cause, the chemistry between them was all bad.

Nate had heard nothing but good things about Hunter as a producer, and he suspected the DJ would love an opportunity to work with Ivy. Maybe he'd have better luck dealing with the pop princess. And if Hunter was reluctant to tackle Ivy's album, maybe he'd be interested in her personally. She was beautiful and talented enough to appeal to him.

And that was the second reason to push them together. Weeks earlier Trent had signed Hunter to a one year contract as a DJ with Club T's, which meant Hunter was going to be spending a lot more time in Las Vegas. While he promised to be a huge draw on Sunday nights, Nate was worried this might further disrupt Melody and Kyle's relationship.

A year earlier Melody had been dating Hunter. They'd been together eighteen months and she found him lacking in the commitment department.

Kyle was Trent's best friend since high school and had always treated his buddy's little sister like family. After listening to Melody complain about her relationship woes, Kyle insisted that if Hunter thought he had competition, he would stop taking her for granted.

At some point during their six-week ruse, both of them got caught up in their pretend romance. But it wasn't until Hunter came to his senses and realized he was about to lose Melody that she and Kyle admitted to each other that they'd fallen in love.

For a while things were going great between them. But then Melody had gone on tour with Nate and the separation had taken its toll on the fledgling romance. Melody and Kyle were committed to making the long-distance thing work right up until Melody got caught by the paparazzi coming out of a New York City club hand-in-hand with Hunter.

The whole incident had been innocent enough. He'd taken her hand to keep from being separated in the crush leaving the club, but there was too much history between Melody and Hunter for Kyle to dismiss the episode.

Seeing that Ivy was utterly absorbed in the DJ, Nate caught Mia by the arm and drew her away.

"Where are we going?" she asked, as he guided her toward the stairs once more.

"Somewhere I can put my hands all over you."

"I really shouldn't be gone for very long."

"Hunter will keep her busy. Let's you and I find a private spot and make out."

She glanced back over her shoulder. "Twenty minutes. No more."

He could definitely work with that. Nate led her through the club to a discreet door that opened into a

nondescript hallway. Mia blinked in the sudden brightness of the florescent lighting.

"Where are we going?"

"Somewhere we won't be interrupted." He pulled out
his phone and shot Kyle a quick text, warning his business partner that he was going to use Trent's office for a
private meeting and didn't want to be disturbed.

While Nate had mentioned to Kyle that he was seeing
someone, he hadn't revealed that it was Mia. It wasn't
that Nate was keeping her a secret—Melody and Trent
knew—but the friendship between the two men was
strained because of what was happening between Kyle
and Melody.

Nate hadn't exactly taken sides, but Melody was one
of his favorite people and she wasn't the one behaving
like an idiot. The way Kyle had reacted after her New
York club incident with Hunter made Nate feel less than
friendly toward his business partner.

Relationships weren't always easy—Nate could at-
test to that with what was going on between him and
Mia—but when you loved someone, you should trust
them. And from what he was seeing of Kyle, the guy
was worrying more about guarding his heart than opening it to Melody.

And that was the last thought Nate intended to have
on that subject for the next hour. He ushered Mia in and
closed and locked the door to Trent's office, sealing them
inside the space. He didn't bother to turn on the overhead
lights. One wall of floor-to-ceiling monitors, tuned to
various locations around the club, provided enough light
to highlight the wet bar, Trent's neat desk and, most important for Nate's purposes, a comfortable couch.

"Now that you have me here," Mia said, dropping her
purse on an end table, "what do you plan to do?"

Was she kidding? He swooped her into his arms and deposited her on the couch. His lips found hers even as her fingers skimmed his suit coat off his shoulders. Fortunately, he wasn't wearing a tie and she was making quick work of the buttons on his dark gray shirt. He barely restrained a groan as her palms slid over his abs and skated around to his back.

As much as he enjoyed that her skill as a translator kept her at his side, he really wanted his voice back so he could tell her all the delicious, wicked things he intended to do to her. Although he could easily spend the near future indulging in one slow, drugging kiss after another, he was afraid they might interrupted by yet another summons from Ivy.

He kissed his way down her neck and across her shoulder. The dress she wore zipped up the back and he cursed himself for not taking it off her before he got her onto the couch. He slid his hand up her bare thigh, hearing her gasp as he hooked his fingertips into her panties and gave a tug. With a little help from her, he got her underwear off. Then she eased the hem of her dress upward until she'd exposed her lower half.

Smiling at the gorgeous picture she made, Nate settled his shoulders between her thighs and pressed his mouth against her. Everything about the moment was perfect, from the way she tasted to the sweet, mewling sounds of pleasure that escaped her lips as he pushed her to the edge of desire and held her there.

She clutched and released his hair as her thighs began to tremble and her back arched. She sighed his name on a ragged breath as he slid two fingers inside her and made her climax. Her hips lifted as she came, body tensing as her release crashed over her. As always he marveled at the power and duration of her orgasm. The only thing he enjoyed more than watching her come was being with her when it happened.

Mia went limp beneath him. "That was just…wow." She panted. "Give me a second and I'll return the favor."

Nate grinned as he stripped off his clothes, slipped on a condom and returned to the couch. Mia had been watching him the whole time, grinning like a satisfied cat.

"You are gorgeous, do you know that?" she murmured as he lay flat on his back and repositioned her so that she straddled him.

"So are you, but I like you better naked." He reached behind her and managed to unzip her dress. In seconds it was on the floor. Her bra followed. He traced her breasts with his fingertips and smiled. *"Much better."*

She lifted her hips and closed her hand around his erection. Nate hissed between his teeth, but before he could react further, she'd settled herself over him. While stars exploded in his vision, Mia leaned forward and kissed him, with such tenderness Nate's heart nearly stopped.

"No," she corrected him, sucking his lower lip between her teeth. "This is much better."

"I stand corrected."

With a husky laugh, she began to move. And suddenly they had no further need for words.

Eight

Five days following that epic night with Nate at Club T's, Mia decided she couldn't put off taking a pregnancy test any longer. While it wasn't unusual for her to miss an occasional period due to stress, or if she was doing a lot of traveling with Ivy, it was over two months since that night in Sydney and time she pulled her head out of the sand.

Part of Mia recognized the old adage that what you don't know can't hurt you. Until she took the test, she didn't have to think about the future. But each day she delayed, the worry consumed her more, and she couldn't decide if her queasy stomach was morning sickness, plain old anxiety or a little of both. Today, however, she'd decided to stop procrastinating.

It was the morning of the AMAs and Ivy was scheduled for a video interview at eight thirty. As soon as her twin slapped on the headphones, Mia made a break for the door. In ten minutes she'd bought the pregnancy test and returned to the television studio. Although taking the test in the bathroom there wasn't ideal, it was better than taking it at home.

She now had ten more minutes until Ivy would be done. Fortunately, she had a full bladder and the test took only three minutes to show results.

She sat on the toilet to wait. Head down, eyes closed, Mia sorted through her tangled emotions for a bright thread of certainty. How did she want things to turn out?

Pregnant? Joy at the possibility filled her like a crystal-pure note perfectly sung. But almost immediately anxiety rose up in her, drowning out the happy emotion. If she was pregnant, her life as she knew it was over. Nothing could possess her to keep being Ivy's assistant, and when Ivy found out who'd fathered her child, Mia would probably find her relationship with her sister over, as well.

And what if she wasn't pregnant? She'd feel a mixture of relief and disappointment. Everything would be easier. She wouldn't have to change a single thing about her life.

But was that really what she wanted? How long did she think she was going to be Ivy's assistant? Was she going to be forty or fifty and still following her sister around? Fetching for her. Putting up with her insecurities. With no husband and children and few friends.

Tears welled up in her eyes. She fought them off by taking several deep breaths and stabbing her fingernails into her palms. A baby would change everything. She could make a case for choosing her child over her sister. The guilt her parents heaped on her shoulders would lose its power.

Three minutes had never felt longer. Mia watched the seconds tick by on her cell phone; she'd started the stopwatch as soon as she took the test. While the seconds ticked off, she stayed in the stall, too afraid to stand in the bathroom proper and get caught with a pregnancy test in her hand. Not that anyone would know who she was or care what she was doing. Sometimes being invisible was nice. But there was that tiny chance that someone would be interested in what was going on and that information could leave the bathroom and cause her a lot of trouble.

When the time was up, Mia found herself unable to look at the test. She sat with it in her lap, the indicator facing downward. She didn't need to look to see the answer. She already knew. She was pregnant. Her phone buzzed, scaring her. She dropped the test. It clattered to the floor and landed faceup.

These days the tests were easy to read. No more questionable results. Depending on which one you chose, there was a line, the word *yes* or the word *pregnant*. In Mia's case it was "pregnant." She swallowed a hysterical laugh. Her whole life had just changed inside the bathroom of a TV station.

No, that wasn't quite true. Her whole life had changed the day she'd met Nate.

Mia had about thirty seconds to absorb the reality of her situation before the bathroom door opened and two women entered with a gust of animated chatter. She recognized the voices and quickly snatched the pregnancy test off the ground and dropped it into her work tote. She would just have to dispose of it later, when no one was around. Opening the stall door, Mia stepped out.

Skylar and Riley were standing at the sink, touching up their already flawless makeup. The key to being one of Ivy's friends was to be beautiful without being too beautiful. No one was allowed to outshine Ivy Bliss.

That had never been a problem for Mia. She barely

had enough time in the morning to shower and brush her teeth. Maybe apply a little eyeliner. A slash of neutral lipstick. Tucking her hair behind her ears, she'd don her uniform of black skinny pants and some sort of blouse. Her only jewelry was a pair of diamond studs she got for her sixteenth birthday.

"What are you two doing here?" Mia asked as she exited the stall. She stepped to the sink to wash her hands, avoiding eye contact with either of Ivy's friends.

"We're here to spend the day with Ivy and help her get ready for the AMAs."

"She doesn't need your help." Mia didn't make any effort to hide her impatience and didn't care if she sounded rude. She'd had enough of these two. "Ivy has a team of professionals to get her ready."

Skylar pouted. "She wants us."

"She told us to come," Riley echoed.

Mia wasn't sure what to believe, but didn't get a chance to argue further because the bathroom door opened and Ivy walked in. She glanced from her two friends to Mia and frowned.

"What are you doing in here?" she demanded. "I've been looking for you all over."

"I was explaining to these two that you don't need them around today."

Ivy pouted. "I invited them."

"You need to focus on tonight." Mia eyed Skylar. "They will just distract you. Come on. Jennifer is going to be at the house in an hour for your massage and Yvonne and her team are coming by at eleven."

"In a second." Ivy headed toward one of the stalls. "Can you go get the car? My feet are killing me in these shoes and I don't feel like walking all the way out to the parking lot."

"Fine."

Mia didn't want to argue with her sister. She was too excited about her own plans for later that day. Nate had pulled out all the stops to make her AMA experience special. He'd arranged for her to have a hotel suite where he was staying, and his stylist would be there at two o'clock with a designer dress and all the trappings to get Mia award-ceremony ready.

Ten minutes later, after Mia had fetched the car and picked up her sister, they were heading back to Ivy's house. "How did the interview go?"

"It went okay. Didn't you stay to watch?"

"I had a quick errand to run."

Ivy yawned. "I'm dead. Can you stop and get me my usual with three shots? I need a pick-me-up."

"Sure." Mia resisted the urge to talk her sister out of such a massive caffeine hit. If Ivy was ever going to start taking care of herself, Mia would have to stop making all her decisions for her.

She drove to Ivy's favorite coffee shop near her house, parked and grabbed her wallet out of her tote. "Anything else?"

"One of those scones with the raspberry."

"The white chocolate one?"

Ivy nodded and Mia headed off. Thanks to the long line, it took her fifteen minutes to get back to her sister.

"They didn't have any of the white chocolate so I got you one with orange and cranberry." Mia set the coffee cup in the drink holder and held out the bag containing the pastry.

Ivy took it without looking up from her phone. She was idly scrolling through pictures and acted as if Mia hadn't spoken. The change of mood wasn't unexpected. Ivy hated being kept waiting for anything.

And then as they pulled up in front of the house, Ivy spoke. "I'm going to get Hunter to produce my album."

"What?" Mia glanced at her sister in confusion. "Are you sure that's a good idea? I mean, he's had some success, but at the same time he's still pretty new to that side of the business. And the label is expecting Nate to be involved."

"I don't like the direction Nate is taking my album. I want to do things my way."

Often when Mia dealt with Ivy she felt as if she stood between a rock and a hard place. Part of her job was to keep Ivy happy. The other part was more difficult. She needed to keep her sister's career on a strong trajectory. That meant keeping the label happy.

"Of course you do. But at the same time you have to consider the best for your career."

"You don't think I know what's best for my career?"

"Sure. Of course." Mia decided retreat was the best option.

Ivy got out of the car, and once she was in the house, headed straight to her room without saying another word. After checking in with the housekeeper, Clara, Mia grabbed her overnight bag and left. She was too excited about her own plans to stick around and let Ivy's drama spoil the rest of her day.

Mia had booked a spa appointment for herself as a special treat. She'd planned for a facial, pedicure and manicure to get her in the perfect mood for the festive event. It was rare for her to get so much uninterrupted time to herself, and several hours later she felt both relaxed and refreshed as she headed to the suite Nate had booked and put herself into his stylist Patricia's capable hands.

Although Mia had watched Ivy get ready for dozens

of award shows and thought she knew what to expect, when she saw her dress for the first time she nearly started to cry.

"That's the most beautiful thing I've ever seen."

Patricia smiled at her and Mia wondered what she must be thinking of this silly girl Nate had asked her to dress for the event.

"I'm glad you like it. When Nate described you to me, I knew immediately this dress would be perfect for you. There's so much going on with the wildflower print that I think we should keep your styling simple."

Patricia directed the hairdresser to sweep her hair back into a sleek bun. A smoky eye shadow and rose lipstick accentuated Mia's features. By the time they were done even Mia believed she looked presentable enough for the red carpet. Not that she would be walking with Nate. She'd put her foot down on that score. He had his bandmates to speak for him. Her appearance at his side would only lead the media to ask questions.

"You look fantastic," Patricia said as Mia finished slipping into sparkling sandals and straightened so the stylist could assess her total look. "I know several stars who would kill to have that cleavage."

Mia's fingers coasted over her still-flat belly as she stared at herself in the mirror. The neckline of the gown plunged to her waist, yet somehow managed to look elegant rather than sexy. Mia guessed it was due to the delicate sprays of sequin-accented wildflowers that covered the skirt and halter-style top.

"I'm pretty sure I'll never wear anything so beautiful again." The dress fit as if it had been made for her and had required only a few minor alterations. "What time does it turn into fairy dust?"

Patricia laughed. "So I'm your fairy godmother?"

"You had to work some serious magic to get me looking this good."

"You underestimate how beautiful you are. I suppose it's hard to feel pretty when you're constantly comparing yourself to Ivy Bliss."

"I don't compare myself," Mia said without a hint of bitterness. "Everyone else does that for me."

"I know one person who doesn't. Nate. You are his star."

Mia's cheeks heated at Patricia's knowing grin. Because she doubted the stylist would believe anything she had to say to the contrary, she said nothing at all.

Twenty minutes later she was in a car heading for the venue. She'd followed Ivy's day on social media and saw that her sister was excited about her look for that evening. She'd teased bits of the dress all day for her fans. It was a toss-up which Ivy loved more, fashion or performing. She talked all the time about starting her own clothing line and sketched ideas in her free time.

Determined to bridge the gap developing between her and Ivy, Mia texted her twin to ask if she liked her gown, but received no reply.

She decided to go early in order to slip past the media while they were still in setup mode. Her decision turned out to be sound, but she was surprised at how many people wanted to talk to her. Unlike the commotion caused when Ivy and other big stars walked the carpet, Mia was able to take her time with several of the reporters she knew. If they were surprised to find her walking the red carpet on her own, they made no mention of it.

Once she was inside the theater, several producers Ivy had worked with in the past approached her to chat. Apparently word had gone around that Mia had been working with Nate these last few weeks. Most everyone wanted to know if she was writing as well as producing. She kept her answers vague, but by the time she reached her seat, she felt as if she belonged.

It was a heady sensation, but one she reined in almost immediately. So what if she belonged? It wasn't as if she was free to pursue her dreams. Not as long as Ivy needed her. Yet Nate's question continued to plague her. How long was she planning to keep her life on hold so she could watch over her sister? Ivy was a grown woman, no longer a fragile seventeen-year-old girl getting a taste of stardom for the first time.

Besides, in seven months, Mia's priorities would undergo a massive change. She fanned her finger over her stomach. Pregnant. A chill raced through her at the thought of how everyone around her would react to that news. She imagined her parents would be disappointed in her for not being married. Despite having a daughter who pranced around half-naked onstage, they were conservative when it came to family values. Mia was afraid of how Ivy would react. She hoped her twin would be happy for her, but Ivy rarely liked it when good things happened to Mia.

And how would Nate react? What was going on between them was fun and exciting, but it was also new and undefined. They'd known each other only a few months and weren't exactly dating. To go from lovers to parents without all the stuff in between would be a huge leap. But there wasn't any question in Mia's mind that it was one she was ready to make. So when did she tell Nate?

Tonight was too soon. When Ivy's album was done? Mia shook her head. At the rate things were going, with her sister lobbying to switch producers from Nate to Hunter, getting the recording finished by the end of November wasn't going to happen.

Tomorrow they were heading back to Las Vegas. Thursday was Thanksgiving and she and Nate had talked about spending the day together, cooking a special dinner for Trent, Savannah, Melody and hopefully Kyle. She would tell Nate then.

Blinded by the flash of dozens of cameras, Nate squelched his irritation as he walked the AMAs' red carpet with the other members of Free Fall. Although he'd convinced Mia to accompany him to the event, he'd been unable to persuade her to walk beside him past the gauntlet of paparazzi and press. Nor had he caught a glimpse of her to see how Patricia had styled her. The curiosity was killing him.

Behind them Ivy posed and vamped for the cameras. Tonight she'd abandoned her signature high ponytail for a sleek side bun that complemented her romantic red ball gown with its tiers of gauzy layers. The halter top bared her back and shoulders, but offered full frontal coverage. Fabric roses circled the high neck and waist. The deep scarlet tint showed off her light olive skin and caught every eye.

Nate put on his easy grin and posed with his bandmates. They took selfies and signed autographs for their fans. It was great to step away from his role as front man and let the other guys answer the interviewers' questions. All the while his mind was on what awaited him at the end of the red carpet.

After what felt like a ridiculous amount of time, but was only about a half an hour, they entered the theater and headed to their seats. He saw a woman sitting in one of the seats assigned to Free Fall, her brown hair knotted at the nape of her neck. All Nate's tension fell away as he reached the row and realized it was Mia. While his heart thundered in his ears, he suddenly realized he'd half expected her not to show.

She stared straight ahead with fixed concentration, as if by holding herself perfectly still no one would notice her. She was completely mistaken. For starters, she was wearing the exact opposite of Ivy's gown. This dress boasted a deep V that bared Mia from throat to waist, yet somehow managed to look elegant rather than overly sexy. Nate realized it was the gown's off-white background and the sprays of vivid printed flowers with their hints of sparkle that gave the dress a feminine vibe.

Her expression softened as she saw him approach. Nate's pulse hitched at the relief in her eyes. Or maybe it was just how perfect she looked. And smelled. This last he noted as he sat beside her and brushed her cheek with his lips.

"You look gorgeous," he signed, not trusting his voice. Although he'd been cleared by Dr. Hansen to talk a little, he'd grown accustomed to communicating with her in ASL.

"You look pretty great yourself." She glanced past him at his other bandmates and gave them all a sweet smile. "Are you guys nervous?"

"Nah." Mike, their keyboard player, had his arm wrapped around his smiling wife.

Their base player, Dan, was riding solo tonight. His very pregnant wife had opted to cheer from home. "Hell, yeah."

"Sort of." This last came from their drummer, Brent, who had a stunning blonde in a sequined mini on his arm.

Mia laughed, the sound light and musical. "I would think you guys are old pros at this. How many Grammys have you won?"

Nate took his seat as he listened to Mia banter with his

bandmates. Sitting beside her, he was a little surprised at his light-headedness. The weight he'd been carrying all afternoon lifted. He took her hand, lacing their fingers together, and brought it to his lips.

The theater was filling with musicians. They were fifteen minutes away from the start of the show. Beside Nate, Mia was a bundle of restless energy.

"Did you see Ivy?" she asked.

"She was behind us on the red carpet."

"How did she look?"

"Beautiful as always. She was wearing a red dress."

Mia nodded. "I saw bits of it on Instagram. The style is a departure for her and I think she was both excited and a little nervous about wearing it."

Nate was slightly surprised she'd let him tuck her arm through his. Then he realized, given the way she was looking around at all the celebrities, she probably hadn't even noticed the intimacy between them.

The same couldn't be said for him. He was hyper-aware of every little thing about her, from her muted squeal when Taylor Swift walked past to her soft gasp when Luke Bryan winked at her. Given how often she must have seen these people at other award shows, her starstruck behavior amused him. She was like a kid at Disneyland for the first time.

"It's different sitting in the audience among them," she explained when she caught him grinning at her. "I don't have to be professional."

By professional he sensed what she meant was invisible. She'd learned how to bottle up all her emotions, good and bad. He'd realized this when they first met on tour. They'd hung out for almost three weeks before he realized she liked him the way he liked her.

Excitement hummed in her slim body. "I don't think I could ever get used to this."

"They're all just people, like me and you."

"You're not just people. You're Nate Tucker." She stated his name as if that explained everything.

"I'm just a guy."

She shook her head as if he could never understand. Her voice was soft as she spoke. "I still have a hard time believing you ever noticed me."

Conscious of their surroundings, he resisted the urge to sweep her into his arms and kiss her soft lips. *"Let's go find a quiet corner and I'll notice you plenty."*

Even now after everything they'd shared, she still blushed when he stared at her intently. That she'd somehow maintained such innocence while immersed in show business craziness continued to enthrall him.

"I'm glad you came tonight."

"Me, too." But there was a hint of hesitation in her answer.

She was still worried about Ivy. Nate was of two minds. Part of him was irritated at the hold her sister maintained over her. The other part sympathized with Mia. He knew firsthand the effect of being bullied by family. His father hadn't treated his wife and child as though they mattered to him. On a good day he'd settled in front of the television with a whiskey and ignored them. On a bad day he'd led with his fists.

Music began to play, signaling that the show was getting under way. Mia relaxed and snuggled a bit closer. Had she been worried that her sister might stop by and make a scene? What was it going to take for Mia to get out from beneath Ivy's thumb?

It was nice for a change to not have to worry about performing. The only time he needed to leave Mia alone was a little over an hour and a half into the program, when Free Fall presented the award for Favorite Male Country Artist. He stood to the side while Dan and Mike took turns reading off the nominees. While the winner thanked family and fans, Nate shared a smile with Mia. She looked so perfect sitting there, her eyes bright, her gaze all for him as she waited for him to come back to her.

All of a sudden he couldn't wait for the show to be over so he could take her to the after-party and spend some time with her in his arms on the dance floor. Since she was officially his date, Mia couldn't possibly use her sister's presence as an excuse to keep him at bay the way she'd done on the tour.

But he'd underestimated Ivy.

When the pop star stepped onstage to perform, something was definitely off with her. Nate doubted most people would notice, but he'd watched her rehearse and perform for weeks while on tour. She was a beat behind the music and she was walking through her complicated choreography. Mia sat forward in her chair, her expression tightening with concern.

"What's wrong with her?"

Mia shook her head, but he knew her well enough to know when she wasn't telling the truth.

"Is she drunk?"

Mia's gaze was glued to Ivy. Nate wasn't sure if she'd even noticed his questions, until she shook her head again after a minute.

"Maybe high." Mia set her fingertips against her mouth and blinked rapidly. The bright glint in her eyes was from tears. "I need to get backstage and be there for her."

"Then we'll both go." He wasn't letting Mia run off without him. She might never come back.

"You can't leave in the middle of the ceremony."

But she could. It was her way of highlighting the difference in their status. She was a lowly, anonymous assistant, while he was a celebrity. Nate was getting tired of it.

"Contact your dad. He's her manager. Let him deal with her."

Mia bit the inside of her lip, looking concerned at his insistence. "I'll call him when I get backstage."

Nate cursed long and viciously in his head. Leave it to Ivy to upset her sister just when Mia was having fun. Nate reached for her hand, but Mia pulled it out of reach before he made contact.

"I'll be back in a little while."

Then, as the performance ended and the crowd politely applauded, Mia slipped away. And Nate wondered if he'd see her again before the evening was over.

Nine

It was a little after midnight when Nate returned to his hotel suite without his date for the evening. He wasn't surprised that Mia hadn't reappeared after heading backstage to check on her sister. At least she hadn't left him hanging. She'd sent him several texts as she assessed the situation and waited for her father to show up and take charge of Ivy.

Now, his cell phone pinged and his screen lit up with a text.

I'm back at the hotel. Sorry about what happened tonight.

The tightness in his chest eased as he texted her back, letting her know that he was also at the hotel and asking her to come to his suite. It was time he and Mia had a serious conversation about what was going on between them and where he saw their relationship going. He needed to know where she stood.

A soft knock sounded on his door. When he opened it, Mia stood in the hallway holding a pint of his favorite ice cream and two spoons.

"What's that for?"

"Girls always eat ice cream after a big disappointment."

He wondered which disappointment she referred to: the fact that Free Fall didn't win their category or that her sister had ruined his evening.

"I'm not a girl. And I don't care that we lost." He plucked the ice cream from her hand and gestured her in.

"I am a girl and the ice cream is for me. I just thought I'd share." She swiped at the container, but he moved beyond her reach.

He set the ice cream on the coffee table and sat down on the couch. *"It's my favorite. And what do you have to be bummed about?"*

"You're mad at me."

"I'm not."

"Liar." She followed him and sat down cross-legged, facing him. "I'm sorry I ruined our night."

"You didn't. Your sister did."

"I shouldn't have left you."

In five minutes she'd managed to dispel his annoyance and arouse his sympathy. Here he'd been feeling sorry for himself, and she was the one who'd had to disrupt her evening to take care of Ivy.

"How come you didn't tell me your sister has a drug problem?"

The question had been burning up his thoughts since he'd realized what's going on.

"She doesn't have a problem."

Mia's evasion annoyed him. It wasn't just that she was keeping a whopping huge secret from him. Ivy's career was something Nate and Trent were investing time and money in. If there was a problem, they needed to know.

"You don't think I can see what's going on? You forget, I've been there."

Mia wouldn't meet his gaze. "I know, but you got clean and Ivy can, too."

"Who knows about this?"

"Just my immediate family."

"How long has this been going on?"

"It started when she had plastic surgery at seventeen. She got hooked on the painkillers. She was on Broadway at the time and I was finishing up my senior year of high school in LA. No one knows this but my parents and me, but she almost died after overdosing." Mia looked miserable. "That's when it was decided I should become her assistant so I could keep an eye on her."

"But it's been eight years." At least this explained Mia's dedication to her sister. *"How long is everyone expecting you to sacrifice your life for Ivy?"*

She didn't answer his question. "She doesn't always make good choices. I've been worried about her spending so much time with Riley and Skylar. They are far more likely to drag her into trouble than they are to keep her out of it."

"How bad are things with her?"

"She's been mostly clean since what happened in New York."

"Mostly?"

Mia winced. "Except for a setback a couple years ago."

"She seemed fine on the tour."

"She was. It's the album. She's really struggling. But I don't know what happened tonight. Usually she loves performing."

Nate had a pretty good idea. *"It's because you're here with me. Your sister loves to spoil things for you."*

"That's not true." But she didn't sound or look convincing.

When Mia offered nothing else, he asked another question. *"Does your father know what's going on?"*

"Before. But not this time around."

"You should tell him. He's her father." Nate thought that Javier needed to act like her father for a change and put his manager role on the back burner. "This could ruin more than just her career."

Mia dropped her gaze to her hands. Misery radiated from her. The tour had offered Nate plenty of chances to observe the family dynamic and he sensed more at work here that Mia wasn't saying.

"What?"

"They'll blame me." She leaned forward and dug her spoon into the ice cream. "That's not true. I don't mean that." But it was obvious that was exactly what worried her. "It's just that I'm supposed to keep an eye on her. And I've been distracted." The sly smile she shot him wobbled at the edges.

His heart broke. *"Why do you let them do that to you?"*

"Because she's my sister and I'm…"

"Responsible for her?"

He'd never had a brother or sister and didn't understand the connection these two had. To make matters worse, Ivy and Mia were twins. Granted, they were fraternal rather than identical twins, but still, sharing a womb with someone for nine months must take the bond to a whole different level.

"Where does it end?" Hopelessness overwhelmed him as he suddenly realized his plan to disengage Mia

from her sister had been doomed from the start. *"When do you get to live your life?"*

"I don't know."

His mother had stayed with a bully too long and she'd ended up beaten and bruised on too many occasions. Mia wore her wounds on the inside.

On the other hand, he wasn't sure if Mia was ready to leave her situation. Shucking off her family's expectations couldn't be easy. He'd seen firsthand the pressure Javier exerted on both his daughters.

"Have you asked yourself what you owe her?"

"I know you don't think I owe her anything," Mia said. "Maybe I don't. I just know if I leave and something happens to her again, I would never be able to forgive myself."

That sort of emotional blackmail was nearly impossible to walk away from. Nate wished he could somehow make her understand what they were doing to her. Or maybe she did. Maybe the way she coped was to pretend it didn't bother her.

More than anything Nate wanted to protect her from herself. He'd be her champion if she'd let him. But he couldn't force her to get out of the bad situation she found herself in. Unlike when he'd stepped between his parents and wrestled the knife away from his father, the danger to Mia wasn't tangible. But that didn't make it any less dire.

"How much longer can you keep it up? Following Ivy around. Keeping her out of trouble. Catering to her every whim. When do you get to live your life?"

He'd posed this same question several times on tour. Each time Mia had given him the same answer.

"It's what I need to do right now. Once Ivy's new album drops and it's a sensation, I'll have more options."

Her eyes pleaded with him to understand. "I promised my parents to watch out for her. She doesn't take good care of herself. That leads to people taking advantage of her. Like Riley and Skylar are doing right now."

"You say you're going to leave after this album launches, but what if she needs you more than ever?"

That Mia didn't answer immediately told him a lot.

"You know I'm in your corner, right?"

"I do." But she didn't look at him.

For a moment he felt as if she didn't want him to be in her corner. As if having him on her side created a whole new set of problems for her. How was that possible?

"Where does this leave us?"

"I just need some time to sort things out."

"How much time?" He had to head back to Las Vegas tomorrow, but hated the idea of leaving her behind in LA.

"My parents are sitting down with Ivy tomorrow. I'll know more then."

"Are you coming back to Las Vegas?"

"I promised I'd help with Thanksgiving dinner." She gave him a wan smile. "We can talk then."

The morning after the AMAs, Mia drove Nate to a checkup with Dr. Hanson and then to the airport. As delighted as she'd been to hear that Nate's progress was good and he was able to start speaking again, she would miss being his voice. That he'd needed her to translate for him was a great excuse for why she was spending so much time with him. Now, she'd have to come clean about their relationship and face Ivy's displeasure.

When Mia got to her sister's house, she saw their mom's car parked in the driveway. Mia approached the front door with a sick feeling in her stomach. Her mother stood in the foyer as Mia entered the house. As Ivy's career had taken off, Sharon Navarro had changed from an average housewife and mother who'd homeschooled her three daughters and shopped discount stores for her clothes to a designer-label-wearing middle-aged woman with large diamonds at her ears and on her fingers. Despite what must have been a harrowing night worrying about Ivy, she looked as if she was ready for lunch at a fancy restaurant.

In contrast, Mia felt disheveled and gritty despite the shower she'd shared with Nate that morning. "What are you doing here?" she asked, hoping nothing worse had happened to her sister overnight. "Is Ivy okay?"

"She's fine. Where have you been?"

"At the hotel. I told Dad last night where I was going. I needed to return the dress."

"And you stayed?"

Although they'd spent the night together, talking and making love until dawn, she couldn't help but feel as if Nate had put a wall up between them. He wanted her to leave Ivy and be with him. Mia thought that's what she wanted, too. So why couldn't she just walk away? Because Ivy needed her? How long was she going to use that as an excuse? Especially now that she was pregnant.

"I knew Dad was here. Ivy didn't need us both." Mia's tone contained a touch of belligerence. "I had a whole night planned." To her own surprise, she sounded like Ivy, petulant and frustrated.

"Do you mean to tell me you went to the after-parties after dropping your sister off here?" Mia's mother looked appalled.

"No, of course not. I just wanted to point out that I had my own plans for the evening that didn't involve my sister getting high and making a fool of herself on live television."

"Mia," her mother admonished. "Your sister works so hard and is under such pressure."

Fury rushed through Mia's body as she thought of her high hopes for last evening. It was supposed to her magical night. Her chance to appear in public with Nate and behave like a couple. To dance and mingle and have fun while not giving her sister a single thought.

"She spoils everything," Mia countered.

"She supports all of us."

"Well, maybe I'm tired of being supported by her. Maybe it's time I started supporting myself."

When had her level of resentment risen so high? How had she not noticed that each day of acting as her sister's assistant grew harder than the one before? Nate's constant pointing out how badly Ivy treated her didn't help.

Mia's mother retreated a half step beneath the rush of her daughter's emotional tirade. "You can't turn your back on her sister. She isn't strong enough to do this on her own."

"I'm not turning my back on her." All the energy drained from her. No matter what she said or did, Mia was never going to win this battle. It all came down to guilt. Responsibility. "She's my sister and I love her. But my life revolves around her and I want a little something for myself."

"You mean your songwriting," Mia's mother said. "I'll speak to your father. Maybe there's room on Ivy's next album for a few of your songs. And this time you should get the credit."

"That's not what I mean." But Mia could tell her mother wasn't listening.

Her fingers shifted to her abdomen and the child that

lay there. Now wasn't the time to get into this with her mom. She needed to talk to Nate first.

But right now, Mia needed some sleep. The past twenty-four hours had been a roller coaster of highs and lows, all of which had taken every ounce of Mia's energy.

"Can we talk about this later?" she said. "I'm exhausted. Are you going to stick around for a while?"

"No. I have a meeting at the foundation."

Sharon Navarro ran the Ivy Bliss Foundation, a program that promoted hearing health and helped low-income children with hearing impairments. It was a charity near and dear to her heart because of her eldest daughter's hearing loss at age two.

"Where is Dad?"

"Your father's meeting with Trent Caldwell about Ivy's album. It looks as if she's going to finish recording it with Hunter Graves." Mia's mother picked up her purse. "He'll come by afterward."

"Then I guess it's just me keeping an eye on her." Again.

"I don't understand what has gotten into you lately. You used to be happy for your sister's success."

"I still am. But she's become such a different person. There are times when I don't recognize her anymore."

"She's a star," Mia's mother said, as if that explained everything.

Overwhelmed by defeat, Mia watched her mother depart before shuffling toward her bedroom. She shut the door behind her and glanced around the space. Besides the clothes in the closet, barely anything in the room belonged to her. Mia dropped her overnight bag on the floor and flung herself on her bed, where she lay on her back, staring at the ceiling. Her eyes were dry despite the lump in her throat.

She didn't remember ever feeling so alone. And yet, what about her situation had changed? Acting as her sister's full-time personal assistant and keeper had kept Mia from forming lasting friendships, and interfered with every man she'd ever tried to date.

Except now, Mia had been given a glimpse of what her life could be. A career as a music producer. Friendships with Melody, Trent and Savannah. A relationship with Nate. Motherhood.

Mia closed her eyes. Ready or not, everything was going to change.

Nate was surprised when the person picking him up at the Las Vegas airport was Kyle and not Melody. As he slid into the passenger seat of Kyle's bright blue BMW convertible, he glanced at his business partner and thought he looked as exhausted and miserable as Nate felt.

"I didn't expect to see you," Nate said.

"Melody asked if I could get you. Seems she had a small window to get Hunter's input on her album—" Kyle's eyes widened. "Hey, you're talking again."

"My doctor gave me the go-ahead to start using my voice, but I'm not supposed to overdo it. So you and Melody are finally talking?"

"If by talking you mean she sent me a text saying she was stuck at the studio and would I pick you up, then yeah."

Nate winced at the other man's bitterness. "You two have got to sit down and chat. Why don't you come for Thanksgiving." Nate had extended the invitation to Kyle once already and been turned down. This time, he decided to push harder.

CAT SCHIELD   143

"I don't want to spoil the day for you guys."

"You won't." The only thing that could spoil the day for Nate was if Mia found a reason not to show. "The longer you and Melody keep up whatever it is you're doing, the harder it's going to be to reconcile."

"What if we're not meant to be together?"

Kyle's question hit at the heart of what Nate himself had been grappling with these last few weeks. And after last night, he was more convinced than ever that when the time came, Mia was going to bolt the same way she had that last morning in Sydney.

And what then? What was he planning to do without her? He couldn't bear to think about it.

"You and Melody love each other," Nate said. And in less than six months they were going to become parents, whether either of them was prepared or not. "You'll find a way to work it out. Just remember why you fell for her in the first place."

"But I've really messed up. I pretty much accused her of cheating on me with Hunter."

Nate could appreciate his friend's predicament. Kyle was a well-known player. Before realizing he was in love with Melody, he'd dated lots of women and committed to none of them.

"Have you asked yourself why?"

"Many times. It's the way Melody and I got together. She was trying to make Hunter jealous. I keep thinking maybe she picked the wrong guy."

Nate didn't think this was the heart of Kyle's troubles. It seemed more likely that he was afraid to give himself over to the intense feelings Melody aroused in him. Nate got it. Falling in love was a big, scary deal. As he was discovering.

"You don't really believe that?"

"That picture of them together in New York. She looked so happy with him. It's been months and months since she's been like that with me..." Kyle's voice trailed off and silence reigned in the car for a while. "And now he's here and working at your studio," he finally added. "I'm sure she's spending tons of time with him. He's going to win her back," Kyle grumbled. "If he hasn't already."

"So that's it then?" Nate's tone was harsh. He wanted Kyle to man up and fight for the woman he loved. "You're giving up?"

"I didn't say that."

"It sure as hell sounds like it."

Kyle opened his mouth but no words came out. Nate would love it if the only problem between him and Mia was a stupid misunderstanding about a photo of her with an ex-boyfriend.

"You're both acting like a couple of idiots," Nate declared. "Things between you might have moved fast, but that's no reason to freak out. Stop being so dense. Tell her you love her and make her believe it."

For a long time Kyle didn't say anything. Then, as he turned the car onto Nate's street, he said, "Thanksgiving, huh? What time should I be there?"

"Dinner's at five, but you're welcome at any time. Trent and Dylan are coming early for the Vikings-Lions game. Savannah and Melody plan on coming midafternoon."

"Can I bring anything?"

Nate grinned. "Just your best behavior. Mia and I will provide the rest."

Twenty minutes later, after switching to his own car at home, Nate was pulling into the studio parking lot.

The receptionist greeted him with a wave when he went inside. He popped into a couple different control booths to see how things were going. He found Melody on the couch in studio C with Hunter at the boards.

When she spotted him, Melody jumped up and rushed across the room to throw her arms around his neck.

"Thanks for sending Kyle to pick me up."

"Sorry about the switch, but Hunter had a free hour to help me out. Hey, you got your voice back." Melody beamed at him. "But you shouldn't overdo it."

"I won't." Nate turned to Hunter. "How's it going with her album?"

"She's got a lot of great songs here. We'll just have to whittle it down." The look he gave Melody sent a wave of apprehension through Nate. "It might take a while."

Maybe Kyle had reason to be concerned, after all. Not because Melody was falling for her ex-boyfriend, but because Hunter had a very possessive look in his eye when he gazed at her. As if he might be planning to work damned hard to win her back.

"Not too long, I hope," Nate said. "I'd like to have it ready to go by the beginning of next year."

"I'll put all my energy into making that happen." Hunter shot Melody a fond look. "But now I've got to get going. Dinner later?"

"Ah, sure."

"I'll pick you up at six."

When Hunter left the control booth, Nate turned on Melody. "What the hell is going on between you two?"

"Nothing. We're just friends."

"And Kyle?"

Melody toyed with her phone. "Kyle and I need some space."

"That's the last thing you need. Have you forgotten that you two are going to be parents? When do you plan to tell him about the baby?" Nate saw the excuses gathering in her eyes and shook his head. "I've invited him for Thanksgiving. You'll be surrounded by family. We'll all be there to support you. Plan on telling him then."

"But that's only three days away."

"The sooner the better."

"So tell me what happened with Ivy at the AMAs last night. She looked out of it."

"Apparently she's been addicted to painkillers on and off for the last eight years and recently suffered a relapse. Mia stayed behind in LA while they figure out the best way to handle things."

"Trent is meeting with Javier today." Melody's features wore a worried expression. "Do you think he'll postpone her album?"

"The way things have been going, it might be a good idea to push it out until later next year. She needs to focus on getting clean again." Nate thought about his plunge down the rabbit hole of drug and alcohol abuse and didn't envy Ivy for what she had to look forward to. "I'm off to get some work done." He leaned over and kissed Melody on the forehead. "Give what I said about you and Kyle some thought before you head off to dinner with Hunter tonight, okay?"

Melody nodded and Nate left to make some music and figure out what he was going to do about Mia next.

Early Tuesday afternoon, Mia was in her bedroom at Ivy's LA house, sorting through recipes and planning the shopping list for her Thanksgiving dinner with Nate and his friends when the door burst open and Skylar plunged into the room with Riley on her heels.

Since she'd returned from dropping Nate at the airport the day before, Mia had either been holed up in her room to escape the thick tension filling the house, or popping in every couple hours to check on Ivy. So far, her sister hadn't shown much interest in anything besides binge watching *Pretty Little Liars* on Hulu.

"You bitch!" Skylar shrieked, her wild eyes fixed on Mia.

"What?" Mia stared at her dumbfounded, unsure what Skylar and Riley were doing in Ivy's house, much less Mia's room.

Ivy must have let them in. Why couldn't she understand that she was supposed to cut all ties with these two? They were the ones who'd been supplying her with the prescription drugs. Mia jumped off her bed as Skylar advanced toward her.

"You have some nerve," Ivy's friend said in a threatening tone.

Mia glanced from Skylar to Riley. "You need to leave. Now."

"We're not going anywhere," Riley piped up. "We know it was you."

Mia shook her head. "It's not just me. My father wants you to stay away from Ivy, too." But she could tell the two women weren't listening to her.

"Haven't you sponged off your sister long enough?"

These two were the most clueless women on the planet. "Sponged? Do you have any idea what I do for Ivy?"

"Well, you don't write her music. That's for sure."

Skylar's words made Mia go cold. Everyone who knew the truth behind Ivy's songwriting worked awfully hard to keep it hidden. Neither one of these two was trustworthy enough to be told such a damaging secret.

"Of course not," Mia said calmly, while her heart thundered.

"Then why did you tell the media that Ivy didn't write any of her songs?"

"I didn't." Mia was besieged by panic. Such a disclosure would devastate Ivy. "I wouldn't do that."

"Sure you would," Riley said.

Skylar nodded. "You resent her."

"I don't." But she could hear the lie in her voice.

She did resent Ivy, but not for the reasons these two thought. Mia didn't care that Ivy had been gifted with all the looks and talent. Up until the last few years, when Ivy had started behaving more and more like a diva, Mia had been happy to be her assistant and do whatever she could to bolster her twin's career.

"Sure you do." Riley exchanged a look with Skylar. "You have a thing for Nate."

"We all noticed."

"But he doesn't know you're alive. He wants Ivy. So you decided to discredit her by lying to the media and saying you're the one who writes her music."

It was on the tip of Mia's tongue to argue that she did write all Ivy's music, but too many years of living with that secret kept her silent now. "I need to talk to Ivy."

Mia started toward Ivy's bedroom, but Riley stepped in her way.

"She doesn't want to talk to you."

Irritation flooded Mia, loosening her tongue. "If you want to talk about people who sponge off my sister, look in the mirror." Imbued with strength she didn't know she possessed, Mia pushed past Riley and headed toward her sister's bedroom. She had to explain.

Ivy was standing by the open sliding glass door that led onto the pool deck, Mia's song journal in her hand.

Mia stopped halfway into the room as Ivy turned her tear-streaked face in her direction.

"I didn't tell anyone about the songwriting," Mia said, her voice clogged with emotion. "I swear."

"Not even Nate?"

"He figured it out all on his own." Mia advanced toward her sister, but Ivy went outside, maintaining ten feet between them.

"You're such a liar." Ivy held out the notebook. "I read this. It's all about him."

Mia's song journal was more than just a place for her to jot down music and lyrics. She also used it as a diary, and although she'd never used Nate's name, many of the entries had described incidents that made it pretty clear who she was talking about.

"I'll bet you couldn't wait to tell him," Ivy continued. "You probably thought he'd be into you if he thought you were a songwriter."

"I swear I didn't tell him." But in her heart, she knew she'd wanted him to figure it out. And maybe she'd helped that along. "It was just that I wrote songs with Melody on the tour and you never showed any signs that you wrote, too. He got suspicious."

"What other bad things have you been telling Nate about me?"

"I haven't said anything."

Ivy gave a bitter laugh. "I see the way you moon over him. He's never going to be interested in you."

"Why do you care how I feel about Nate?"

"I don't." But it was obvious that she was bothered. "I just hate to see you make a fool of yourself over someone who is so out of your league."

"Nate doesn't see himself that way." The instant the words were past her lips, Mia wished them back.

"He should."

Without warning, Ivy launched Mia's song journal through the air in the direction of the pool. Mia watched in horror as hundreds of hours' worth of angst and love hit the water with a splat and began to sink.

"My journal." An anguished cry broke from her as she rushed forward. She stood at the edge of the pool with her hands over her mouth, unable to believe her sister could have done something so cruel. "What the hell, Ivy?"

Her twin glared at her. "Now there's no proof who wrote those songs."

"You forget that I have years' worth of those journals. Every one of them proves you've been taking credit for my songs. Are you planning on destroying those, as well?"

"Yes."

"Why are you doing this? All we have to do is release a press statement that confirms you write your own songs."

"Why did you have to ruin everything?" Ivy demanded.

"I didn't do anything."

"It's all your fault. Every bit of it." Tears streamed down Ivy's cheeks. "I can't look at you anymore."

"Ivy, why don't you calm down and let's talk about this." Her sister's behavior was scaring Mia. She started to put her hands on Ivy's arms in an effort to connect with her, but her twin threw her off and backed up.

"There's no need to talk. I hate you. I want you out of this house and out of my life. I'm sick of having you telling me what to do and where to go."

"I only do that because I'm your assistant." Mia's frustration was continuing to build; she was at her breaking point. "It's my job to keep you on schedule."

"Well, I'm sick of it. I don't need you."

"What are you saying?"

"I'm saying I don't want you around anymore. Get the hell out of my house."

Ten

Tuesday night after a lonely dinner by himself, Nate sat in his living room with his guitar for company and came to terms with just how miserable he was being a bachelor. He was sick of coming home to an empty house and sleeping alone in his big bed. Sexy Skyping with Mia last night had been more frustrating than fun. He needed her here and now. Tomorrow couldn't come soon enough.

His phone buzzed. Hoping it was Mia calling, Nate reached for it. "Hey, Trent."

His business partner got right to the point without preliminaries. "Someone leaked that Ivy doesn't write her own songs."

"What?"

"Was it you?"

"No." Nate cursed, half wishing he had done it. But Mia would never have forgiven him. "When did this happen?"

"This afternoon. I just found out."

"This afternoon…" Why hadn't Mia called to tell him? She had to know. "Have you spoken to Javier?"

"Not yet. I thought, given your connection to Mia, that we should talk about how you'd like the label to handle things."

While Nate appreciated his friend's consideration, he had absolutely no idea what would be best for Mia. "I think West Coast Records should come out saying we have no knowledge of this."

"But is that true?" Trent sounded tense and weary. "I don't have any idea what sort of unscrupulous business practices the label was engaged in with my father or brother at the helm."

Where was Mia?

Was she corralled with her family as they strategized damage control? Ivy must be near hysterical. First there was the misstep at the AMAs on Sunday. And now this. But why hadn't Mia called or texted?

"What if you make a personal statement that you had no knowledge of the situation and that you will investigate and correct whatever mistakes were made."

"That feels a little bit like we're throwing Ivy under the bus." Trent's tone was neutral, giving Nate no idea which way he was leaning. "Bottom line—do you want Mia to get credit for the songs or not?"

"Let me talk to her. Can you give me a couple hours?"

"I'm not going to rush into anything. Tomorrow morning is soon enough."

Nate hung up with Trent and dialed Mia. He wasn't surprised when he got her voice mail. After leaving a message, he began to pace. Not more than five minutes later, his doorbell rang. Expecting to find Melody on his doorstep, he was shocked to see Mia.

"I was on my way here when I got your message."
She looked miserable as she stood outside his front door.

He reached for her hand and pulled her inside. "Are
you okay?"

"No." Mia pressed herself against his chest and mumbled her next words into his shirt. "She thinks I did it."

"You didn't, did you?"

Mia pushed away and glared up at him. "Absolutely
not."

Of course not. He wasn't even sure why he'd asked.
"But now that the truth is out there, Trent and I will back
you one hundred percent."

"She threw my journal in the pool. There was almost
six months' worth of ideas and melodies." Her small
frame shook. "And she fired me as her assistant."

Nate tightened his arms around her and buried his
face in her hair. It was probably best that she couldn't see
his face at the moment because the news that her sister
had fired her pleased him. He knew she wouldn't agree
that it was the best thing for her.

She pulled out of his arms and wiped at her eyes. "I
can't believe she did that."

He drew her from the foyer and into his living room.
Her expression was blank, her gaze turned inward as he
settled her on the couch. Once she was tucked against
his body with her head resting on his shoulder, he gave
a contented sigh. Her life might be falling apart, but in
the depths of her despair, she'd come to him.

"I don't know what happened," she murmured after a
long, long time. "One second I was working on a shopping list for Thanksgiving dinner, the next Skylar and
Riley are bursting into my room and accusing me of
being the one who told the media I wrote all Ivy's songs.
And when I told Ivy that I wouldn't have done that, she

didn't believe me." Mia's breath came in unsteady gasps as she relayed her tale. "She was half out of her mind, saying all sorts of crazy things that made no sense."

"She'll realize it wasn't you."

"I don't think she'll ever believe that. She threw me out. I don't know what that means. I've always lived with her."

This was sounding better and better by the second. "You can move in here," he said, keeping his voice as calm and gentle as possible. Mia was vulnerable. He didn't want to spook her. "Maybe this will all work out for the best," he began. "It'll be a fresh start."

"A fresh start?" She echoed the words as if she were tasting some strange and suspicious dish. "It's not over."

"I thought you said she threw you out and fired you."

"She didn't mean it."

"What if she did?" Nate intended to capitalize on this turn of good fortune. "You could come work for me. Live in Las Vegas." *Be with me.*

It was the same offer he'd made to her in Australia. The one she'd turned down without giving it a second's consideration.

"I could." Her shoulders slumped. She shook her head. "But this isn't how I wanted things to happen."

"What did you want?" Nate couldn't stop his expression from turning grim. "Her blessing? She was never going to give you that."

"I know, but this seems so abrupt. It's like she hates me. Knowing how important my song journal is to me, she ruined it. That's six months of work. Gone."

His eyebrows went up; he couldn't help it. "You forget you have the demos you made." What he'd heard was pretty fantastic. "And you'll write plenty more songs."

She made a face at him. "You make it sound so easy."

Taking him by surprise, she set her hand on his cheek and brought her lips to his in a sweet, poignant kiss. "Besides, those songs were special. They were about us. How I feel when I'm with you."

Nate's heart gave a mighty thump. For a second he lost the ability to breathe. "How do you feel?"

"Like I exist."

"You've always existed to me."

"I know."

When he'd left LA yesterday morning, he'd promised himself to keep his distance until she was ready to commit to being in a relationship with him. That vow went up in smoke as she eased closer and sifted her fingers through his hair.

He had no words to deny her and no willpower to push her away. Letting his eyes close, he absorbed her breath on his skin and the gentle sweep of her lips against his. She touched him tentatively, as if she expected rejection at any second. Even if he had the strength to push her away, he'd never be able to do it. She soothed the places inside him damaged by his father's abuse and the years he'd spent drowning in forgetfulness. Until she came along, he'd filled the gnawing emptiness first with reckless amusements, and then music.

That he couldn't hold on to her, couldn't convince her his need was greater than her sister's, had nudged him close to the dark places he'd once lost himself in. Good thing he was no longer a stupid twentysomething. He might have sought the oblivion of those earlier days in his career before he'd hit rock bottom and cleaned himself up.

"About what you said to me the other night," she said. "Nate, there's something you should know—" she began, but he shook his head, cutting her off.

"Don't talk."

If they started a conversation he wouldn't be able to take her in his arms and show her how much she meant to him. Standing up, he scooped her off the couch and headed for his bedroom.

"Are you sure?" she asked, when her feet touched the floor beside his bed.

"Very sure."

He lowered his lips to her soft neck and breathed in her clean fragrance. Her fingers coasted down the front of his shirt, unfastening buttons as they went. Anticipation coiled in his gut below where she laid her palms against his skin. He shuddered, eager to revisit the heat of her body sliding against his.

"Tonight it's just you and me." And the beginning of everything.

Mia stood in Nate's kitchen, surrounded by the leftovers from their Thanksgiving dinner, and smiled in blissful contentment. In the family room, Nate, Kyle and Trent sat on the couch in front of the big screen television watching football. It was the third game of the day and Mia wondered if men ever grew tired of watching a bunch of beefy guys pass, run and tackle.

"What can I do to help?" Melody slipped into the kitchen and gazed at the packed countertops.

"I've got this," Mia said with a wistful smile. "But if you'd hang out and keep me company, that would be great."

"But you did all the cooking," Savannah said as she passed with her infant son in her arms. She placed the boy in his father's care and returned. "You shouldn't have to clean up, as well."

"I'm happy to do it. Today was one of the best Thanksgivings I've ever had." She pulled out plastic storage containers and began making meals that she intended to send home with everyone.

She'd made enough food for twenty people and what they hadn't finished was way more than she and Nate could eat by themselves.

"I agree," Melody said. "Last year Nate and I were on the road. Kyle and Trent went to Miami." She paused and glanced at Savannah. "Did Rafe make you spend the holiday with Siggy?"

"Unfortunately." Savannah shuddered.

Mia remembered hearing how Melody and Trent's father was a terrible bully who treated Trent like the black sheep of the family for no good reason.

While the two women began sharing tales of Caldwell Thanksgivings past, Mia worked methodically to restore order to the kitchen. Listening to their stories of family dysfunction eased some of her angst. Although she'd called her parents and Ivy to wish them a happy Thanksgiving, not one had picked up.

It seemed impossible that after everything she'd done for Ivy her family could believe she was responsible for the leak. And with each hour that went by, it seemed as though Nate was right about her being permanently fired as Ivy's assistant.

No more demands for coffee or frivolous errands. No more being awakened at three in the morning when Ivy returned home from partying with her entourage, and having to fix waffles or quesadillas, depending on what her sister was in the mood for. Mia still wasn't accustomed to the peace and quiet that came from not being her sister's assistant any longer.

It was nice playing house with Nate. Her gaze traveled toward the couch and lingered on the three men. Was this what a normal Thanksgiving was like? A house filled with great friends, good food and football.

"Oh, I know that look," Savannah said with a wistful sigh.

Melody chuckled. "Do you recognize it every time you look in the mirror?"

"I recognize it from when you and Kyle first started dating." Savannah eyed her sister-in-law. "Don't you think it's time you two stopped playing games and started acting like you're in love once again?"

"Have you told him?" Mia kept her voice low.

Melody shook her head. "I was supposed to today, but there never seemed to be an opportunity."

"We all gave you plenty of chances," Savannah pointed out.

It had been easy to isolate the pair several times over the course of the day, but neither Melody nor Kyle seemed at ease with each other. Three times Mia had watched them engage in awkward conversation before separating. Each time her heart had ached for the pair.

With Savannah gently pressing Melody about her urgent need to talk to Kyle, Mia's own mouth went dry. She'd made a similar promise to herself about telling Nate that he was going to be a father. With all the drama surrounding Ivy, and the frantic meal preparations, it had slipped Mia's mind.

She sipped from her water bottle to alleviate her sudden cotton mouth. Anxiety made her stomach churn. As soon as she told Nate he was going to be a dad, her life would completely change.

Together they would have to decide how to move forward. Mia's hands shook. Despite his declaration that he wanted them to be together, there was a huge difference between building toward a committed relationship and becoming parents.

Well, there was nothing she could do until everyone was gone. Melody was staying at her brother's house while she worked on her album at Ugly Trout Records, and had ridden with them. When Kyle offered to give her a ride home, Mia and Nate exchanged a satisfied look.

It took an hour for Savannah to pry Trent away from the game. Dylan was sacked out in his father's arms and she declared it was time to head home and put him to bed. As the door closed on Savannah, Trent and Dylan, Nate turned to Mia.

"And then there were two," he said, his smile conveying both tenderness and desire.

Mia couldn't resist the invitation in his eyes. She lifted herself onto her toes, but just as her lips made contact with his, her phone buzzed in her back pocket and she instinctively flinched.

"Ignore it," Nate said, gathering her into his arms for a proper kiss that left her gasping for breath and aching for more.

She wrapped her arms around his neck and trembled as he slid his palms beneath her shirt and up along her rib cage to her breasts. Her nipples turned to hard buds as electric impulses sizzled and snapped along her nerve endings.

Her phone buzzed a second time. Nate dragged his mouth from hers and cursed.

"It might be my family," she said, hope tugging at her voice. "Let me check."

"Sure. I'll meet you in the bedroom."

She blew him a flirtatious kiss and went into the family room to shut off the television and close the sliding glass doors that led out to the pool. As she walked, she pulled her phone out and keyed her message app. To her disappointment, the text hadn't come from her family, but Yvonne, Ivy's stylist. The dire message had her clicking on the attached link. A second later, she gasped at what appeared.

For the last forty-eight hours Mia hadn't had time to pop on to social media to see what her sister had been up to. And it had been a relief to be completely disengaged from all the Ivy drama. Nor had she felt any guilt, mostly because of the way her twin had behaved since the truth had come out about Mia's songwriting.

Now, however, all it took was a single Instagram post and she was right back in the thick of the craziness. Mia stared at the picture on her screen. It was a photo of the contents of a very familiar tote. Hers. Including the positive pregnancy test. Also hers.

When had Ivy taken the picture? The answer came at once. The morning of the AMAs, after the television interview. Ivy had asked Mia to get her some coffee. She'd left her tote behind.

Mia's skin turned to ice. All this time her sister had known? Why hadn't Ivy said anything? Suddenly Mia couldn't breathe.

"Mia?" Nate's voice came from the direction of the master bedroom.

"I'll be there in a second."

Her attention returned to her phone. Suddenly, the screen lit up with her mother's number, but Mia doubted she was reaching out to wish Mia a happy Thanksgiving. She let the call go to voice mail and blocked all incoming calls. Then she went back to staring at the picture.

Before she spoke with anyone, she and Nate needed to have a conversation. Ivy's bid for attention on social media had highlighted that Mia's secret was out of the bag. Was it in retribution for her belief that Mia had spilled Ivy's own secret? If so, why not announce that Mia was pregnant?

Because this created a huge buzz. One that might distract everyone from the songwriting scandal and create confusion about the authenticity of all the latest Ivy Bliss stories.

"Mia?" Nate sounded closer.

She'd sat down at the breakfast bar when the room started spinning. Now she looked up and spied him standing a few feet away.

"Sorry," she murmured, struggling to focus, with her thoughts in turmoil. "Did you say something?"

"I asked if you're okay. You've gone awfully pale."

"I'm…"

It was time to tell Nate that she was pregnant. In truth, she'd already delayed too long. The words were on her lips. She just needed to get them out.

"I'm…"

About to be very, very sick.

When Mia rushed out of the room, Nate picked up the cell phone she'd left behind and looked at the photo on the screen. A positive pregnancy test lay nestled atop a wallet, a familiar shade of lipstick and a teal-colored journal, which was probably the one Ivy had ruined when she threw it into the pool. His brain was slow to process the tableau.

What was Mia doing with a pregnancy test in her purse? From down the hall came the sound of retching. Answers from that quarter weren't going to come as soon as he liked. Nate glanced at the text below the photo. It was not Ivy's feed, but that of her friend Skylar. Nowhere in the description was Mia's name mentioned. The photo was teased with Ivy's name and…his.

Now Nate understood Mia's abrupt flight from the room. Fury exploded inside him. Did she seriously in her wildest imagination think he'd ever touched Ivy? That he would do something so cruel to her? Was this why she'd been acting so strange lately? How long had she thought this of him? Obviously, she'd known her sister was pregnant since before they'd gone to the AMAs. Why hadn't she asked him about it? That she had so little faith in him cut Nate to the core.

And what of Ivy? Nate doubted this little stunt had been accomplished without her approval. She'd never tolerate such betrayal from her posse. He couldn't imagine what this would mean for Mia. Would she see herself even more firmly bound to her sister? Or could this be an opportunity for her to break free of her family?

Before he could ask that question, he needed to sort out what was going on in Mia's head. Nate headed down the hall and found Mia on the floor in his master bathroom. She sat with her back to the soaker tub, knees drawn up to her chest, arms wrapped around her legs. Although she'd doubtless heard his approach, she didn't look up from the floor when he stopped in the doorway.

"Are you okay?"

"No." Despite her stricken expression, the word came out with a sarcastic twist. She pushed to her feet and crossed to the sink. After splashing water on her face, she reached for her toothbrush.

"You know I never slept with Ivy." He paused, waiting for her reaction, and when none came, he continued, "I never touched her, never even looked at her in that way."

Mia closed her eyes and didn't respond. Did she not believe him? Was that really possible, given everything they'd been to each other? Nate joined her at the sink and met her gaze in the mirror. Her only acknowledgment was a slight frown before she bent down to rinse the toothpaste from her mouth.

"Why don't you believe me?"

"I do." A tear trickled down her cheek. Air hissed between her teeth as she dashed it away. "But the fact is, it is your baby."

Nate couldn't believe what she was saying to him. "That's both ridiculous and impossible."

Mia turned to look at him at last. "The piece of the puzzle that you're missing," she said, her voice breaking on the words, "is that the pregnancy test doesn't belong to Ivy."

"If it doesn't belong to her, then…" The impact of understanding was like trying to walk through a closed glass door. He bounced off the invisible surface, his whole body rattled by the impact. "You're pregnant?"

"Yes." She nodded as if for emphasis.

Shock reverberated through him like thunder. "How long?"

"Sydney."

"I meant how long have you known?" A voice in the back of his mind told him this was the best thing that ever happened to him. But it was a quiet reminder, easily drowned out by the anger that licked through him because she'd kept this a secret. "It had to be before Ivy threw your journal in the pool. I saw it beneath the pregnancy test."

"The morning of the AMAs."

"Why didn't you say something?"

Her eyes widened. "It was a huge event for you. I didn't want to ruin…"

When she bit her lip and didn't finish, he jumped in.

"Why would you think finding out I was going to be a father would ruin anything?"

She frowned at his aggressive tone. "I didn't plan this. I didn't want you to think I was trying to trap you."

"Trust me, that's the last thing I'd ever think." He gave a bitter laugh. "In fact I'd be overjoyed if that had truly been your motive. At least then I could count on you and me being together."

She didn't immediately respond to his accusation, but a hot burst of color flared across her cheekbones. "That's unfair."

"Is it? You still haven't explained why you didn't tell me as soon as you realized you were pregnant."

"I was scared, okay?"

"Of what? Me?"

"Of everything changing."

"What's so horrible about that?"

"You just don't understand."

But he did. She'd rather remain in her sister's shadow, where she thought it was safe, instead of taking a chance with him.

"When are you going to stop hiding behind Ivy?"

"Hiding? That's not it. You know how she is. What she's struggling with. Every time I'm not there for her something terrible happens."

And there was the core of their problem.

"You can't be your sister's keeper forever." Nate lowered his voice as he fought for calm. "She's never going to take responsibility for herself if you and the rest of your family don't stop enabling her."

"I can't have this conversation again." Mia's lower lip quivered. She caught it between her teeth and pushed away from the sink.

Nate was on her heels as she reentered the master

bedroom and made a beeline for the door. He caught her arm and spun her around to face him. "Where are you going?"

"I need some time to think."

"You've had months and months to think. What you need to do is make a decision about us."

She crossed her arms over her chest. "You don't think I know that?"

He stroked his palms up her arms to her shoulders, but made no move to draw her close. "We are having a baby." He emphasized each and every word, hoping to penetrate the wall of stubbornness she erected around herself. "I intend to be in my child's life. And not in a long-distance sort of way." He didn't mean to sound so angry. He loved her. He wanted to be with her. To marry her and raise their child together. Instead he'd declared a challenge, bordering on a threat. "I've asked you to stay in Las Vegas with me. You haven't said yes. So, what's it going to be, Mia?"

"I want to." Her eyes pleaded with him through the tears. "You want me to choose between you and Ivy. I can't do that."

"Are you going to choose between our baby and Ivy?"

He might as well have hit her. She reeled backward two steps and stared at him in dismay. "That's not fair. Our baby comes first."

Our baby. He liked the sound of that. But what about him? Was she going to choose him?

"Look, I'm sorry." It was inadequate, but he made the apology sincere and heartfelt. "Let's sit down and start again, only calmer this time."

Her hands shook as she dragged them through her hair. "Okay."

She let him guide her toward the bed. They settled

onto the mattress with their backs against the headboard and said nothing for a long time.

"I'm sorry." She set her head against his shoulder and reached for his hand.

"For what?"

"This is not at all how I wanted you to find out that you were going to be father."

"It's not how I expected it to happen, either." He gave a soft chuckle. "Actually, I'm not sure I have any idea what I expected."

"Are you really okay with this?"

"So okay." He threaded their fingers together and gave a gentle squeeze. "It's pretty amazing, in fact. Every time my dad came after me when I was a kid I thought about what being a father entailed. Not everyone is cut out for it, but I knew I'd work twice as hard at it to make up for the hell my dad put me through."

"You're going to make an amazing father. We'll figure out everything. I just need some time to talk to my family. It's pretty obvious from the way Ivy is acting out that dealing with her is not going to be easy."

"You don't have to do it alone. Let me be there for you when you go talk to them." He knew better than to suggest he go with her to confront Ivy. Mia knew how to handle her sister better than anyone.

But to announce a false pregnancy on social media and name him as the baby's father was beyond disturbing. Nate swallowed an I-told-you-so. As much as he wanted to reiterate his opinion on how the entire family's pandering had created the monster that was Ivy Bliss, Mia needed his support, not his criticism.

"Don't be mad," she began, trying for a smile and not succeeding. "I really think I need to go explain things to my dad on my own. Having you there will just complicate the whole situation."

Nate shrugged off his disappointment. He'd like to be at her side, presenting a united front to her father. For support and because he worried that she'd cave to her family once again. "I'll let you handle your family, but I'm telling you right now that I'm calling my publicist and having her deny that your sister and I have had or are having any sort of relationship."

The last thing he intended to do was get into a social media pissing match with Ivy. At least she'd had the sense not to post a picture or the caption herself. She would have plausible deniability.

Suddenly, he was sick to death of talking about Mia's sister. "For the next twelve hours we are not going to talk about a certain pop star. Can you do that?"

"I don't know. I'm not sure I've ever gone that long without talking about her." A cheeky grin spread across Mia's face. "Actually, now that I think about it, there were a couple nights I'll never forget with a handsome guy."

Damn if his pulse didn't kick up a notch. She had the most amazing effect on him. It was what he kept coming back over and over despite how much her obligation to her sister irritated him. But they would worry about her sister later. Right now, it was all about Mia. He eased her back against the headboard and slid his fingers into her hair. She sighed in delight and tilted her face to receive his descending mouth.

Eleven

The next morning, Mia packed a bag and let Nate drive her to the airport to catch a ten o'clock flight to LA, where Ivy and their father were meeting with Trent about the album and their interest in having Hunter Graves produce it instead of Nate.

To her surprise, she hadn't received a single call or text from her family. No doubt they were all in crisis mode over the Instagram post. Mia wondered how her sister was coping with the fallout. Nate had done as he'd promised and released a statement through his publicist. And then he'd watched her fidget as the night stretched on with none of her family reaching out to her.

Was she crazy to resent being shut out after everything she'd sacrificed for her sister and her career? And then she realized how foolish that sounded. None of her family were avoiding her; more likely they just hadn't bothered to bring her into the loop. Resentment flared.

As he pulled to a stop at the terminal, Nate put his

hand on hers and gave a reassuring squeeze. "Are you sure you don't want to just forget about coming clean with your family, and stay with me?"

With each minute that passed she felt less confident about going alone to LA, but she'd put off telling her family about Nate and her pregnancy long enough.

"I appreciate your offer, but I think it will go better if I talk to them in person." She exited the car and waited while Nate pulled her suitcase out of the trunk. "I'll call you later."

But as Mia headed to the counter to check in and drop off her luggage, she was overwhelmed by a mixed bag of emotions. Annoyance. Dread. Her relationship with Nate had been a secret she'd kept to herself for almost four months. Loving him had given her greater joy than anything she'd ever known, and yet she'd hidden her happiness for fear of it being taken away if the truth came out.

It was something she hadn't explained to Nate. He'd assumed that she was afraid of moving forward because her identity was trapped in her sister's shadow. After she'd told him about Ivy's near death experience thanks to the painkillers, he'd been more understanding about the burden of responsibility she felt toward her twin. But he resented that she couldn't leave her sister to make mistakes and face consequences.

Well, Ivy was on her own right now and look what had happened. Hunter Graves was probably going to produce her next album, and while the man was nearly as talented as Nate, Hunter's vision for her music was in line with Ivy's own. They weren't going to record a breakout album. If Ivy had only listened to her...

Mia cut off the thought. Nate was right. She was too caught up in her sister's career and life. Even now, with things so strained between them, even though Ivy had fired her, Mia remained emotionally invested in what her sister was doing.

When it was Mia's turn to step up to the counter, instead of presenting her ticket to LA, she checked to see if there was a flight to Chicago. Suddenly, more than anything, Mia craved some advice from her older sister, Eva. She didn't pause to wonder whether Eva would be happy to see her. Many times in the last five years Eva had also questioned her dedication to Ivy, and as much as they loved each other, Mia's stubborn refusal to leave her twin had led to some tense discussions between Eva and her. Despite this, Mia knew Eva would welcome her with open arms.

After successfully switching her ticket and getting through security, Mia raced to catch her flight and emailed her sister about the surprise visit, mentioning the post on Instagram and offering a brief explanation about the trouble she and Ivy were having. Normally Mia didn't involve Eva in her Ivy issues because she knew how Eva would respond, but Mia wanted her sister's expert opinion.

She had to shut her phone down before Eva replied. Most likely she was in the middle of a session with one of her patients. As a deaf psychiatrist, Eva had a unique niche: almost two thirds of her patients were hearing impaired.

Once she landed in Chicago, Mia exited the airplane and headed for O'Hare's baggage claim. The plan after she collected her luggage was to take the blue line downtown and then the purple line north to her sister's condo in Evanston. The trip would take around an hour and a half. But as Mia entered the baggage claim area she saw a familiar face and sped toward her older sister.

She was so overwhelmed by surprise and relief, she forgot to sign as she blurted, "What are you doing here?" It was the last sentence she uttered before sobs overtook her. Eva's unexpected appearance and the relief of not having to wait two more hours to hug her pulled the cork from the bottle containing Mia's turbulent emotions.

Eva didn't ask questions; she merely wrapped her arms around Mia and let her release all the pent-up sadness that had been building for the last few months. When Mia got herself back under control she realized Eva had coaxed her out of the flow of people and toward the wall. With the initial rush of her tears slowing to a trickle, Mia gave her sister a watery smile.

"What are you doing here?" Mia repeated the question out loud as she wiped her eyes. Eva could read lips and also speak. The sisters usually communicated in a combination of both. "I was going to take the train to your office."

"I canceled my last two appointments," Eva signed. *"You didn't seriously think I was going to let you take the train."*

It seemed impossible that Mia had more tears to shed, but as she and Eva walked arm-in-arm to the baggage claim, Mia's cheeks remained wet. Her initial outburst had lasted long enough for the luggage to make its way from the belly of the airplane to the terminal. Mia collected her suitcase and followed her sister to short-term parking, where she'd left her car.

Because it was impossible for them to have a conversation while Eva drove, they sat in the parking lot long enough for Eva to ask several questions.

"Have you spoken to Ivy and asked her what she was thinking?"

"No. I was afraid what I might say."

"Have you talked to Mom and Dad?"

Again Mia shook her head. "I'm also afraid of what they'll say."

"Do you want to tell me what happened now or wait until we get to my condo?"

"I'll wait."

While Eva drove, she shared with Mia bits of what had been going on in her job. Although Eva preferred to sign, she'd also learned how to speak. She'd had to in order to communicate with their father and sister, neither of whom had learned more than the most basic of signs. Mia knew this hurt Eva, but she was a pragmatist. Which was why she'd left California to pursue psychiatry. Her life in Chicago was the sort of normal Mia craved.

"Are you hungry?" Eva signed as they waited at the bottom of the freeway ramp for the light to turn green. *"We can go to a restaurant and you can tell me what's going on. Or we can go home."*

Mia grew confused by something in her sister's manner. An evasiveness so unlike Eva that Mia grew immediately suspicious. She had to wait until the next stoplight to ask her question.

"What's going on at home?"

"I thought you might be more comfortable talking without anyone around."

"At a restaurant?" Mia eyed her sister intently. "What's at home that you don't want to bring me there?" Not for one second did Mia think it was anyone from their family, and she knew Nate wasn't aware she'd taken a detour. "Jeremy? Did I interrupt your evening? I'm so sorry."

"Nonsense. I haven't seen you in six months." She shot Mia a wry grin. *"Him I see all the time."*

Eva had been dating Jeremy for the last year. He was a

pediatric doctor at Evanston Hospital. They'd met when she'd done her residency there and had been friends for several years before deciding to give dating a try.

Joy flooded Mia. If anyone deserved to be happy it was Eva. "It's gotten serious then?"

The joy shining in Eva's eyes was answer enough. *"We're living together."*

"Wow."

A spike of envy drove through Mia's heart. She didn't resent her sister's happiness, but it shone a light on her own failure to grab the brass ring. Mia's eyes went to Eva's bare left hand as her sister rubbed her ring finger in an unconscious gesture.

"Are you engaged?"

Eva nodded but looked pained. Mia flinched as the subtext hit her in the chest.

"How long?"

"Six weeks. We wouldn't be living together otherwise."

Eva had been engaged for six weeks and had kept it secret from her family. Or perhaps *secret* wasn't the best word. Their parents, Ivy, even Mia, were so focused on Ivy's career that there wasn't room for anything else.

"Where is your ring?"

"My purse."

Mia opened her sister's purse and dug the diamond ring from a zippered interior pocket. She drew it out and handed it to her sister, who slipped it on. "I'm sorry I didn't know."

The stoplight turned green and Eva started the car forward.

"My fault. I should have told you."

But it wasn't Eva's fault. With their lack of interest and support, her family had failed her. It was almost as if once Eva went off to college and then moved to Chicago to do her psychiatric residency she'd been forgotten. Maybe that wasn't completely fair. Mia and their mom flew out to spend long weekends with her a couple times a year. And Eva tried to get back to the West Coast at least once a year, either around the holidays or when Ivy took a break from promoting, recording or touring.

But there was no avoiding the fact that the Navarro family revolved around Ivy and her career.

"Why did you keep it from me?" Even as she asked the question, Mia knew the answer. "Because of what happened to me? Did you think I wouldn't be happy for you because I've royally screwed up with Nate?"

Eva shook her head and Mia saw how her sister's situation was similar to her own. They'd both kept the men they loved from their family in order to savor the joy for as long as possible. It wasn't as if anyone would actively disapprove, but their family had a knack for spoiling things without trying.

"I want to tell him congratulations. Let's go to your condo."

But it turned out that Eva was wrong about her fiancé being at home. He'd left a sweet note explaining that he'd gone out for drinks with his buddies and would catch dinner and be back late. That left hours and hours for the sisters to talk and for Mia to unburden herself.

She started by explaining about how she and Nate had discovered their mutual connection through sign language and then described their secret rendezvous and their one night together in Sydney.

"Very romantic," Eva signed with a hearty sigh.

"And stupid. Looking back, I regret hiding what was happening."

"But you knew Ivy would spoil things."

Mia had known that. *"Why is she like that?"*

"Insecurity. She thinks everyone is happier than she is."

"With all her beauty, fame and success, how is that possible?"

Mia hadn't yet come clean with Eva about being pregnant, and before she could, Jeremy returned home. Mia rushed to congratulate him on convincing the best girl in the world to marry him. By the time they'd finished discussing wedding plans it was late. Both Eva and Jeremy had to be at work early the next morning. They said their good-nights and Mia went to the guest bedroom.

Despite her lack of sleep the night before, Mia was still on Pacific time. Once she'd changed into her sleepwear, she sat wide-eyed and cross-legged on the bed in the beautifully decorated guest room.

She picked up her phone and puzzled over the lack of messages and emails. And then she realized she'd not taken her phone off airplane mode. She swiftly restored her cell service and watched the red notification indicators explode.

Even before his car cleared the airport, Nate started kicking himself for not accompanying Mia to LA. He never should've let her talk him into staying behind. They were in this together and together was how they should have tackled her father and sister.

If he wasn't so damn busy with the studio he would circle around right this second, drop his car in short-term parking and chase after her. But he had a business to run and artists he couldn't let down. Maybe he could reschedule his day tomorrow and fly to LA tonight. Nate headed for the studio to see what could be done before he let Mia know his plans.

Two hours later he'd spoken with all the artists who were coming in to work with him the next day. Each of them was fine with a short postponement. It meant Nate was going to be working extra-long hours in the days to come, but standing beside Mia as she told her father that she was pregnant was worth it.

Nate called Mia to tell her his plans, but got her voice mail. He'd expected as much. She was probably midflight on her way to LA. She would get the message when she landed and know to put off meeting with her father until later that night.

Pleased with the arrangements he'd made, Nate headed into the studio. He got a text from his publicist letting him know his statement had gone out to news organizations denying that he was the father of Ivy's baby. An hour later his phone lit up with Javier Navarro's number. Nate was in the middle of a recording session and let the call go to voice mail. He knew it would only annoy Mia's father, but Nate wanted to pick the time and place for his conversation with Javier.

Forty-five minutes later he turned the session over to one of his assistants and headed to his office. Nate dialed Javier and braced himself for what was to come. Ivy's dad could be hotheaded when it came to his daughter.

"How dare you call my daughter a liar," was the first thing out of Javier's mouth.

Nate sighed and pinched the bridge of his nose. "I think you need to have a conversation with your daughter," he said. "I am not the father of Ivy's baby."

"She says you are."

"That's impossible, since she and I don't have that sort of relationship." Nate wanted very badly to tell Javier exactly what he thought of his spoiled, childish daughter, but he owed it to Mia to try to keep from exacerbating an already tricky situation.

"That's not how she sees it."

Nate was over trying to keep his cool and remain polite, but recognized if he blew up Mia would catch the brunt of the trouble. "Look." He paused to suck in a calming breath and even out his tone. "Ivy and I never... I don't know why she picked me, but I'm not the guy."

"What reason would my daughter have to lie about something like that?"

"I really couldn't say." He was really trying not to go there with Javier. Nate leaned back in his chair and stared at the ceiling. "I think your daughter is incredibly talented and has the potential to be a huge star. Our relationship is and always has been professional."

"Not all that professional. You've done nothing but badger Ivy the entire time she was recording at your studio."

"That's not what happened." But Nate knew he was wasting his breath. Still, he persisted. "Ivy and I had creative differences, that's all."

"Well, Ivy wants Hunter Graves to step in as the producer."

"Trent and I have already spoken about this and I understand." Nate didn't add that he'd thrown Hunter at Ivy hoping for this exact result. "I'm sure they'll work well together."

"She has a lot riding on this album," Javier said. "I hope the label is ready to get behind her."

"Of course. Ivy is very important to West Coast Records. The intention is to get behind her one hundred percent."

This last seemed to mollify Ivy's father and the conversation ended more cordially than it had begun.

After Nate hung up with Mia's father, he raked his fingers through his hair and spent several minutes calming down. He couldn't call Mia, given his mood. When he felt sufficiently chilled, he dialed her number. Once again it went to voice mail. He left her a quick message, summarizing his conversation with her father. And then he returned to the recording studio to wait for her to call him back.

That call didn't come until a little after nine. He'd just let himself into his hotel room in LA and was about to leave Mia another text when she called.

"Hi."

"Hey." Air gusted from his lungs. He was so relieved to hear her voice. "Did you get my messages?"

"Ah…" She drew the word out. "Not until just now. I'm sorry."

Nate reined in his concern. She sounded mortified, but her voice lacked the tense edge from that morning. He realized that whatever she'd been up to, she'd discovered some peace.

"I cleared my schedule and came to LA. Where are you?"

"Ah…" Again that strange little pause. "I'm not in LA. Last minute, I decided to visit Eva in Chicago."

"That's not what we discussed this morning."

"I know, but I just needed a little more time to think things through and Eva has always been the voice of sanity in our family."

Nate was torn between frustration, relief and concern. Frustration, because he wanted Mia's priorities to shift from her family to him. What would it have taken for her to text him before her flight and let him know where she was bound? But he wasn't going to react as her family would, pushing her around, telling her what she should and shouldn't do.

He was relieved because when he hadn't heard from her since dropping her at the airport, he'd begun thinking all sorts of terrible things. Didn't she realize she meant the world to him, even before he found out she was carrying his child? Why was it she refused to believe anyone would want to put her first? Surely it couldn't all be laid at Ivy's feet.

And lastly he felt concern because if she'd fled to Chicago instead of confronting her problems and going to LA, then she was a lot more out of sorts than she'd let on.

"What did Eva tell you?" Nate made his voice as calm as possible.

"Nothing that I didn't already know. That Ivy is insecure and has a knack for spoiling other people's happiness."

"So what are you going to do about that?"

"Be happy in spite of her?"

"You don't sound very convinced."

"What is wrong with me?" Mia blurted out.

He wished he was there to offer her support, but as he'd often remarked about Ivy needing to become more responsible, Mia also needed to not only claim her independence, but also accept that she deserved to be happy.

"There's nothing wrong with you. It isn't your fault that your parents put too great a burden on you at such a young age. They pushed Ivy to be a star and made you her keeper." Nate paused and listened, wishing he could see Mia face. "There's nothing wrong with you," he repeated, more quietly this time. "Tomorrow you'll fly back to LA, and then you and I will go talk to your parents together."

"Okay." It was a squeaky whisper, as if something was blocking her voice.

"I have your back."

"Thank you." She sounded clearer and more confident.

"You don't have to thank me. It's time someone took care of you. And from now on that someone is me."

Her laughter was the most wonderful thing he'd heard all day. He wished he was there to see happiness brighten her eyes and soften the curve of her lips.

"You know I love you, right?"

She tossed out the phrase with such an ease that he wasn't sure if she meant it as a heartfelt pledge or if they were just words that conveyed her fondness. She still hadn't committed to moving to Las Vegas to be with him. And instead of going to LA to confront her family, she'd run off to Chicago.

"I do now," he teased back, but his heart was a brick in his chest. "Get some sleep. I'll see you tomorrow."

Nate's presence was a solid comfort at her side as Mia pushed the doorbell of Ivy's house the next afternoon. It felt weird to not just let herself in. She'd lived here with Ivy for nearly two years, coming and going at will. But it had never been her home, and since Ivy had tossed her out four days earlier, it didn't feel right to just walk in.

Clara answered the door. The housekeeper gave Mia a tentative smile as she stepped back to let them in, but sadness overcame her features as Mia's eyes fell on the stack of boxes in the foyer.

"I'm so sorry. She made me pack up all your things."

Mia gave the woman a hug. "It's okay." The pile was small enough to fit into their rental SUV: just her clothes, her journals and a few mementos. It was a sad reflection on Mia's personal life to this point.

"How is Ivy doing?"

With a furtive glance over her shoulder, Clara shook her head. "She's…"

"Mia?" Javier Navarro stood at the far end of the foyer, radiating impatience and disapproval. "We're waiting for you in the living room."

Nate squeezed her shoulder and Mia gave Clara a reassuring smile. As the housekeeper stepped aside, Mia lifted her chin. Then, fortified by Nate's support, she headed toward her father. Javier's eyes flickered from her to Nate.

"I don't think it's a good idea that he's here."

"We have something to tell you." Mia's stomach was a knot of anxiety as she and Nate entered the living room. Only her mother occupied the space. "Where's Ivy?"

"She doesn't want to see you," her mother said.

Mia frowned. "I imagine she doesn't want to face up to what she's done."

"And what is that, exactly?" Javier asked, stepping to his wife's side.

"Lied about being pregnant for one." Mia wasn't surprised at her parents' relief. A baby wouldn't be good for Ivy's career. "It was my test she splashed all over social media." Mia glanced up at Nate. "We're going to have a baby."

Mia's mother gasped. "Why would she do that?"

Her spirits plummeted at her mother's words. She'd just announced the most amazing thing that had ever happened to her, but all her parents could think about was Ivy. Her throat tightened.

"It's a cry for help."

"Then you should be here to help her," Javier said.

Beside her, Mia felt Nate tense as the familiar scene played out. "She doesn't want me around anymore," Mia explained.

"I take it back." A soft voice spoke up from the glass doors leading out to the pool. Ivy stood just outside. Wearing workout clothes and no makeup, she looked fragile, unsure and younger than her twenty-five years. "I don't want you to leave me."

Mia glanced over her shoulder at Nate and saw his dismay. He was her future. She couldn't imagine her life any other way. But Ivy was her twin and she couldn't go with Nate until she'd made peace with her.

"Let me go talk to her," Mia said, her gaze lingering on his as she silently pleaded with him to understand.

A muscle worked in his jaw, and then he nodded to the boxes beside the front door. "I'll take those out to the SUV."

Before he could go, Mia stepped into his space and wrapped her arms around his waist. "I love you," she said, her cheek pressed against his chest.

His arms bound her to him until she could barely breathe. "I love you, too."

The words made her smile. She pulled back and looked up at him. "And I'm choosing you."

The relief on his face made her heart stop. He set his forehead against hers. "Thank you." With a quick, hard kiss he let her go. "I'll wait for you outside."

Ignoring her parents, Mia ran across the room and put her arms around Ivy. At first her sister resisted, then her body went limp and she hugged back.

"Don't leave me," Ivy murmured again, her voice muffled against Mia's shoulder.

"You know I have to go. I love Nate. I can't live without him."

"I can't do any of this without you."

"You can and you will. Stop letting Dad pressure you into doing things. Fire him if you have to. Ditch Skylar and Riley. Get clean. Forget about the stupid album. Start a fashion line. Do what you want. I'll support you."

"I'm so sorry about how I treated you."

"I know." As she hugged Ivy she felt as if she got her sister back.

"I'm glad you and Nate are together."

"That means a lot to me."

"We never hooked up, you know."

"I do."

"He's only ever had eyes for you. I saw that while we were on tour and I was so afraid he would take you away from me. But in the end I knew that you needed to go." Ivy gave her a sad smile. "That's why I leaked that you wrote all my songs. I needed a reason to fire you."

Mia was stunned. "You did that?" Her throat closed up. "For me?"

"I knew you wouldn't stop worrying about me."

"But you just asked me to stay."

"I didn't realize how lonely it would be not having you around." Ivy dashed tears from her cheeks. "Now, get out of here before I stop being nice and go all Ivy Bliss on your ass."

Mia laughed. "I love you."

"And I love you."

With one final hug, Mia left her sister and retraced her steps through the living room. She gave her parents a brief nod and burst through Ivy's front door, feeling free for the first time in eight years.

Nate waited for her by the SUV, his tall figure relaxed as she sped across the distance between them. His broad smile became her whole world as she flung herself into his arms and kissed him.

"Let's get out of here." Taking her by the hand, he led her to the car, opened the passenger door and ushered her inside. Seconds later he was sliding behind the wheel and starting the engine.

"Where are we going?"

"To the shipping store for these boxes, and then the airport. I intend to get you settled in Las Vegas before you change your mind."

"I'm not going to do that," she assured him.

An hour later they were walking hand in hand toward the security checkpoint at LAX when Nate pulled her out of the traffic flow. She gazed up at him in surprise as he gave her a sheepish grin.

"This isn't at all how I'd planned to do this, but it occurs to me they're going to make me empty my pockets." He pulled out a small box and popped the lid. Nestled in the black velvet was a diamond ring. "Mia Navarro, love of my life, will you marry me?"

Stunned to silence, she stared at the gorgeous ring and then lifted her gaze to his.

When she didn't speak, his brows drew together. "I'm not asking because you're pregnant. I'm not that guy."

"You are exactly that guy." She gave a self-conscious laugh. "Which is why I love you."

The look on his face set her heart to pounding. "Say that again," he demanded.

"Say what?"

"That you love me."

"I love you."

"And," he prompted.

"And I absolutely will marry you."

He took her hand in his and slid the ring onto her finger. "You are my world."

Mia put her palm against his cheek and leaned close. "You are mine. Forever and always."

And after a tender kiss that sealed their vows, they headed for the plane that would take them home.

* * * * *

*If you liked this story of romance in Vegas
pick up these other* LAS VEGAS NIGHTS *novels
from Cat Schield*

*THE BLACK SHEEP'S SECRET CHILD
AT ODDS WITH THE HEIRESS
A MERGER BY MARRIAGE
A TASTE OF TEMPTATION*

*And don't miss these other great reads
by Cat Schield*

*THE NANNY TRAP
ROYAL HEIRS REQUIRED*

Available now from Mills & Boon Desire!

* * *

*If you're on Twitter, tell us what you think
of Mills & Boon Desire! #MillsandBoonDesire*

Everyone went into the room but Nate. He hung back.

Kinley shook her head.

"What are you doing here?" "I'm the big brother of the groom. He asked me to come, so I did," Nate said. "This is why I wanted us to chat earlier. Just to clear the air. Like I said, I was a jerk, and I'm sorry. I don't want anything to mess up Hunter's wedding."

Oh.

When he said it like that, he sounded so reasonable. And she realized that coming to Cole's Hill had more consequences than she'd thought. She was losing her professional edge because of Nate. Part of it was the way he made her pulse speed up. A bigger part was the fact that he was her daughter's father and she hadn't told him. And the cost of keeping that secret seemed higher than she might be able to pay.

"Sorry. I'm just a little short-tempered today. Must be the jet lag."

"Don't be. It happens to the best of us. After the tasting, can we get a drink and talk? It's obvious we're going to need to."

* * *

Tycoon Cowboy's Baby Surprise
is part of The Wild Caruthers
Bachelors duet: These Lone Star
heartbreakers' single days are numbered…

TYCOON COWBOY'S BABY SURPRISE

BY
KATHERINE GARBERA

First Published in Great Britain 2017
By Mills & Boon, an imprint of HarperCollins*Publishers*
1 London Bridge Street, London, SE1 9GF

© 2017 Katherine Garbera

ISBN: 978-0-263-92820-4

51-0517

Our policy is to use papers that are natural, renewable and recyclable
products and made from wood grown in sustainable forests. The logging and
manufacturing processes conform to the legal environmental regulations of
the country of origin.

Printed and bound in Spain
by CPI, Barcelona

USA TODAY bestselling author **Katherine Garbera** is a two-time Maggie Award winner who has written more than seventy books. A Florida native who grew up to travel the globe, Katherine now makes her home in the Midlands of the UK with her husband and a very spoiled miniature dachshund. Visit Katherine on the web at www.katherinegarbera.com, or catch up with her on Facebook and Twitter.

To Courtney and Lucas,
who showed me that being a mom is
about the best damned job any woman can
have and for making my life so much richer.

As always special thanks to Charles
for being a wonderful editor and for getting me.
Also thanks to Nancy Robards Thompson,
who originally brainstormed a
version of this story with me.

One

"Pack your bags, kid, we're taking the show on the road," Jacs Veerling said as she swept into Kinley Quinten's office. The term was a stretch for the large workroom she shared with Willa Miller, the other wedding planner who worked for Jacs.

Jacs had the smarts of Madeleine Albright, the figure of Sofia Vergara and the business savvy of Estée Lauder. She was fifty but looked forty and had made her career out of planning bespoke weddings that were talked about in the media for years, even after the couples had split up. She wore her short hair in a bob, and the color changed from season to season. As it was summer, Jacs had just changed her color to a platinum blond that made her artic-blue eyes pop.

"Who's going on the road? Both of us? All three of

us?" Kinley asked. Based in the Chimera Hotel and Casino in Las Vegas, they did in-house weddings, but the bulk of their business came from destination weddings all over the world. Wherever their A-list clients wanted.

"Just you, Kin," Jacs said. "I've inked a deal to plan the wedding of reformed NFL bad boy Hunter Caruthers. It's taking place in your home state of Texas, and when I mentioned your name, he said he knew you. Slam dunk for us. I think that might be why he picked our company over one in Beverly Hills."

Caruthers.

At least it was Hunter and not his brother Nate.

"I can't."

Willa abruptly ended her call with a client, saying she'd call back, and turned to Jacs, who gave Kinley one of her patented she-who-must-be-obeyed stares.

"What? I'm sure I heard that wrong."

Kinley took a deep breath and put her hands on her desk, noticing that her manicure had chipped on her middle finger. But really she couldn't help the panic rising inside her. She had no plans to return to Texas.

Ever.

"I can't. It's complicated and personal, so I really don't want to go into it, but please send Willa instead."

Jacs walked over and propped her hip on the edge of Kinley's desk, which was littered with bridal gown catalogs and photos of floral arrangements. "He asked for you. Personally. That's the only *personal* that matters to me. Will you die if you go to Texas?"

"No. Of course not." Kinley just didn't want to see

Nate again. She didn't even want to see her dad again in person. She was content with their weekly Skype chats. That was enough for her and for her two-year-old daughter, Penny.

"Is it because of your baby?" Jacs asked.

She'd told Kinley when she started that even though Jacs had made the decision to never have children herself, she understood that being a mom was an important role. She was very understanding about Kinley's needs and had a generous child-care policy for their small office.

"Sort of. She has just really settled into the day care here at the casino. Is it just a weekend trip?"

"Uh, no. I said pack your bags. You're going to be out there for the duration. That means six months. I'm taking on two more clients in Texas—one is a Dallas Cowboy and the other plays basketball for San Antonio. I think you'll have plenty to keep you busy."

"Where would I stay?" Kinley asked, realizing there was no way to get out of the trip.

"I've rented a house in a nice subdivision…something called the Five Families. What an odd name," Jacs said.

"Is there anything I can say that will make you change your mind?" Kinley finally asked.

"Not really," Jacs said. "The client wants you, and you really have no reason not to go, do you?"

Yes. Nate Caruthers. The man who'd rocked her world for one passion-filled weekend, fathered her child and then interrupted her when she called later with that important news, telling her what happened in Vegas needed to stay there. He was her new client's older brother and still lived on the family's ranch outside Cole's Hill. But she didn't want to tell Jacs any of that. And she wasn't prepared to lose her job over it.

The only thing that was vaguely reassuring was that Nate would be too busy running the Rockin' C Ranch to be all that involved in wedding planning.

Fingers crossed.

"No reason. When do I need to start?" Kinley asked.

"Monday. I'm having Lori take care of all the details. You'll fly out on Friday, so you have time to settle in over the weekend. I've even included your nanny in the travel plans. Keep me posted," Jacs said as she turned on her heel and walked out of the office.

Kinley glanced down at the framed picture of Penny on her desk and felt her stomach tighten. After that disastrous call to Nate, she'd vowed not to allow him to let Penny down the way her own father had let her down. She just hoped that promise would be easy to keep once she was back in Cole's Hill. All she had to do was avoid Nate. Surely she could handle that except in this town she knew it would be impossible.

Nate Caruthers was a little bit hungover as he pulled his F-150 into the five-minute parking outside the Cole's Hill First National Bank. He reached for his sunglasses as he downed the last of his Red Bull before getting out of the cab of his truck. His younger brother was back in town, and that had called for a celebration that had lasted until the wee hours of the morning.

He tried the door on the bank, but it was locked. He

leaned against the brick wall and pulled his hat down over his eyes to wait the five minutes until it opened.

"Nate? Nate Caruthers?"

The voice was straight out of his past and one of his hottest weekends ever. He pushed the Stetson he had tilted to cover his eyes back with his thumb and looked over.

Kinley Quinten.

He whistled.

She'd changed. *Again.* Wearing some kind of lacy-looking white dress that ended midthigh and left her arms bare, she looked sophisticated. Not like the party girl he'd spent that weekend with almost three years ago in Vegas. His gaze followed the curve of her legs, ending at a pair of impossibly high heels. She looked like she'd stepped out of one of his mom's Neiman Marcus catalogs.

There may have been five years between them but none of that had mattered since he'd seen her in Vegas. She'd been twenty-three and he'd been twenty-eight.

"Eyes up here, buddy," she said.

He straightened from the wall and gave her a slow grin that many women had told them would get him out of any tight spot as he walked toward her. "Sorry, ma'am. Wasn't expecting you to look so good."

"Is that supposed to be a compliment?" she asked, opening her large purse and pulling out a pair of dark sunglasses, which she immediately put on.

"How could it not be? I guess the men in California must be blind if you're not sure."

She crossed her arms under her breasts. "I live in Las Vegas."

"Really? Since when? I thought you were only there to celebrate graduating from college," he said. "You should let me buy you a coffee after I'm done at the bank and we can catch up."

"Catch up? I don't think so. I'm in town for business, Nate," she said. "Plus, I think we said all that needed saying two years ago."

The door next to him opened with a gush of cold air-conditioning, and Kinley gestured for him to go first, but he shook his head. "Ladies first."

She huffed and walked past him.

He watched her move, her hips swaying with each of her determined steps. She probably wouldn't appreciate his attention, but he noticed that Stewart, the bank manager, was watching her, too.

Nate got in line behind her to wait for the cashier.

"I'm sorry I was such a douche on the phone. Can we please have coffee?" he asked. His mom always said, "If you don't ask, you don't get," and he wanted Kinley. Or at least to spend a little more time flirting with her before he headed back to the ranch.

She sighed. "One coffee, and then that's it. Okay?"

"Why will that be it?" he asked. "Maybe you'll want to see me again."

He grinned at her, and she shook her head. "I won't have time. I'm here for business."

"What business?" he asked. "Are you working at the NASA facility out on the Bar T?"

"No. I'm a wedding planner. I'm here to plan Hunter's wedding," she said.

"Well, I'll be damned."

"Yes, you will be," she said. An emotion passed over her face but too quickly for him to interpret it.

The cashier signaled Kinley over, and Nate stood where he was and observed her. She'd changed more than just her wardrobe, he realized. There was a core of strength that he hadn't noticed in her when they'd spent the weekend together. Maybe that was because they'd both been focused on having fun.

She concluded her business, and Nate stepped up to do his. He talked with Maggie, the cashier who'd been working the opening shift since before Nate had been born. When he was done, he looked around and noticed that Kinley was waiting for him by the exit.

She had her smartphone in her hand and was tapping out a message to someone. She'd pushed her sunglasses up on her head and was concentrating as she typed. She looked so serious.

He wondered what had happened in her life in the last three years and then realized he really had no right to find out. He'd ended their affair because her dad worked for his family and Nate wasn't really big on monogamy or commitment.

But seeing her again reminded him of how good that weekend had been and how hard it had been to hang up on her when she'd called and said she wanted to see him again.

She glanced up as he approached her.

"I hate to do this, but I can't make coffee this morning. I have to get my office set up here, and my boss has a potential couple scheduled for 10:00 a.m."

"Rain check, then?" he asked.

"Yes, that would be great," she said. She held her hand out to him.

She wanted to shake hands. Did she think this was a business deal? He took her hand, noticing how smooth and small it was in his big rough rancher hand. He rubbed his thumb over the back of her knuckles and then lifted her hand to his mouth to drop a kiss there.

"I'll be in touch," he said, turning and walking out of the bank. He went to his truck and realized his hangover was gone.

Kinley put Nate out of her mind as she unpacked the office and got the client meeting room set up. She glanced at her watch as she worked. The day care she'd signed Penny up for was two blocks down. Kinley wanted to get the room ready for the meeting with the basketball player and his fiancée and then go to see Penny before the meeting.

Her thoughts drifted back to Nate.

Damn.

He'd surprised her. Though she'd known she would run into him, she hadn't been prepared for it to be today. She'd sort of hoped to establish herself here first. She stood in the doorway and looked at the table she'd set up with a variety of faux cakes and flower arrangements.

Her phone rang and she glanced down. It was Jacs on the Skype app. She answered the call.

"Do you hate me now that you're back there?" Jacs asked.

"No. I don't hate you. But I could have used a little

more time before seeing the client this morning," Kinley said.

"Sorry about the rush, kid, but these two are hot to get married. They want to expedite the timeline but still make sure everything is one of a kind. You are going to have to really work your contacts to get this done. But I have confidence in you. Also don't let Bridezilla bully you. She was full on this morning with me."

"I won't," Kinley said. Actually, it would be good to get straight to work. "I'm seeing the local baker this afternoon for the Caruthers-Gainer wedding. If she doesn't work, I'm going to see if I can get Carine to fly in from LA."

"Good. Do you need anything from the office here?" Jacs asked.

"I might after I talk to my ten o'clock. We still have the dress from the O'Neill-Peterson cancellation. She was very demanding. Maybe it will work for this bride if she doesn't know it was designed for another woman," Kinley said.

"I like your thinking. I'll have Lori email the sketches so you can use them," Jacs said. "Have a good one."

Jacs disconnected the call, and Kinley gave the room a final once-over. She nibbled on her bottom lip as she realized that she was rubbing the back of her right hand…the hand Nate had kissed.

She shook her head. This was a horrible idea. For one thing, she'd never really gotten over him. She hadn't been pining over him; she was too sensible for that, or at least that's what she told herself. But she still thought about him.

Still remembered all the things that had gone on in that big king-size bed in the Vegas penthouse suite. Sometimes she woke up in a sweat thinking about Nate.

Usually it only took a moment to shove those thoughts away. She'd been telling herself that he wasn't as good-looking as she'd remembered, but the way those faded jeans had hugged his butt this morning had confirmed he was.

And the spark of awareness that had gone through her, awakening desires that had been dormant since she'd given birth to her daughter, couldn't be ignored. Maybe it was like Willa had suggested to her last month. It was time to start dating again.

Yes, that was it. She'd find a nice guy, a townie, and ask him out for a drink. Or maybe she'd go to the local bar and see if she could find someone…to do what? She wasn't the party girl she'd once been.

She was a mom, and frankly the idea of going out and hooking up sounded like too much work—and not the kind she wanted to do.

She left the office, grabbing her purse and keys on the way out and locking the door behind her. She needed to see Penny.

Her daughter grounded her and made her remember what was really important.

As she walked down the streets of the historic district, she took stock of how far she'd come. When her parents had divorced, Kinley was a tomboy, the daughter of a housekeeper for one of the wealthiest families in Cole's Hill. Now she was living in one of the houses her mom used to clean and planning a wedding for the son of her father's boss. She felt like she'd come a long way.

Not that there had been anything wrong with her parents' careers, but she was different. She always had been.

She entered the day care facility and was shown to the room where Penny and the other two-year-olds were playing. Her daughter was right in the middle of a group that was clustered around some easels. She walked over to her daughter and stopped next to her.

"Hi, Mama," she said, dropping her marker and turning to hug Kinley's legs.

"Hey, honey pie," Kinley said, stooping down to Penny's level. "What are you making?"

"A horsey. That boy said he has his own," Penny said.

Kinley tucked a strand of her daughter's straight red hair behind her ear and brushed a kiss on her forehead. "There are a lot ranches around here."

"Like Pop-Pop's?" she asked.

Penny had seen the ranch on the many video chats they'd had with her father. And the last time they'd talked, her dad had taken his tablet into the barn and shown her his horse. The toddler couldn't wait to visit her Pop-Pop and meet his horse.

"Just like that one. But Pop-Pop just manages the hands. It's not his ranch."

"I can't wait to see it," Penny said.

"We might not get to go out there," Kinley said. She didn't want to take Penny to the Rockin' C and chance her running into Nate. She had no plans to tell Nate about Penny; he'd made it clear a long time ago where his interest lay, and it wasn't with raising a family. "Pop-Pop is going to come to town and visit us."

"Okay," Penny said.

Kinley hoped that would be the last of Penny talking about going to the ranch. She visited with her daughter until snack time, and when it was over, Kinley left after giving Penny a hug and a kiss.

She got through her meeting. She'd talked the bride, Meredith, into looking at the sketches for the dress they'd already had made. Meredith liked the design but wanted a few changes. Kinley was still thinking about that as she drove over to the Bluebonnet Bakery to sample the cakes for the Caruthers wedding.

She saw a familiar pickup truck with the Rockin' C logo on it parked out front but told herself not to jump to conclusions. The Rockin' C probably had a lot of F-150 pickups. It was probably just Hunter.

But when she walked into the bakery, she found her gut had been right. Nate stood at the counter along with his middle brother, Ethan, Hunter and a woman who had to be Hunter's fiancée. Derek, the second-oldest Caruthers, was a surgeon and probably not available to sample cake.

"Hello, everyone," Kinley said.

She just had to be professional. She could do that.

"Hi, I'm Ferrin Gainer," the woman said, stepping over to her. "It's so nice to meet you."

"I'm looking forward to working with you and helping you plan your special day. I've arranged for us to have a tasting in the back room," Kinley said, motioning everyone in the right direction. "Why don't you go through there and I'll be right with you."

Everyone went into the room but Nate. He hung back.

She shook her head.

"What are you doing here?"

"I'm the big brother of the groom. He asked me to come, so I did," Nate said. "This is why I wanted us to chat earlier. Just clear the air. Like I said, I was a jerk, and I'm sorry. I don't want anything to mess up Hunter's wedding."

Oh.

When he said it like that, he sounded so reasonable. And she realized that coming to Cole's Hill had more consequences than she'd thought. She was losing her professional edge because of Nate. Part of it was the way he made her pulse speed up; another, bigger part was the fact that he was her daughter's father and she hadn't told him. And the cost of keeping that secret seemed higher than she might be able to pay.

"Sorry. I'm just a little short-tempered today. Must be the jet lag." Though with only a one-hour time difference between here and Vegas, she knew jet lag was a bit of an exaggeration.

"Don't be. It happens to the best of us. After the tasting we can get a drink and talk. It's obvious we're going to need to."

She nodded. She had to check in with her nanny, Pippa, and make sure that Penny would be fine for the evening. "I have one more appointment, and then I can meet you for a drink."

It would have been so much easier to just say no if

Nate wasn't…well, so likeable and charming. And if she didn't have Penny. But she did. And now she was going to have make a decision that she'd thought she'd already made.

Two

Cake tasting. There were times when Nate wondered what had happened to his family. Though he didn't begrudge Hunter his happiness or his wedding, Nate liked things the way they'd always been: when the Carutherses were out working hard, playing even harder and making respectable mamas lock up their daughters.

"What do you think?" Hunter asked, pulling Nate aside so that they could speak privately for a moment.

"About what?"

"The cake. Do you have a preference?" he asked.

Nate shook his head. "I do like the idea of your groom's cake being shaped like a football field."

"That was discussed fifteen minutes ago. Where is your head?"

He looked over at the pretty redhead taking them

through the different types of jam and icing that could be used between layers. Kinley. She was too much in his head. Going for a drink had *stupid* written all over it, but he'd never been one to back down from anything, even when it went against his own better sense.

"Don't do it," Hunter said.

"Don't do what?" Nate asked. Though he knew what his brother was talking about.

"She's practically family," Hunter said. "Marcus is like a second dad to us. Don't mess with her."

Too late. Nate recalled every detail of the weekend that he and Kinley had spent together; a part of him didn't want to ever forget it. Another part didn't believe it could have been as good as he remembered. But he knew it was. Then he remembered that silly little handshake she'd limited him to this morning at the bank and the rush of energy that had gone through them when they'd touched.

"I'm just looking."

"Make sure that's all you do," Hunter said.

He clipped his brother on the shoulder with his fist. "I don't take orders from you."

"You do now. Ferrin really wants this wedding to be special. And that means not letting you, Ethan or Derek screw anything up. So be good."

"When have any of us ever been good?" Nate asked. He wasn't going to mess up Hunter's wedding. As much as he was against marriage himself, he really liked Ferrin and thought she was perfect for his brother. Hunter hadn't enjoyed being single the way the rest of the Carutherses did. His college girlfriend had been murdered and suspicion had fallen on Hunter for a good ten years before the real murderer had been convicted. So the only women Hunter had dated were those looking for a thrill...until Ferrin came along.

"I won't do anything to hurt your wedding," Nate promised.

Hunter reached over and squeezed his shoulder. "I know you won't. You've always looked out for me."

"Someone had to," Nate said. He loved his brothers and had always been the one to stand up for them.

"You two done over there?" their mother asked.

"Yes, ma'am. I was just saying how much I liked the mandarin filling," Nate said, luckily recalling the last cake he'd tasted.

"That's the one I am leaning toward as well," Ferrin said.

"Honey, that's my favorite, too," Hunter said, giving his fiancée the sweetest, sappiest smile Nate had ever seen. What the hell had happened to his brother?

"Then it's decided," Kinley said. "I have your other preferences marked down. Are you happy with this bakery? We can have one of our specialty bakers from Beverly Hills fly in and talk to you as well."

"We'd like to keep it local as much as we can," Ferrin said. "Hunter and I want this to be as authentic as it can be."

Kinley made some notes in her notebook, her hand gliding across the page. Nate couldn't help remembering the tomboy she'd been and the time he'd caught her sitting under one of the scrub oaks out in the pasture crying because her teacher said she had the worst handwriting in the class.

He shook his head. Where had that old memory come from? He had spent hours under that tree showing her how to write until her handwriting had been passable. It wasn't that he'd had the greatest handwriting, but Nate had never liked to be second best at anything. So he'd practiced a lot, and he remembered how grateful little Kinley had been that he'd helped her.

The women had moved to leave the room, but Ethan and Hunter hung back. Hunter just shook his head, but Nate noticed that Ethan watched until Kinley had rounded the corner.

"Dang. That Kinley sure has changed," Ethan said. "She makes a man—"

"Don't. She doesn't make you anything, Eth."

Both of his brothers turned to stare at him, and Nate knew he'd showed his hand without meaning to. But he wanted her. She had been his once and he knew himself well enough to know that he was going to try to make her his again. He didn't think it would last longer than it took her to plan Hunter's wedding, but damned if he was going to let any other man—especially one of his brothers—make a play for her.

"The lady might have something to say about that," Ethan said.

Nate shrugged. "We're having drinks tonight."

Ethan put his hands up. "Fair enough. I was just saying she sure isn't the girl who used to follow us around on horseback."

"No, she isn't," Nate agreed. He thought of all the changes he'd seen in Kinley and how much he appreciated each one of them. She'd been a party girl once, but she'd matured past that and he could see that she was stronger now. She'd changed and he acknowledged that he hadn't really, but one thing he knew for sure was that he still wanted her. And he was pretty sure they weren't finished with each other yet.

There had been something in her eyes when he'd shaken her hand earlier, maybe attraction, maybe something more. Whatever it was, he was hungry to explore it.

Ferrin was a marked contrast to the bride Kinley had been working with that very morning. They were in the office at the bakery discussing a few details. Where a true bridezilla would never take any of the first things that Kinley offered, Ferrin pretty much did. Her mom was a professor at UT Austin and wasn't able to make the cake tasting, so Ferrin did ask if Kinley would mind very much if they waited to finalize the cakes until her mom drove over on Saturday to give her opinion.

That was a very easy yes. Food was easy, Kinley thought, or it should be most of the time. It was a little bit funny to see all of the Caruthers brothers sitting around trying cake and pretending they cared what it tasted like, because even Ma Caruthers—as she'd always insisted Kinley call her—knew her boys weren't interested in cake flavors. They were here because Ferrin had asked Hunter to give his opinion and had suggested his brothers might want a say as well.

It was sweet.

The bond between the Carutherses was one of the many things that Kinley had always envied about them.

Being an only child hadn't been a burden, but it had been lonely. Her parents both had demanding jobs that kept them away from home most of the time. She'd spent a lot of her childhood alone or tagging after the Carutherses. Now she was planning a wedding for Hunter… It was almost too much to be believed.

She made a few more notes. "Ferrin, what's your schedule like for the rest of the week? I'd love to get your dress selected. I have some designers that I like to use who are in New York and Beverly Hills, but also I have a friend from London who is just starting out. Her dresses are exquisite and I think they would flatter you."

"I'm teaching at Cole's Hill Community College on Thursday and Friday morning. But I'm free in the afternoon," Ferrin said.

"That's fine," Kinley said. "I can forward you the look books so you can go through the sketches and photos before you start narrowing down your choices."

Hunter came in as they were talking, and Kinley was very aware that Ethan and Nate were right behind him. She wasn't sure what they had been discussing, but given the way all three men stared at her…she guessed she'd been the topic.

"Hunter, y'all are free to go. We are going to be discussing the dress, and I want to surprise you on the big day," Ferrin said.

"Sounds good to me," Hunter said, coming over and giving her a kiss before leaving the room with his brothers behind him.

"Do you want my opinion?" Ma Caruthers asked.

"I know you have your mother and you might want to make the decision with her."

"I'd love your opinion," Ferrin said, then turned to Kinley. "Tell me more about what will happen after I look at the designs in the books. Pretty much my entire bridal experience has been limited to episodes of *Say Yes to the Dress*. And I don't know how much of that is real or not."

"Well, once we have an idea of the type of dress you want, I'll get samples in similar styles shipped to us and then we'll arrange for you to try on all the different dresses until you narrow it down to a designer or a type of dress you like. Then someone from the designer you've chosen will be assigned to you to come out here and fit and measure the dress properly," Kinley said. Finding the perfect dress was really Kinley's favorite part of the wedding planning service. She was naturally organized, so the other parts of her job were easy and almost routine. Every wedding had food and cake and wine and music. But it was the dress and the theme that the bride selected that set each wedding apart.

"That sounds…exhausting," Ferrin said. "Also a little daunting."

Kinley walked over to the bride-to-be, who was a few years older than she, and put her arm around her shoulders. "Don't worry about anything. I will be by your side the entire time and we are going to plan the wedding of your dreams."

Ferrin turned and hugged her, and for the first time since she'd gotten off the plane in Texas, Kinley was glad she was here. Ferrin was the kind of bride that made her glad she was a wedding planner.

"Thank you."

"Told you you'd be in good hands with this one," Ma Caruthers said. "She's always had a good head on her shoulders."

"You've been wonderful to help me so much. I really appreciate it," Ferrin said to her future mother-in-law.

"Well, I never had any daughters and am hoping that you are going to give me a granddaughter one day. Thank you for letting me help out," Ma Caruthers said.

Kinley felt the heat in her chest and cheeks as she blushed. She hadn't considered anyone besides herself and Nate when she'd made the decision to keep Penny a secret from him. He was wild and not ready to settle down—she wasn't sure he ever would be—but his mother and father…they were nice people. People who wanted a grandchild.

And they already had one.

Kinley excused herself and left the bakery. Guilt weighed heavy on her shoulders as she walked to her car. It was hot on this summer afternoon, and she wished she could blame the heat for the feeling in the pit of her stomach. But she knew the truth. She'd let the secret of Penny go on for too long. There was no way to casually introduce her daughter to the Carutherses without them getting angry—justifiably so. She realized she might have bitten off more than she could chew by agreeing to come to Cole's Hill.

Now she was stuck between a rock and a very hard place. She could either stay here and hope that no one noticed Penny and that the guilt that had started to grow inside her would be bearable, or she could quit her job and run away from life.

She knew which option she wanted to choose. But she'd never been a coward, and she didn't want Penny to grow up thinking that she could run away from her problems. Kinley was going to have to figure out how to tell Nate he had a daughter, and she knew the sooner she did it the better it would be for everyone.

Nate had half expected Kinley to cancel on him and had gone to the Bull Pit with Ethan to have a drink while he was waiting for her to finish up with her afternoon appointments. What was it about Kinley that always made him feel on edge? With most of the women he dated he usually fell into a comfortable feeling pretty quickly. He knew what they liked and how to give it to them.

But not with her.

"Dad wants me to go to San Angelo to check on one of our mineral contracts. It's set to renew, and he's not sure if we should renew it or sell it," Ethan said. He was the family lawyer but also worked for a big-time law firm. He used to work in Houston but now handled his clients from his home office here in Cole's Hill. "Then I'm probably going to fly to LA and be back a few days later."

Ethan had a woman in Los Angeles. They all knew it but he never mentioned her, so Nate had figured she was either casual or married. And since he didn't want his brothers nipping in his own business, he'd never asked.

"Sure thing. We aren't doing anything major this week. Mitzi is looking for men for the Fourth of July bachelor auction… She's suckered a few of those astronauts into doing it and has a theme of American Hero for this year's event. She wanted Hunter, but since he's off the market he promised to get a friend from Dallas."

"Then why does she need me?" Ethan asked.

"Well, we all know lawyers are sharks, so it must be that she remembers your gold buckle rodeo days and wants to have you as a cowboy in the lineup." Nate liked to rib his brother about being a lawyer but he'd be welcome at the auction.

"How about I just make a large donation and sit on the sidelines?" Ethan said.

They all felt about the same way when it came to participating in events like the charity auction. "You can't. One of the Carutherses already did."

"Derek? He's a doctor—he should be used to this kind of thing," Ethan said.

"He is and he likes the attention, so he said yes as soon as she asked," Nate said.

"You?"

Nate shrugged. "I have been dating her off and on, so she was willing to let me out of it."

"Well, damn. Okay, I'll do it," Ethan said.

"Good," Nate said. He thought it would do his brother some good to find a woman here in Cole's Hill whom he liked instead of driving to Midland whenever he wanted to hook up. Or whatever Ethan did over there.

"So when's your date with Kinley?" Ethan asked as he took a swallow of his beer.

"We're having drinks tonight," Nate said.

"Drinks? That's not a date," Ethan said.

"Isn't it?"

"Hell, no. You and I are having drinks and this sure as hell isn't a date," Ethan said.

"Damned straight," Nate said. "I've never had any problems turning drinks into something more."

"None of us have," Ethan said. "Can you believe Hunter is getting married? I thought…well, I guess we all thought that he was never going to find a woman who'd trust him."

"I know," Nate said. He didn't like to think about how many times he'd defended his brother in places like the Bull Pit and in boardrooms whenever someone had brought up Hunter's past. Gossip had it that their family had bought Hunter's freedom, but the truth was the cops never had enough evidence to charge him with murder. Not that that had made any difference in the court of public opinion. "I'm glad to see him so happy. Damned if I could have ever seen any of us as married, but being engaged looks good on him."

"It does. Ferrin seems to be an important part of his new life. And I'm going to deny saying this if you bring it up, but he seems like a new man now."

Nate had to laugh at that. Hunter was a new man. A man freed from the past and the guilt that he'd carried for ten years.

"Guilt did weigh on him. That's why I lead a free and easy life. The only thing that weighs on me is the family business, and to be honest I like a good tussle in the boardroom, so that's not really a big deal."

Ethan laughed. "You said it, brother. Speaking of a business, Dylan Gallagher has a Cessna he wants to sell us. He's thinking of buying a big jet."

"What does he need a jet for?"

"Apparently, he has a lady friend on the East Coast he wants to visit," Ethan said. "I'll drive over and look at it this afternoon. It would be nice to have it as a backup for the older one we've been thinking of getting rid of."

"It would be. Ranch assets are your domain, so if you think we should buy it, I'll agree with you."

"Wish all things with you were this easy to settle," Ethan said.

Before Nate could respond, his phone beeped and he glanced down at the screen to see he had a text message from Kinley. Nate finished his beer and stood up. "I'm easy to get along with. You're the troublemaker."

Ethan's laughter followed him out the door. He left his pickup in the parking lot at the Bull Pit and walked across town to the restaurant where Kinley was waiting for him. The sun was setting as he came around the corner and he saw her standing to the left of the entrance. She was backlit by the sun, which silhouetted her curves and seemed to highlight her reddish-brown hair. He stopped for a minute as he realized that he didn't want to screw this up.

He'd hurt her with the way he'd behaved when she'd called him from Vegas, and this was a fresh start. The kind of thing that he needed with her, because no matter what he'd said to her on the phone, one weekend hadn't been enough to get her out of his system.

Three

Kinley had a rushed dinner with Penny and her nanny before leaving to meet Nate. Tonight was important, and she needed to be stronger than she'd ever been before. She'd dressed carefully, choosing a gray cap-sleeve dress that nipped in at the waist before ending at the knees. She'd paired it with a piece of costume jewelry she'd purchased at a vintage shop in Melrose the year before her mom had died.

Wearing it always made Kinley think of her mom. She touched it like a talisman, trying to glean a little of her mom's courage before Nate showed up. She was scared.

She'd made the only choice she felt she could make when she'd decided to have Penny and to raise her daughter on her own. But circumstances had changed, and it was time to make another choice.

She pulled her phone out of her purse for the tenth time since she'd texted Nate that she was waiting for him at the Peace Creek Steak House, not because she expected him to respond, but because she felt so vulnerable just standing there waiting for him.

She heard a group of people approaching the entrance and looked up to see Bianca Velasquez walking toward her. Her mom had cleaned the Velasquez home way back when, and Bianca and Kinley had been really good friends. She smiled when she noticed Kinley, waved her friends on and came over to give her a hug.

Her friend had thick black hair that she wore long and falling around her shoulders and olive skin Kinley had always envied. She was wearing a pair of slim-fitting white jeans and a flowy navy-colored blouse.

"I didn't know you were back in town," Bianca said.

"I didn't know you were, either. I thought you were still in Spain," Kinley said. Bianca's young husband had recently died in a fiery car crash, leaving the window with an eighteen-month-old son to raise. Kinley and Bianca kept in touch by email and had a lot to share since they both were single moms.

"I recently moved back. Mom and Dad were really persistent. And I missed Texas," Bianca said. "Do you have plans tonight? You can join us."

"I'm only back for a few months to plan Hunter's wedding," Kinley said. "I'm meeting someone but I'd love to catch up sometime."

"Me, too. I'm looking for a job, believe it or not," Bianca said in a sort of self-effacing tone. "I have your number, so I'll text you and we can find some time to meet up with our kiddos."

"Sounds great," Kinley said, hugging her friend and realizing how nice it was to see Bianca. The combination of secrets and guilt had been weighing on her, but seeing a friendly face, making some normal plans, made her feel better.

Bianca waved goodbye before going into the restaurant. Kinley felt someone watching her and glanced up to see Nate at the end of the driveway, walking toward her. He hadn't changed since their earlier meeting; he still wore dark jeans paired with what she knew was a designer shirt and hand-tooled, custom-made leather boots. He walked like a man who knew his place in the world. He was confident and sure, and a part of her truly resented him for it.

She'd been struggling to figure out her place her entire life. She might not have been aware of it when she'd been younger, but these days it felt like a yoke around her neck. Like she'd been carrying it for too long. Part of it, she knew, was the burden of what she had to tell him and her own uncertainty about how to do it, but she knew another part was the fact that she felt like she was always running to catch up.

Probably that could be traced back to living two different lives for most of her upbringing: the weeks in town with her mom at the Velasquez home and the weekends on the ranch with her father.

"Nate, I'm glad you could make it," Kinley said. To her own ears, her voice sounded too bright. Like she was trying to force out a happiness she didn't feel. But she put a smile on her face, determined to keep it in place until she actually could smile around him.

"It was my idea, so I wasn't about to say no." He winked at her as he reached her, putting his hand at the small of her back to turn her toward the entrance.

She moved forward, trying to ignore the pulsing that had started as soon as she felt his hand on the small of her back. His hands were big and hot and made her very aware of the last time he'd touched her there.

They'd both been naked and he'd rolled her onto her stomach in that big king-size bed to give her a massage, which had ended with him deep inside her as she'd climaxed again and again. A shiver of pure sexual need went through her.

It had been a long time since any man had touched her save for her ob-gyn, and Kinley, who had been too tired to think of dating before this, now thought that might have been a huge mistake.

She wished she'd had at least one other man since Nate so she'd have some sort of buffer. He reached around her to hold open the door, and she was both elated and disappointed that he broke contact.

She stepped inside, waiting a moment for her eyes to adjust to the dim interior. She was losing control of herself, which would mean loss of control of the situation if she didn't pull herself together.

She skimmed the bar and spotted a booth in the back that looked like it would give them some privacy from the other patrons in the steak house.

"I see a spot," Kinley said, walking toward it quickly, not giving Nate a chance to touch her back again.

* * *

Touching her had been a mistake, because as he watched her walk through the bar, images of the last time he'd touched her back ran through his mind. He remembered the afternoon sunlight shining into their room and how creamy her skin had looked against the white hotel sheets. She had freckles on her back, and he'd taken his time to touch and caress each of them before he made love to her.

A jolt of need went through him, and he knew whatever lie he'd been telling himself about meeting up with Kinley to clear the air was paper-thin. He wanted her. And pretending that there was anything other than that motivating him would be a mistake.

She slid into the booth she'd spotted in the corner. It was darker back here, lit only with an electric fixture mounted on the wall that was made to look like a gas lamp. The bulb flickered like a live flame. They had more privacy than he'd expected.

He started to slide in next to her, but she shook her head and gestured for him to sit across from her. He sat down on the hard wooden bench, hoping it would cool him down, but it didn't. Instead his legs brushed against hers under the table, and every time he inhaled all he could smell was her perfume. It was some kind of flowery, summery scent that made him more determined that they should spend the summer together.

He was a temporary guy and she was here temporarily; it should be easy enough for both of them. But his gut warned it wouldn't be. It couldn't be. First of all, her job was going to bring her into contact with his family—a lot. Second, her dad was his foreman, and Nate didn't want to do anything to compromise that relationship. Plus—and this was the big one—he was pretty sure that Kinley had already written him off.

So he was going to have to figure out how to convince her that he was more than a wealthy playboy. Was she worth it?

Even as he asked himself that question, he knew the answer was yes. There was something in her big chocolate-brown eyes that made him determined to figure out what he needed to say or do to claim her as his own.

"What are you drinking?" he asked. His voice sounded almost too loud in the quiet intimacy of the booth.

"Sparkling water with a twist of lime," she said.

"I can't order that at the bar or they will laugh me out of here," he said.

"Then I'll order it. What do you want?" she asked. He noticed that her tone was all business, and he realized that while he was thinking this was the first step to renewed intimacy, she wasn't.

"I was joking, Kin. I'll get the drinks," he said. "I'm ordering something to eat as well."

"Thank you," she said as he left the booth to go and place their order.

A good five minutes had passed before he returned to their table. He put the glasses down before retaking his seat.

"I'm sorry about overreacting about the drink. I'm a little on edge tonight," she said.

"Planning weddings is stressful work?" he asked. He

took a swallow of his beer and leaned back, stretching one arm along the back of the wooden bench.

"Sometimes. Ferrin's such a sweetie, so she's making my job pretty easy. But I'm working with another client who is a bit more demanding," Kinley said.

"I never would have pictured you as a wedding planner," Nate said. When he'd known her as a child, she'd been so rough-and-tumble. The kind of cowgirl who could do anything the boys could on the ranch. His parents had always treated his brothers and him the same way they did all the kids whose families worked on the ranch. That meant they all did chores together and they all got a horse of their own to take care of. It was a tradition that Nate had followed when he took over running the ranch from his dad a few years ago.

The Caruthers fortune derived from the cattle they ran on their property as well as oil and mineral leases they'd had for generations and the newer stud operation that was just fifteen years old. The stud farm had been Kinley's dad's idea for diversifying the ranch.

"I guess you don't know me," she said. "I like planning weddings."

"You might be right that I don't know certain things about you," he said. "But I'd argue there are parts of you I know very well."

She flushed. Her skin was so creamy and pale that any time she was aroused, angry or embarrassed it flashed in a pinkish red across her face.

"Don't, Nate," she said. "Please do not bring up that weekend in Vegas or our intimacy again. I really would rather your brothers and parents didn't know about it."

He leaned forward over the table. "There isn't anyone here but you and me, Kin, and we both know what happened."

"We do. And we both remember how it ended…or is that just me?"

"I already apologized for that," he said, sitting back. Damned if it wasn't just like a woman to keep reminding him of how he'd screwed up.

"I know. And I accepted your apology. All I meant by my comment was that we're like oil and water—we don't mix very well."

He thought they'd mixed just fine. But arguing now would just get her back up more and not move them any closer to the ending he wanted for them. He knew he had to ease up, and he did. "I'm not the same man I was three years ago."

She gave him a small smile and nodded. Then she laced her fingers together, and he noticed she wore a small thin ring on her middle finger. "Fair enough. I'm definitely not the same woman. So what's changed with Nate Caruthers?"

Kinley knew she was stalling, but honestly she needed more time. She toyed with the lime on the side of her glass, rubbing it around the rim to distract her from the fact that Nate's big frame dominated the corner booth. His legs were on either side of hers, the rough fabric of the denim abrading the bare skin of her legs. She tried to shift but just ended up rubbing her leg against his.

She glanced over at him to see if he'd noticed. He had. He didn't say anything. Instead he took a sip of his beer, and she watched the muscles of his throat work as he swallowed and then leaned back, stretching his legs out under the table, brushing them against hers again.

"I'm still doing some investment stuff, but my main focus now is running the ranch. Dad wanted to ease off on the everyday running of the Rockin' C. And as you know, it's a full-time job. So I stepped up," Nate said.

The Rockin' C was one of the largest ranches in Texas. They ran cattle, had oil, operated a stud farm and employed more than one hundred families on the property. They weren't gentleman farmers; they were more like the Ewings of TV's *Dallas*.

"Where are your folks living now?"

"Still on the property. Mom wanted a smaller house, so they built a five-bedroom ranch house out near the small lake."

"That's small?" she asked with a laugh.

"For her. Plus she said she wanted enough room to spoil her grandkids once we all settled down," Nate said.

Once again Kinley felt the white-hot needle of guilt pierce through her. "When is that going to happen?"

"Not any time soon, as far as I'm concerned. Hunter is the only one who seems interested in getting serious. But after ten years of hell, I think it's about time he had a break."

"That stuff about him… It was really hard to watch when I was in California. I mean, there was the Hunter I grew up with and then this other guy I was seeing stories about on TV. I'm glad they finally caught the man responsible."

"We all are. Mom spent a lot of time at St. Thomas Aquinas Church praying," Nate said.

When he spoke about Hunter, Kinley heard the love and concern in his voice. She'd been in high school when Hunter had first been accused of murder, but all that was in the past now. And Hunter had Ferrin.

"He's got the happy ending he deserved," Kinley said. It gave her hope that once she came clean with Nate she'd be able to move on. Maybe keeping Penny's paternity a secret was one of the barriers that had kept her from dating over the last few years.

But she knew it wasn't. She knew it was her own fear of trusting a man again. Or, to be more honest, trusting her heart. She'd thought what she felt for Nate had been the beginning of something more solid, but in the end it had only been lust.

Which was raising its hotter-than-hell head once again.

"He has. How many weddings have you planned?" Nate asked. "How did you get started doing that?"

She sipped her sparkling water and took the reprieve he'd unintentionally given her. "I've planned close to twenty weddings. All of them high-end, destination-type affairs. I got started when I answered an ad for a personal assistant and starting working for Jacs. She had one of her planners flake out and gave me a trial run. I guess she saw something in me and decided to promote me to planner."

"I'm not surprised she saw something in you. I've never known you to be a woman to back down," Nate said. "No matter how much the outer packaging has changed over the years, that solid core of steel still remains."

It was one of the nicest things that anyone had ever said to her. That Nate Caruthers was the one saying it made her heart heavy. "Thank you."

"It's okay. I should have remembered that when you called me. Instead I felt trapped, and I wasn't ready for that. Despite the fact that we spent a weekend together, you're not the kind of woman a man should ever be casual about."

She didn't know what to say to that. The fact that he hadn't been ready to settle down gave her pause in her determination to tell him about Penny. Was he ready now? How would she know for sure?

She wanted to make things right. For Nate. For Ma Caruthers. For herself. But her duty was to Penny. And Kinley had to determine if it would be better for her daughter to never know who her father was or to know and have him disappoint her.

It was a tough call.

One that was going to take more than a sparkling water and a single conversation to figure out. She wasn't sure if it was cowardice or not, but she decided she needed to get to know the man that Nate was today before she let him know he had a daughter.

It was the only fair thing to do for herself and Penny. And for Nate, who was still running wild, if word around town could be believed.

"I'm not sure that I was ready for anything more during that weekend in Vegas," she admitted. "But I am definitely not as casual now."

"Can I talk you into dinner?" he asked.

She hesitated, but she'd already said good night to Penny, so she knew her daughter wasn't expecting her home until after bedtime. Kinley had promised to call at seven thirty and could still do so.

If she was going to figure out how and if to tell Nate, they were going to have spend more time together, and dinner seemed like a safe enough way to start.

Four

Nate normally would have gone to the country club for a midweek dinner and then played a few games of pool with Derek before hitting the Bull Pit for more drinking and carousing before heading home. Instead he was seated across from Kinley eating a steak and listening to her talk about the latest book she'd read.

He didn't want to dwell on the fact that this was shaping up to be one of his best weeknights in a long time. She was animated when she talked, and now that he'd put the brakes on anything too sexy, she'd relaxed. Her hands moved as she explained a part of the book she really liked, and then she laughed and his gut clenched and his blood seemed to flow a little heavier in his veins.

"It's just the funniest thing I've read in a long time

and I thought while I was reading it, *this girl could be me*. Have you ever felt that way?" she asked.

He hadn't. "Not really, but then, I've always had Dad to show me the kind of man I wanted to be."

"Your dad is the best," she said.

There was a note in her voice that made him wonder if Marcus hadn't been the same kind of dad as his was. His father lived for his sons and made sure they knew it. They'd all been very certain that he had a strong moral code for them to live up to and he expected a lot from them. But he'd always treated them with love.

"Was your dad?" Nate asked.

"He wasn't horrible or anything like that. But he did tend to work a lot on the weekend when I was out there. Mostly I think I saw your dad more than I saw my own."

Nate hadn't realized that and now wondered if he was keeping any of his employees from seeing their kids as often as they liked. He never really thought about the ranch children. His life was very different from his employees', since his days of working the ranch were long gone. He spent most of his time in his high-rise office building here in Cole's Hill doing deals and managing the business that the Rockin' C had blossomed into.

"I didn't know that," he said, at last understanding that there was a lot to Kinley that he didn't know.

In his mind he always imagined that she'd had the same sort of upbringing he had. He remembered Kinley being on the ranch on the weekends. He'd thought of her as a sort of girl version of himself.

"Why would you?" she asked. "It would be weird if you had. Besides, my dad and I have a pretty good relationship now. It's just different than yours is with your parents."

Nate shook his head. "I was very glad to move them into their own home, not that I forced them out. But as much as I like having my town house in the Five Families area, I do prefer to be out on the ranch."

"Couldn't you have lived there with your parents?" she asked.

"Of course, but if I did, then Mom wanted to meet any of the women I brought home, and sometimes that could get awkward."

"I bet," she said. "Are you still mostly keeping it casual?"

"Mostly. But I am here with you tonight."

"Tonight? Should I just be thinking of this as temporary... What am I talking about? We're having dinner to clear the air and give us a friendly base so that we don't make Hunter and your family aware of what happened between us."

He should have been very happy that she understood the kind of man he was.

But...

He didn't want her to dismiss him so easily. Yeah, he was a temporary cowboy, the kind of man who knew how to show a woman a good time for a short stretch, but he might change for the right woman.

That was a big ask, though. And Kinley was perfectly within her rights to friend zone him the way she had.

"Fair enough. But for the record, you're not like everyone else," he said.

She paused for a second, her eyes widened, and he realized that a part of her wanted him to be Mr. Right. He could see it there in her gaze, and he'd never been anything close to that.

"Really?"

There was so much hope in her tone that it was almost painful to listen to it. He was afraid of hurting her and before this moment hadn't been aware of how likely it was that he could. He'd thought she was like him. The female version. Party girl to his party boy and that like him she'd segue into the next phase of her life as a successful businesswoman. But in her eyes was a hope that he hadn't counted on or ever seen before.

She wanted him to be a hero.

Not a bad boy.

Could he do it? Could he be the man she wanted?

The selfish part of him wanted to pretend he hadn't noticed and maybe just go with it. But he had always prided himself on being honest in all of his relationships, and pretending was a form of lying. Some would say the worst form.

"Yes. You are very special," he said at last.

She fumbled for her water glass and took a sip before placing it carefully back on the table.

"You're kind of unforgettable, too," she said.

Just like that he knew he could have Kinley again if he wanted to. If he kept his mouth shut and acted the part. But he'd already decided that would be the kind of low-down behavior he wouldn't indulge in. But, oh, he was very tempted.

Her mouth was full and peach colored in the ambient lighting of the restaurant, and he was so tempted to just lean across the table and kiss her. To stop talking before he did anything that would ruin whatever it was she thought she saw in him.

Kinley was teetering on the edge. There had been a flash of something in Nate that made her want to believe he could be the kind of man who would spend the rest of his life with her. And though she was killing it—or at least managing it—as a single mom, there were times when she fantasized about having the perfect family that she'd always dreamed of having as a child. Growing up her family hadn't been perfect, and she'd believed when she finally had kids she'd do it the right way. Have that perfect family from television and magazine ads that she'd always craved.

And now Nate was here sitting across from her saying things about how she was different from other women and looking at her…like he might have changed in the last two years. But she couldn't just take a chance on that being the truth. She needed to be logical with this man whom she'd never been able to be logical about.

He'd always fascinated her. When she was younger, Nate had been the Caruthers who'd always looked out for her when she'd been on the ranch for the weekend. Then when she'd grown into her awkward preteen self, she had crushed on him—hard.

Now he tempted her again. Not with his easy charm and good looks, but with the slightest hint that he might be the partner she lacked. The father Penny needed.

She reached for her wineglass and took a sip. She was riding the crazy train straight to some sort of dream-like existence that she knew didn't exist. She knew that Nate was a great guy, sexy as hell and able to make any woman feel like she was the center of his world. And there were times when Kinley was able to make herself believe that she had been the center of it for that weekend in Vegas. But then he'd moved on.

A new business interest caught his attention, probably a new woman and a new expensive toy. She had to keep her wits about her.

But she liked him.

She'd always liked him. And it had been a really long time since a man—any man—had looked at her the way Nate was now.

And she'd left herself the slightest bit vulnerable when she'd just gone with her gut and told him he was unforgettable. He was. Even if she hadn't had Penny to remind her of him every day, she doubted she would have been able to stop thinking about him.

"So...?" she said at last. Yeah, she was great at conversation, she thought. She could handle a full-on bridezilla on the warpath trying to make her special day the most fantastic ever, but put her across the table from this man and her verbal skills suddenly dropped to nothing.

"How do you feel about getting out of here and taking a walk around the plaza? The city commission is sponsoring a light show on the side of city hall that I've heard is pretty amazing," he said.

It sounded so nice and normal. Like a real date. Except, was this a date? She wasn't about to ask him and make herself look silly. But they'd said drinks, and now it had turned into dinner. She was holding a secret she needed to share and no closer to actually figuring out how to do it. And he had invited her to do something that sounded so normal.

So not a part of the chaos in her mind.

"I'd love to," she said. She glanced at her watch, realizing it was almost time for her to call Penny and say good-night. "I need to make a call first."

She reached for her wallet to leave some money toward the bill, but he stopped her. "I've got dinner. Go make your call. I'll meet you out front."

She got to her feet, put her purse over her shoulder and left the table. She glanced up and noticed that Bianca was watching her. Her friend waved. Kinley waved back, realizing how much she'd missed living in a town like Cole's Hill. These people were part of her past, and they knew her. She had a connection here that she'd never have in Vegas.

She'd missed it.

She wanted so much for Penny. Not just that perfect fantasy family in her mind, but also to have friends like Bianca, a solid base for her childhood so she'd always know where she came from.

She stepped outside, noting that the sky was clear and the sun was starting to set. She walked away from the entrance of the restaurant. At a safe distance, she hit the video call app on her phone and dialed Penny's iPad. Her daughter would be waiting for their good-night ritual.

"Mama!" Penny said as the call connected.

"How are you, sweet girl?" Kinley asked.

Her daughter was nestled into her pink cotton pajamas with her red ringlets fanning out behind her head as she lay propped up in the bed. She had her stuffed rabbit, Mr. Beans, tucked under her arm, and her eyes looked sleepy.

"Good. We just read the fishes," she said.

Which was what Penny called Dr. Seuss stories. All of them. Kinley had started reading her *One Fish, Two Fish* from the time she was tiny. And now anything that rhymed was *the fishes*. "Yay. Those are our favorites. Good night, sweet girl."

"Night, Mama."

"Love you."

"Love you, too," Penny said, waving her chubby little toddler hand at the screen. "Bye-bye."

Kinley waved back. "Bye-bye."

She disconnected the call and then held the phone to her chest for a long minute. She had never realized she could love anything as much as she loved her daughter, and she would do anything to protect her.

Never had the challenge of ensuring that been harder, she thought as she heard voices at the entrance and turned to see Nate talking to a group of three women. They were all Texas beauties with straight blond hair and charming accents, and Nate was being his usual flirty self with them.

Had whatever she thought she'd seen in his eyes just been her projecting what she wanted to see?

Most Texas towns prided themselves on their history, and Cole's Hill was no different. Unlike other towns that could trace their history back to the original Spanish land grants, Cole's Hill had been a dusty stop on cattle drives from Houston and little more for a long time. It had gotten steadily bigger in the 1800s and 1900s until it was one of the fastest-growing small towns in the United States by the early 2000s. Today it blended the broader Texas history with the local traditions that had helped build the community.

The five families who'd originally settled in Cole's Hill were still a big part of the town. Nate's family was one of them, and he served on the Cole's Hill Committee along with several other members of the Five Families. This summer's light display was just part of their yearlong heritage celebration.

Something had changed between the time Kinley had left the table and when he met up with her outside the restaurant. She was more subdued than before and seemed to have her barriers up. She wasn't as chatty as she'd been, and he noticed when she spoke she wasn't as animated.

"The light display is being put on by the local community college and high school multimedia programs. We asked them to take the history of the town and turn it into a show. I haven't had a chance to see it yet," Nate said as they walked into the town square.

"It sounds pretty interesting," she said. "How long is it running?"

"Every Friday, Saturday and Sunday evening during May, June and July," he said. "With the new space facility here we are getting a huge surge in population, and we want to make sure that we don't lose anything that makes Cole's Hill special."

He had no idea why he was talking about the town so much when what he wanted to do was tell her how pretty she looked tonight. But instead he was sticking to the safer topic.

At the end of the meal, he'd run into a few of the women he dated casually over the years, and it had made him aware of the fact that those women knew him pretty well and knew what to expect from him. Not one of them had ever looked at him the way Kinley had at dinner—like he was more than just a good time. That look she'd given him was making him want to believe he could be more with her.

"I'm really glad to hear it. Is there a good spot to view it?" she asked.

City hall dominated one side of the square. Two more sides were lined with shops and restaurants. On the fourth side was a mixed-use luxury high-rise that had both offices and penthouse apartments, including his own. The square itself was dotted with trees and benches and a statue of Jake Cole, who had given the town its name. During the war of Texas independence, he'd made a stand here.

"I'm told that anywhere we can see the front face of city hall is good, but I have a special viewing area in mind," he said.

He'd texted his assistant, Ben, and asked him to set up the balcony for them to watch the light show. He put his hand on the small of Kinley's back again, this time spreading his fingers wider to touch more of her.

"Stop doing that."

"What?"

"Touching me. I don't need your hand to steady me," she said.

He dropped his hand, then lifted it up toward her shoulder. "My father raised me to be polite to ladies."

"Well, thank you. I appreciate that," she said. "Where is this spot that you think we should view it from?"

He pointed up to his balcony.

"From your apartment?" she asked.

"It really is a better view," he said. "And I thought we were friends. Surely if Bianca invited you to her place to watch the light show, you'd have no problem with that," he said.

She tipped her head to the side and studied him. She nibbled on her lower lip, which just made him want to groan, as it drew his attention to her kissable mouth. It was full and lush and it didn't matter to him what she said. He always wanted to feel it under his.

"Are you saying that you and Bianca are interchangeable?" she asked.

What? He wasn't even paying attention to anything other than the fact that there was a spark in her eyes as she teased him. Teasing him was a very good sign, and he knew he was one step closer to having her where he wanted her: in his apartment, where he could maybe convince her to give him another shot. Another chance.

"Not at all," he said. "Bianca is a lovely person, but she and I are very different."

He took a step closer to Kinley until barely an inch of space separated them and leaned in closer, giving in to the temptation that had been taunting him all evening. He brushed his lips across hers and felt a jolt go through his entire body. He pulled back, because they were in the square and crowds were starting to build. And what he wanted from Kinley was too private to be shared in public.

"I want something from you that I don't think Bianca does," he said, then put his hand on the small of Kinley's back again and turned her toward his building. She didn't flinch or pull away but just walked next to him.

Five

Kinley stopped thinking about everything and reminded herself she was twenty-six years old. Sometimes she felt ancient, but when Nate kissed her she felt a spark of the young woman she was and she wanted to run with it.

She smiled at several people who looked vaguely familiar as they walked past her. She had a feeling that Nate was her kryptonite, that he was the one man she'd never be able to resist.

She'd been right to have that jolt of fear when Jacs had first told her she was coming back to Cole's Hill. The completely crazy thing she was just now realizing was that her secret about Penny hadn't been the reason for her apprehension.

She knew it wasn't the smartest choice and that tomorrow she'd have to deal with that, but for right now there was a pulsing in her body and an empty ache that she wanted to fill. She walked slightly ahead of him on his left. His hand was like a hot brand on the small of her back as he urged her toward the luxury condo building. When they arrived, the doorman smiled at Nate and greeted him. She was sure Nate answered, because she felt the rumble of his deep voice like a caress against her body, but she didn't really hear the words. They walked across the marble floors in the lobby, and the sound of her Louboutin heels seemed overly loud to her when matched with the heavy footfall of Nate's boots.

"This is a really nice building," she said, inwardly smacking herself for the inane comment.

"It's part of the downtown revitalization project. Most of the city development has taken place on the outskirts, and we didn't want to lose the charm of Cole's Hill."

"It's hard to think of Cole's Hill as so…trendy and metropolitan. When I was growing up here, it felt like a tiny redneck town."

He laughed. "I bet it wasn't just the town that felt that way. Some of the people here are still good old boys, but we've got some style now."

"I can see that," she said.

They had crossed the lobby, and she noticed there were two banks of elevators. Nate steered her toward the ones on the right.

He reached around her with his free hand to hit the elevator button, and as they stepped inside the fingers of his hand dipped lower, brushing against the top of her buttocks.

She shuddered and leaned back as the elevator door closed, enveloping them in a world all their own. He used his hand to push her toward the back of the car and then he stepped in behind her, his chest pressed along her back and his free hand pressed against the wall of the car as he leaned in close to her.

"I want you, Kin," he whispered right into her ear. "It's as if I've never had you and I'm on fire for you."

She shivered again and turned her head to face him. His blue eyes were sincere and she saw there was a flush of arousal on his face.

"I want you, too," she admitted.

"Good," he said, bringing his mouth down on her lips. She opened to him, his tongue brushing over her teeth and tangling with hers. She half turned in his arms and put one hand on his face as he deepened the kiss. There was the slightest hint of a five o'clock shadow on his jaw, and she ran her fingers back and forth over the stubble as he thrust his tongue in and out of her mouth.

She tried to turn more fully into his body, but he lifted his head and stepped back just as the elevator pinged to signal their arrival on his floor. She noted that he had the timing of the ride down and hoped she wasn't making as big a mistake as she had in Vegas.

But honestly, she wanted him. It felt good to be with him, and it had been way too long since anyone had made her feel this way.

Again he put his hand right at the small of her back as they walked off the elevator and down the corridor to his apartment. She heard the lock disengage as they approached and he reached around her to open the door. She stepped inside and away from him, hoping that the break from his touch would bring some clarity.

Was she really doing this?

"Second thoughts?" he asked.

"A few, but I'm still standing right here," she said. She hadn't come up to his apartment just to turn and walk away. "But there is something I should tell you before we go any farther."

He reached for his belt buckle and slowly undid it, then drew the belt through the loops of his jeans, holding it loosely in one hand.

"I remember what you like," he said.

She blushed even harder, and a pulse of liquid desire went through her. Her fantasies had always leaned a little bit toward the dirty side, and Nate had been more than happy to play his part in them with her.

"Not that," she said.

But her mind wasn't on the secret she'd meant to share as he came closer to her. "Put your hands behind your back, Kinley," he said.

His voice was straight out of her hottest dreams, and she turned and did what he asked. He let the thick leather of his belt brush against her skin before he drew her wrists together behind her back and looped the belt around them. He tightened it, but not so firmly that she was uncomfortable. The position drew her shoulders back and pushed her breasts forward. She felt her nipples tighten against the fabric of her bra.

He wrapped one hand around the side of her neck

and shoulder and pushed her slightly forward so that she was almost off balance. His other hand was at the small of her back again, gathering the fabric of the skirt of her dress and drawing it slowly up until she felt the cool air brush against the backs of her thighs and then her butt cheeks. She wore a thong, so when he lowered his hand to cup her it was bare skin on skin.

She felt another one of those liquid pulses in her center and shivered as he held her with one hand on her neck and the other on her ass. He stroked his finger between her legs, tracing the fabric of her thong as he came back up. She felt his finger nestle in her and then skim up to where the lacy waistband was. He hooked his finger in the top of it and drew it slowly down her legs. She felt the heat of his breath against her back through the fabric of her dress, and then he moved lower, nipping against her exposed backside and then kissing the back of her knee. She tottered in her heels.

But he steadied her with both hands at her waist as he pushed her panties to the floor.

"Step out of them," he said.

She did as he commanded, and then his mouth moved back up her body, stopping to kiss and nibble wherever he wanted. He slowly stood up behind her. "Ready to watch the light show?"

She nodded, but honestly the answer was no. She was ready for him to stop teasing her and get down to business, but he just let the fabric of her skirt drop to cover her nakedness and then put his hand on the small of her back and urged her to walk toward the French doors that led to his balcony. He opened the door, and the warmth of the night surrounded her as she stepped out onto the balcony. Her arms behind her back didn't feel awkward at all as he urged her forward toward the railing. He stood behind her, and her fingers brushed over the crotch of his jeans against his erection.

She stroked him through the denim and then fumbled around until she could undo the button and zipper of his jeans. She felt his fingers brush over hers as he reached between them and freed himself from his underwear. The next thing she felt was his hands in her hair sweeping it to one side as he lowered his mouth against the back of her neck. He had one hand on the railing of the balcony and the other lifted up the back of her skirt.

She felt decadent as she realized how exposed they were on the balcony, but no one could see anything other than the two of them pressed together given the height of the balcony and the darkness. They were the only two who knew that his hands were on her naked buttocks and her hands were wrapped around his erection.

She stroked him as the music started to blare in the town square. Then his hand moved around under her skirt to her stomach. He drew her back against him, and his hard length slipped from her fingers to nestle between her legs. His fingers moved lower until he was stroking her most intimate flesh.

She rocked against him, trapped between his erection and his fingers and his mouth on her neck. He suckled the skin at the base of her neck and she shivered and shuddered in his arms. Her eyes closed as the lights in the town square dimmed and the music swelled.

He parted her and tapped his finger against her before he rubbed in a circular motion that made her legs weak. She sagged against him, and he chuckled against her skin.

"You like that?"

She nodded. Words were beyond her at this point. He pulled her back into the curve of his body, his fingers moving lower to plunge in and out of her center. She felt his erection moving between her legs and realized he was going to keep teasing her. She reached lower between his legs and cupped him, teasing him with her fingers and then scraping her nails over the lower part of his shaft until he drew his hips back and took his fingers from between her legs.

She felt his hands on the belt that held her wrists together and then it was off. Before she could do anything, he took both of her hands in his and put them on the railing in front of them. She wrapped her hands around the cool wrought iron and canted her hips back toward him.

Below the images flashed on city hall and the music swelled, but there was a storm brewing inside her that put all of that to shame. Nate had one hand on the small of her back under the fabric of her dress and she turned around to look at him, seeing him holding a condom packet in one hand.

He ripped it open and put it on with one hand then pulled her hips back toward his. She felt his erection slide against her most intimate flesh and then he entered her. He stretched her as he thrust into her, and his other hand went between her legs to fondle her clit. She moaned and tried to make him move inside her, but his hips stayed still as his one finger tapped out a rhythm against her. His mouth was against the side of her neck, and she groaned as she felt her orgasm approaching. She wanted to stop it from coming, but it had been too long and he felt too good.

She groaned again as her climax washed over her and everything inside her clenched, squeezing his erection. He continued to rub her. He started to move, slowly pulling out of her and then plunging back in, deeply. He moved slowly at first and then started going more quickly. She turned her head, trying to find his mouth, and he accommodated her, kissing the side of her neck and then her jaw as he continued to drive himself deep inside her until she felt that tingling along her body and she knew she was about to come again. She did as he continued thrusting and then he gripped her hips, driving hard into her with more intensity. Then she felt him shudder against her back and moan against her neck. He thrust into her a few more times and then wrapped one arm tight around her stomach, holding her to him as he put his other hand on the railing next to hers.

The kisses he dropped on her neck now were softer as he cradled her to him. She closed her eyes and stood there, wrapped in his arms. He was still inside her as the light show concluded.

He finally pulled himself free of her body and then lifted her in his arms, carrying her back into the apartment. She wrapped her arms around his shoulders, put her head against his chest and closed her eyes.

There was no running away from this night and her

actions, and she was honest with herself, admitting she wasn't ready to leave him. Not yet. But she knew she had to talk to him.

She had to tell him about Penny. But when he put her on her feet in the living room, she found it was harder than ever to find the words. She wobbled a little for a second. She felt the moisture between her legs and knew she should excuse herself to go clean up. She caught a glimpse of herself in the mirror and was surprised to see how normal she looked. Her clothes were still in place, her hair just a tiny bit rumpled, but otherwise she looked the same as she had at dinner.

She was the only one who knew how much she'd changed. That the storm that was Nate had once again swept through her life and this time was more unsettling than the last. She hadn't known what she was letting herself in for the last time, but this time…there was no excuse.

He had tucked himself back into his pants and zipped them but left the button undone. His shirt was untucked… He looked more unkempt than she did.

She wanted to believe that this was more than just something physical, but she wasn't naive. Not where he was concerned. He had been too practiced…well, in the elevator. On the balcony that hadn't felt like a routine.

"I missed the light show," she said at last. She glanced around for her purse and saw she'd dropped it by the door, but she didn't remember that. She'd been so focused on Nate when they'd entered his apartment she was only just now taking notice of the decor. It was modern and masculine. There was a Georgia O'Keeffe painting of skulls that dominated the living room wall mounted above a river-stone fireplace. The ceilings were high and vaulted.

"Should I apologize?" he asked. "I hope you still enjoyed yourself."

"You know I did," she said.

He brushed past her, walking toward the kitchen, which was nestled against the wall and opened into the living room. He went to the fridge and took out a bottle of sparkling water before coming back to the breakfast bar and getting two glasses and filling them with water.

"Do you wish things had been different?" he asked.

She shrugged. "I don't regret this."

"Good," he said, holding out one of the glasses to her. She walked over, took it from him and had a sip. "I meant to wait until later, but there is something about you, Kinley…like I said at dinner, you're different from everyone else."

She felt that same spark of hope that this was more than just a good time, but she ruthlessly shoved it back down. One night wasn't going to change Nate any more than one night could change her… But one night had. One night in Vegas had altered her life and made her into the woman she was today.

So one night could have a huge impact.

Was that what was going on with Nate?

She needed to tell him about Penny. Now, so that if this really was a different Nate they'd have a chance to be together. Forever. Or he could let her know that he wasn't interested.

"Do you want to spend the night?" he asked.

"Do you want me to?" she countered. But she knew she couldn't. In fact, this was the perfect opening for her to finally come clean about her daughter. "Don't answer that. I can't stay the night. I have to get home."

"Why?" he asked. "No one is going to be upset if you stay here with me."

She took a deep breath and put her glass down on the countertop. "I have a daughter."

There, she'd said it.

"A daughter?"

"Yes. Her name is Penny, and she's two years old."

He rubbed the back of his neck. "Well, that is a complication."

"It doesn't have to be," she said. "I just thought you should know."

She felt better having told him. He must know by the age that Penny was his.

"I'm guessing the dad is out of the picture."

She stared at him for a moment. Did he think she'd slept with someone else so quickly after she'd been with him?

"Yeah, he is," she said at last. Realizing that even though she thought she knew Nate, he had no clue about her at all. Though she'd partied hard with him, she'd never given herself cheaply or easily to anyone…but Nate.

She was too stunned to say anything else to him or try to explain. How could he think so little of her? Or miss the obvious: that Penny was his daughter.

Six

Memorial Day was a big celebration in Cole's Hill. All of the businesses on Main Street had flags flying and patriotic displays in their front windows. Kinley and Penny were joined by Pippa as they searched for a good spot to see the annual Memorial Day parade.

"I've never been to a parade before," Penny said in a very singsongy voice. From the moment that Penny had woken up this morning she'd been singing everything. She'd insisted on wearing her newest T-shirt that had a horse on it with her red, white and blue–striped shorts. It didn't match and Kinley had thought about arguing with her daughter about her clothing choices but then asked herself why it mattered what Penny wore if the outfit made her happy. So she let her wear it.

"Me, either," Pippa said. Her nanny, a twenty-three-year-old from the UK, had dyed her hair red and blue on the tips in support of Memorial Day.

"Well, I have, and y'all are in for a treat," Kinley said. She led the way toward the studio Jacs had rented for them to use for their business, which was along the parade route. They set up the portable chairs they'd been carrying for the adults and placed a thick picnic blanket on the ground between the chairs for Penny. Kinley started to get settled in when she noticed Bianca and her son walking toward them.

"Hey! Do you mind if we sit with you?" Bianca asked as she approached.

"Not at all," Kinley said. "Bianca, this is Pippa, who helps out with Penny. And this is my daughter, Penny. Everyone, this is Bianca."

"Hiya," Pippa said with a wave.

"Hello," Penny said. "Who's that?"

She pointed to Bianca's son, getting up from her chair and moving closer.

"This is Benito," Bianca said.

Penny and Benito stared at each other for a few minutes and then Kinley heard her daughter start talking about horses. She offered to let Benito share her blanket and her toys.

"May I, mama?" Benito asked.

"Si, changuita," Bianca said, kissing her son on the head as the two kids settled on the blanket.

Bianca set her chair up next to Kinley's.

"Did you just call your son little monkey?" Kinley asked trying to remember the Spanish she'd heard growing up.

"Yes. My *papi* used to call us that when we were little," Bianca said.

"I think I'm going to take a walk while we're waiting for the parade to start and see what the town has to offer," Pippa said. "Wanna come with me, imp?"

"No, Pippy, I'm playing with my new friend," Penny said.

"He can come, too," Pippa said.

"Wanna go?" Penny asked Benito.

He leaned around Penny and looked over at Bianca, who nodded at him. "*Si.*"

"*Si?* What's that mean?" Penny asked.

"Yes," he said. They both clambered to their feet and Pippa held out her hands to the kids, leading them toward some of the tents that had been set up along the parade route.

"What happened the other night with Nate Caruthers?" Bianca asked as soon as they were alone. "Are you two dating?"

Kinley should have been ready to have people ask about her and Nate. Cole's Hill was getting big and more cosmopolitan, but the Five Families all knew each other's business and Nate and Bianca were both part of that group.

"I don't know," she answered honestly, though she probably should have said no and then meant it. She couldn't date a man who was the father of her child but didn't know it.

Of course, that was easier to commit to when Nate wasn't around and she wasn't thinking about him. Just thinking about the other night made her pulse race and her skin feel more sensitive. She remembered everything they'd done together. For a moment she wished she'd never brought Penny up and had spent the night with him.

"That sounds interesting," Bianca said. "If I'm being too nosy just tell me, but I'm so tired of only talking about shows on PBS Kids and I need something adult and gossipy to remind me there is life outside of my son."

Kinley laughed. "You should start working. I think it's the only thing that saved me when Penny was born. I mean, I had to work—not like you—but it gave me something to think about instead of worrying if I could raise her on my own."

"My parents have suggested I start working as well, which is why I'm interviewing at the Caruthers, Parker and Zevon Surgical Group on Monday. I remember how much your job changed you," Bianca said. "The tone in your emails changed. You seemed…in a better place."

"I was," Kinley said. It was ironic that the job that had saved her from dwelling on Nate and his absence in her life was directly responsible for bringing them back together. "Benito is cute as a button."

"So is Penny. She seems to really love horses," Bianca said. "Have you had her out at the Rockin' C?"

"No. Not yet. I've been busy with the wedding planning. Jacs didn't want to send me out here for just one client and has been arranging for new clients all over the state. I'm pretty sure she has no idea how big the state of Texas is. She wanted me to drive down to Galveston to check out a venue in the morning and see a client in Dallas for lunch."

Bianca laughed. "Did you set her straight?"

"I tried," Kinley said. "But she mentioned she was trying to find me a private plane so I could get to all the appointments. Next week is going to be very busy for me."

"Wow, sounds like it. Don't you miss Penny when you're traveling for work?" Bianca asked.

Kinley knew her friend meant well and wasn't being critical of her, but she still felt a twinge of guilt...something she thought all working mothers must experience. "I do miss her, which is why Jacs is arranging for the plane. She knows that I like to be home every night for either dinner or bedtime with Penny."

"I didn't mean anything by that," Bianca said. "Everyone keeps telling me to give Beni some breathing space and to get a job. Mainly because of everything with Jose's death. They think it's not healthy for either of us. No one really gets what it's like to be the only one there for him."

"I do. From the moment I found out I was pregnant it's just been me. Sometimes I don't make the best decisions, but they are the only ones I can make," she said. The guilt that had been a knot in her stomach since she'd returned loosened a little bit.

"That's really all we can do. I didn't realize Penny's father had been gone from the beginning. Is he dead?" Bianca asked.

"No. He just didn't want to listen when I tried to tell him he had a child," Kinley said.

Luckily Pippa and the kids came back then so she could stop thinking about Nate and how she was going to tell him about Penny. And what impact that was going to have on all of their lives.

Memorial Day was a huge deal on the Rockin' C ranch. Everyone had been given the day off after the morning chores were completed. After all, cattle didn't know it was a holiday. Most of the ranch hands and their families were in town watching the Cole's Hill annual parade and then they would be back for a barbecue by the Samson Lake. One of Nate's ancestors had named the lake after he'd been wronged by a woman and felt like Samson.

The lake had started life as a fishing hole and been dug out and expanded to its current size, which was big enough for fishing and water sports. A creek that ran off a spur of the Guadalupe River fed it. There was a dock with seating for about twenty and two speedboats that were set up for taking the ranch staff and the families out tubing or water skiing.

Marcus Quinten, Kinley's dad, was in charge of the annual fest and was supervising his team at the grills. Nate had stayed behind to help out as well but also because he'd wanted to talk to Marcus and try to learn more about the guy who had fathered Kinley's child.

Marcus was getting older and his brown hair was mostly gray now. He was still one of the strongest men on the ranch, but at fifty-two he was getting a little soft around the middle. He shaved every Sunday, so today he was clean shaven but by the end of the week stubble would be covering his cheeks. He was a genius with horses, and there were days when Nate thought that Marcus could forget more about ranching in a day than he'd ever know in a lifetime.

"Just get the pits going," Marcus said as Nate walked over to him. Marcus had served in the military right after high school, just one stint before coming to Cole's Hill and being hired on a ranch hand. "I think this year is going to be one of our best. Our beef was superb this year."

"We got top dollar for it. Your new breeding and grazing program is paying off. Thanks," Nate said.

"That's what you pay me for, son," Marcus said.

A twinge of guilt went through him at Marcus's nickname for him. He hadn't been a very good honorary son to Marcus. Not when it came to Kinley. He had a lot of respect and admiration for Marcus, but there had always been that crazy, wild part of him that he'd never been able to control.

"Marcus, mind if I ask you a question?"

"Not at all," Marcus said, straightening his cowboy hat. He looked over at Nate with those same dark brown eyes that Kinley had.

"What do you know about the father of Kinley's kid?" Nate asked.

Marcus inhaled sharply and then put his hands on his hips. "Why do you want to know?"

"I like your daughter. I'd like to ask her out, but I wanted to make sure there wasn't someone else in the picture," Nate said, which was pretty damned close to the truth.

Marcus nodded slowly and then gestured for Nate to follow him, leading him away from the ranch hands who were tending the grills. Marcus walked up the dock and stood there at the end staring out at the lake. The sound of the water lapping against the pilings that held the dock up was the only thing to break the silence.

Finally Marcus turned to him. "I don't know a damned thing about the father. Only that when she asked him if he wanted to be a part of their lives, he said no. She's been on her own since."

Nate thought that guy must be a big asshole to not want to be in his kid's life but then wondered how he would have reacted almost three years ago if she'd told him he was going to be the father of a child. He hadn't been ready to settle down or even be serious about one woman.

"What a jerk," Nate said.

"Well, I had some other words I used to describe him, but that works," Marcus said, turning to fully face Nate. "I don't mind if you date my daughter, Nathaniel. I've known you since you were born and you might be a little wild, but underneath all that I've always believed you are a decent man. But she's been screwed over enough, so make sure whatever your intentions are, she knows them up front. I won't hesitate to come after you like I wanted to go after the sumbitch that knocked her up and left her behind."

Nate respected that. He had no intention of leading Kinley on. He didn't know what the future held for the two of them but he intended to let her know exactly what he wanted right from the start.

"Fair enough, sir."

* * *

Penny ended up sitting on Kinley's lap during most of the parade, while Bianca held Benito. Kinley watched the parade and felt a keen sense of longing for her hometown, which was silly, since she was sitting right here in it. But she knew that in six months she'd be heading back to Las Vegas and her old life.

While Vegas was very good at putting on a show, there was nothing like this. She had seen people she'd known as a kid and new friends she'd made through Penny's day care. She had a sense of civic pride that she hadn't realized she was missing. This town felt like a community, one she wanted to be a part of.

It would be difficult to start a business on her own and just move here. So she wasn't sure what she really wanted. Plus there was the fact that she might not really want to stay, depending on Nate's reaction when she told him about Penny. But for this moment she wished she could.

As the parade ended, Kinley gathered together their stuff while Benito and Penny both continued talking to each other and comparing the candy and toys they'd caught during the parade.

"Mama, can I go with Benito to a barbie?" Penny asked.

"Do you mean a barbecue?" Kinley asked her daughter, smiling down at her.

She nodded vigorously, her red ponytail bobbing up and down.

Kinley glanced over at Bianca. "Are you having people over?"

"Not me. We are going to the Rockin' C barbecue. Aren't you going?" Bianca asked.

Her father was in charge of the annual event and had asked them to come out there for it. But since she'd been trying to figure out how to tell Nate about his daughter before he met Penny, she'd thought she should skip it.

"I wasn't going to."

Bianca shrugged. "It's up to you, but my brothers are going to be there. If you aren't going to date Nate, maybe one of them will interest you."

Kinley shook her head. Life was crazy enough already without adding another guy to the mix. "I remember your brothers when they used to torment us as kids."

"They've turned out pretty good," Bianca said with a wink. "I know how to keep them in line now."

"I bet you do," Kinley said.

"Mama? Can we go?" Penny asked, tugging on the hem of Kinley's shorts.

She looked down into her daughter's face and saw the hope and expectation and wanted to say yes. But she was afraid.

It was the first time in a really long time that she'd felt this kind of fear. The last time had been right after she'd brought Penny home from the hospital and her daughter wouldn't stop crying all night. Kinley had been scared that she would ruin Penny's life with her ignorance when it came to mothering.

"Hmm… I'm not sure. We had plans to go to the movies this afternoon," Kinley said. "Are you sure you want to miss that?"

"Yes," Penny said. "I really, really, really want to go."

Knowing that Bianca would probably be suspicious if she made up some excuse not to go out to the Rockin' C and might even ask questions that Kinley didn't want to answer, she decided to give in. She'd try to locate Nate and talk to him before he saw Penny.

"Okay."

"Yay! Thank you, Mama," Penny said, throwing her arms around Kinley's legs and hugging her tightly. Penny turned back to Benito. "I can go."

The two kids chatted all the way up Main Street and it was only when they got to the cars that they hugged each other and waved goodbye.

Pippa helped Kinley buckle Penny into the car seat and then turned to her out of earshot of her daughter. "I thought we were avoiding the Rockin' C at all costs."

"We were. But I didn't want to make Bianca think I was avoiding something. It's bad enough that Dad is on me for not coming out to the ranch," Kinley said. "I'm going to try to find Nate and tell him when we get there. Do you mind keeping a close eye on Penny? I imagine she's going to want to hang out with Benito."

"I got your back, Kin. Whatever you need, I'll be there for you and Penny. You two are like family to me."

Impulsively Kinley hugged Pippa. "It's the same for us. I don't know how I would have managed the last two years without you."

"To be honest, me, either," Pippa said. "Now let's go see what a real American barbecue is like. I've never been to one."

"It's loud and fun and hot. The food will be delicious and I recommend you try it all. My dad has a secret rub he makes for the meat…he's really good at that," Kinley said.

They got in the car and started to drive out to the ranch. Penny was playing an interactive game on her tablet and wearing her headphones as they drove.

"You don't talk about him much," Pippa said.

"I know," Kinley said. She and her dad had been close until her mom had moved them to California after the divorce. After her mom died, they'd started talking again, and maybe they would have had a chance to be closer if it weren't for that weekend with Nate.

After Nate had told her what happened in Vegas needed to stay there, Kinley had been too embarrassed to think of visiting Cole's Hill and her father ever again. And of course having Penny had just given her one more reason to stay away. Her father had come to Vegas twice but those were always very brief visits usually around the Professional Bull Riding finals that were always in Vegas.

"He's a good guy and wants to protect me and Penny. But I know I can't tell him about Nate, because it could cost him his job. Which is the last thing I'd want. So I've kept him at arm's length."

"That secret is taking over your entire life," Pippa said. "Just like mine did before I ran away from England. Are you sick of it? I know I am."

"Yes. But telling the truth is harder than I ever thought it would be."

Seven

The DJ had been flown in from Nashville and was blasting a mix of old country classics that had formed the soundtrack to Nate's childhood, like George Jones, Bocephus and Willie Nelson, as well as newer artists like Florida Georgia Line, Zac Brown Band and Kenny Chesney. Right now "Sinner" was playing, and he and his brothers were all doing their rowdiest singing along with Aaron Lewis while their dad chimed in on Willie Nelson's parts.

Nate had spent the morning on the water, taking kids and ranch hands tubing behind the speedboat. He'd lost his shirt along the way and as the afternoon lengthened into twilight he had started drinking. He'd caught a glimpse of Kinley earlier, but his talk with Marcus had made him realize that rushing things with her probably wasn't a good idea.

His dad had his long hair pulled back in a ponytail and looked like the redneck hippie he'd always been. He had been drinking hard as well, and when the song changed to George Jones's "He Stopped Loving Her Today," his mom had come to grab his dad and claim a dance. Nate and his brothers just sat down on the edge of one of the bales of hay that had been set up around the dance floor and watched them.

"Look at them. Still crazy for each other after all these years," Ethan said. There was a hint of wistfulness in his voice.

Nate felt that same longing deep inside, and he realized that all his running around had been to fill up the need for this thing his parents had found. He hadn't really recognized that until this moment. He scanned the crowds and saw Kinley again on the other side of the dance floor talking to Hector Velasquez. Then she threw her head back and laughed at something Hector said and Nate was on his feet before he realized what he was doing.

He didn't stop as he wove his way through the crowd and over to where Kinley was.

"Excuse me, Hector, the lady and I are going to dance," Nate said, putting his hand on Kinley's hip and turning her toward the dance floor.

"We are?" she asked as he pulled her into his arms and started doing his version of a country waltz around the dance floor.

God, he'd missed her. Her face showed the effects of being out in the sun all day, and a few tendrils of her red hair had escaped her braids and curled around her face and neck.

She wore a pair of white shorts that ended midthigh and showed off her legs. They were long and skinny and he remembered exactly how good it had felt when he was between them. His erection stirred as he danced her around to the music, and he realized that this was what he'd been missing in his life—this feeling of excitement that he only got when he was with Kinley.

"Yes, ma'am," he said. "I owe you something nice after the way things ended the other night."

"I don't think you owe me anything," she said. "Actually, I was hoping to run into you today."

"You were?" he asked, pulling her closer to him as the music changed to "Sangria" by Blake Shelton. Nate put his hands on her hips as she wrapped her arms around his shoulders. Nate lowered his head toward hers and looked down into her eyes. He wanted her. He might have had a few too many beers this afternoon, but nothing was clouding his judgment right now.

"I was. I wanted to talk to you again."

"I want something from you, too," he said, kissing her neck as he danced them off the floor toward a secluded area away from the crowd where they could still hear the music.

She looked up at him. "I'd like that, too."

"Good. We always seem to be on the same page romantically," he said. It was one of the things he really liked about Kinley. She wasn't coy about wanting him and never played games.

"We do. But we need to talk first," she said. "I don't want it to be like last time."

He didn't, either.

"Where's your daughter?" he asked.

"She went with Bianca. Her son is about Penny's age and they wanted to hang out."

"I'm looking forward to meeting her. But let's find somewhere to talk." He took Kinley's hand and led her farther from the crowds down the path that wrapped around the lake. He was careful to stay on the lighted path as he led the way to the old homestead cabin.

"Where are we going?"

"Somewhere we can be alone," he said. "Do you remember the old homestead cabin?"

"That creaky, falling-apart shack that you and your brothers used to dare me to go into?" she asked.

"Yeah, that one. A few years ago we had it redone. It's still rustic and authentic-looking, but it no longer creaks and has all the modern conveniences. I lived in it for a while," Nate said.

"Why?"

"Dad and I were butting heads about the business and fighting a lot. It was before I bought the penthouse in town," Nate said.

"What were you fighting about?"

"Dad was stuck in the old ways of doing business. He sent me to business school and I have an MBA, but he was still treating me like his second in command even though I…well, I wanted to be in charge. Finally, he decided to retire and then I took over."

"When was that?" she asked.

"Right about when I got back from that weekend in Vegas with you, Kin," Nate said. "He decided to step down, and I knew it was going to take a lot of work to make the changes I wanted at the ranch and in the Rockin' C business. Not making excuses for what I said to you, but I just wanted you to know where I was in my life back then."

Kinley's heart was beating too fast as she stepped into the cabin after Nate. She wanted to tell him where she'd been in her life, but the words just wouldn't come. He went to turn on the air-conditioning as she looked around the one-room cabin. It had been enlarged and the kitchen was to the right of the door, with an old 1950s stove against the wall and an open-front china hutch. There were mugs and matching blue-and-white plates in the slots above them. There was a chandelier with wicker lamp shades that complimented the wrought-iron base over the butcher-block island in the kitchen.

She turned to her left and saw a king-size bed with a wrought-iron headboard and a thick hunter's plaid bedspread on it. She skipped past the bed, but her pulse had sped up at the sight of it.

Next was a fireplace that would be cozy in winter with two rocking chairs positioned in front of it, and then an antique postmaster's desk in the corner with a big leather chair.

"I like it. It's not creepy at all," she said. "Looks like it's your little love nest."

Nate rubbed the back of his neck. "I'm not going to lie to you, Kinley. I've had a lot of women in here over the years, but since you…well, it hasn't been the same. Every time I close my eyes, I've seen you."

She wanted to believe that. She wanted it more than

she wanted just about anything else, but she'd been lied to before. She'd bought his lines one time…though to be fair, he'd never promised her anything other than a weekend. It had been her own hopeful heart that had painted in the rest of that fantasy, weaving her hopes and dreams into something Nate wasn't able to provide.

But he was here now.

She wanted to tell him the truth about Penny but the words were trapped in her throat.

He stood there in a pair of navy swim trunks that hung off his hips. His chest was bare, suntanned and muscled from a lifetime of work. He looked more like a cowboy today than the CEO she'd seen in town, but either way he was Nate Caruthers, the one man who was more like her Achilles' heel than she wanted to admit.

"It doesn't matter. I was just being difficult because when I'm around you all the stuff I tell myself I'm not going to do, I end up doing," she said.

She knew she couldn't be with him again. Not until she told him about Penny. But he had tipped his head to the side and canted his hips toward her as he stood there watching her.

"Did you promise yourself you wouldn't let me kiss you?"

He was hard to resist. She arched both eyebrows at him and tried to look prim and proper. "Yes, I did."

"I guess I should be a gentleman and not try to tempt you," he said, walking toward her with intent in his eyes.

"You should," she said, but she took a step forward to meet him. And then they were standing close together, as close as when they'd been dancing, and she could smell his cologne and his sweat and the faintest whiff of barbecue sauce. He lowered his head toward hers and she had plenty of time to back away, but she wanted this. She wanted to be with Nate one more time before she told him about Penny and everything changed.

She knew some people might say she was being selfish, but she'd taken very little for herself in the last three years. She had focused on raising Penny and starting a career, and she wanted this for herself. The other night on the balcony had been fire and passion.

This was deliberate. It was her taking what she wanted with Nate because she had missed him. His mouth was full and sensual and he moved it over hers with intent, his hands skimming up and down her back as he drew her closer to him.

Their hips brushed against each other, and she felt the tip of his erection rub over her center. He was humming the song they'd danced to as he moved his body against hers, and she realized that she was starting to fall for him.

He was complex and complicated and absolutely the last thing she needed in her life at this moment, but she wanted him—and even more important, she liked him. She could see a future for herself and Nate together once she finally told him about their daughter.

What if he rejected her when he found out that he was Penny's father? What if he couldn't understand why she'd kept silent? What if he didn't realize that telling him now was the only option she had left? She pulled her mouth from his and looked up into those blue-gray eyes, and her heartbeat was so loud in her ears that she couldn't hear Nate when he spoke.

"What?"

"Isn't that what you wanted from me?" he asked.

It was. But she knew the guilt inside her would keep on growing unless she told him her secret.

"It is. But I wanted to talk to you. I have something you need to hear first," she said. "It's important."

He took her hand in his and drew it to his chest. He held it over his heart, and she felt the steady beat under her hand. He rubbed her hand over his body, down over his rib cage and his rock-hard stomach and lower, to his erection.

"More important than this?" he asked then pulled her back into his arms, kissing her slowly and deeply and seducing her with his body.

His kisses said not to worry about anything and that this was going to make everything okay between them. And though she knew it wouldn't, she wrapped her hand around his erection and her free arm around his shoulders and met his passion with her own.

Talking had never made anything better as far as Nate was concerned. Especially not with Kinley. He lifted her off her feet, one arm right under her buttocks and the other around her back, swung her around and walked toward the bed. He'd been living here when they'd hooked up in Vegas, and in the nightstand was a picture of the two of them from their first night together. They'd gone into one of those photo booths and he had a strip of four photos of the two of them. He tried to avoid looking at it, because it had always stirred up regret. Despite what he'd told her, he hadn't brought any other women here. This place reminded him of the time he'd had with Kinley in Vegas, and the last thing he'd wanted to do was to have another woman interfere with that.

He turned so that he sat down on the edge of the bed and she straddled his lap. Lifting his mouth from hers, he reached for the buttons of her blouse and undid them slowly.

She put her hands on his shoulders at first as he took her blouse off and undid her bra before tossing it aside. Her skin was so soft and creamy and her torso was covered in freckles. He leaned forward, licking one of the bigger ones just above her left breast. He put his hands on her tiny waist and rubbed his thumbs up and down against her body.

She sat back on his thighs, her shoulders back and her spine arched, and he looked at her and caught his breath. Logically he knew there might be women as beautiful as her in the world, but when he looked at her, for the life of him, he couldn't remember seeing anyone as breathtaking as Kinley.

His hands looked too big and rough as he caressed the side of her neck and then her collarbone. He drew his finger down her arm and noticed that her nipple beaded as his hand came closer to her breast. She shifted on his lap as he cupped one breast in his hand and leaned forward to lightly lick her nipple.

She put her hands on either side of his head and held him to her. Her back arched even more, and her hips were rubbing against his thighs. She made a soft little sound in the back of her throat that drove him wild.

His swim trunks were too tight against his erection,

and he lifted his head and shifted her off his lap to her feet. He undid the button latch of her shorts and then slowly lowered the zipper, drawing her shorts and then her panties down her legs. She stepped out of both of them. Her hands went to the tie fastening of his swim trunks, and soon they were both naked. He lifted her back onto his lap as he sat back down on the bed.

She scooted forward and wrapped her arm around his shoulders as the tip of his erection nestled against her center. She was warm and wet and ready for him and it was only as he felt her nakedness on him that he realized he didn't have a condom close by.

"Dammit," he said. "Wrap your arms and legs around me."

She did as he asked, and he stood up and walked the short distance to the bathroom, which was the only room with a door in the open-plan cabin. He set her down on the countertop as he reached around her to the medicine cabinet and found the box of condoms there. He shook one out and Kinley caught it.

She tore open the packet and put the condom on him and then shifted so that he was poised at the opening of her body. He made a shallow thrust into her and then drew back, lowering his mouth to her nipple and sucking on it as he drove his hips forward, plunging fully into her body this time.

He felt her nails on his back and her legs tighten around his hips as the rhythm between them intensified. He put one hand between their bodies and rubbed her clit as he kept up the pace until he felt her tightening around him. Shivers went down his spine and he lifted his head from her breasts, tightening his hold on her as their mouths found each other.

He sucked her tongue into his mouth as he drove into her harder and faster. She bit the tip of his tongue and tore her mouth from his, crying out his name. He felt her clamping down on him.

Every muscle in his body was tense and he was driving into her, focused on the sensation of her long limbs wrapped around him and her center pulsing around his length. Then he felt that feathering along his spine as he started to come. He buried his face against her neck and pushed into her three more times until he felt empty.

He kept thrusting a few more times because it felt so good. Her arms loosened around his shoulders and she stroked her hands up and down his back. When he turned his head on her shoulder, she was looking down at hm.

There was something in her eyes that looked like... well, he wasn't too sure, but it was a mix of sensual satisfaction and something a little bit like apprehension. He wondered if she was worried he'd ask more questions about her past.

He hated to see that look on her face, so he lifted her off the sink and carried her to his bed and held her in his arms. He just held her, not talking, until he started to drift off to sleep. He wasn't sure how long he slept, but when he woke Kinley was gone and he was alone again.

Eight

Kinley was so ready to be back in Las Vegas. Especially after the other night with Nate, when she'd left him sleeping at the cabin because she'd chickened out. Since then she'd been busy with work, and if she were being completely honest, with avoiding him. She'd stayed away from the downtown area where she knew his offices were. So when the opportunity to fly with a few of her brides-to-be to Vegas for dress shopping arose, she'd jumped on it.

Penny and her nanny made the trip as well. Now they were back in Kinley's home in Henderson enjoying playdates with Penny's friends and giving Pippa a chance to meet up with some of her friends.

Ferrin, Joie, who was engaged to the professional basketball player, and Meredith, who's fiancé was a Dallas Cowboy, along with their closest friends, mothers and soon-to-be mothers-in-law were all staying in suites at the Chimera Hotel, and Kinley had about thirty minutes before the brides were due to arrive. They'd landed last night and Kinley had been in Jacs's showroom since six this morning getting it set up for the dress shopping. They had accounts with all of the major designers, and since Jacs did a lot of business with them, they were always sent the latest designs.

Kinley thought it was funny that she worked as a wedding planner since the bride fantasy had never really been one of hers. She'd been a tomboy more into daydreaming about winning a rodeo buckle or living on an island with wild horses than planning her perfect wedding day.

But as she moved through a sea of ivory, cream and pure white dresses, fingering the satin and lace, she did sort of feel a little bit of longing. Since the moment she'd hung up the phone with Nate a few years ago and realized that he wasn't going to be in her life, she'd focused on having her baby and being a single mom.

She thought she'd put away her dreams of a white wedding with all of her friends and family looking on, but she was starting to wish it was her trying on dresses.

"Well, kid, looks like Texas didn't kill you," Jacs said as she swept into the room in a cloud of Chanel perfume wearing an all-white pantsuit and waving her manicured fingers at Kinley.

Kinley turned to look at her boss, trying to school her features into something confident and nonchalant.

But she noticed the concern on Jacs's face and realized she hadn't been quick enough.

"What happened?"

"Nothing that matters to the job. I'm killing it as a bridal planner," Kinley said.

Jacs put her arm around Kinley's shoulders and drew her over to one of the love seats that had been positioned all over the room. There were actually five dressing rooms in this area and each would be used for a different bridal party. The teams from the design houses would be making their way through the rooms so that each bride would have private attention.

"What happened?"

Kinley looked at Jacs. She was her boss, but they were also friends. "I don't think you'd understand. I made another one of the stupid, impulsive decisions that will have consequences, and I don't know how to fix it."

"Why wouldn't I understand?" Jacs asked.

"Because you're smart."

Jacs threw her head back and laughed with that loud, booming sound that made Kinley smile despite the fact that her life was one big mess at the moment.

"I wish I was as smart as you think I am. I'm guessing this problem involves a man, given that you didn't want to go to Texas and now you're saying things are a mess."

She took a deep breath and held it.

"You really don't want me to get into this," Kinley said.

"Hon, you are more than an employee. When you came in here looking for a job with just your sense of style and that tiny baby, I took a chance on you because I saw something more—a determination to make a good life for yourself and your baby. There's nothing you can say that will change my opinion of you," Jacs said.

"Penny's father is one of our clients' brothers. I never told him," Kinley said, looking down at her hands and neatly crossed legs. There were no chips in her manicure. If only she were as calm and put together on the inside as she was on the outside.

"Did you try to tell him? Is he an ass? Is this a problem? Will it affect our client's wedding?"

Jacs's quick-fire questions made Kinley's head spin. "Yes. Sometimes. Yes. And I hope not," she answered. "I thought telling him about Penny and how old she was would make him realize she was his daughter and if not, I'd just tell him. But instead he asked me if the dad was still in the picture… Jacs, he thought I was with another guy almost at the same time I was with him."

Jacs squeezed her closed. "Men can be dimwitted. Maybe he didn't realize when you would have had to be pregnant to have Penny. You should try to tell again."

Kinley nodded. "I know. I'm planning to. And it's even more complicated, because Nate's mom is so sweet and she told me how she wants grandchildren and I know she has one…"

Jacs put her hands on Kinley's as she nervously twisted her fingers together. It was funny that Kinley had been able to be confident when she was by herself, but having her friend and mentor here with her gave her a chance to talk about all the things that were weighing on her mind.

"She is always going to have that grandchild. You already said you are going to let the father know, and then she will have a chance to build the relationship. If there is one thing I know for sure about you, Kinley Quinten, it's that you are unstoppable when you make up your mind. You'll make this work."

She knew Jacs was right. A lot of people—her friends and even her dad—had expressed concern about her being able to raise a child on her own, but she hadn't let them dissuade her from having her daughter and finding a well-paying job. And on most days she did a really good job of being a mother.

"You're right. Thanks, Jacs. I needed that."

Jacs winked at her as she stood up. "We all need someone in our corner who sees our strengths. It's way too easy for us to focus on the negatives at times. I've got Willa coming in and I'm here to help out, too. Which one of us do you want with which bride?"

Kinley and Jacs finished talking business and were ready when the first bride arrived. It was Ferrin, accompanied by her mom and Nate's mom, along with Ferrin's maid of honor, Gabi de la Cruz. This time Kinley didn't feel swamped by guilt when she saw Ma Caruthers, and as she shepherded the party into one of the dressing rooms she noticed Jacs watching her and gave her friend the thumbs-up sign. She would figure out how to make this work. As Jacs had said, she was smart and capable. But somehow all of those things seemed to fly out the window when Nate was in the picture.

* * *

Los Angeles was a far cry from Cole's Hill, and as much as Nate loved to travel, he was glad this was his last night away from Texas. He had come to Ethan's Beverly Hills office to sign a new contract with a long-running television series that liked to use part of the Rockin' C for exterior shots and some on-location filming. He was having dinner tonight with Ethan and Hunter at a trendy new restaurant. A few of his brothers' friends—Kingsley Buchanan and Manu Barrett, whom Hunter knew from his NFL playing days, and Hayden McBride, a partner in the same firm as Ethan—had joined them.

The group was boisterous. There was a lot of good-natured teasing of King and Hunter, who were both recently engaged. King had an adorable three-year-old son who was spending the month was his maternal grandparents. Nate had caught a glimpse of Conner, King's son, earlier when King and Hunter had video called him. Hunter was very close to them both.

Nate had never paid much attention to kids, but given that Kinley was still on his mind and now that he'd had a week to think about things, he realized he should have talked to her more about her daughter after she'd brought the subject up. He was jealous of the man who was the baby's father. It seemed to him that he must have had a powerful hold on Kinley to talk her into bed after Nate had left Vegas… and, well, rejected her.

"Tell me about being a dad," Nate said to King once dinner was over and they'd arrived at a cigar club Manu had recommended.

"What do you want to know?"

Nate shrugged. "I'm sort of dating a girl who has a kid."

"Wow. That's not like you at all," King said.

"Which is why I'm asking you about kids," Nate said. Already he was regretting this. It wouldn't be long until King told Hunter and then Hunter would tell his brothers and everyone would know about him and Kinley. Not that he was hiding her or anything, but he would have liked to have sorted things out privately before his entire family guessed that he had a thing for her.

"What do I need to know? She said her daughter is two. The dad is out of the picture…hell, I'm not really even sure when he was last in the picture."

"Did you ask her about him?"

"Just if he was still around. Why?" Nate asked, leaning back against the thickly upholstered bench and taking a puff of his cigar.

"Women always wanted to know about Conner's mom. I think they were being careful to make sure she wasn't still in the picture. I was pretty up front about everything, telling them I was a widower, mentioning the cloud of doubt that was hanging around me from the Frat House Murder."

Hunter's college girlfriend had been murdered after a frat party and Hunter and his best friend Kingsley had been questioned in connection to the crime. The culprit hadn't been caught for ten years and the stigma of the suspicion of being a murderer had hung around King and Hunter until the actual murderer had been caught last year.

"She said she had a kid and I asked if the dad was still in the picture. I didn't want to know too much about the dude since I'm pretty sure Kinley hooked up with him after—" Nate broke off. He hadn't meant to share any of that. But he knew the guy had to have come along pretty soon after he and Kinley had been together in Vegas. And he didn't blame her for moving on. He'd pretty much told her it was that weekend and then goodbye.

But knowing she'd found someone else so quickly… well, it stung. It didn't matter that he knew he had no right to be upset or angry about it. He still was.

"Well…I'd ask her about him. He might be dead or he might be making child support payments. I'm sure Ethan will tell you the same thing. Legally, you should know what is going on."

Nate already had plans to talk to Ethan about it if things moved forward with him and Kinley. "Thanks, but what I really want to know is how to treat a kid. Can they talk when they are that young? I don't want to be awkward and freak the kid out."

King started laughing, which drew the attention of everyone else in their group, who demanded to know what was so funny. And of course King told them. Hunter came over to Nate, draping his arm around his brother's shoulder. "Why didn't you come to me? I know all about this thanks to Conner."

"Because you can be an ass when you think you know more than me," Nate said. Plus, he hadn't really been ready to talk about Kinley or anything else until he'd seen King talking to his son.

Nate wasn't getting domestic and he sure as hell wasn't sure he wanted to settle down, but he knew he was going to see Kinley again and that meant figuring out how to deal with her kid.

"Just give me some clue of how to deal with kids," Nate said. "Kinley has a two-year-old girl."

Hunter leaned in close. "It's easy, Nate. Kids are the world's greatest BS monitors, she'll know if you're being fake. Just relax and do your thing. She'll react better to you the more honest you are."

"Honest how?"

King leaned over. "Don't be fake nice to her because you want her to like you so you can hook up with her mom. That's what Hunter is saying. It's better to just leave the kid out of the picture if you can't get along with her. I dated a woman for a very short time who had a son Conner's age, but we just never connected and eventually the relationship ended."

Everyone else shared stories of dating, and though he wasn't a huge fan of sharing details of his personal life, Nate felt much better about meeting Kinley's daughter after talking about it with the guys. And he knew he was going to have to get some answers about the father of the baby at some point. But he figured it was better to do one thing at a time.

Kinley got home late from a long day and Pippa was waiting at the door for her. Today she wore her dark hair in a bob with purple-tinged ends. She had a small nose ring and always wore the brightest red lipstick that Kinley had ever seen. They were more like friends than boss and employee since they were only a few years apart in age, and more importantly they both were carrying around big secrets.

Pippa was on the run from her family in the UK. Having decided not to marry the wealthy aristocrat her family had selected for her, she'd escaped to Las Vegas, assumed a new identity and had been struggling to get work when Kinley met her. Kinley had been nine months pregnant, her water had broken and she'd been freaking out when Pippa had stepped up to help her.

A strong bond had been forged between the women and working for Kinley enabled Pippa to stay off the grid and away from the private investigators that her family had looking for her.

"Penny is in a mood today. She's cranky and I think she might be getting in one of her molars. I need a drink and a break."

"You've got it. I could use some Mommy and Penny time," Kinley said. "Are you going out?"

"Not likely," Pippa said. "I spotted a guy at the airport who I thought might be following me, and I'm pretty sure I saw him at the park when Penny was playing today. I wonder if I've been caught."

Kinley hugged her friend. "Let me see Penny and then we'll figure this out. Go and get yourself some wine and sit by the pool."

"Thanks, Kin."

"No problem," Kinley said. It was nice to have someone else's problems to worry about instead of just her own. Pippa had lived with them since Penny was born and Kinley considered her a heart sister.

She went down the hall to Penny's bedroom, and as soon as she stepped inside she saw what Pippa had meant. All of Penny's stuffed animals and dolls were lined up facing the wall.

"Hey, sweet girl," Kinley said as she walked into the room. "What's going on here?"

"Hi, Mama," Penny said. "Someone was bad."

"Want to tell me about it?" Kinley asked as she came into the room and sat down next to Penny. Kinley dropped a kiss on the top of her daughter's head, and as she did so she noticed that there were marks on the wall in front of Penny's toys. Kinley leaned in for a closer look and realized it was lipstick.

"Did you write on the wall with lipstick?" she asked.

Penny shook her head back and forth. "Not me. But one of them."

Kinley had spoken with her daughter about lying before. Every time Penny got in trouble there was usually a stuffed animal to blame. "Who do you think did it?"

"Mr. Beans," she said. The large fluffy bunny rabbit was dressed in overalls that had jelly beans on it. He was the closest to the lipstick stains on the wall, and as Kinley leaned over she noticed that it looked as if Mr. Beans had tried putting the lipstick on himself. And then she groaned when she realized it was the expensive tube of Marc Jacobs lipstick that she'd splurged on last month.

"I think someone had to help Mr. Beans," Kinley said to Penny. "Someone who knows where Mama keeps her lipstick. And who may have tried one on this morning when Mama was getting ready."

Penny stared up at her with those wide gray-blue eyes of hers. Kinley kept her stare level until finally Penny ducked her head. "It was me."

Kinley put her finger under her daughter's chin. "I know. How did it happen?"

"During nap time," Penny said.

Kinley knew that Penny slept in Kinley's bed during nap time because she liked to be closer to her. Pippa usually worked on an anonymous blog she wrote that focused on commentary on high-end fashion and beauty during that time.

"So you finished up your nap and decided to do Mr. Beans's makeup?" Kinley asked.

"He was having a down day. Lipstick always cheers you up," Penny said.

"It sure does. But you have to ask and you need supervision to use it," Kinley said. "Come on, let's go get our cleaning supplies. And I think you owe Pippa an apology. She said you were cranky."

Penny got to her feet and Kinley led the way back to the kitchen. When they got there, Penny went over to the screen door, which was closed, and put her face against it. "I'm sorry, Pippa."

Pippa looked over from her spot on the pool deck and smiled at Penny. "It's all right, imp. We all have bad days."

Penny came back over and together they attempted to clean the lipstick off the wall. As they were working, Kinley realized just how busy she'd been with her job lately, mostly to avoid seeing Nate, and that she hadn't been spending as much time with her daughter as she'd like. So she spent the rest of the night playing with Penny and getting in as much good mommy time as she could.

Kinley knew whatever happened in her life, she couldn't let her daughter suffer for it. Penny needed her mom. Kinley had always promised herself that she'd put her child first and not her job, but it felt like she was falling into the same habits her parents had, which worried her, because Nate was a workaholic as well. But she remembered her own parents and how each of them had given her something different. She'd always thought she was enough for Penny, but now that Nate was back in her life, she wanted Penny to know her dad. And Penny deserved two parents who were there for her all the time.

Nine

Nate took an early morning flight back from LA and drove himself home from Houston. He stopped at a coffee shop on Main Street, groaning when he realized the line was long and he probably should have gone to his office, but then he caught a glimpse of Kinley's red hair pulled back in a ponytail. She was toward the front of the line. He opened the door and walked inside, doffing his Stetson and putting his sunglasses on top of his head. He skimmed his gaze down her back, remembering how much he missed her when he noticed she held a little girl's hand.

Her daughter.

He almost turned around and walked out the door and away from her. But when he'd been in Los Angeles, he'd thought of Kinley the entire time. Not just hot, sexy daydreams, which could be justified, but other dreams where he held her in his arms all night, and even better still, where he was sitting and talking to her. He remembered their dinner conversation and wanted to spend more time with her.

He liked the woman she was and needed to continue getting to know her. And despite the fact that he wasn't anyone's first choice when it came to being a parent, he was very good at maneuvering around circumstances and making things work. He could do this.

He remembered what King had said about kids being BS meters and decided he'd just be himself. But just then, Kinley looked over her shoulder at him and then looked down at her daughter. The little girl wore a pair of jeans and a flowery shirt and had her hair in a ponytail similar to Kinley's. There were several customers between them in the line and the entire time the line moved, even while making small talk with men he knew from high school or business, Nate kept his eyes on Kinley.

His attention stayed on Kinley and he wondered as he watched her. Who was the man who'd convinced her to have a child with him? Then it hit him that the baby might have been accidental. Was that why the father wasn't in the picture?

He hated to think of the kind of man who would have abandoned Kinley when she'd been pregnant. That wasn't a real man, he thought.

She ordered her drinks and her daughter skipped away from the counter over to a table in the corner, where a woman with purple-striped hair was waiting.

Kinley took their tray and came over to the table and he noticed that she leaned in and talked to the other woman. Then she scooped her daughter up and gave her a hug and kiss before shouldering her large work-bag and walking out of the coffee shop.

Nate was next in line. He ordered his drink and then quickly followed Kinley outside. She hadn't gone too far; in fact, she was leaning against his pickup truck when he walked up to it.

"Hiya, Nate," she said. "I wanted a chance to apologize for the other night."

"There's nothing to apologize for. I meant to call you and see if you wanted to go on another date," he said. "But I was in LA and I heard you were out of town."

"From Hunter?" she asked.

"Yeah. Though it is hard to keep secrets in this town," he said.

Kinley turned away, opened her bag and began searching for something. She found her sunglasses and put them on. "Yes, it is. I haven't dated at all since I had Penny, and I think I might have been a little awkward when I told you about her. I'd like another chance, so I was wondering if you wanted to join me for dinner tonight…at my place. My daughter will be there, too."

Kinley sounded nervous and unsure of herself. Not at all like the Kinley he knew. He realized that his reaction to her daughter had probably spooked her a bit. It made him realize that whatever had happened with the man who had come after him had shaken and changed her. Maybe as much as having a daughter on her own.

"I'd love to. But I can't tonight. I was gone for four days and I have a board dinner tonight."

"Of course. It's an open invitation. Just text me when you have some free time in your schedule," she said. She glanced at her watch. "I have to run. Have a good one."

She turned before he could say anything else, and he almost let her walk away, except he was a Caruthers. He caught up with her in two steps and caught her wrist, stopping her.

"Nate?"

"Sorry. I forgot to say that I missed you and that I'm sorry I wasn't better prepared to hear that you had a kid. It shook me, but it didn't change the way I feel about you, Kin," he said.

"How do you feel about me?" she asked.

"I want to get to know you better. I want a chance to see if that weekend we spent together was just a fluke or if we have something solid," he said. "Will you take a chance on that?"

She bit her lower lip and then pushed her sunglasses up with her free hand. "I'd like that, but we need to talk a little more. There is something I have to tell you."

"Go on then, girl," he said.

She glanced around as early morning commuters streamed past them on the sidewalk, and she shook her head. "Not here. Let me know when you're free and we can talk."

He wasn't sure what it was that she had to say that had her so spooked. He let her hand drop and then nodded and walked back to his truck without a backward glance. He hoped she was watching him leave, but he couldn't confirm it. *Wouldn't.*

He was pretty sure that she wanted him with the same intensity that he wanted her, but there was unfinished business in her mind. He only hoped it wasn't her trying to get even for the callous way he'd treated her almost three years ago.

Kinley's heart was racing like a prize thoroughbred nearing the finish line at the Kentucky Derby as Nate turned and walked away from her. She waited until he got in his truck and took a deep breath. This was getting more and more complicated.

It reminded her of something her mom used to say: "Don't start lying unless you want to keep doing it for the rest of your life." Kinley wished she'd remembered it sooner. Jacs had said that everything would work out, and Kinley knew that she absolutely couldn't let any more time go by before she told him. But blurting it out on the sidewalk while everyone was heading toward work wasn't the right thing to do.

She wasn't exactly sure how Nate was going to react when he learned that he was Penny's father, but she was pretty sure he wasn't going to be calm and collected. He was a man of passions and, if town gossip was to be believed, a quick temper.

She was sweating. Not from the heat, though the temperature in southern Texas was rising already on this hot June morning. It was from her own fears.

"Mama!"

She turned to see Pippa and Penny walking toward

her, and tears stung the back of her eyes as she looked at her daughter. She'd only ever wanted what was best for her, and now she was afraid, really afraid that she might have made the wrong decision when she'd let Nate push her aside when she'd called.

Now she could think of a bunch of scenarios where maybe she could have flown to Texas or written him a note, but at the time, his words had been blunt and hurtful. But now he definitely wasn't the same man he'd been three years ago. For one thing he was hanging around her and there was a sense of real commitment in him. Still, she worried that the man he was today wasn't going to understand her motivations for her keeping Penny secret.

Pippa took one look at her face as she got closer and picked Penny up in her arms.

"Are you okay?"

"Yes. Sorry. I'm just trying to figure out how to do what I have to do, and it keeps getting harder."

Pippa nodded. "Want me to do it?"

Kinley smiled at her friend. "It would be easier for me but I'm pretty sure that it would only make it worse."

"Make what worse, Mama?" Penny asked.

"Just something I have to do, sweet girl," Kinley said, reaching over and stroking the back of Penny's head. Her daughter shifted and reached for her and Kinley took her from Pippa, holding her close. Penny put her little arms around Kinley and hugged her, giving her a sloppy kiss on the chin. Kinley felt a little bit of peace stealing through her.

She'd make it right for Nate once she told him and

found out how much he wanted to be in Penny's life. He might not want to, she realized. And that made her sad. Really sad. Because she wanted the man she kept getting glimpses of to be the kind that would want his own child.

"Would you like to come to work with me today?" she asked Penny.

"Yes! Pippa can come, too," Penny said.

"I can?" Pippa asked. "Maybe I need a break from you, imp."

"Nah, you love me."

"I do," Pippa said as Kinley put Penny down.

They all started walking up the street toward her offices. She and Pippa each held one of Penny's hands. Then they counted to three and swung her between them. And Kinley realized as they walked that of all the regrets she had about Penny, she never had any doubts she'd provided a good, solid home for her daughter. Pippa was like an aunt to Penny and the three of them were close. She wondered how Nate would fit in with the dynamic, but she refused to worry about it any more. She would tell him.

He said he had a meeting tonight. She should text him and push him to get a time for dinner scheduled. She made up her mind to do it as soon as she had a free moment at work.

But when they got to her office, Meredith, the bride from Dallas, was waiting in her Porsche Cayenne in the parking lot. She got out as soon as she saw Kinley walking up. She pushed her sunglasses up on her head, and Kinley saw that the other woman had been crying. Her makeup had run, and she looked like she was about to lose it.

"Pippa, can you take Penny inside and let her play in my office?" Kinley said, handing her key ring to Pippa. "Mama will be in soon."

She kissed Penny as Pippa took her toward the building.

"Meredith, are you okay?"

"No. Everything is a complete mess. Someone else has my dress," Meredith said.

Kinley didn't think that was possible, since Meredith had picked out every item that would go on her dress, but she put her arm around Meredith and led her into the office, which Pippa had already opened up. Kinley got Meredith seated and talking about her concerns.

They made a video call to the designer in Beverly Hills to talk about the changes Meredith wanted. She had confessed to Kinley that the bride whose dress was similar to hers was her fiancé's former girlfriend.

It took Kinley most of the day to get her calmed down. Six hours later, Meredith was in a hotel room in the Cole's Hill Grand Hotel and her fiancé was on his way down from Dallas to join her. But the crisis was averted.

She finally had time to text Nate. She told him they needed to talk.

She saw that the text was delivered and kept checking her phone all night, but there was no response.

Nate went to the Five Families Country Club after he finished the board meeting. It was close to midnight by the time he finally had a moment to think. He'd had two whiskeys with beer chasers so he knew his responses were alcohol driven. He was in the mood to do something to prove that Kinley didn't have the power over him that he knew she did. So when Derek showed up straight from a late-night emergency surgery with that wild look in his eyes, Nate knew that his brother needed him, and maybe he needed Derek, too.

Reprieve, he thought. He would text her in the morning when he was less likely to say something rash.

Early on, right after Derek had become a surgeon and he'd lost his first patient, Nate had been the one to spend all night drinking with his brother until he could talk about it.

Derek had started college when he was fifteen and had graduated from medical school at twenty-one. He was one of the youngest in his field but one of the brightest.

Then he'd held him until he fell asleep. There were times when Nate knew exactly what someone needed from him. And as the oldest Caruthers, he usually was pretty good about figuring out what his brothers needed. He'd done the same thing for Hunter when he'd first been released from police questioning in the Frat House Murder.

"Rough night?"

"I don't want to talk about it," Derek said.

"Drinking, fighting or pool?" Nate asked.

"Drinking and pool. Maybe if you cheat, some fighting," Derek said.

"You go rack 'em up. I'll grab the drinks," Nate said.

Derek walked past him into the game room at the club. It had been built in a Spanish style with large, sweeping arches and lots of rooms for events, games and televisions for game day. There were three restaurants: one upscale, one with counter service and one that women really seemed to like because they served an afternoon tea and brunch. In the summer kids from Cole's Hill's Five Families neighborhood could use their parents' accounts to charge food and play games. It had been like a second home to the Caruthers growing up, since their dad was a descendant of the Five Families.

Nate signaled one of the waitresses and told her to get him a bottle of Jack and two glasses and bring it to the Caruthers' room. He walked into the room to find Derek leaning forward with his hands on the bumper of the pool table. He cleared his throat so Derek would know he wasn't alone.

Derek straightened up, turning to look at Nate as he entered. His thick blond hair was rumpled, as if he'd spent a lot of time running his hands through it. Derek liked to wear suits, but he'd loosened his tie, taken off the jacket and rolled his sleeves up. Nate went to the paneled wall and took down two cue sticks.

He handed one to Derek just as Carly, the waitress, brought in the bottle and glasses.

"Thanks, Carly."

"No problem. I'm off in twenty minutes if you want some company," she said.

He thought about it for a split second but knew that the last thing he wanted was to complicate things with

Kinley any more than they already were. He shook his head. "Not tonight."

She looked disappointed but nodded and then disappeared. As soon as the door closed, Derek arched one eyebrow at him. "Sorry to cut in on your action."

"You're not."

"I'm not?" Derek asked. "You got a woman now?"

"I've been sort of seeing Kinley," Nate said. "You can shoot first."

"Wait a minute. Marcus's daughter? That Kinley?"

"Yeah," Nate said. "But we're not in here because of her. You are the one who—"

"Needs a distraction," Derek said. "And listening to you try to get out of talking about her is pretty damned amusing."

"I haven't had near enough to drink to be amusing," Nate said.

"So there's a chance you could provide entertainment later," Derek said, leaning over the table to break.

They played pool until three in the morning and eventually ended up just sitting on the floor with the bottle of Jack between them and talking.

"Did you lose a patient?" Nate finally felt like it was the right time to ask.

"Yeah. I was on call. An accident out on the highway. I thought I had him, and I did for a short while and then…" Derek poured more than two fingers of liquor into his highball glass and swallowed it, putting his head back against the paneled wall. He drew his knee up and rested his hand on it.

"What's going on with Kinley?" Derek asked. "She's not your type."

"You couldn't be more wrong," Nate told him.

"Truly?" Derek asked, arching one brow. His eyes were bloodshot—he'd probably had enough to drink.

"Yeah. She's different," Nate said. He took another swallow from his glass and realized it was empty, so he poured himself another one. He thought about how Kinley for him was like those photos his mom loved so much, where everyone in the background was in black-and-white and then in the forefront there would be an image or a person in color.

Kinley was in full-blown color and other women were starting to fade to black-and-white. But he knew better than to say that out loud. Despite the fact that Derek had drunk more than he had, Nate knew his brother would recall every moment of the evening. It had happened before.

"Good. I always thought you should settle down before Hunter," Derek said.

"Why the hell?"

"Oldest and all that. It won't be long before you start losing your hair like Dad and maybe getting a beer belly," Derek said.

"You're an ass," Nate said. Their father still had a full head of hair and didn't have a belly.

"I am," Derek said. "An ass who can't save everyone."

Nate reached over and draped his arm around his brother's shoulders. "No one can save everyone. Did you make any mistakes?"

"No. I've been over it again and again in my head. I tried to figure out if it would have mattered if the ambulance had gotten to us five minutes sooner or if I had shaved off a few minutes when I scrubbed up…I just don't know what else I could have done."

"Life is like that, D. Sometimes we have to accept that things are out of our control."

"I can't. I'm supposed to be able to save everyone," he said. "Natey, don't tell anyone else I can't."

"I won't, D," he said to his brother. "I promise."

He kept his arm around Derek and thought about the mistakes he'd made with Kinley and knew it was past time he made up for them. He didn't need alcohol to show him what he wanted to say. He just needed honesty, and sometimes that was the hardest thing to find.

Ten

Nate didn't dwell too deeply on the fact that he was driving around the Five Families neighborhood looking for Kinley's rented house early the next evening. He hadn't had to be Sherlock Holmes to get the address—a call to Hunter had been sufficient—and now he was sitting in front of her place, wondering if she'd let him in if he knocked on her door.

He also wondered what time a two-year-old kid went to bed. He put his head forward on the steering wheel. It wasn't like him to be indecisive.

But the kid had thrown a monkey wrench in his plans.

Rekindling things with Kinley was one thing. He had been fairly confident that a summer affair would suit them both. But not now.

He saw the front porch light come on and the curtains move in the front window. Now he looked like a creeper sitting out here. He opened the door to the cab of his truck and hopped down, walking up the front path toward the door.

He hit the doorbell and stood back to wait. He wasn't standing there long before it swung open and he found himself staring into Kinley's warm brown eyes. She wasn't wearing any makeup and had her hair pulled back in a ponytail, with only a light fall of bangs hanging down on her forehead. She had on a pair of leggings and a sleeveless T-shirt that fell to her thighs. Her feet were bare and next to her was a little girl in a matching outfit with the same red hair. But her eyes were blue. A beautiful light blue that seemed to sparkle.

"Hello, cowboy," the child said.

"Hello," he replied, stooping down so he was on eye level with her. She smiled at him, her grin just as sweet as Kinley's. "I'm Nate."

"I'm Penny," she said, holding out her hand.

He shook it carefully before standing up. "Sorry to drop by without notice," he said. "Work has been keeping both of us busy, but I wanted to see you."

"Work has been crazy lately. What did you want?" she asked.

Penny kept staring up at him. He wondered what it was that she was staring at, so he took off his Stetson and held it out to her in case it was his hat.

She started to reach for it, but Kinley stopped her. "What are you doing here, Nate?"

"I missed you. I regret the way things ended the other night, so I thought I'd stop by and apologize—damn—

I mean darn. I do that a lot with you," he said. It was true. She seemed to be the one woman in the world who could rattle him with little effort.

"I think we both are to blame for the other night," she said. "We are baking cookies. Would you like to come in and help us?"

He looked down at Penny, who was smiling and nodding up at him. "Mama is making horsey cookies."

"I'd love to help," Nate said.

Penny reached for his hat again, and he let her have it. She plopped it on her head and it fell down to cover her eyes, but she pushed it up so she could see before she turned and ran up the hall.

She was charming; he had the feeling that she got away with a lot. He knew that he'd easily say yes to anything she asked him if she smiled up at him with that gap-toothed grin of hers.

He stepped inside the foyer and closed the door behind him. The floor was Spanish tile and the ceilings were high and vaulted. As Kinley turned and he followed her, he noticed that despite the fact that she would only be in Cole's Hill for six months, she'd hung pictures on the wall.

He knew they were hers, because all of them were of her daughter, save for one of Kinley with her parents at her high school graduation. When he entered the kitchen he saw it was spacious and there was a large island in the middle with a sturdy-looking wooden step next to one side of the counter and cookie sheets as well as a bowl of dough in the middle.

Penny was nowhere to be seen. The kitchen was

modern and sleek, and he noticed that there were two double ovens that were both preheating.

"How many cookies are you making?" he asked.

"Two dozen. It's Penny's turn to bring the snack in at her day care tomorrow," Kinley said.

Nate was having a time trying to reconcile the two versions of Kinley. She was very domestic now, which he hadn't expected or truly caught a glimpse of before this.

"Where's your daughter?" he asked.

"Over here," she called, as she reentered the room on a broomstick horse that made a clip-clopping sound as she rode it around the kitchen. "I'm a real cowgirl."

"Yes, you are," Kinley said. "But it's time to put Buttercup back in her stable so we can finish making our cookies."

"'Kay," the little girl said.

"She has a stable?"

"We made one in her room out of one of the moving boxes. She's horse crazy," Kinley said a bit nervously. "Dad has been showing her the horses on the Rockin' C every time they have a video chat."

"Did he tell you that your mama used to be a cowgirl?" Nate asked.

"Yup. And he showed me her bucks."

"Bucks?" Nate asked, looking at Kinley.

"My buckles from the rodeos I competed in," she said.

He remembered another girl who had been horse crazy. And it made him realize that something inside him was changing. He couldn't say why, but he didn't want to stay here in this warm kitchen with Kinley and

Penny. The two girls talked and laughed, and he felt out of his element. But just like when he'd first stepped into the boardroom to take over his father's position, he also felt something like excitement in the pit of his stomach.

Kinley was surprised to see Nate in her home, being so charmingly awkward around Penny. When he showed up here tonight she'd seen it as fate's way of forcing her to talk to him about his daughter. And this was a chance she couldn't let slip by again. She took her iPhone out when they were both concentrating on the cookies and snapped a few pictures of the two of them together.

A heavy weight was on her heart, and she knew that the time had come. No more delays or excuses. It was harder this time than it had been after their recent times together, because tonight she could see the softer side of Nate. And she knew that once he learned Penny was his, he wasn't easily going to forgive Kinley for not telling him.

Part of why Nate had softened up was because their daughter was being very sweet with him tonight. Penny always had been a bit of a flirt with men. Pippa had said it might be due to the fact that she didn't have a father.

But she did have one.

And he was here now.

He was definitely out of his element. He had worn his Stetson, faded jeans and a designer shirt with leather loafers. He was not exactly full-on cowboy tonight, but he was quintessentially Nate. He was a mix of rancher, businessman and jet-setting playboy. And he was sitting in the breakfast nook next to Penny, helping her decorate horse-shaped sugar cookies. He was patient as she directed him on the different colors and patterns he should put on each horse.

"Mama, what did your horse look like growing up?" Penny asked.

"She had a paint," Nate said. "I remember what it looked like."

"You knew her?" Penny asked.

"Yes, I did. Your grandfather works for me," he said.

Penny put her tiny hand on Nate's shoulder and leaned around him to look over at Kinley, who was standing by the sink.

"Pop-Pop," Kinley said.

"Oh. So all the horsies belong to you?"

"Some of them, but not all. Do you want to come and see the horses?"

"Yes. Mama, did you hear that?"

"I did," Kinley said. But she wasn't too sure the invitation would stand after she and Nate spoke later this evening. She wasn't going to let him leave without telling him the truth. "We will figure out a time for a visit. Pop-Pop already wants us to come out there."

"Just let me know," Nate said. "I think that's the last cookie. What do we do now?"

Penny clambered over his lap and then turned around on the bench to slide down feetfirst. "This."

She reached for the tray with her tiny, chubby hands, holding it very carefully. Kinley was already on her way to the table as Penny tipped it to lift it. Nate reached underneath the tray and steadied it for her until she was on her feet. Then he helped her readjust her hold.

Penny walked over to her, carrying the tray, and Kinley blinked as she realized for the first time what she'd unintentionally stolen from Nate. He might have said he didn't want to hear from her again, but he had missed out on fatherhood, which wasn't fair.

Kinley hurried over to take the cookies from Penny. "Why don't you show Nate where the bathroom is and wash up?"

"'Kay. Come on, Nate," she said, taking his hand.

Nate didn't hesitate, just took her hand in his and followed her down the hall. Kinley grabbed her phone and texted Pippa, who was in town doing some grocery shopping. She wanted to warn her before she came home. She was definitely going to go to a special kind of hell if she didn't finally tell Nate her secret. And she was going to do it tonight. But she didn't want Pippa to walk in on them fighting if he got angry.

Kinley began typing.

Nate's here. Penny already likes him. I'm so scared.

The response was immediate.

You got this, girl. Want me to come and get Penny?

I think it might be better if I put her to bed with Nate and then tell him. He seems to like her.

Of course he likes her. Okay, want me to stay in town?

Yeah, for now. I don't know how long it will take to tell him.

I'll go to a movie. Text me when it's safe to come home. I'll get groceries tomorrow.

Thanks, Pip. Wish me luck.

She closed the text app on her phone as she heard Nate and Penny coming back down the hall.

Penny tried to climb up on one of the breakfast bar chairs and Nate scooped her up in his arms and turned to Kinley. He and their daughter both had the same expression on their faces, and her heart broke. It just broke right open, because she wasn't sure what was going to happen when she told Nate. But she knew things were never going to be the same, and she was pretty sure Nate was never going to look at her with that happy expression in his eyes again.

"What do we do now?" he asked.

"We get to eat 'em," Penny said, turning her head toward Nate's. She noticed his five o'clock shadow and lifted her hand to his face. "You're prickly."

"Not all the time," he said, smiling at her. "You're sweet."

"Not all the time," she said back to him. "Sometimes I'm naughty."

Kinley rolled her eyes. "Okay, missy, that's enough. You can put her down on the chair."

"I like him, Mama."

Kinley took a deep breath and let it out. "I do, too."

* * *

Nate had never expected to be a part of a bedtime ritual. But helping with Penny reminded him a lot of when his brothers were younger. By the time Nate was ten, his mom had been tired from riding herd on him and his brothers every day and had put Nate in charge of bedtime. That meant he'd supervised everyone getting into their PJs and brushing and flossing their teeth. Then they'd all go into their parents' bedroom and climb up on their big bed for a story. When they were done, they'd kiss their parents good-night and head to bed. Nate always turned off the lights in his brothers' rooms before going to his own.

And then they stayed in their rooms until it was time to get up in the morning.

Not so with Penny.

"I'm thirssy," Penny said the first time she'd come back into the living room, where Kinley had suggested they sit down.

Kinley got up and poured her a glass of water and put her back in bed, then came out and sat down next to him again.

"Sorry about that," Kinley said. "Usually she goes right to sleep, but I think she's afraid she's missing out on talking to a real cowboy."

"It's okay. Wait until you take her out to the ranch. She'll go nuts," Nate said. He was slightly surprised that Kinley hadn't already taken her out there, except on Memorial Day. Given the fact that her daughter was clearly horse crazy and her grandfather was there, it seemed like they'd be visiting more often. "Why haven't you brought her out before this?"

"Actually—

"I'm scared. Something's under my bed," Penny said again from the hallway.

"Penelope Grace, stop getting out of bed," Kinley said in a very stern voice.

"But Mama," Penny said.

Kinley got up and scooped her daughter into her arms and went down the hall again. This time she was there for about fifteen minutes, so Nate put on ESPN and noticed they were rerunning a one-hour special they'd made about King and Hunter being cleared of all suspicion in the Frat House Murder. As happy as he was that his brother had been cleared, Nate definitely didn't want to watch that, so he flipped channels until he found an NBA playoff game and then settled back to wait.

He had enjoyed spending the evening with Kinley and her daughter. It was so different than what he'd expected, but the longer he'd been in the house the more natural it was to him to see Penny and Kinley together. It had seemed at first as if Kinley was different here, but she was the same way with her daughter as she was with everyone else. Only more relaxed.

She laughed more easily, and she watched her daughter constantly with love in her gaze and more than a little bit of pride. He could easily see himself fitting into their lives, but the one thing he wasn't sure about was his own track record with long-term relationships.

His mom had always said when the right girl came along he'd know it.

Was Kinley that right girl?

He was beginning to think she might be.

"Okay. Sorry about that. I think she is going to stay put now," Kinley said.

"I know I would. You sounded very stern," Nate said.

Kinley shook her head. "Sometimes I have to be firm. Otherwise she thinks I'm not serious."

"I'm beginning to see that all that charm she was showing me earlier could be hard to resist," Nate said. "I wanted to ask you about her father. I'm sorry I didn't the other night."

Kinley nodded. "We both didn't handle things very well. I wanted to talk to you about that very same thing."

"Good. I wasn't feeding you a line the other day in town. I do want us to date. And I know Penny is part of the package. She's too cute for words."

Kinley crossed her legs underneath her body and then wrapped her arms around her waist as she leaned forward. "She is adorable. I feel so lucky to have her."

"You are," he said. "What kind of jerk wouldn't want his own kid?"

She took a deep breath. "Um…it's sort of complicated, and once you hear the story, please understand I did the best I could."

"Okay," he said. "I'm not going to judge you, Kinley. I know you're a sweet girl, and the way I rejected you on the phone must have sent you into a tailspin. I'm not judging you for hooking up with someone else after our weekend."

Kinley suddenly stood up and walked away from the couch toward the entertainment center and then turned to face him again. Her face was ashen, and she put her hands on her hips then let them drop to her sides.

"There wasn't anyone else, Nate. There was only you. When I called you, it was to tell you I was pregnant. I didn't know what else to do after you said what you did, and honestly, I never thought I'd see you again. The other night when I mentioned Penny's age, I just assumed you'd figure out you were the dad. That was my bad, but you are Penny's father. There wasn't anyone after you. Just you."

He stared at her, trying to process the torrent of words coming from her mouth but he'd stopped listening after she'd said he was Penny's father.

He was a father.

A father.

Penny was his daughter.

He stood up and looked at Kinley. He watched her shrink back from him—not that he'd ever hurt her, but he was pissed and he knew it showed. Pissed at her for telling him now and not telling him then. Pissed at himself for not figuring it out earlier. Just good and pissed.

He turned away from her and walked down the hall to Penny's bedroom and stood there in the doorway, watching her sleep with a stuffed bunny tucked under arm in the illumination of her night-light.

His daughter.

Eleven

Kinley watched Nate watching Penny and waited. While she felt guilty about not telling him before they'd recently slept together again, she didn't regret not telling him before she came to Texas. Even now as they were starting to get to know each other, she still wasn't sure exactly what he was going to want from her.

How involved would he want to be in Penny's life? She suspected his parents were going to be very excited to have a grandchild, but what about Nate? And where did that leave Kinley?

She'd told him because she'd started to care for him again. Which was a total lie, she thought as she realized she'd never really stopped caring for him. It was like that stupid, secret fantasy from her childhood when she'd seen the other kids at school with their perfect nuclear families and longed for that for herself.

He turned to face her, and the raw emotion on his face made her want to comfort him. She walked closer to him, intent on hugging him, but he held his hand up and shook his head. He stalked past her in the hall, back toward the living room.

She checked on Penny and noticed her daughter was sleeping peacefully with Mr. Beans tucked up against her side. Her daughter was completely unaware of the storm that was raging in the house.

Kinley closed the door, leaving it slightly ajar, before going back into the living room. It was empty, but she followed the sound of the china cabinet's doors opening and closing into the dining room, where she found Nate with a bottle of Glenlivet that she and Pippa drank occasionally.

Nate had a squat glass in one hand and had poured several fingers of scotch into it.

"So... I think we need to talk," Kinley said. She had one arm around her waist but remembered an article that Jacs had made her read about how the posture made a person seem defensive.

But she was sort of defensive. She'd done the best she could.

"I'm sorry I didn't tell you before," she said. "But you weren't exactly listening to anything I had to say on the phone."

"I know," he said, grinding the words out between swallows. "Give me a few minutes, Kinley, or I might say something I'll regret."

She nodded and left him alone in her dining room with the scotch and went into the kitchen to clean up the counters. They were already spotless but a little extra polish wouldn't hurt.

"Does your father know I'm Penny's dad?" Nate asked, startling her as he entered the kitchen.

She pivoted to face him and saw him leaning against the arch that led to the dining room. He held the bottle loosely in one hand and the glass in the other.

"No. I told him that the father isn't in the picture," she said.

His eyes narrowed. "Did you say I didn't want her?"

"No. I didn't tell him it was you. I did tell him about the phone call and hanging up on me, but not that it was you. Do you remember that? How I was trying to talk to you and you said we both had fun, but it was over and we should go back to our normal lives?" she asked. She was trying to be calm and let him work through things, but she wasn't going to allow him to try to reframe the past. The truth was she'd tried to tell him, and he hadn't wanted to hear anything she had to say.

"I do remember that. I'm trying to make myself feel better for missing out on two years of my daughter's life, but there is nothing that can change that, is there?"

"Not really," she said. "I have tried to think of a better way that I could have handled things, but honestly I was alone and scared and didn't want Dad to lose his job, so I stayed in Vegas and did the best I could."

Nate put the bottle and glass on the countertop and walked over to her. He stopped when there were a few feet of space separating them and then tipped his head to the side. "Did you hate me?"

"A little bit," she admitted. "But mainly I was mad at myself for not being more careful. All of those feelings went away the minute Penny was born and I held her in my arms. And then, Nate, even though I believed I'd never see you again, I was grateful to you for giving her to me. She's made my life so much richer and forced me to grow up."

He stared at her and didn't say anything else for a long time. Kinley wondered what he was thinking. But now that she was talking about Penny, all her anger had evaporated. And she knew that they needed to make some plans…if he wanted to be involved in Penny's life.

She licked her suddenly dry lips, trying to figure out how to ask him. What if he said no? He might need time. She'd had nine months to get used to the idea of being a mom—well, more like seven, since she'd been in denial after she'd first found out.

"What do you want to do next?" she asked.

"About what?"

"Penny," she said. "Do you want to be her father? Do you want to be in her life? Or do you want to keep things as they are?"

He cursed and looked down at the floor. "Boy, you know how to kick a man when he's down."

Kinley stared at him. "What do you mean?"

"Just that you must think I'm some kind of scumbag to not want my daughter to know I'm her father. What kind of man do you think I am?"

Kinley looked at him and answered honestly. "I have

no idea. We've had sex and talked a few times, but we don't know each other, Nate. I don't know what is in your heart or in your mind when it comes to raising a family."

This night just kept getting better and better, Nate realized. If he'd needed a stark reality check, then Penny and Kinley had definitely provided him with one. He'd always thought of himself as a protector and told himself he'd left no damage behind when he moved on from his relationships, but now he saw that might not have been true.

"I want my daughter. I will be claiming her and I will be raising her," Nate said. "In fact, I've already texted Ethan, and he's going to start working on the papers needed for me to officially be named as her father. In my heart and mind is that sweet little girl who has been living without me."

Kinley let out a long breath. "I'm glad to hear that. I think kids need both parents. I am happy to have my attorney look at whatever papers Ethan draws up. We can have your name added to her birth certificate in Nevada, and then we can work on some sort of visitation for you."

"Visitation? I'm going to be her father, Kinley. I'm not going to be one of those dads that drifts in and out of his kid's life. We are going to figure out a way to share custody and make sure that Penny has the best damned childhood ever."

Nate already had a few ideas of things he was going to have to change. In fact, drinking was probably one of them. And he lived equally between the ranch house and his penthouse here in town, but Kinley would probably prefer to live on the ranch, so Nate could easily work from there until Penny was older and started school.

"We can discuss it, but for right now you are going to have to transition into her life. You and I can come up with whatever plan we think is best for her, but the truth is, change is hard on kids. I have a nanny who watches Penny while I work," Kinley said. She moved to a drawer in the kitchen and opened it, taking out a pen and pad. "Do you want to hash this out tonight or wait and do it tomorrow?"

Tonight. But he wasn't thinking clearly. He was still mad and trying to process that he had a daughter. He was afraid he was going to react instead of think things through. Ethan was one of the best lawyers in the country, so Nate had no doubt his brother would get him whatever Nate asked for. But once he spoke to his brother, he was going to have to tell his mom and dad he had a kid.

"I have to tell my parents," he said. It hit him that his mom was going to be over the moon to find out she had a granddaughter. She'd always wanted a little girl, and he felt a spark of anger toward Kinley and himself for keeping Penny a secret for so long.

"I know. I have to tell my dad," she said. "This is complicated."

A twinge of guilt and embarrassment went through Nate. He had always respected Marcus and thought that Marcus had grown to respect the man Nate had become, but he knew this would change things. He'd made a clean break with Kinley because he hadn't wanted complications almost three years ago, and now he had more snags than he'd ever guessed he could have.

A daughter.

Nothing had been farther from his mind before this night. He'd thought about dating a woman with a kid, not about being a father himself. But tonight when he'd sat on that bench in the kitchen nook with Penny, he'd fallen for her charm. Nate had thought it was because she was Kinley's daughter, but now he was going to put it down to some sort of latent paternal instinct.

"It is…they are going to expect me to marry you," Nate said.

"Marry you? We aren't living in the 1890s. This is the twenty-first century. Parents don't have to be married."

"In Cole's Hill they do. Your dad isn't going to be happy knowing I knocked you up and told you to get lost," Nate said. "Either I make this right—the way our parents would expect me to—or we have to come up with some sort of better story than the truth."

"No," she said, shaking her head. "No more lies. And we can't just marry. We don't even know each other and I'm not sure if we'd even get along."

"We get along in bed," he said.

"There's more to life than that," she said. "I…I can't marry you just because of our daughter."

Nate could see that Kinley was going to be stubborn about this. He wanted to understand her reasons, but now that the thought had entered his mind, he knew he wasn't going to be happy with anything less than having Penny and Kinley both in his life permanently. "Why not?"

She chewed her lower lip and wrapped her arms around her waist again, then dropped them and put her hands on the countertop behind her. The action thrust her breasts forward, and for the first time since she'd dropped her bombshell he saw Kinley as the woman who had him tied in knots and not as the woman who'd kept a huge secret from him.

"I'm waiting," he said.

"My parents married because of me. And they didn't get along and hated each other. They were miserable, and my mom took a job that kept her away from my dad. I always wanted something better for Penny."

Nate wanted the best for Penny, too. He doubted that he and Kinley would end up resenting each other, but if she needed time maybe he'd give it to her—at least in terms of getting married. Penny was going to know she had a father now.

Kinley realized that things were no longer in her control. Nate was talking about marriage…marriage! There was no way that was happening. She'd watched her mom blossom as soon as she'd divorced Marcus and left Texas. And to be honest, Kinley might have thought it would be nice to have that perfect image of a family, but in reality she wasn't too sure she could live with someone else.

There was Pippa, but they were both pretty independent, doing their own thing. Maybe if Nate would agree to an arrangement like she and Pippa had, it could work. But she doubted he would. She also knew he'd want them to sleep together and she wasn't saying no about that. But marrying a man she wasn't in love with?

That wasn't something she was prepared to do.

When he didn't respond to her explanation of the difficulties in her parents' marriage, she raised another point. "Also, Hunter's wedding should really be the focus of the family right now. We don't want to steal any of the spotlight from him or Ferrin. Why don't we date? That's what you suggested earlier."

"Because when I suggested that, I had no idea that I had a daughter. I don't want to simply be dating a woman with a child. I want everyone to know she's mine," Nate said.

"I think you should tell everyone that you're her dad and then we can figure out us. I'm fine with dating or if you'd rather figure out the parenting thing first, we can wait," she said.

"You're saying that parent and partner are two different roles and I should just separate the two?" he asked, moving a bit closer to her. She dropped her hands and eased subtly down the counter to put more distance between them.

The more she thought on this idea, the more she liked it. Nate had always been one of those guys she just couldn't resist, so it might be for the best if they kept things on a dating basis—at least until they got used to co-parenting Penny.

"I have a counterproposal for you," Nate said. He came closer to her, and she realized that his anger was gone now. In its place she noticed his steely-eyed determination to have things the way he wanted them.

"Go ahead."

"We try it your way. Tell Penny, and then our folks and my brothers, and explain that we are going to try living together to ease Penny's transition and give us a chance to get to know each other better."

She wasn't too sure she wanted to live with Nate. "I have a nanny, so I think we will be okay if you live in your house and I stay here."

"I don't think that," Nate said. "I want to meet the nanny and I'll decide if she can stay on—"

"No. You aren't coming in here and changing everything. We've been living our lives this way for a long time, and Pippa is the only person on the planet who has been with me from the beginning. I was alone in Vegas. Dad couldn't come out until after the baby was born, and when my water broke I was using public transportation and freaking out a little bit, but Pippa— a perfect stranger—helped me. She's not going anywhere," Kinley said.

It wasn't until she started talking that she realized how much she resented Nate for not being there for her. She'd thought she'd adjusted to everything. To having to do it all on her own. But hearing him say all the things he wanted…well, it ticked her off after she'd had to figure out so much of it by herself.

She blinked as she realized she was going to start crying. Dammit. She wasn't about to let him see her cry over something that she'd dealt with a long time ago. She blinked again, trying to keep the tears in her eyes, but she felt her nose and her cheeks heat up and knew they were probably bright red at this moment.

Nate walked toward her, and she put her arm up to keep him at a distance. "Don't."

He stopped, put his hands on his lean hips and looked at her, his blue-gray eyes filled with remorse and something else she couldn't read. "I'm sorry. I hadn't thought about what it was like for you to deal with a pregnancy on your own," he said at last. "I wish I'd been there for you."

"But you weren't," she said. She reached for the dish towel she'd left hanging on the handle of the stove and wiped her eyes with it. "I want us to figure out something that will be in everyone's best interest, but you must understand I'm not going to just blindly let you sweep in and make changes. I know that it isn't your way to let someone else take the lead, but in this case we are going to have to work together."

Nate nodded. "Fair enough."

Kinley took a deep breath. "You can spend some more time Penny tomorrow if you'd like, but I think you should go home now. I have a meeting in the morning, but it's with Ferrin so I might be able to postpone it. I'm not sure how your day is."

"I'll clear my schedule for you," Nate said. "I'm working out of the ranch office tomorrow. When you're done, bring Penny out to the ranch and we can tell her I'm her daddy and show her the horses and introduce her to her grandparents."

Kinley wasn't ready to face her dad and Nate's parents, but she had been mentally preparing herself for it after the cake tasting, when she'd seen the look on Ma Caruthers's face as she'd talked about grandchildren.

"Yeah, that sounds good," she said. She walked Nate to the door, but when they got there, he stopped her from opening it, pulling her into his arms and lowering his head to kiss her. When he lifted his mouth away from hers, he looked down into her eyes.

"Thank you for my daughter," he said, then turned and walked out into the night.

Twelve

Kinley texted Pippa that it was okay to come home and then went and climbed into Penny's bed, holding her daughter close as she slept. She didn't know what she'd expected would happen when she told Nate everything, but a part of her had expected to feel more relieved.

But to be honest, she felt more confused and conflicted than before. Talking about when she'd found out she was pregnant had brought back all of those emotions from when she'd been lonely and scared. She held Penny tighter and her daughter snuggled closer and Kinley let herself cry like she'd wanted to earlier in the kitchen.

It wasn't as if things were going to magically fix themselves. She was going to be in for some tough questions from her dad, and she wasn't sure how Ma Caruthers or Nate's father and brothers would react to her news.

A part of her wanted to pack her bags and Penny and leave. Just get in the car and pull a disappearing act like Pippa had. But the truth was that she couldn't do it. She'd never been one to run from trouble. She could take whatever they dished out to her.

She was used to fighting and being on the outside… *Oh, no.* That was it. What she truly feared was being alone again. When she had her secret about Penny, she'd been guaranteed to have her daughter with her. But now that Nate was back in the picture, everything was going to change—and she was very afraid of that.

She rolled onto her back, staring at the stars that Penny's night-light projected on the ceiling. When she was little sometimes her mom would climb into bed with her after a long night working in one of the houses and hold her. Kinley had always cherished those nights. Her entire life she'd been isolated a little by circumstances and by her nature.

She was very much afraid of trying to have a relationship with Nate, because none of hers really lasted. Sure, she had Pippa now, but once Pip decided to stop running and claim her real life, she'd leave.

And Pippa was different than Nate.

He was complicated and he made her feel things she wasn't sure she understood. Even when she was mad at him—and for a while when she'd been pregnant she'd tried to hate him—she couldn't stay mad. Even though she'd known it would have been smarter to stay away from him when she returned to Cole's Hill, she'd gone to dinner with him, slept with him.

And now…now she was going to have to figure out

how to have a family with him. How to co-parent with a man who still intimidated her a little.

She kissed Penny's forehead and quietly let herself out of bed. She needed a plan. A real plan so she could manage herself and Nate. Otherwise she was going to find it hard to be strong tomorrow. And seeing Nate, his parents and her father was going to be difficult.

She had to be like Jacs. Tough but fair.

She would do it.

She was sitting on the couch working on her pro and con list when Pippa let herself in. She plopped down on the couch next to Kinley and gave her a sympathetic look. "How'd it go?"

"Awful. He wants us to get married," she said.

"What?"

"You heard that right. I said no. I mean, we hardly know each other."

"Didn't you sleep with him when you got here?" Pippa said, setting her purse on the coffee table and moving around on the couch until she was wedged into the corner and curling her legs up underneath her.

"I knew I shouldn't have told you about that," Kinley said. That was it. She couldn't resist him at times. He appealed to something inside her that felt wild and untamed. She didn't want to end up living her mom's life. She'd been miserable and hadn't really gotten any happier until they'd moved to California.

"You needed someone to talk to," Pippa said. "And I'm not bringing it up to be a bitch. I'm just saying you're not exactly immune to him."

Kinley groaned as she pulled her knees up to her

chest and put her forehead on them. "What am I going to do?"

Pippa didn't even try to answer. No one could tell Kinley what to do in this situation.

She lifted her head. "The thing is, I don't regret telling him. You should have seen him with Penny tonight. I think he is going to be a way better dad than I ever would have suspected."

She scrambled to grab her phone from the coffee table and opened up the photo app and showed Pippa pictures from tonight. Of Nate helping Penny to decorate cookies, both of their heads bent over the cookie tray.

"Oh, Kinley, this is bad. He does look like he is going to be very involved in his daughter's life. Honestly, this is such a sweet picture…was this before you told him?"

Pippa handed her phone back, and Kinley took it and looked down at the screen. Nate was really an expert at being a good ol' boy and everybody's friend in Cole's Hill, but the expression on his face in this photo showed him as the real man. One who only let a few people in.

"Before," she said to Pippa.

She remembered the one other time she'd seen that softness in his expression. It had been their last morning together in Vegas, when the sun was creeping in and they were both trying to pretend that the weekend wasn't ending. That look had made her believe…

…in fairy tales.

But this was the real world, and she doubted tomorrow everyone in the Rockin' C kingdom was going to be excited to hear that she'd kept Penny a secret as long as she had.

But that wasn't what worried her the most. What worried her was her own soft heart and the fact that she might give in to Nate despite the fact she knew it would be a bad idea.

Nate drove straight from Kinley's house to the Rockin' C. As always when he drove onto the family land, he felt that sense of being where he belonged. The Texas summer sky looked huge illuminated by a full moon as he drove up the two-lane road that led past the bunkhouses and ranch family homes. He steered his own big inherited mansion and around onto a small, packed-dirt road that led to his parents' new place. He turned off the engine and coasted down into the driveway before putting the vehicle in Park and sitting there.

He wasn't about to wake his parents up at this time of night, but this had been the only place he'd thought to come. Now that he was here…what was he going to say to them?

He had a feeling they were going to be overjoyed about Penny but disappointed in him, and he couldn't really blame them. He was disappointed in himself.

Tonight he'd had a glimpse of something he had never realized he'd wanted. When his mom had said there was a solace in having a family that couldn't be explained, he always thought it was just her trying to get him and his brothers to settle down.

He'd never known that love for a child could completely overwhelm a person. Could completely over-whelm *him*.

He'd spent his entire life thinking he had it all and only tonight realized that something had been missing. Something he'd almost lost out on because he'd been too busy running around proving to everyone that he was the shit.

Except now he felt like shit. He should have known that Kinley might be pregnant. He should have listened to her instead of hanging up the phone the way he had.

He leaned forward and put his head on the steering wheel. How was it that he could handle troubled cattle, cantankerous business executives and rowdy rednecks, but one woman threw him into a tailspin?

There was a knock on the driver's door, and he turned to see his dad standing there with a flashlight.

Nate opened the door and stepped down onto the ground. "Hey, Dad."

"Son. You okay? Your mom thought she heard something and sent me out here to investigate... You know Derek showed up last night."

Nate hadn't known that. "Sorry for coming out here. I just didn't know where else to go."

"What's the matter?" his dad asked, walking back toward the house and the front porch.

Nate followed him up the steps and onto the porch toward the large rocking chairs that were waiting. His dad sat down in one and gestured for him to sit in the other. But Nate felt too restless to sit down. Instead he walked to the porch railing, put his hands on it and looked up at the moon.

"Son?"

"Sorry, Dad. It's just…I found out I have a kid tonight," he said.

"Congratulations," his dad said, clapping him on the shoulder. "How old is she or he? Who's the mom?"

His dad sounded so normal—too normal—that Nate turned to face him to see what he was thinking. This was the hardest part of all, he thought. How did he tell his dad this? He understood why Kinley had waited so long to tell him. It was a difficult thing to say. "I have a daughter, Dad. She's two, and Kinley Quinten is the mother."

"Marcus's daughter?" his dad asked. "Damn, boy, you know how to stir up a hornet's nest, don't ya?"

"Yes, sir," Nate said, coming over and sitting down next to his dad in a rocking chair. "Marcus doesn't know yet."

"Figured he didn't. He would have come after you with a shotgun," his dad said. "So I guess it'll have to be a double wedding."

Nate knew it. He was tempted to text Kinley and tell her to expect parental pressure tomorrow. But he didn't. "I'm not so sure. Kinley and I are still trying to figure that part out. For now, I've got a daughter, and I'm going to be a part of her life."

"Fair enough," his dad said. "But you know your mama isn't going to let you get away with waiting too long. You best get to winning that gal over."

For the first time since he'd found out he had a daughter, Nate felt some of the tension seep out of his neck. His dad made it sound so easy. Like there were steps he could take to make Kinley fall for him. If he knew the actions that would make that happen, she'd already be his.

But he didn't.

With her he was always operating on gut instinct and wild lust. Not the best combination to win. "How'd you do that with Mom?"

His father gave him a devilish smile and wriggled his eyebrows at him. "You're still not old enough to know those secrets, son. But I will say this—every woman has something she wants. Not gift-wise, but man-wise. You have to figure out what that thing is and show her you can deliver."

"Sex?" Nate asked.

"Hell, son, if it were that easy, you'd have been married ages ago."

"Funny, Dad, real funny."

"I know. You want me to tell your mom about your little girl… What's her name?"

"Penny. Well, Penelope Grace," Nate said, smiling when he remembered her hopping in and out of bed so many times. It felt like a million years ago instead of just a few hours. "No, I'll tell her. I think she'd rather hear it from me."

"Can't wait to meet her," his dad said.

"I feel like I've let you guys down," Nate said at last. "She's two."

"You haven't. We all make mistakes. The key is to fix them and move on. Don't let them define you."

Nate said good-night to his dad and drove home. He spent a restless night in bed thinking of how he was going to move forward as Penny's father and Kinley's man.

* * *

Kinley got out of bed at six o'clock after one of the worst nights of sleep she'd ever had. Penny woke up while Kinley was in the shower. Her daughter came in to talk to her, went potty and then headed back to Kinley's bedroom and climbed into Kinley's bed.

Standing under the shower spray, Kinley wondered how she was going to tell Penny about her father. She toweled off before putting on her robe and walking into the bedroom. Penny had turned the TV on and was lying at the foot of Kinley's bed watching her favorite show. She had her head propped up on her hands.

"Morning, sweet girl," Kinley said, sitting down next to her and giving her a kiss.

"Morning, Mama."

"So…you know how we talked about your daddy?"

Penny rolled over at her side and then sat up, crossing her legs underneath her little body. "Yeah."

"Well, he is ready to meet you," Kinley said. "How do you feel about that?"

"Yay. I want a daddy," Penny said, jumping up and then using the bounce from the bed to launch herself into Kinley's arms. She caught her easily and hugged her close.

"Good. You actually met him last night."

"The cowboy? My daddy is a cowboy?" Penny asked.

"Yes, he is."

"And he owns all those horsies," Penny said. "I am gonna have my own horsey."

Kinley had to laugh at the way her daughter said that. "Yes, you are. You have some other relatives, too.

You're going to have some uncles, and your daddy has parents, so you'll have a grandma and a grandpa."

Penny stared at her, and Kinley wondered if she understood everything that she was being told. "Does Pippa know?"

"She does. And we are going to see your daddy after I go to work for a little while this morning."

"I have to go to school. It's my day to bring the snack," she said.

"I know. We can drop the snack off and then go meet your daddy. What do you think?"

Penny tipped her head to the side, pushing her long curls out of her face, and then nodded. "Okay, Mama."

Kinley finished getting dressed, answering questions that Penny came up with as she did. First she wanted to know where her daddy lived, and Kinley explained he lived on the same ranch as Pop-Pop, where they'd gone for the cookout. When Kinley was done putting on her clothes and makeup, they went to Penny's room to get her dressed. Penny wanted to look her best, so she wore a pair of cowboy boots, a pink skirt and her horse T-shirt.

She was squirmy while Kinley braided her hair and then raced to the kitchen, where Pippa was making breakfast, to tell her all she'd learned about her daddy.

Kinley was a little slower, texting Nate to see if he wanted to come to town and see Penny without his entire family and her father around. He texted back that he'd see her at the ranch house.

It was pretty abrupt, and she wondered if he was still mad at her. She suspected he was, and on some level she didn't blame him. But she thought they'd gotten closer to an understanding last night before he left.

"Pippa, can you take Penny to school to drop her snacks off and then bring her to my office around eleven? We are going to go out to the Rockin' C today."

"Yes, I can. Do you want me to come with you?"

"I think that would be a good idea. Someone is going to have to show Penny all those horses while I talk to everyone," Kinley said. She didn't want Penny to witness whatever the outcome was of telling the Caruthers and her dad about her and Nate. Her daughter was only two, so Kinley wasn't too sure how much adult conversation she'd understand, but she didn't want to chance it.

She poured her coffee into a to-go mug and gave her daughter a kiss before heading into her office. As soon as she was at her desk, she emailed Jacs and gave her a heads-up on what was going on. She didn't believe that Hunter would be so upset by the news that he'd fire her, but just in case, Kinley wanted her boss to be ready.

Then she picked up the phone to call her dad. She had no idea how she was going to ask him to meet with her without telling him why.

But she didn't want to tell him over the phone.

The call went to the answering machine. It really was an old answering machine and not voice mail, because her dad didn't like newfangled gadgets.

"Hey, Dad, it's Kinley. I'm coming out to the Rockin' C later," she said. "I'm bringing Penny and I have something to talk to you about."

She hung up and then started looking through her wedding books and planning the happiest day for the brides she was working with. She wanted to pretend that her heart didn't ache just a little bit at the thought of her own love life, which was in the gutter as she planned perfect days for these other women.

Today it didn't seem as much fun as it always did, and maybe part of that was because Nate had offered to marry her not because he wanted to, but because he thought he should.

Never in the history of the world, she thought, had a woman ever wanted to be married to a man because he felt obligated. She knew this firsthand. She'd seen what that kind of marriage was like. As she told Nate last night, she'd grown up in a house where resentment and hatred had simmered between her parents.

And she didn't want that. But she looked down at the sketch of the dress that Ferrin had picked out and admitted to herself that she did want a husband of her own. It was just her bad luck that she had fallen for Nate again and he was the only man she could picture as her groom.

Thirteen

Nate was waiting for Kinley on the porch of the main ranch house when she pulled up. She got out of her car, wearing a short skirt and a fitted top. Another woman stepped out of the passenger side of the car. He'd seen her before, with Kinley and Penny at the coffee shop.

Kinley had her hair pulled up in one of those sophisticated updos that women seemed to love to wear. A pair of large sunglasses covered her face, and he wondered if she'd slept any better than he had the night before. She opened the back door of her car and stepped back so that Penny could get out. Their little girl hopped out of the car and then reached back inside to get a stuffed bunny and a brightly colored gift bag.

She saw him waiting for her and stopped in her

tracks. The other woman called over to Kinley. "I'm going to wait over there. Holler when you need me."

Kinley gave the woman the thumbs-up sign, and Nate guessed she was the nanny.

Kinley crouched down to talk to Penny. They were too far away for him to hear what they were saying, but it seemed obvious to him that his daughter was afraid to come and meet him. So he went to her. He stooped down next to Kinley, and Penny turned to him.

"Penny, honey," he started but then realized he didn't know what to say. Blurting out that he was her father didn't seem the right thing, and just asking her if she knew also felt awkward to him. He touched the stuffed bunny under her arm with the lopsided lipstick marks on its mouth. "Who's this?"

"This is Mr. Beans," she said. "He wanted to come with me today to see my daddy."

"I'm glad he did," Nate said, holding his hand out to Mr. Beans. "It's very nice to meet you, Mr. Beans."

Penny set her bag down on the ground and then turned Mr. Beans so he could shake Nate's hand. Then she leaned in close to the stuffed bunny. "He is happy to meet you, too. We've been wantin' a daddy."

Nate scooped her into his arms and stood up, giving her a great big bear hug. She wrapped her little arms around his neck and hugged him back, and he realized that his life was never going to be the same again. He had a daughter.

Last night when he'd gotten the news, he hadn't thought of the long-term impact. The shock of learning he had a daughter had been enough to occupy him, but today, when he held her in his arms, he knew he never wanted to let her go.

He looked over at Kinley, who stood patiently watching them, and felt a little bit of resentment toward her that she'd had Penny all this time and he'd had nothing. Nothing but work, the ranch and temporary relationships. He knew that it had been his own choices that had given him that life, but he wanted something different now.

"Are you going to give me a lot of horsies?" Penny asked.

He shook his head. "No. I will probably give you a horse one day but you have to start learning to ride on a pony. Why is this bunny wearing lipstick?"

"He was feeling sad and needed cheering up," Penny said.

Nate turned toward his house as Kinley walked over to him. "I think we are going to need to talk about the horse. Penny can't have a horse in Nevada. My house is in a subdivision."

"I don't think that will be a problem," Nate said as they entered the house. "Since my daughter will be living with me."

"We still have to discuss where we are going to live. Penny, why don't you give your daddy the cookies we made for him, and then I'm going to get Pippa so you can play with her while we talk," Kinley suggested. She walked back to the front door and signaled her nanny.

"Thanks for the cookies," Nate said to Penny as he set her down.

"Nate, this is Pippa. Pippa, this is Nate," Kinley said as the other woman came into his home. "Where is a good place for them to hang out?"

"The game room is down the hall, second door on the right. There's a television and some board games and video games and a pool table."

"I think that will keep us busy," Pippa said in a crisp British accent that sort of surprised him.

But before he could ask her any questions, she'd taken Penny's hand and led her away. Nate turned to face Kinley and noticed she had a very stubborn look on her face.

"I have a list of things I think we should discuss," Kinley said. "First of all, don't make promises to Penny before we've had a chance to talk. She can't stay on the ranch with you, since our being in Texas is temporary."

He shook his head. "You've had too long being the only one who made decisions for our daughter. I'll make any promises I want to her. And your stay in Texas might be temporary, but Penny's isn't. She's my daughter and I want her here with me."

"Nate, be reasonable. She can't just start living here with you. She barely knows you. And my work is in town now, but I'll back in Vegas after Hunter's wedding."

"I think she'll know me well enough by the time you have to return to Nevada," he said. "Or you can reconsider my offer and stay here with me."

"No. It doesn't work that way. You gave up your rights when you hung up on me. You can get to know her now, but only because I'm letting you."

* * *

Kinley could tell already that today wasn't going to be a good one to talk to Nate. She didn't blame him for his anger, but she wasn't going to allow him to walk all over her, either. But she missed him and she wanted what she'd never had: Nate in her life, and not just for Penny. She didn't want to start off talking about how they'd co-parent like this. And it was even harder, because she'd sort of hoped that he'd have taken the night to realize that he wanted to be with her. That he'd say he wanted them to be a family. The three of them.

She wanted him to love her. Because she needed to know that he wanted her for herself and not just because they had a child together.

Instead he seemed set on telling her what to do.

"Letting me?" he echoed. "She's my daughter, too, Kinley. Don't forget that."

"I have never forgotten it, Nate. I can promise you that. Now, are you going to be reasonable?"

"Define reasonable," he said. "Because I think me having her on my own for two years would be a nice place to start."

Never. She would never give her daughter up, and she could see now that talking to him was getting her nowhere. She had an attorney that she'd visited in Nevada right after Penny was born who'd done the paperwork for her to leave the father's name blank on Penny's birth certificate. She also knew that Nate had no rights to Penny because he wasn't named as her father. But Kinley didn't want him to be cut out of Penny's life if he wanted to be part of it.

She took a deep breath. Nothing was going to be solved by being angry and fighting.

"I don't want either of us to be isolated from our daughter. Let's figure out a way that we can make this work," Kinley said. "I have already drawn up a list with a few ideas of ways we can try it out while I'm living here."

Nate took a deep breath and then turned away from her. "Let's discuss this in the den. Mrs. Haskins is around here somewhere, and I probably shouldn't have been yelling the way I was."

"You weren't that loud," Kinley said, following him into his den. It was decorated in very dark, masculine colors. The room was large and there were two guest chairs in front of a big mahogany desk. Bookcases lined the left wall, and the right wall had a big bay window that looked out over the pool. Behind his desk was a huge TV screen. He went around the desk and sat down, and she took a seat in one of the leather armchairs that had been provided for guests.

She set her bag on the floor by her feet and took out the notepad she'd jotted her thoughts on last night.

"To start with, I thought we could try letting her come out here during the day, and maybe on the weekends we could stay with Dad so you can see her," Kinley said.

"I want her to spend the night at my house," Nate said. "I'm her dad. How is she going to get to know me if she just visits?"

He had a point. But if Penny stayed here, then she'd have to as well. "I don't know if she'll spend the night away from me or Pippa. She's only ever stayed with the two of us."

"So you and Pippa can stay here with me. The house is big enough for the three of you to join me. Also, I want to decorate a room for her. Tell me what she likes and I'll get my decorator to start on it. I've already got her scheduled to come out here later in the week."

Kinley again felt like everything was spiraling out of her control; she wanted to run out of the room, grab Penny and drive far away from here. But she knew she couldn't. That it was too late for that. "Okay. I'm happy to work with your decorator, and Pippa is a great resource as well."

"I'll need Pippa's contact details," Nate said.

"Of course," Kinley said, but she wanted to talk to Pippa before she shared any information with Nate about her. She was on the run and only let a few people close enough to know her secret. "We should probably draw up some paperwork that has all of this spelled out."

"I'm not sure how we went from being lovers and starting to be friends to ending with paperwork to figure out how we'll raise our daughter. What is it you are so afraid of happening?"

Kinley sat back in the chair and had to force herself not to cross her arms over her chest. She didn't want to admit that trusting him was still hard for her. She didn't know if Nate was going to be there when things got real or if he'd flake out again.

"I'm not sure I trust you," she said at last.

"You can trust me," he said.

"I hope so. Because Penny deserves the best, and I'm not going to let you hurt her," Kinley said.

"Nice opinion you have of me," he said.

"Sorry. It's just been my experience."

"Three years ago," he said. "You're the one who left me the last time we slept together."

"I'm sorry about that. I just didn't know how to tell you about our daughter, and I didn't want to let myself believe that there could be something between us until you knew the truth."

"Do you still think there could be something between us?" he asked.

Yes. But she didn't want to say that or admit to feeling anything for him until she knew how he felt. He might be saying whatever he had to in order to get her to give up her rights to Penny.

She rubbed her forehead, feeling a headache coming on.

"Kinley?" he asked.

She licked her lips and looked over at him. Into those very serious blue-gray eyes that she knew she'd fallen in love with.

She started to tell him what he needed to hear. But what she wanted to say was that she wished there were something between them, because she was falling in love with him again.

But the door burst open behind them and her father was standing there with his shotgun in his left hand and his hat in the other.

"You son of a bitch, you better be prepared to do right by my daughter."

* * *

"Daddy! Stop it," Kinley said, jumping to her feet and rushing over to Marcus.

Nate stood up as well, feeling a heavy lump in the pit of his stomach. It wasn't only Penny and Kinley that Nate had to make up to for the last three years. He was going to have to make amends with Marcus and his own parents, too.

Marcus tossed his hat on the empty chair and then stood there with the shotgun held loosely in his arms. "Someone want to tell me what's going on? Babs only heard that you are Penny's father." Babs was the ranch's housekeeper.

"It was news to me as well," Nate said, putting his hands up. "There's no need for the gun. Why don't you put it down."

Marcus walked over to the sideboard under the window and set the gun on it and then turned back to face them both. The door opened again, and Nate groaned when she saw his parents standing there along with Derek and Hunter.

What the hell were they all doing here?

"Babs said that Marcus was headed over here with his gun, so we thought we'd better get over here, too," his father said.

"Dad, we don't need an audience right now."

"Why is Marcus here with his gun?" his mom asked.

Kinley stood up and cleared her throat. Everyone turned to look at her. She knotted her fingers together and then opened her mouth to speak, but no words came out.

She tried again. "Um…well, Nate and I have a daughter. But he's only just found out about her. Dad didn't know who the father was, either, and I think he's here to make sure that Nate does right by me. Which is silly, since it's the twenty-first century and I've been raising Penny on my own for two years."

"I have a granddaughter?" his mom asked. "Where is she? Can I see her?"

Kinley nodded. But Nate thought it was best to defuse this situation first. "Yes, Mom. To all of it. As soon as we get this sorted out, you can see her."

"What is there to sort out?" Marcus said. "You two getting married or not?"

"Your daughter just said she didn't want to marry me," Nate pointed out.

"That's not exactly true, but okay," Kinley said.

"Why didn't you tell Nate?" Marcus asked her. "And why did you tell me that story about Penny's dad?"

Blushing, Kinley looked down at her shoes and then over at Nate. She hadn't told them anything about his behavior, and now she was trying to find some way to save him. To keep everyone in this room from knowing he was an ass.

He realized how much he loved her in that moment. And how much he didn't deserve her.

"It wasn't a story, Marcus," Nate said. "It happened just like she told you. She called me and I told her to get lost before she had a chance to tell me about her pregnancy."

Marcus made a grunt and exploded across the room, punching Nate in the jaw. For an older man, he packed a lot of power; the punch snapped Nate's head back and sent pain shooting through his jaw and down his neck.

His father ran toward Marcus, probably to stop him…or maybe to help him. And then Marcus's face convulsed. He grabbed at his chest and started to crumple right in front of Nate.

He reached for Kinley's dad as he started to fall, and Derek yelled for someone to call 911 as he rushed over from the doorway and started to do CPR.

"He's having a heart attack," Derek said. "Get the medevac out here."

Kinley was pale and shaking as she stood next to Nate and her father and waited for help to arrive. Nate put his arm around her, offering her some comfort. She patted his hand. Then clung to it. Even to Nate it felt as if time was moving in slow motion. He wasn't sure how long it was until Hunter came back in leading the EMTs.

"Can I go with you?" Kinley asked the medevac team.

"Only Dr. Caruthers. We don't have room for a passenger."

She nodded, and Nate grabbed his keys and put his hand under Kinley's elbow. "Come on. I'll drive you. Mom, Penny is in the game room with her nanny. Will you make sure they get to Cole's Hill?"

"Sure will, honey. You go with Kinley. I'll take care of our granddaughter."

"Are you sure, Ma Caruthers? I don't want to impose," Kinley said.

"Girl, you're family. There's no way you can impose. Now go on and make sure your daddy is all right."

Nate ushered Kinley into his truck, with Hunter in the backseat. Now and then, he looked over at Kinley nervously as they drove through town to the new medical facility on the outskirts of Cole's Hill. "Derek is one of the best cardiologists in the state. You know that he will save your dad."

Even as Nate said that, he remembered the other night and how Derek had lost a patient but told himself that was the exception. Derek was one of the top-rated cardiologists in the country and he would do everything in his power to save Marcus.

Kinley was white as a ghost as he pulled up in front of the medical center. He put the truck in Park and Kinley hopped out of the vehicle, heading toward the front door. He followed her, knowing that Hunter would park the truck for him.

When Nate caught up with her, Kinley was at the desk trying to get some information, looking very small and very alone. He came over to her and put his arm around her and then signaled for a nurse to come and help them. Kinley looked up at him, almost surprised that he was still here, and he realized that this was how she'd been for the last three years—on her own and having to deal with everything. She didn't know how to lean on someone, because no one had been there for her. But now he was here.

Fourteen

The hospital where Derek performed the emergency operation on Kinley's father was on the outskirts of Cole's Hill in a new medical park that had opened five years ago. She'd been sleeping in her dad's room since he'd come out of surgery two days ago. She hovered over him, seeing to the oxygen tube in his nose, watching his pale face for any signs of trouble as he slept.

The only way he could sleep was when the nurses gave him sleeping pills. They hadn't had a chance to talk about anything since his heart attack. She felt guilty; maybe learning that Nate was Penny's father had brought it on, though Derek had been pretty clear that her dad's arteries had been in bad shape for a while. If she was grateful for anything, it was that Derek had been at the Rockin' C when her dad had the heart attack.

She still replayed in her mind the moment when he'd started to collapse and she ran toward him. She'd never get over seeing him like that.

Her dad.

The biggest, strongest, toughest cowboy she knew, crumpling to the ground as they all stared on in shock. Derek had been the first to know what was happening.

"Kinley?"

"I'm here, Daddy," she said. "What do you need?"

"Some water would be nice," he said. "I'd get it for myself, but I'm too damned weak."

"I don't mind doing it for you," she said. "That's why I'm here." Kinley poured him some water from the pitcher on the nightstand and then adjusted his bed, being careful of the IV in his arm as she did so. His left arm was completely black-and-blue, and just seeing it made tears sting her eyes. She blinked them back as she handed him his cup of water.

He took it from her, his hand shaking as he tried to lift it to his mouth. She put her hand under his and helped to steady it as he drank. He didn't say anything to her as he let go of the cup and she put it back on the table.

She leaned over him and hugged him carefully. With his free arm, he hugged her back.

"I'm sorry if hearing about me and Nate shocked you," Kinley said at last.

"It did, but that's not what caused this. Derek has been after me for the last six months to cut back on my salt," Marcus said. "I was surprised you didn't say anything about Nate earlier."

She paused and searched for the right words to tell him how embarrassed she'd felt and how she knew if she'd told him about Nate it would make things awkward for him. He loved the Rockin' C. It was his home. She'd never wanted to jeopardize that.

She nibbled on her lower lip. "I wanted to, but I knew that it would put you in an awkward situation."

"So instead you isolated yourself," he said. "Do you know how that makes me feel?"

"Pretty awful, I'd guess," she said. "But that might be the effect of your heart attack." She hoped he'd smile, and he did manage a weak one.

"It might be," he admitted. "You look tired. Why don't you go home and get some rest?"

"I don't want you to be alone." And she'd never say this out loud to him, but she was afraid to leave him. Her dad was the only parent she had left, and his heart attack had scared her and made he realize how much she still needed him.

"He won't be."

Kinley turned to see Ma Caruthers and her husband, Brody, standing there in the doorway. "We will keep an eye on him while you go rest."

Kinley looked at her dad and he nodded. She walked over toward Nate's parents, a million words that she hadn't had a chance to say swirling around in her head. She hoped they didn't hate her, but wouldn't blame them if they did. But instead of saying anything to her, Ma Caruthers pulled her close and hugged her. And then Brody clapped a hand on her shoulders.

"You have to take care of yourself as well," he said.

"Thank you," she said to them both. They were nice people, and with everything that had happened in the last few days and her lack of sleep, Kinley knew she was on the edge of crying again. She tried to keep it together, blinking like crazy.

"Call me if anything happens with Dad. I'll be back in a few hours," she said and walked away before she lost it completely.

When she got out to the parking lot, she couldn't remember what her car looked like and just stood there staring at the vehicles, waiting and hoping she'd remember.

A black pickup truck pulled up in front of her, and Nate leaned over to open the passenger door. "Want a ride home?"

She did. But she remembered the fight they'd had in front of his family, and she wasn't too sure leaning on him and taking a ride from him was the best idea.

"Nate—"

"Don't worry about anything. Your dad just had a heart attack and you're tired. I'd have to really be a bastard to be anything but a friend to you right now."

She nodded and climbed up into the cab of the truck. Putting on her seat belt, she realized that everyone was being very nice to her. And for the first time since her mom had died, she truly felt like she was part of a family.

"Thank you."

"You're welcome. I hope you don't mind, but I told Penny I was coming to get you."

"I don't mind," Kinley said.

When they got to her house, Penny stood in the doorway wearing the horse shirt that her grandfather had given her, jeans, her cowboy boots and a pair of fairy wings.

"Where did the wings come from?"

"She heard my mom say that your dad needed lots of angels around him and wanted her own wings, so I got her some," Nate said.

Kinley nodded her thanks to Nate and got out of the truck as Penny ran down the walk toward her. She scooped her little girl up and held her close, finally letting the tears that had been threatening fall.

"Your pop-pop is okay," Kinley told her. "We're going to go visit him after I get some sleep."

Nate waited until Kinley was sleeping before he checked his phone. He had a text from Ethan telling him he needed to stop by the office.

Pippa was in the kitchen with Penny, who was decorating heart-shaped cookies for Marcus.

"Hi, Daddy," Penny said.

She'd been calling him Daddy every time she saw him. And it warmed his heart to see how happy she was to have him in her life. He wished he'd handled things with Kinley better, but his temper had always had gotten the best of him and he'd reacted without thinking things through.

Now he had to figure out how to make it all up to her. "Hi, angel. How are the cookies coming along?"

"Good. Pippa is already baking them."

"That's right, and then we'll frost them," Pippa said.

Nate came over to the breakfast table where Penny was sitting and dropped a kiss on the top of her head. "I have to run over to my office to do some work. Will you be okay with Pippa until I get back?"

"Yes, Daddy."

"Pippa, is that okay?"

"Sure is," she said.

"Good. I'll be back in an hour. If Kinley wakes and needs anything, let me know," he said.

By the time he got finished with his meetings, it was nearly three in the afternoon. The board was discussing fracking for shale oil on their property. Oil was one of their income streams, and Nate knew that many members of the board wanted to try to diversify. But he wasn't satisfied yet that fracking was the way forward. They agreed to table the issue for now. He adjourned the board meeting and then went into his office to finish up some paperwork so he could have the next few days free to help Kinley and her dad with whatever they needed.

He'd already arranged to have an in-home nurse stay with Marcus until he was fully recovered. Once Nate talked with Kinley, he'd figure out if she wanted her father to stay in town with her or if the nurse would stay with Marcus at his house on the ranch.

"You have a call on line one," Nate's assistant called from the outer office.

He lifted the handset. "This is Caruthers."

"Nate, it's Ethan. How's Marcus doing? Is he okay?"

Nate rubbed the back of his neck, tucking the phone between his neck and shoulder. "Yeah, Derek thinks he's going to make a full recovery, but it will take some time for him to be back to normal."

"Thank God. I'm heading toward the airport now. I'll be back on the ranch tonight. I wanted to talk to you about your daughter. I started working on the papers you requested for custody—"

"I've changed my mind. Obviously we can share custody, as long as Kinley will agree to it," Nate said. He knew that he'd felt backed into a corner when he'd made the decision to sue for full custody.

He'd been angry and disappointed by all he'd missed out when he'd thought about suing for full custody but even as he'd pursued that by asking Ethan to look into it, he knew he'd never go through it. Penny and Kinley belonged together. A part of him had been worried he wouldn't fit in.

And if he were being brutally honest, he wanted to hurt Kinley a little. But that had been anger and not the rational man he was.

Part of it had been because of the disappointment on his mom's face, and the other part had been guilt and anger at himself for not being the better man. He'd thought if he had full custody he could make up for that... Hell, he'd wanted to hurt Kinley, too.

But Marcus's heart attack had taken the teeth out of Nate's anger, and he'd realized that when it came to family, there wasn't any reason to be selfish. Penny was his, and Kinley hadn't denied that. They'd figure out something that worked for them without involving lawyers.

"I'm glad to hear that. I would have done what you wanted, but the whole intent of this call was to talk you out of it," Ethan said. "I'm pretty sure you would regret taking Kinley to court. If we won, things would always be weird between you, and I think that would affect your daughter."

"You're right," Nate said to his brother. "I have an idea and I could use your help with it."

"Whatever you need," Ethan said.

Nate described what he hoped Ethan would do for him. And Ethan laughed as he heard Nate's plan but just said he'd do it. After he hung up the phone with Ethan, Nate called Derek and got an update on Marcus's condition.

"He's doing good, Nate. One of the best things was that the air ambulance was nearby, thanks to the NASA facility, and they were able to get us to the hospital so quickly. The surgery went well and when I was him a few minutes ago he looked good. Well, aggravated but also pretty good," Derek said.

"Why was he aggravated?" Nate asked. He knew he still needed to make his peace with Marcus now that the other man knew he was Penny's father.

"He didn't like it when I told him it was going to be at least six months before I cleared him to go back to work," Derek said.

"That sounds like Marcus," Nate said. "Did the news about me and Kinley affect him? Did it bring on his heart attack?"

"Not at all. This was a long time in the making," Derek said.

Nate wanted to believe his brother, but he had seen how purple Marcus's face had gotten when he'd punched him, and Nate was not going to be able to forgive him-self for putting Marcus in that position for a long time.

He drove back to Kinley's house and arrived just as Kinley and Penny were getting ready to go visit Mar-cus. He offered them a ride, but Kinley declined, say-ing she would drive herself.

He wanted to argue with her, but he'd done enough of that for this week and instead simply followed her to the hospital in his own truck.

When they got to the hospital, Penny ran to Nate as soon as he got out of his truck and he scooped her up. It was hard seeing Penny run to him the way she did, and Kinley realized that her daughter had missed hav-ing a father. She wished she'd found a way to tell him sooner. Things had gotten so out of hand between them, and then her dad had punched him...

"I don't know if they are going to let Penny in to see Dad," Kinley said, walking over to them. "If they don't—"

"I'll keep her with me. Where's Pippa?"

"She's going to pick Jacs up at the airport," Kinley said. Her boss had insisted on flying out to Texas and taking over all of Kinley's appointments for the next week to give Kinley time with her father.

"Who is Jacs?" Nate asked, shifting Penny to his other arm so he could reach out and hold open the hos-pital door for her. She walked in front of him and then stopped inside, taking off her sunglasses.

Nate was wearing suit pants, a dress shirt and tie. He looked every inch the CEO today, but then she noticed his cowboy boots and realized he hadn't left the ranch behind.

"My boss," Kinley said. It was funny to her that Nate knew so much about her but not something as simple as her boss's name. There were a lot of things to work out, she realized. She and Nate needed to sit down and talk.

"We really need some time to discuss Penny and the future," she said. After the way the entire Caruthers family had rallied around her and her dad, she knew that she wanted to be a part of the family, and she was hoping that maybe Nate would feel the same way.

"Of course. But let's sort out your dad first," Nate said.

She nodded. Dad was everyone's top priority. She led the way down the hall to her father's room, but when they got to the nurses' station, they hesitated.

"Is it okay if my daughter comes in to see her grandfather?" Kinley asked.

"It sure is," the nurse said. "Dr. Caruthers already cleared her for a visit."

"Thanks," Nate said.

Kinley finished leading them down the hall, and Nate set Penny on her feet. "Go in and visit with your pop-pop. I'll be right out here."

Kinley opened the door for Penny and then looked back at Nate. "Why aren't you coming in?"

"The last time he saw me, he threw a punch. I'm not sure your dad is going to want to see me again so soon."

"I'll let you know," Kinley said. Remorse was a tough thing to live with, and Kinley was feeling it in spades today. She'd come between her father and Nate. She'd come between her daughter and Nate, and she was pretty sure she'd ruined any chance she and Nate had for a future together that didn't involve just parenting their daughter.

And that hurt more than she expected it to.

"Hi, Pop-Pop," Penny said, running toward his bed.

Kinley hurried after her, catching her and lifting her up before she reached the bed. She didn't want to take a chance on Penny pulling on any of the IVs.

"Hi, there. Is that my granddaughter or a little angel?" Marcus asked, holding out his arms for Penny.

Kinley carefully set her daughter on his lap. "Watch out for these tubes, Penny."

"I will," she said as Marcus snuggled her close to him with the arm that wasn't attached to the IV. "I'm an angel, Pop-Pop. Grandma said you needed them."

"I do need them," he said to Penny.

Penny continued doing what she did best—talking and laughing—and Kinley noticed that her father seemed more relaxed with Penny in his arms. Now she had another regret to add to the many that she'd been carrying with her today—that she'd limited them to a relationship conducted by video chat instead of one that was in person.

Derek came into the room with an orderly. "How are you feeling today, Marcus?"

"Better than I did yesterday," her father answered.

"Good to hear it," Derek said.

Derek asked Marcus a bunch of questions about how

he was feeling and made some notes in his file. "I want to check your heart."

Marcus lifted Penny up, and Derek took her and set her on her feet next to him. Kinley came and got her and they both stood over near the guest chair while Derek finished checking her father out. "My office manager will be calling you to set up an appointment. It's important that you don't miss any of the pills I've prescribed. Nate has arranged for an in-home nurse, and he asked me to recommend a few. Two of the candidates will be by later and a third tomorrow morning. It's going to take you months to recover, Marcus, so make sure you select the nurse you think you can work with for that long."

"I don't need a nurse," Marcus said. "I'll be fine on my own."

"Don't be stubborn, Dad. He's going to stay with me in town—"

"He's sitting right here, daughter. I'll stay at my own place. You have enough to worry about with Penny," Marcus said.

Kinley took a deep breath and realized just how hardheaded her father could be. "We haven't decided anything yet."

"Fair enough," Derek interjected. "Colin is here to take you for some blood work."

"Can I go with him?" Penny asked.

Derek looked at her and then stooped down to Penny's level. "You can push him down the hall to the elevator with me, and then I'll bring you back to your mom. How's that sound?"

"Perfect."

Kinley stepped into the hallway and watched as her little angel pushed her grandfather down to the elevator. Then she glanced up and saw Nate waiting there, and she knew it was time to sort out her future. And she hoped that there would be one with this man.

Fifteen

Nate went by the hospital the next evening when he knew that Kinley, Penny and his parents were all having dinner together. He wanted a chance to talk to Marcus, to make things right.

He knocked on the hospital room door and stuck his head in before entering. "Do you mind if I come in?"

Marcus was sitting in bed watching PBR on the television. He muted the TV before motioning for Nate to come in. Nate closed the door behind himself and walked over to the bed. He knew that Marcus was recovering well from his heart attack; Nate had seen him a few times through the door, but it did him good to see the older man sitting up in bed after the last time he'd seen him crumpling in front of him.

"What's up, son?" Marcus said.

Marcus's kind tone humbled him and made him realize that he had been right to wait and come and talk to him alone. "I wanted to apologize, sir."

"Kinley already explained things," Marcus said.

"She did?"

"Yes. But you and I both know that girl is sweet on you, so I'm not buying half of what she said," Marcus explained. "I think it did happen the way she originally said, and I'm pretty sure you're not in the same frame of mind you were three years ago when she got pregnant."

"You're correct, sir. I want to make it up to her. Figure out a way to show her that I have changed and that she doesn't have to be on her own anymore."

Marcus nodded, crossing his arms over his chest as he leaned back against the pillows. "That might not be easy. She might like you, but…her mom and I married because of Kinley, and Rita never really forgave me for it. She and I were never meant to be together forever and neither of us really tried. Our folks said we should marry, so we did."

Nate remembered how he felt when Marcus had burst into his den with the shotgun and could understand why that wouldn't be the best start to a marriage. But he wanted to spend the rest of his life with Kinley, and he wanted Penny to have some siblings, too. So Nate knew he was going to have to figure out how to change her mind. Figure out how to show her that he was the kind of man she could count on.

"I'm not going anywhere, and I'll wait as long as it takes for her to see that I'm serious about her. I want your permission to ask her to marry me," Nate said.

He knew Kinley would take some convincing, but he wanted to make sure that Marcus understood that he did respect him despite the behavior that had led to this situation.

"You have it, son, but I don't think it's going to be easy to convince her to say yes."

Nate didn't, either. Which was why he was starting with the tough guy in the hospital. Marcus was daunting, but Kinley was doubly so, and Nate was only starting to realize just how tough and self-reliant she was.

"You're not exactly telling me news I don't know," Nate said. "But I have a plan."

"Good. You're going to need one. And you might need a few allies," Marcus said.

Nate already had his brother helping him set up everything so that it was just right, and it had taken a lot of talking but eventually he'd gotten Pippa on board to help him out, too. He would have gone to Penny, but it seemed like cheating to use their daughter so he'd ask Pippa to just tell her they had a surprise for Kinley, and he didn't want Kinley to feel trapped. He wanted her to only say yes when she was convinced that he was the man she wanted by her side for the rest of her life.

He stayed with Marcus for another hour, talking to him about ranch business and reassuring him that his job would be waiting for him when he returned. "It's not like anyone else can do you job."

"Damned straight. No one knows that place like me. Except maybe your dad, but he's retired now," Marcus said.

Nate was thinking it might be time for Marcus to retire, too, but Derek had recommended putting off talking about that until he was fully recovered. Derek said state of mind made a huge difference in the speed of recovery, and men who thought they had someone waiting for them recovered quicker.

"My dad's not really that retired. He still shows up unannounced at my office in town when he feels like it. I'm hoping that Penny will take up some of his time. Can you believe that Kinley hasn't had her on a horse yet?"

"It's a sin. I was thinking we could start Penny out on Abigail. She's such a sweet mare. She'd be perfect, and you could ride double with her until she gets used to being up there on the horse."

Nate had been thinking along the same lines. "I'll do it until Derek gives you the okay to ride again. You're a genius with horses, so maybe she'll pick up some of your skills."

"Deal," Marcus said.

Nate checked his watch and realized he needed to get moving so that he was at the ranch when Kinley got there. He had talked Pippa into bringing her out to pick up some stuff for Marcus.

Twenty minutes after saying his goodbyes to Kinley's dad, Nate pulled up to the barn at the Rockin' C and parked his truck. He walked into the barn to see if everything was set up and was pleased to discover that Ethan had taken care of every detail just as he'd requested.

Penny and Pippa were up to something. She could tell by the way Penny kept trying to wink at Pippa when she thought Kinley wasn't looking. Her daughter couldn't really wink; she closed both eyes and then opened one up with her fingers instead. It was one of the most adorable things Kinley had ever seen.

As soon as Pippa said they needed to go to the Rockin' C, she suspected that whatever they were up to involved Nate. She was happy enough to go along with it, since she had missed Nate. He'd been very sweet since her dad's heart attack.

In a bunch of different, quiet ways he'd made her feel that she wasn't on her own when it came to dealing with her father's heart attack and the aftermath.

The live-in nurse he'd hired for them was very nice and efficient and seemed charmed by her father's gruff manner. Nate had also offered his penthouse apartment to Jacs for her to stay in while she was in town. When he'd realized that Pippa didn't drive, he assigned the task to one of his ranch hands so she had her own driver.

And of course Kinley couldn't really forget that moment before her father had burst into the den, when something had passed between the two of them and she'd almost told him she loved him.

Pippa directed her to park in front of her father's house, which was located adjacent to the barn.

"Penny and I will go and gather some of Marcus's things. He wanted you to check on his favorite horse. Take as long as you like. We've got things to do, right, imp?"

"That's right. Take as long as you want," Penny said, then blew Kinley a kiss as she got out of the car.

Kinley waited until they were both inside her dad's house before walking to the barn. As soon as she got close, she noticed that there were lights on inside, and she heard the sound of music.

When she opened the barn door, she saw that twinkle lights had been draped over the beams and a table and chair sat in the middle of the main aisle. On the table was an old-fashioned telephone. She walked farther into the room and looked down at the tabletop.

But there was no note.

The phone started ringing, which she thought was odd, since it wasn't attached to the wall. But she answered it.

"Hello, Kinley," Nate said. His voice was deep and husky. She smiled to herself as she sat down in the chair next to the table.

"Hello, Nate," she said.

"I know we said that everything between us would just be for one weekend," he started.

She swallowed the lump in her throat as she realized he was using the exact words she had when she'd called him almost three years ago.

"We did say that."

"But circumstances have changed. I know that I said what happens in Vegas stays there, but do you know what happens in Cole's Hill?"

She shook her head and then wondered if he could see her.

"No, I don't."

"Well, what happens in Cole's Hill is forever, and I'm not sure how you feel after the way our last call ended, but I want to spend the rest of my life with you," he said. Now she heard him next to her, not through the phone. She turned to see him standing there.

He held a ring box in one hand. She put the phone back on the table and turned to face him. "I know I haven't made things easy for us, but I love you, Kinley. And I want to spend the rest of my life with you. Not because we have a beautiful daughter, though I want her, too. But because you are you, and my life will not be complete without you."

He went down on one knee and held the ring box out to her. "Will you marry me?"

"Are you sure you are doing this because you want to marry me and not because you think you have to?"

"Kin, have you ever known me to do anything because I have to?"

"No. Is it because my dad had a heart attack?"

"Not at all. Though you should know I asked him for his permission to marry you, and he gave it to me."

She chewed her lower lip. *Yes* hovered on her lips. She loved him and wanted to marry him. It was the secret she'd kept closer to her heart than Penny's dad.

"I need to make this right for us, because when you and I are sixty and our grandkids ask us how we fell in love, I want them to know that I fell for you so hard that I couldn't imagine living another day without you."

"Me, either," she said. "I love you, too, Nate. And I will marry you."

Nate let out a whoop and lifted her out of the chair

and swung her around in a circle. He held her tightly to him as he kissed her.

He put her on her feet and took the engagement ring and put it on her finger. She looked down at it. It was simple and elegant and absolutely perfect.

Kinley remembered how afraid she'd been to come back to Cole's Hill, but now she was glad she had come. She had been afraid of the unknown and of facing Nate again, but together they were going to have a wonderful future together.

"We have to tell Penny...unless you already did?"

He shook his head. "Not a chance. I had to ask you before I started telling anyone else."

"I love you, Nate Caruthers."

"Not as much I love you, Kinley soon-to-be-Caruthers."

He pulled her into his arms and kissed her. Finally it felt like coming home. Like the place that she'd been searching for was really a person. Nate. It was hard to believe it after all they'd been through and how she'd almost given up on him...*had* given up on him.

But now he was holding her as if he'd never let go and looking down at her with love in his eyes and she knew deep in her soul that this was what she'd been missing.

Being a mom had satisfied something inside of her but being in Nate's arms, knowing he was going to spend the rest of his life with her made her realize this was what she'd secretly wanted all along.

They told Penny, who was very happy. Pippa also

congratulated them. Then they drove back to Marcus's hospital room, and all of the family gathered there to hear the news. Kinley, who had felt alone for so long, had the family she'd always dreamed of and the only man she'd ever loved by her side.

* * * * *

Don't miss any of these sweet and sexy reads from USA TODAY *bestselling author Katherine Garbera.*

HIS BABY AGENDA
HIS SEDUCTION GAME PLAN
HIS INSTANT HEIR
BOUND BY A CHILD
FOR HER SON'S SAKE

Available now from Mills & Boon Desire!

* * *

If you're on Twitter, tell us what you think
of Mills & Boon Desire! #MillsandBoonDesire.

MILLS & BOON®

Desire™

PASSIONATE AND DRAMATIC LOVE STORIES

A sneak peek at next month's titles...

In stores from 18th May 2017:

- **His Accidental Heir** – Joanne Rock
  and **Unbridled Billionaire** – Dani Wade

- **A Texas-Sized Secret** – Maureen Child
  and **Hollywood Baby Affair** – Anna DePalo

- **Claimed by the Rancher** – Jules Bennett
  and **Reunited...and Pregnant** – Joss Wood

Just can't wait?
Buy our books online before they hit the shops!
www.millsandboon.co.uk

Also available as eBooks.

MILLS & BOON®
are delighted to support
World Book Night

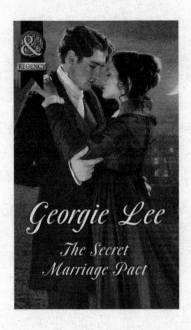

Georgie Lee

The Secret Marriage Pact

World Book Night is run by The Reading Agency and is a national celebration of reading and books which takes place on 23 April every year. To find out more visit worldbooknight.org.

www.millsandboon.co.uk

WB0517_2